# WHY WE
# Play
## with Fire

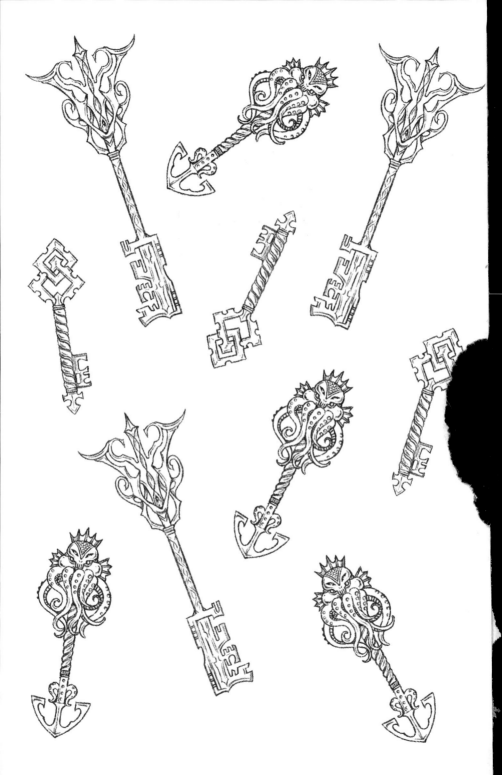

# WHY WE
# Play
## with Fire

## Giselle Vriesen

futures

futures

*Because we at 100 Block Futures and Row House Publishing believe that the best stories are born in the margins, we proudly spotlight, amplify, and celebrate the voices of diverse, innovative creators. Through independent publishing, we strive to break free from the control of Big Publishing and oppressive systems, ensuring a more liberated future for us all.*

*Protecting the copyrights and intellectual property of our creators is of utmost importance. Reproducing or republishing any part of this book without written permission from the copyright owner, except for using short quotations in a book review, is strictly prohibited.*

*Send all press or review inquiries to us at*
*100 Block Futures, PO Box 210, New Egypt, NJ 08533*
*or email publicity@rowhousepublishing.com.*

Library of Congress Cataloging-in-Publication Data
Available Upon Request

ISBN 978-1-955905-31-2 (TP)
ISBN 978-1-955905-66-4 (eBook)

Printed in the United States
Distributed by Simon & Schuster

First edition
10  9  8  7  6  5  4  3  2  1

To Alexandria, I love you.

# PART

# One

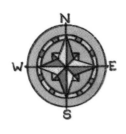

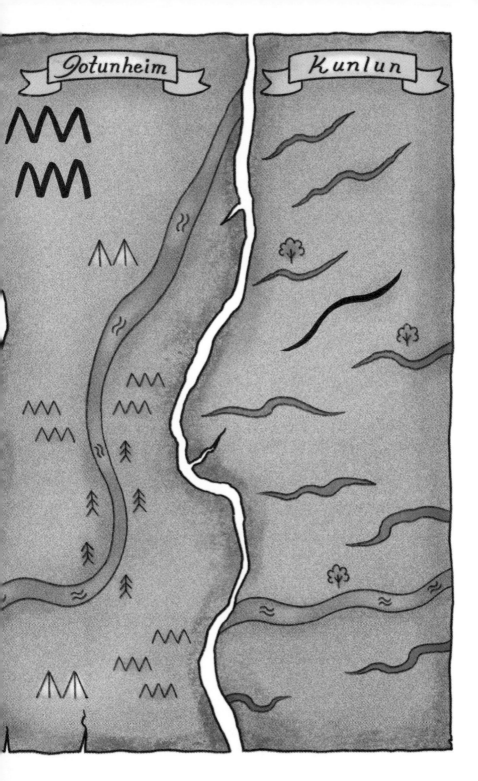

# 1

*WHERE ARE THEY?*

A plume of dust rises from one of Mom's discarded dresses as I fluff it off the ground in her closet. It's funny how such a small space can hold so many memories: the skirt she wore when we moved to Salt Spring Island from Toronto, the belt I coerced her into buying during our one-month stay in southern Saskatchewan—before she started going out less and less—before we settled down. *There it is*, the object of my desires. My heartbeat drowns out the sound of clinking pots and pans as Nana cleans up in the kitchen and the simultaneous sounds of her scolding my mother for throwing away perfectly good rice. All I see is the shoebox.

When Auden invited me to come to Matthew's with her a few days ago, I wanted to give an instant *no* because I wasn't technically invited. She assured me it "wasn't a big deal" and insisted that I'm friends with everyone she's friends with. What Auden doesn't understand is that I'm not *actually* friends with anyone but her.

She doesn't notice the weird glances and withheld energy I get from our classmates. In such a small town, no one knows what to say or how to speak to me. Ever since we moved here, I can tell that all my classmates see when they look at me is "Black girl," while Auden sees "girl who is Black." *Well, tonight I'm not going to let anything hold me back from having a good time.*

I push aside the edge of my slightly too-long bangs as I look down at the box in question. It tingles with a forbidden energy. Inside are brown leather shoes with wooden soles, my mother's favorite and the nicest pair of shoes in our whole house. I have coveted them for as long as I haven't been allowed to wear them, forever. But, now that I'm sixteen and Mom is more forgetful than ever, what could the harm be in wearing them out just this once?

I imagine the faces of my peers as I, the Blerd, arrive at the party wearing these beautiful, vintage Fluevog shoes. In this daydream I'm lounging against the doorway acting as cool as a glass of ice water. I can practically feel the envy in mean-girl Emily's eyes as I stride in, one leather-clad foot after another. Suddenly I'll stand out for all the right reasons.

I lift the box up with two hot palms, pulling it onto my lap on the floor of Mom's bedroom. *Strange, this box is heavier than I remember.* I can wait no longer; the hairs on the back of my neck stand as Mom's and Nana's voices rise in the kitchen. A little part of me wonders if maybe I should put the box back and wear my usual flats. *Why are you overthinking this?* I lift the top of the box with my breath held in the center of my chest, then exhale in a burst when I find something unexpected inside.

A statue, as long as my forearm and carved from smooth black stone, stares back at me. It has no eyes and no mouth, just large hands folded on top of one another. Its body is curved like a woman, though it has no discernible face. When I pick it up, its smooth exterior sends an electric shiver down the palm of my right hand. My shoulders sag. *Where are those shoes?*

Nana keeps statues all around the house, the Buddhas beside her easel in the corner of the living room where she does her paintings, the small African masks in the kitchen, even a Mother Mary statue in the bathroom. All stuff she collected when she and my mother were younger and traveled the world before I was born. I've avoided paying attention to any of it.

I'm about to tuck the statue away when something in its small face—or lack thereof—catches my attention. Looking at the space where eyes should be, a shiver runs down my spine, suspending my racing mind. Then I hear it, a prickly voice in the back of my head. Over my shoulder I find Mom's room as empty as it was before, but still the whispering voice creeps like vines inside my skull.

*There are tales of foes and fate, with heroes never asked to wait. A chance to come and sweep the stars aside at night with wanting arms.*

*But when a hero is born to earth, chased by a villain of shadow and mirth,*

*To steal and thwart a girl of age, to seal a tale of oppression and rage,*

*There will come a point in this young life when waiting could bring forth the knife.*

I inhale; the voice continues.

*The journey is long, and some will desire more, but she should not forget the key came before.*

I balk at the strange rhyme and glance down at the innocent statue. This must be me cracking under the stress of winter break being nearly over and having to go back to class, or maybe it's the lack of sleep given all my anxiety about this party—or it could be something more. I shove the statue and the box deep into Mom's closet.

I power through and pack an overnight bag, get dressed, and find my ferry card. I let myself get lost in my routine: forgetting the strangeness of the little statue intentionally. Half an hour later I am tucking the edges of my bangs behind my ears, determined to get to the front door and out of the house, until a roadblock presents itself.

"Do you have your phone charger?" my mother asks. She stands between me and the sweet release of arriving ten minutes early to the ferry. I bite the inside of my cheek.

"I have everything." I reach out to hug her. When my skin connects with hers, I feel a familiar wave of energy—her worry and love—but there's also something else too, something darker and metallic. Frowning, I pull away and remind myself that I can't *actually* feel her feelings. *I'm just imagining it.* A mantra I repeat to myself most days.

When I was little, I invented a game where I pretended I could feel someone else's feelings by touching their skin: love, sharp distaste, cold anger. As I got older, it became less of a game, more of a habit. One I am ashamed to have not grown out of.

"I'll be back in less than twenty-four hours, don't worry." I say this even though my mother never looks worried, just practical and hawkish. She surveys my clothes, internally assessing whether they're weather appropriate, before nodding once.

"Okay, well, I want to talk to you when you get back, all right? There's something—"

"Seriously, I *have* to go, I don't want to be late." Even the word *late* causes my already damp underarms to moisten, my breath to tighten in my chest. "And I have to work tomorrow, so I will see you after my shift."

This is a conversation we have already had twice today; she forgot about it each time. Her memory slips away like the tide going out to sea: the conversation gone with it like a toppled sandcastle. Usually, I would spend at least another five minutes comforting her—this stage of menopause is a lot stronger than I think it should be—but as it stands, I *cannot* miss this ferry. I plant a kiss on either of her cheeks and rush for the door. I wave as I pass Nana where she sits at her painting station. She doesn't look up at me as I make my exit.

Once outside, I hesitate, wanting to sprint off, but instead I look at my mother where she stands in her robe and slippers in the doorframe. We wave at each other in unison.

Mom's hair is darker and longer than mine, unmarked by gray though slightly thinned with age, and her smooth brown skin holds the same freckles as mine. This is where our resemblance ends. Mom's features are more prominent than mine, with wide, thick lips and intense piercing eyes. Her mix of Black and Chinese heritage gives her features a smooth, upturned look, while my features fall flat. Potentially a bit resting-bitch when I'm not smiling. I blow a kiss and set off.

The roads in Crofton are frozen and black. My flat boots skim the ice precariously as I slide down the hill toward the ferry. I have no idea where those Fluevogs are—a mystery for another day.

The houses all look the same here, light-colored stucco with closed curtains over the windows no matter the time of day. This is a place I think people go to die, no matter how old they are when they move in. When I get older, this is the last place I'd like to end up. This is the armpit of Vancouver Island. As much as I hate moving and as much as I want to belong, I can't imagine staying here much longer. While I walk, I think about the future: exams, more studying, what comes after high school, if I can get my grades up high enough to get a good scholarship for university, and what happens after that? Each familiar thought barrels into the next, causing such internal chaos, I almost miss the figure on the road ahead of me.

The icy sidewalk, dark save for sparsely hanging streetlights, curves right as it slopes toward the ferry, but up ahead on the deserted street is one other person: a boy. There aren't usually many people walking in Crofton at this time of night. Whenever I've walked to the 7:45 ferry, I have done so completely alone.

The boy stands beneath a broken streetlight. He isn't dressed in the uniform of everyone who lives here (Costco jeans and Joe Fresh jacket). Instead, he has on a long black leather coat, unfit for this frigid weather, with dark hair tousled away from his face. Beneath the coat is a black-and-white-striped uniform that contrasts the casual fashion of this town.

I pause and he looks at me, and it feels like even from a block away he truly *sees* me. It's an unfamiliar feeling. Usually when people register me, they either make it their abject mission to *not* see me, to stare over my head or just to my right, or to look at me like I'm a puzzle they can't quite make out. It's as if they're always trying to pin down exactly where I "came from." But this boy, obviously handsome despite the strange lighting and distance, stares me dead in the eyes with such force that I forget the icy condition of the road and take a confused step back. Like a deer when it hesitates in crossing the road, I rear back. Except unlike a graceful animal, I slip.

The edge of my foot glides over the hard ice, right off the side of the sidewalk. The skin poking out from beneath my pants and above my shoes grates against the cement like Cheddar cheese. I wince in pain and look down at my twisted ankle. My heart soars to my throat just thinking of him witnessing this, but when I look back, the boy isn't there and the streetlight is once again lit.

*I'm seriously losing it,* I decide. Now I'm both hearing voices *and* inventing a boy wearing a weird black-and-white uniform. *What if my mother's memory loss is rubbing off on me? What if this is yet another reason to feel like a freak?* I bite the inside of my lip while the pit of my stomach, already wrung tight in anticipation of going to Matthew's house, suddenly pitches right at the concept of hallucination. *At least if I am losing it, I don't have to worry about finals.*

*I can do this,* I tell myself. *I can go to this party. I can act like a normal person, and everyone will think I'm cool.*

**WHEN THE BOAT SWAYS** jarringly as we pull into the Salt Spring harbor, I stand up from my seat and walk past seven rows of empty seats in this bright room that smells of pleather to the observation deck window. A twinge of pain slices up my ankle, so I glance down at the haphazardly wrapped Band-Aid I got from the kiosk upstairs. It's tinged red at the edges. *Less elegant than I hoped.* I frown down at it before scanning the dock ahead for my ride.

The second I see Auden's Jeep waiting for me, I take a deep breath and hobble down the narrow metal staircase to the car deck where I then weave through twenty cars all bearing THERE IS NO PLANET B stickers.

"What's wrong?" Auden asks as soon as I slide into her passenger seat after disembarking the boat.

"Nothing, I just—nothing," I say, shutting the door beside me. My hands are stiff from the cold.

"You have a weird look on your face," Auden assesses as she pulls out of her parking spot and joins the rush of cars driving off the ferry.

I school my features into something blander. "I messed up my ankle on the walk to the ferry."

"Oh, boo," Auden says flatly, eyes glued to the road ahead of her.

Auden likes to dress like a Pinterest board come to life and spends most of her waking hours living up to the soft-girl aesthetic. To her credit, in this moment, she's achieved it: vintage Redline Levi's, little fur-trimmed knit pink shirt that matches her clutch purse, French tips, slicked-back auburn hair threaded with delicate gold pins, and the Celtic knot necklace she always wears no matter the occasion. I wish I could hold it against Auden, how seemingly perfect her life is. In reality, she basically lives alone because of how often her parents work. I know how anxious she secretly is in relationships too. When I don't text her good night, she immediately worries we're in a fight. Auden wordlessly unplugs her phone from the aux and holds it out to me as an apology for my twisted ankle. I avoid brushing her hand with my own, plug it into my phone, then shuffle my liked songs.

"If you don't want to go, we can just head back to my house for the night and watch some movies." She smiles and turns to look at me.

Auden's pretty when she's kind, so much so it often catches my breath. But she's rarely kind when there are other people around. I like to think this version of her, the one I get when it's just the two of us, is the real Auden, and that any other version is an amalgamation of every other high school "it" girl she watched on TV as a kid—not a real person, just an idea.

"No, it's fine," I say.

"Okay, cool, because I talked to Emily and she said that we can go to her house afterward and have like a midnight debrief of everything scandalous we saw at the party, and then tomorrow morning we can all go to the diner for breakfast. We'll have a blast!"

I nod along since this is a discussion we have already had via text.

Auden continues chatting about who will be at the party, how excited she is to see Dom after they kissed for the first time last week. I itch the center of my right palm. Outside the window of Auden's Jeep, the world is a wall of black, no streetlights, no houses, just dense forest. *It's so dark here.* While Auden talks, I try to summon my earlier excitement, or at least my earlier determination, but all I can focus on now is the boy I saw in the dark and the pulling pain in my ankle. The lamp over him was dim and empty—*so strange.* I wrap my arms around my stomach, pressing my wrists into the puffy down of my winter parka. What would Auden think if I told her what I saw or what I heard? *She'd probably tell me I was crazy or offer me a protein bar and blame it on low blood sugar.*

When we pull up to Matthew's house, Auden bolts, carrying her six-pack under one arm. I look up at the enormous compound, wide windows and four stories of sheer glass. If I had a house this big, I'd throw parties too. But with me, Mom, and Nana all cramped into a two-bedroom house, I'd be lucky to squeeze in three friends.

Outside the house is a group of about ten parents wearing Cowichan sweaters nestled under woven blankets. They smile at us as Auden and I walk up, hold out a wide bowl for Auden to toss her keys in, and ask us each how our parents are doing. I hang back for a second to answer, while Auden disappears into the party.

Inside Matthew's house, every single one of my classmates dances to Frank Ocean while drinking from clear plastic cups. My regret spikes as I walk through the doorframe and not a single person looks my way. My stomach twists until I spy an empty corner of the room. I weave through the crowd, avoiding physical contact, and take a seat, pulling out my phone to scroll through Instagram in ten seconds flat. My entrance was less impactful than anticipated.

"Hey, there you are." Auden approaches, having found Dom, her newest obsession, while I was talking to the parents.

Dom is the type of guy you'd find at the single local diner in town at three thirty in the afternoon, because that's when he woke up. He smiles at me in a glazed way. The smell of alcohol and weed wafts off him in a gust.

"We're going to go dance. Do you want to come?" Auden asks.

Suddenly, the music starts blasting louder. Dom starts bobbing his neck around, pretending to find the beat. As his mouth moves to the words, I realize it's Frank Ocean's "Chanel." Just when I wonder if Dom is going to do what I hope he doesn't, the *n*-word comes flying out of his mouth as he repeats the lyrics to the song.

I recoil. "What did you just say?" My tone is flat while his eyes remain misty with delight, though his singing voice tapers out.

"What?"

"You can't say that word."

Auden tenses and puts a hand on Dom's shoulder. Either he doesn't notice her signal or chooses not to. His eyebrows furrow.

"What are you talking about—*oh.*" Realization hits him, but he rolls his eyes. "It's fine, it's just a song, and it's Frank, so it's like canon."

I squeeze my fist. "It doesn't matter who it is or what song it is, *you* can't say that."

Dom shakes his head and looks to Auden for backup. She shakes her head at him and looks at me with a pained expression. "I mean, why do you even care?" Dom clears his throat, his eyes sharpening. "It's not like you're *Black*-Black," Dom insists.

I want to reach my fist back and propel it outward and hit him in the face. I genuinely do.

"What does that even mean?" I ask.

Dom shakes his head, cheeks flushed. "You're not like *Black* like Frank Ocean is *Black*, you're like half, right? You're barely darker than Auden. You're taking this way too seriously. It's a party. We're having *fun*."

I balk, then look over at Auden. Her eyes widen more than I thought possible, but she doesn't say anything. She just reaches out toward me. I flinch even though I wish I didn't have any reaction at all.

"Hey, let's go get another drink?" Auden suggests to Dom, who doesn't seem to hear her. He just stays staring at me, waiting for a response. I wish my chest weren't so tight. It makes me sick knowing that being ambiguously Black means people like Dom get to both make me feel abnormal and discredit who I am.

"You're a dirtbag," I say to Dom, then turn and walk out the sliding door of Matthew's house. This wasn't at all what I wanted the evening to be.

On my way out, I skim past the shoulders of a few of my classmates and imagine that I'm feeling their mix of discomfort and intrigue at seeing what just happened: sharp and fizzy.

*God, I'm such an idiot! Why did I think today would be any different?* I slam the door shut behind me as Dom's laugh blends with the song changing to something more pop-ish. I rip the hair tie out of my curls and walk so fast I'm nearly jogging.

*I wish he hadn't gotten under my skin.* I'm usually better at hiding it, at knowing when to leave a conversation with people who don't understand. *I can't believe Auden is with that guy.* I mean, she likes him, sure, but we've been friends for three years. *Why didn't she say anything?*

Behind Matthew's house is a short lawn and a staircase leading down the side of a rocky bluff to the ocean. Step by step I fly down the icy planks of slightly molded wood, clutching the splintered railing beside me. When I reach the rocky beach at the bottom, the sting of the cold air whipping off the ocean blows my hair from my shoulders. There are a few deck chairs down here and I settle into one a few feet from the steps, then stare at the sky overhead. It is filled with millions of white stars against inky black.

When we first moved here, I used to look up at those stars and feel just how I do now. Like a tiny speck in an always expanding universe, like no matter what I do, nothing will ever be significant. I press my knees against my chest and let my heartbeat drown out all other noise.

The world is sweeping me up inside of it, and though I might resist, time is dragging me forward. Right now, it's a good thing. I want to leave moments and people like Dom behind, but on the other hand, I'm afraid that's all that's waiting for me outside this island: more awkward encounters and humiliating experiences, more voices in my head. It's all too much. I wish I could keep time in a bottle and pour it out as needed.

"Hello," a soft voice says from beside me.

Outlined by the crash of the waves behind her, a woman approaches through the darkness beside me. Her figure is silhouetted by moonlight casting a halo around her body. She looks otherworldly, and I can't imagine where she came from.

"Hi," I say, pressing my palm against my cheek to make sure it's dry.

The woman is wearing a blue and red quilted wrap around her shoulders, and her hair is curly, soft, and dark brown. She doesn't look like she's from around here, and when she gazes at me, for the second time tonight, I feel like I am truly being seen.

"Thea, do you mind if I sit?" The woman has wide-set dark eyes that twinkle as she approaches. I move over slightly. *How does she know my name?*

# 2

I'M HEATHER," the woman introduces herself as she sits beside me.

I pretend not to notice how beautiful her brown skin is, which shines under the light of the moon and stars.

"You know, the Egyptians have a way of thinking about the stars that I've always found enchanting," Heather says.

I turn and see slight strands of silver weave their way down the sides of her face as she looks up at the sky. "Are you Egyptian?"

Heather continues, "They believed the night sky is just like water. When I saw phosphorescence for the first time here, it reminded me of that—everything is connected in one way or another. What do you think of the stars?"

Maybe if I wasn't raised by an eccentric woman, I might be leaving this conversation. But I was, and there's something about Heather that soothes me, so I stay seated. "I don't know. They make me feel small, I guess." I hold myself against the night chill.

Dark ocean waves bring with them the smell of algae and smoke from across the water.

Heather inclines her head and exhales. "If you connect the stars together, you get constellations, you know. In the old myths and legends, you knew you were a true hero if you became a constellation." She says it almost hopefully.

A tingle winds up the base of my neck, the same sensation I'd get if I locked eyes with a wild animal. Suddenly my body tenses. Just then comes a strain on the wooden steps behind me. I turn in time to see Auden, wearing Dom's sweater, descending the stairs timidly.

"Oh, sorry, I didn't realize you were—should I come back?" Auden stammers.

"No, you girls go ahead. I was just on my way out." Heather stands with a soft, almost mournful smile. Before leaving though, Heather takes my hands and wraps hers around them. Leaning down and pulling me close, a wave of the sweetest intense love washes over me. I'm so moved, I don't know whether to cry or gasp.

"You have it too," Heather whispers, her brown eyes piercing.

"What?" I mutter. "Have what?"

In a flash, she lets go of my hands, waves goodbye, and continues into the dark stretch of beach. I remain frozen in shock while Auden approaches with her hands clasped in front of her body, shoulders tilted down mournfully. I watch Heather disappear around the bend with my mouth slightly open. *What just happened?*

"I just wanted to apologize for—all of that," Auden begins, tugging her Celtic knot with her pinky finger and pulling me back to the present moment. I try to focus on her words, but my mind is elsewhere.

**THE FERRY RIDE HOME** is significantly choppier than the day before. I rest my head against the window beside me as we glide over the narrow stretch of sea separating Vancouver Island from Salt Spring. The cabin smells like the remains of someone's perfume mixed with old vinyl. Both scents cause the headache blooming between my eyebrows to press in closer as I remember the events of last night. *What a disaster.* First there was the Dom thing, then the Heather thing, then the Auden apology—and then having to sleep over at Matthew's because Auden got drunk and couldn't drive us to Emily's.

*I have moved so many times, tried on so many different personalities, and none of them feel right. I thought things would be different here.*

Finally, the ferry pulls into the terminal in Crofton. Rising from my seat, I stumble past rows of empty seats to descend to the car deck. Outside, as I stare up at a sky full of dark gray clouds, I silently curse myself for not listening to Mom and double-checking for my charger. My phone has been dead since the early morning, so I can't even listen to music to block everything out. I make my way off the ferry with my fists shoved in my pockets.

A small yellow building dominates the street corner above the ferry lineup. It is moss-covered and paneled with old wood, unusually soft to the touch due to water absorption and neglect. At this time of the year, the Snack Shack is covered with icicles. The smell of baking rice crisps and the sour tang of lemon bars fill the air as I approach. Both are prepared by my coworker Susan, a twenty-nine-year-old woman who looks about as happy to be here as I do.

Inside the building is a low barn-style ceiling with exposed beams and hints of mouse holes. Across a smattering of eight square tables is the bar. Behind that sits the confining kitchen and tiny employee bathroom. My boss, Greg, sits near the window with his back to the wall and his laptop already open watching television, as he does every day. Greg does not greet me as I enter.

Susan pops her head up to give me a short wave as I wind around the bar of the café and hang my bag on the hook. I wave back.

"Yes," I breathe when I catch sight of the phone charger in the "random things" cupboard beside the till, chock-full of forgotten guitar picks, loose napkins, and about a hundred rubber bands. I look at Greg, as if he'd care that I'm on my phone six minutes before the café opens. He doesn't look up from his laptop screen. After plugging in, I try to turn the black screen on, and it flashes with the "empty battery" sign. Closing my eyes, I rock backward on my heels. *God, this is going to be a long day.*

"Thea, you're here! Help Susan with the cakes, please?" Greg asks, moments after my arrival. *It's not my job to help Susan with the food, I'm just a barista.* I bite my tongue and tie on my apron. As I turn to do as I'm told, the front door to the shop opens with a *ding.*

"Sorry, we're not open for another five minutes," I say, already curt due to my headache and the sloshing in my stomach—*Is that new? Note to self: eat a Tum.*

I turn to face the customer and attempt to replace my frown with a smile when I don't hear them retreat. But then my smile slips because *there he is.* The boy from last night.

He wears a long black leather jacket over what looks like a school uniform: black pants and suspenders over a crisp white shirt with a coal blazer and a striped black-and-white tie. There is a patch on his blazer: a crest that looks like an eye inside of a flame. Behind the eye are two swords, and below it are a few words in a language I don't know, Latin maybe? It's not the crest of any private school around here.

*I didn't make him up, he's real.* The boy looks between me and a piece of paper in his hand three times, not even glancing at our menu.

"But since you're already inside, what can I get for you?" I force a smile and look at the boy head-on. With thick black hair brushed back from his face, a strong jaw coupled with his towering height, he's too attractive to be in a place as ordinary as this. I try to not let it show on my face that I've noticed the symmetry of his dark eyes or the straight line of his nose. I force myself to smile the same way I would if he were an old lady.

The boy continues to look at me with a confused expression, glancing from my name tag down to the paper in his hands. *Maybe he doesn't speak English?* He kicks into motion before I can continue the thought.

"Yeah, yes, um—do you do a macchiato?" he asks, a British accent peppering his speech.

I look over my shoulder at the menu. "I suppose we do," I say, looking at Greg, who promised to train me in drink making before abandoning me with YouTube tutorials and a half-hearted "good luck."

"What size?" I ask.

"What?"

"For the coffee, what size, we have a twelve ounce, sixteen—"

"Twelve is fine." He towers over me.

*He must be a tourist from abroad,* I decide as I ring him up. He pulls out a handful of change, counts it, and holds it forward. I take his money, and as the coins leave his palm, I feel the edge of his finger brush against my skin. I gasp despite myself. When our skin meets, a wave of curiosity, confusion, but also something else—something electric that reminds me of falling—comes off him in a wave.

The hairs on the back of my neck stand, and I pull my hand back. *What was that?* Undeniable electricity races up the bone of my arm and spreads through my whole body. I finally look at him straight in the face. I swallow, no longer just noticing his eyes but also registering a vibrancy in the world behind him—a charge that tingles over the surfaces of all the tables and walls. The room begins to *move*. It's as if there is a bubble beneath the surface of the wall, moving and spreading behind it. Like when I'm making my bed and spread out my sheet, but air gets trapped and creeps toward me, over the still mattress while the fabric settles. Only instead of fabric and air, I'm looking at moving wooden planks. While the scene transforms, I get hints of darkness wanting to burst out. I blink a few times, willing the movement away. The motion becomes more intense and rushes directly toward me as if what is behind the walls is literally bursting. I shout and raise my hands, prepared to fend off a crash of wood, but there is no crash, no sound, nothing. I peek at the room from between my fingers and find Greg looking at me in alarm and the boy staring completely sober at my frantic motion. He opens his mouth as if to ask me something, but I am already moving. I don't waste time telling myself I've made this all up; it feels too real to ignore.

I grab my phone, which has thankfully buzzed to life, and mutter that I need a moment without looking into the boy's dark eyes. I rush into the kitchen. Once I've put a wall between the stranger and me, I register five missed voicemails on my home screen and press my phone against my ear. Mom's voice offers a sense of comfort, until I notice the alarm in her tone.

"Thea, get home as soon as you hear this. As soon as you can, *all right?*" My mother is never frantic. If anything, she usually speaks *too* slow. I look over my shoulder. Around the corner I can see the edge of the mysterious boy's shoulder. I know I should go back and explain myself, but my instincts tell me not to. Instead, I race over to the back door, push my hands flat against the gray metal, and flee.

# 3

I'VE NEVER DONE anything like this before. I'll surely be fired. I keep my eyes fixed forward and my pace quick as I wind my way up the hill toward my house. Halfway there, I realize I forgot my backpack at the Snack Shack, but halfway there means I'm halfway too late to go back. When I get home, I have to rub my eyes. For a split second I think I see a shadow looming over it. *Deep breath, Thea, you need to reign this in.* I push the front door open and call down the hallway.

"Mom? Nana?"

There are three large black bags in the foyer; one of them is mine.

"Thea!" Mom calls from the kitchen. Her voice is usually soothing, but today she sounds as tense as I feel.

"What's going on?" When I get to the kitchen, my mother and grandmother are both standing up, dressed as if they're heading somewhere. My mom is beside the cluttered kitchen table with her arms crossed over her chest. To her right, Nana is leaning onto the counter, vigorously pounding a mortar and pestle filled to the brim with a dusty yellow substance that shines like the powder from the back of a moth's wings.

"What's going on?" I repeat.

"I was hoping this wouldn't happen so soon—" Mom begins but is interrupted by my grandmother.

"Tell us about last night." Nana still doesn't look at me as she continues to grind.

"I—uh, it was fine. I met Auden at the ferry and then ended up sleeping over at Matthew's. He drove me to the boat in the morning."

"Anything unusual?" Nana asks, hand still pounding. She peers at me, just once.

*This is serious. Nana didn't even raise her eyebrows after hearing that I slept over at a boy's house.* Instead, her bright black eyes shine against the glow of the overhead kitchen light as she looks me over like she sees something on me that wasn't there before. Her long salt-and-pepper pin-straight hair is tucked behind her ears neatly. *Why are they acting so weird?*

"One of the boys said the *n*-word and I had to tell him why it was messed up, and I met a woman on the shore. But wait, why did you call?"

My mother stops pacing. "A woman?" she asks.

"Yeah, her name was Heather, she was magnetic and strange. We chatted for a while."

"Heather, you said?" Nana asks.

"Yeah?" I shrug and sink down into a chair beside the dining room table, near my mother. Then I remember her final words to me. "She did say something confusing. As she was leaving, she grabbed my hands and whispered, 'You have it too.'"

Nana's eyes circle the room, skim over her own paintings, over the Buddha across from them, then down the darkness of the hall. She frowns and keeps grinding while my mother sinks down to her knees and faces me.

"What did you talk about?" Mom asks steadily.

"I don't know, the stars. What are you two doing?" I try to stand, but Mom puts her hand on my wrist to hold me in place. As soon as she touches me, I feel her concern, her love, and an oncoming darkness, a metallic terror that makes me stop squirming. When I look into her dark eyes, I find no reassurances.

"Thea, we're going to go soon," she says, hurried. "And before we go, we need to know if anything else has been strange. Anything at all?"

I frown a little at the line of questioning. I don't want to tell them I might be losing my mind, that I may have visual and auditory hallucinations in addition to crippling anxiety and a lack of math skills. I do not need the weight of another self-diagnosed disorder on my shoulders. But then, through my panic, feeling the soft weight of my mother's hand press harder, her love shines stronger than her fear. I let it calm me even if I'm making it up. I exhale a little, *fine*.

"I guess, yeah. Before I got your messages, I thought I saw something weird in the café. The walls, they kind of moved?" I say, expecting some sort of reaction from either of them, but I receive none. My grandmother continues to grind; my mother continues to think.

"Anything else?" Mom asks, very quietly.

"I—don't be mad," I preface, "but I was planning to steal your shoes. You know, the nice leather ones? I was in your closet before I left, looking for them, but instead I found this statue. It looked a little like Nana's Buddha except it had no face, just a body and hands. When I held it, I heard a sort of voice in my head? I know what you're going to say, but it's not like the voices you hear. This was real," I confess.

Moms always said she hears voices, but it's always been jokingly, as if it was our secret. During walks in the forest when I was a little girl she'd whisper compliments from the trees, or as we tended to wild sunflowers in the park, she'd joke about them singing along to our songs.

My grandmother stops her grinding and places her hand on the counter beside her. "What did it say?" Her tone makes it less of a question and more an order.

My mother cuts her a severe look.

I shrug with my palms up and think back to the poem. "I don't know, something about heroes and fate or something."

Nana's pupils narrow and she looks at my mother. A secret conversation passes between them. I have been on the outside of these wordless exchanges my entire life.

"When the keys go missing, you must be the one to find them, and you mustn't trust anyone at first appearances in that house." Nana doesn't blink as she speaks.

"What are you saying?" My pulse quickens as I look between them.

Mom puts her other hand on my upturned wrist and looks at me intently. "I know this is strange. But you'll be okay. I'm sorry about the party. I truly wish we had more time to talk."

"Why are you being so cryptic? I came home because of your messages. You're really worrying me."

Mom's eyes become damp. "I just—

Behind her Nana slams the pestle down beside her mortar and my mother stiffens at the noise.

"Promise me to keep this on, and do whatever Nana says, all right?" Mom gently touches my jade bracelet, a gift from her to me on my thirteenth birthday, just a few days after we moved here. She looks at me with mirrors of my own eyes, and when her hand leaves my wrist, I shiver from no longer feeling her love radiating through me.

Nana turns to the stove just as the hairs on the back of my neck stand on end. As I question the sensation, I hear it. A sound like a drop of rain but flatter, larger. Soon it is accompanied by more. I stand from my seat and walk to the glass kitchen door, pushing open the sheer white curtain to reveal the deck beyond. My eyes widen in confused horror. I take a step back. Big, black, slimy frogs fall from nowhere, over and over. They coat the deck ahead, then begin hopping forward as if incentivized by the sight of my face. My mother pulls me away by the shoulder with an iron grip. What started as three or four frogs is quickly turning to eight, then twenty, now fifty. They drop from the sky with dark eyes that glint even in the morning light and mouths that open to show long, too-sharp tongues.

"What the hell? Where are they coming from?" I ask Mom, who has turned pale under the kitchen light.

"Amina, come," Nana demands, shoving her mortar forward.

My mother bursts into motion, taking the bowl from her hands.

"*What* is going on?" I ask as they begin to move toward the front door.

"Thea, grab the bags!" Mom shouts over her shoulder.

The frogs finally reach the glass of the door ahead of me and begin crawling up the sides. Their little legs push inward, some managing to squeeze under the doorframe. When they do, I notice their amphibious hands darken the wood wherever they touch, as if their skin is leaking hot oil. I scramble to follow behind Mom and Nana. Raising two of the bags into each of my arms, I clutch the third in my hands as my grandmother opens the front door of the house.

Outside, the lawn is as covered as the deck. Hundreds of hopping black frogs coat our car. I'm so shocked I can't even manage true terror at the sight. It's sort of comical how absurd it looks.

Nana and Mom pause on the walkway outside of the house, looking at the frogs approaching with mirrored expressions, not of fear, just determination. My mother then reaches two fingers into the bowl and tosses out a spray of dust from her fingertips. It falls in a yellow-white cloud and wherever the powder falls, like salt on a slug, the frogs shrivel away.

"Come," Nana urges me, "this won't be so easy much longer," she says. Nana's long hair sways behind her as she continues forward, and she looks back at me just once, reminding me why she scared me so much as a child. Without knowing where we're going, I follow Mom and Nana away from the road and the town, into the thick dark forest behind our rented house.

"Are either of you going to tell me what is going on?"

"Look at the house, Thea," Nana says, as if it should be obvious.

I turn over my shoulder again. Instead of looking down at the small black creatures following me, I take in what is normally our beige stucco house. Only now it has become a black writhing mass. I notice the pattern they make over the stucco with their bodies, like a slimy black moving hill. I gasp as I realize—*it looks just like what I saw in the café*, pulsating walls. Only now that mass also spills over the forest floor behind us like a stain.

I increase my pace to stay as close to my family as possible.

Mom and Nana plunge into the forest like they know where they're going, until finally they stop. *I know this place*, I realize as I look at the remnants of an abandoned well I was previously cautioned to stay away from. Its foundation is little more than crumbling stone. Two wooden planks cover its surface.

Mom keeps casting pinchfuls of the shimmering powder in wide arcs the frogs don't dare cross. This is the first time Mom has been outside of the house in over a year. She looks like she belongs here, in the trees and wearing adult clothes, not locked away and lying in bed. My arms strain from the effort of carrying these heavy bags and I scan for a pathway out of the forest.

"Where are we?" I ask as Nana bends over the well, pulling aside the wooden planks. She doesn't answer. With the planks gone, the well is black and deep, like a hole to the center of the earth. The smell of old water and rotting leaves hits my nose.

"Are either of you going to say anything?" I ask.

The frogs begin shaping themselves one over the other, gaining height among the fallen leaves and branches at the very edge of the yellow dust my mother has spread, unable to hop any closer. When some of them do try, as soon as their little bodies come in contact with the dust, they shrivel up as if burned.

Then I hear something. Like the scream of metal, or a car crash on the other end of a tunnel. The screech sends a chill through the roof of my brain. I look instantly to the spot in the distance from where it came.

Stifling a scream, my face goes cold. The creature peels itself forward, rising to at least eight feet tall and only a house-length away. But it isn't the creature's height, corpse-like movements, or even its dense skin made from impossible swirling shadows that makes me take a step back, it is the creature's eyes—or lack thereof. It has two holes where eyes should be and within them exists a darkness deeper and colder than the dark that makes up its flesh.

Mom grabs me by the front of my shirt and pulls me away from the edge of the border she created with her shimmering powder. *Is this really happening?*

"Did you see that?" I ask, trying to look back at the creature over my shoulder.

"Look at me," she says, holding my face still. "Breathe. Just breathe."

I try to force breath through my nose. "What is that?" I whisper.

My mother purses her lips. "It is a demon, my love, but don't worry. It won't get you."

I can see it approaching from the corner of my eye, achingly slow yet confident in its movements. *It's looking right at me.*

"You're going to be all right." Mom says this like a prayer. "You'll *always* be okay. No matter *what.* You have me, but most importantly, you have you."

The surety I feel through the palms of her hands tastes like rose petals.

"The only person you need to survive is yourself, Thea."

"*Survive?* Why are you talking like this?" I want the truth; I want to know what's going on, but Nana cuts me off.

"Come, Amina, don't baby her, she's not a child," Nana says, standing up and wiping her hands on the front of her pants. Mom's hand falls from the side of my face.

My heart is nearly in my throat while the frogs clamor at the border, little veiny black hands sizzling against the yellow dust. I realize that Mom's bowl is empty when a few fall on the dust, burning up immediately, while a few others jump over their carcasses, gaining ground and pressing in closer to our circle. I try to kick them away and not look at the creature in the trees ahead at the same time.

"Here." Nana thrusts a horsehair paintbrush toward me, the one she's used for as long as I've been alive. The tip of it is wet when my palm wraps around it.

"Wait—"

"No time, Thea, come now, get in the well," Nana instructs.

I frown and look between them both, then to the small slice of darkness newly uncovered in the well. The frogs press toward our feet.

"Where does this go?" I shriek, squirming away from the slimy bodies.

I feel the weight of their request; the importance of this moment is in my Mom's and Nana's eyes. But I don't want to move.

Then, one of the larger frogs jumps forward, landing on my exposed ankle with a wet burning sensation. Stifling a scream, I shake my leg to get it off. Nana rolls her eyes impatiently while

Mom wraps her arms around me tight, moving me back a couple of steps. For a second, my eyes are wide open, seeing the frogs growing braver still, sacrificing some of their own into the dust to advance closer in droves; that dark creature is only a few feet away.

*How did it get here so quick?* Then I register Mom's familiar sweet and floral smell. She feels like home. I relax into her embrace, closing my eyes, despite myself. *I don't know what's going on, but if she's here, I'm sure I'll be—Oh, shit!*

Mom pushes me backward. I don't even see her expression as I fall into the well. The corner of my shoulder catches the edge of the stone structure on my way down. All I do see before I hit the cold gripping water beneath me is a single scene. The dark creature without eyes looming over Mom and Nana with long pointed fingernails reaching out—and then the wet is covering my head and I am sinking down, down, down.

# 4

**S**TARS IN A NIGHT SKY, tinged blue and tingling with life, bubble around me. *Phosphorescence.* The word rises in me like a melody as I flail against the water. Salty and thick, it coats my tongue while I struggle for breath and peer through the dazzling dark. The bags on my shoulders weigh on me, my jeans constrict against my body, and there is no bottom, no purchase, no relief—I am drowning.

*I am going to drown in a well, pushed by my own mother, and chased by creatures that can't exist.* The water is cold on my ears and drags at my scalp; I have no idea how deep it is or how wide, and I am sinking deeper and deeper. Then I see it. A light in the distance: a bright circle beckoning me closer. I struggle to swim toward it. I am not a bad swimmer, but every time I push, I barely move an inch. I know the bags are only pulling me down. I struggle against the tangle of the straps until I am free of their weight.

I ignore the burning in my chest and the pain in my throat. I push past the fear that I may have lost too much air already. I push until I cannot push anymore. Then, when I am finally close enough to see, I learn that what first appeared circular from a distance is actually a rectangular length of light. My heart soars as I make out an open door. I don't hesitate. I reach out. The moment my fingers touch the air on the other side, all the water I had been struggling against gushes me forward, pushing me into the world beyond.

I crash into a solid surface, coughing up both of my lungs in the process. Water falls out of my mouth in buckets, and I wipe my eyes until the sting of salt doesn't hurt as badly. After I am finally sharp enough to feel that my throat is as raw as my bones are Jell-O, I look at the room I'm in while I drag myself up to stand. Beneath me and winding ahead is a coarse oriental rug topped with a round table and a vase of flowers; beyond it is an out-of-use fireplace with a shallow mantle, flanked by two large stained-glass windows over two full bookcases. To my left is a staircase that winds to the side for a few paces and then starkly up. This entire entryway is lined in warm-hued wood, and a quaint chandelier hangs over the vase of flowers. I peer over my shoulder at the large doorway behind me, rectangular with a rounded top. It's closed and made from the same wood as the rest of the building. *Am I inside a house?* Or maybe it's a waiting room at an acupuncturist clinic. Either way, it's impossible. *What is going on?*

Immediately, I open the door I just came through and find that yes, I am alive, and somehow, I am no longer in the forest behind my house. I'm not at all prepared for what I see on the other side of the door: a busy road filled with cars, a sidewalk lined with people, and a bright blue sky hanging over it all. I freeze in shock, in fear, in denial. When a voice comes from behind me, casual in tone and just loud enough to be heard over the traffic, I nearly jump out of my sopping skin.

"I wouldn't go out there if I were you."

I turn around to discover someone sitting in the middle of the staircase, nestled against a sunken window. I didn't see him before: he was so well wedged. He holds a book in one hand covering his face. The only feature I can make out is a head of silky dark brown hair and three rings on the hand that holds the book.

"Why not?" I ask automatically. My eyes dart around the room until they snag on my mirrored reflection above the closed-up fireplace: wet hair, frightened eyes rimmed with wet mascara. I look away from myself when he speaks.

"Not safe." The boy finally lowers his book so that I can see his face fully.

I gulp. He's beautiful in the way an intricately carved sculpture is beautiful. His bones look almost sharp, set into tawny brown skin. But then his mouth tightens, and he gives me a sympathetic glance. I bristle.

"I'm Hunar," he says, still sitting casually. "When I came through that door it was the exit of a café in Jaipur."

"Um, okay. Do you know where we are?" I turn to face the undeniable traffic behind me, then look back at him. "I was with my mom. She was right behind me, she—" I shake my head as I remember her pushing me in, the frightened and knowing look in her eyes, the weight of those heavy bags on my arms. My mouth opens to continue, but no words come out.

"It's all right, Reina will be here soon," Hunar assures me.

"Who is Reina?"

Hunar looks to his right and I consider making a run for it. But then I pause and remember the lengths my grandmother and mother went through to bring me here—*wherever here is.* I shake my head. *I need time to think.*

"She's a bit late," Hunar says softly, then unfolds himself before walking down the few stairs and arriving to stand on the same carpet as me. Hunar is so tall his head could easily knock into the chandelier if he weren't hunched over. I stand there, trying not to stare at this kid who is obviously staring at me. The gaze in his eyes confuses me. He vacillates between smiling and turning away when I meet his gaze.

"Well, I don't usually do the introductions, but we might as well start. What's your name?" He approaches, his hand extended.

I look at it nervously, but ultimately reach out and give it a limp shake as water drips from the cuff of my shirt. His grip is loose and his hand quivers inside mine. *He's nervous*, I realize.

When I don't answer, Hunar nods easily and, without missing a beat, continues. "Do you want a towel, or some clothes? There's probably some upstairs."

"I'm fine here," I insist, one hand still on the door behind me.

"All right, well, welcome. This is Malachite. Founded at roughly the beginning of time, it's a home where people like us—"

I throw a hand up. "Let me just stop you. I don't think I am who you think I am. I'll just wait outside for my mom." I begin easing the door open behind me.

"Wait, that's a bad idea. I—I'm not usually the one who does this. Here, let me try showing you instead," Hunar says.

I'm about to throw the door open when he quickly turns and picks up the vase of flowers behind him. Before I can run out, the vase and the flowers he's holding rise into the air and *come apart*. The vase cracks into a neat shatter, pieces of porcelain hovering in the air, and the purple flowers separate from stamen to petal to stem. They just float there, in the air between us—dissected—while I gape.

"Malachite is where people like us live, train, hide, and exist," Hunar says quickly. Three golden earrings glint on the cartilage of his left ear. If I weren't so freaked out, I'd be charmed by his bashful smile. My hand pauses on the door handle. A vein pulses in his neck as he struggles to maintain the exploded vase and its contents, before he closes his eyes, and in a single inhale it all comes back together perfectly, as if it never broke. Hunar catches the vase and flowers and places them back down on the table.

"How did you just do that?"

Hunar shakes his head and looks quite cross with himself, turning away from the vase while I continue to stare at it with wide eyes. *Did that just happen?*

"Look, are you familiar with mythology and the gods, any gods?" he begins. "You know, those giant beings in the clouds who cause mischief, the ones who created the world? Well, they made us. They are our . . . relatives. If you're here—inside Malachite—it means you belong here. And if your family sent you here, it must mean they knew that. So, stay inside, get dry, and relax," he says with wide brown eyes. "You're safe now."

I'm unsure whether to laugh or cry. "Look, I'm sorry, but *no*, you definitely have the wrong person." I say it while tightening my hand on the door handle, but I don't turn it.

He takes a step forward. "Has anything strange happened to you lately? Have you been seeing things, hearing things, *feeling* things that aren't . . . there?"

I pause.

"Have you seen anything unexplainable? Creatures or mysterious people? It's all part of this world. What I'm telling you is the truth."

A shiver passes over me from crown to toes. Then the door behind me suddenly pulls outward again and city air hits the back of my neck in a cold gripping whoosh. I draw away from the opening door into the foyer just as a woman pops her head into the room. She has blonde hair streaked through with a measure of brown that contrasts her sandy complexion and gray eyes. She holds herself tall and proud, giving the perception that she's fully grown, though she looks only slightly older than me and wears loose, light clothes.

"Hunar, did you show her your trick already? That's not necessarily where I would have started," she says, looking between Hunar, the flowers, and my scared wet frame. I notice the very subtle curl of her accent; it reminds me of my Spanish teacher's at school. Hunar visibly relaxes.

"Sorry, Reina, she was going to run out," he says, gesturing to me.

When Reina finally looks into my eyes, hers crinkle with a smile, as if she expected to find me just as I am, wet and afraid, standing in the foyer. Something inside of me relaxes.

"Hello, you. My name is Reina Suárez." She sets down a walking stick beside the entrance, turning to close the door behind her with a flick of her ankle.

I simply stare at her.

"Why don't we get you dry," she says, reaching forward to place a reassuring hand on my wrist.

I KEEP ONE EYE on the door while I stand with a towel around my neck, in the kitchen of this impossible house, a cup of chamomile in my hands. The room is lined with clean white shelves stacked with mismatched bowls and cups. Some are painted pottery; others are ordinary glass. On one end of the room there is a window covered in the same stained glass as the foyer. Through it, I see a moonlit sky, completely at odds with the daylight I spied outside the open front door.

"So, you expect me to believe in what, gods and monsters? That my mother sent me here for you to *train* me?" I shake my head. It's just the two of us now. Hunar left when Reina took over; I don't know why, but I felt a stab of abandonment when he went.

"I am not lying. We both know—even if you choose to ignore it—that you belong here," Reina says, crossing her arms over her chest.

I set my cup down and wrap my arms around my stomach, unconvinced.

"There has always been something different about you, and now you know why," Reina insists.

I swallow and remember the game I made up when I was little, the one where I could feel other people's feelings. It no longer feels like a game to me anymore. Especially when I frame it against everything else that's happened in the past couple of days.

Now I can't help feeling a little flame of hope bursting in the center of my chest as she speaks. I mean, it's everyone's dream, isn't it? To be somehow, inexplicably, unlike your peers in some fantastical way.

"So, gods, are real?" I ask.

"It's likely that every deity you have ever heard of has existed at one point. This house is a link to the gods of the past and present. The blood of old and new gods flows through our veins. It's something to be proud of," she says.

I frown and clamp my hands together. "So, who are your deity relatives?" I ask.

Reina smiles. "My mother is a jeweler in Ecuador but her father is a messenger god named Bochica, worshiped in Colombia for thousands of years as a bringer of civilization. My grandfather on my father's side is Tezcatlipoca, god of destiny," she says with a wink and a smile. "I've never met either of my god relatives, and neither have my parents. They leave us to our destiny from birth." She looks distant for a moment. "Come, I'll walk you through the house and keep explaining as we go," she says, having set down the tote bag she walked in with.

Reina has the air of a camp counselor, one who would sit with you the night after you wet your bunk. She seems like someone who would hold your hair back if you vomited, too. Still, I don't move as she beckons me forward through the doorway at the back of the kitchen. *What if it's all a lie?*

Noticing my apprehension, she says simply, "You say your mother sent you here? What are the chances of her sending you somewhere you would not be safe?"

I leave my untouched tea on the countertop and cast a final look over my shoulder at the wide and imposing doorway, reluctantly following Reina out of the kitchen.

The house opens ahead of us with a wide hallway, carpeted from end to end. There are paintings lining each long wall, some depicting ordinary portraits, others showing stranger scenes: a woman with leathery skin seemingly taking off her face to reveal a more beautiful one beneath, a man drowning himself in a shallow pool of water. A shiver runs up my spine. I wrap my hand around the collar of my shirt and follow Reina another few paces before she comes to a stop.

"This is your room," she exhales.

"What do you mean, *my* room?" I ask, looking at the large wooden door, the light spilling out from beneath its frame.

"This house was built a very long time ago, by the gods who wanted to protect us and other precious things," Reina says, resting her temple on the wall beside her. "My mother told me about it when I was very young. This house was made to fit whoever needed space. All of us have rooms here and we always will." Her words fall from her mouth like water over stone. It's easy to trust someone who sounds this smooth. "The front door changes locations at random every twenty-four hours, so no one can track us. There are many who would like to." She fingers her necklace, an ordinary leather cord that holds an unremarkable river stone.

I raise my hand to the handle of the door and pause. Reina answers my question before I verbalize it.

"If your mother and grandmother find their way to the front door, I will let you know—but you must not leave Malachite. Not until we know who your deity relatives are. The outside world is a dangerous place. I do not wish to scare you, but we are not the only things of legend that exist. Finish getting dry and find me when you're ready."

I walk into the room Reina has called mine and close the door behind me with a firm click, pressing my head into the doorframe a second later. Immediately, questions flood me: *Why would Mom send me here if it weren't for the best? How can Reina trust that I won't run away?* I sigh. *Even if I did run, where would I go?* The world outside that front door is not one I know.

Finally, I turn and look back into the expansive room. Across a peach and blue rug sits a queen-size bed covered in thick down blankets the color of a pink sunset. The windows beside it are circular and bordered by petal curtains with ties on each side. It's the bedroom of my childhood fantasies, as if picked from my thirteen-year-old imagination of what it would be like to live as Marie Antoinette. My stomach rolls to one side in nausea. I walk forward, cautiously placing one foot ahead of the other, unwillingly wondering if that shadow creature has followed me.

I open the curtains covering the round windows and see an impossible sight: an endless ocean churning against the glass without any land in sight. As if I'm gazing out a ship window half-submerged in water, the deep blue of the waves is so dark it could only be the ocean. Overhead, the sky is dusky. *None of this makes sense.* I take a frightened step back, closing the drapes with a flourish, and turn to my right where a doorway leads into a large walk-in closet. I barely look around; instead, I immediately discard my sopping clothes and hurriedly pull on the first things I can find in the drawers just beyond its threshold. As I stand, shivering, halfway through the process, there is the dull thud of something hard hitting the carpet beneath my feet. I turn to look down and find the paintbrush my nana gave me lying against the carpet. I bend down and pick it up. My hands shake as I hold it. Unsure where else to put it, I shove the brush through my curls to hold them out of my face while I finish dressing.

As I head out of the closet, I catch a glimpse of myself in a mirror that's leaning against the opposite wall between two fur coats. Even though I recognize that it's me staring back, now that I'm up close and have wiped the mascara from under my eyes, I find the person looking back at me wildly unfamiliar. There's something about me: a glow that makes my hair seem fuller, my mouth plumper, and my bone structure sharper. The golden glow radiating from my pores does more for me than any filter I've ever tried on. I let myself get lost in my reflection momentarily before I remember all that now awaits me.

Leaving the room, I'm nervous about getting lost in this big house. The eyes in the paintings lining the hall seem to stare at me with an aliveness that sends a gulp down my throat. But, in no time at all, I find that tracing my way back to the main entrance is easier than expected. With my list of newly formed questions for Reina, I approach the kitchen but pause when I hear unfamiliar voices thread toward me. *How many people live here?*

"—and she was all wet," one voice says.

I press myself against the wall beside the door, mortified to realize they're talking about me.

"Hunar said she was old, too. Like fifteen," says a third voice.

"And she's gorgeous . . . could be a selkie, or a faerie."

"*Em*, do you think she could be one of *them*? How are we supposed to know it isn't a trick? I mean, do you think it's a coincidence that the hunt started today? It can't be. I don't know why Reina— Oh—"

All the voices trail off at the sound of shuffling feet. I understand why when I hear Reina's sharp tone.

"What's going on?" she asks.

"Nothing," the few voices murmur.

"Well," Reina begins. I can imagine her pacing across the room as I recognize intentional clicks from her heeled boots. "Why are we gossiping in here? Shouldn't we be in the library working?"

Silence.

Reina lets out a deep sigh. "Remember, we were all new here once. This house is a place for everyone, all right?" she asks.

One by one, each child begrudgingly agrees.

I hold my breath, count to ten, and peek my head around the corner of the kitchen after their footsteps leave through the kitchen's other door. Reina's staring at a cookbook laid out on the kitchen island when I approach.

"I'm sure you heard all that," she says over her shoulder, her voice restored to the soothing, delicate tone with which she first greeted me. "I'm sorry about them."

"Who were they?" I ask, inching into the room.

"Emilio, Aiko, and Ani." She waves her hand in the air. "Nothing to worry about, they're just curious. You'll meet everyone at dinner. They'll be nice once they get to know you."

"I guess I'm not the only distrusting one here," I say.

"They're . . . cautious. It's a tense time you've found us in. We aren't used to newcomers in general. But today—of all days—your arrival has raised a couple of red flags. But don't worry." She forgets the cookbook and walks toward me, placing her hand on top of my left shoulder.

I brace for when she touches me, but when her skin meets mine, I don't feel anything at all except a distant buzzing electricity.

"I trust you," she says, then frowns. "You didn't want to rest?"

I purse my lips. "Can you explain to me again how all this works?"

Reina nods indulgently, lowering her hand from my shoulder and walking back to the kitchen island.

"In the beginning there was nothing but chaos, and then that chaos decided to transform," she begins. "Here, take this whisk while I grind. I will tell you more while we make dinner for the gossips," she winks.

I look down at the whisk like it might be a wand in disguise after I take it from her outstretched hand. *Nothing is as it appears anymore.* I find that the whisk, however, is just a whisk.

# 5

MYTH, LEGEND, GODS, MONSTERS—and me. If what I've just heard is true, this house—Malachite—was built to protect beings descended from multiple gods, mixed with human blood. Some of the Godspring of this house have a literal god as their parent on one side, while on the other they have a great grandparent who is of another mythological lineage. Reina said that there are gods in every part of the world; while many don't live on this plane of existence, they do visit, resulting in us. I look down at my hands under the table before me. *Us.* I still can't accept that I'm a part of this.

*"Gods make children for a reason,"* Reina said, *"to fulfill a purpose, a destiny. We all have a part to play, though it isn't usually our place to ask why."*

The dining room is circular with walls and ceiling made from glass. Outside, the plants and insects of a jungle press against it and a midday sun shines through. I try to focus on what's inside the room instead of the strangeness beyond the glass. To my left,

Reina sits with her linen-clad legs delicately folded. To her left is Hunar, who stores a book just under the table, dressed in cargo like a jungle explorer on rest between expeditions. Across from me is a sullen younger girl with vivid cherry-cola hair and thigh-high red socks.

"I'm Ani." She waved when I first sat down. Next to Ani is Tiana, a Black girl with beautiful, long braids. She hasn't looked at me once since we all sat down, even though everyone else stares in between bites. Beside her is Teal, who stands out with their bald head and alabaster skin.

Meeting so many of the others overwhelms me. I keep thinking: *If only things could calm down for a second, if I could get a moment of rest, I could figure this all out.* But the turmoil continues.

Reina explained that though Godspring live across the world, the people in this house call themselves Malachites. The more she says those two words, *Godspring* and *Malachites,* and the more she speaks about magic, the more convinced I become—the more I begin to accept that what's been happening to me, not just today but my whole life, is a part of this story.

Malachite was founded by the gods when they began spending less and less time on earth. This house was meant to be a haven for the children they left behind, to protect them from the other creatures the gods created.

"Can you pass the salt, please," a soft-spoken young boy asks from beside me. He's maybe ten at the oldest with closely cropped black hair. When I pass it to him, he smiles at me quickly.

Ani visibly kicks him under the table for doing so, hissing "Omari" under her breath.

I smile, grateful to know his name. These kids look like they shouldn't be out of school, let alone in a house with no real adult supervision.

I recall that gods communicate with their descendants only through prayer, but don't raise them, and rarely see them face-to-face. Right now, there are only twelve Malachites, and not many more Godspring in general *"given our high mortality rate,"* Reina says. Looking at her out of the corner of my eye, I recognize that while Reina may appear to be responsible, even she is young, no more than twenty. *How does she take care of everyone?*

I'm now realizing that *I* don't know how to sit or how to act without my mother present. I don't know who I am outside of my house, or at all. I adjust my glasses perched on my nose. As the others eat in relative silence, I watch Reina's movements to try and mimic her confidence, her ease in this strange house with these strange people. I fail and, still clutching my fork, stare down at the meal we prepared: crispy salted chicken, spiced rice, gently tossed salad topped with poppy seeds, a glass of sparkling pomegranate juice so bright it resembles blood.

"So, Thea," a low voice calls. I turn to look down the table at a red-haired boy about my age with folded arms who hasn't touched his food. His light eyes bore into me.

"Um, yeah?"

"I'll be blunt and ask what we're all thinking. How do we know we can trust you? And are you a part of the Arcana?" he asks.

"Ian," Reina says patiently.

"We're all thinking it, let him ask," another Godspring chimes in. She has an animated face and looks beyond cool in a thin-strapped violet shirt.

The whole room is silent. I lower my fork onto the tablecloth beside my plate.

"Marta, don't be rude," Reina says evenly. Still, the whole table looks at me.

"I—I don't really understand how I got here. I don't know anything about the—Arcana? And you don't have to worry about me because I won't be here long anyway. My family is coming for me," I explain. The words fall hollowly in the room. Suddenly, no one will look me in the eyes, not even Reina.

Marta's small mouth doesn't stop frowning. I wish I could press myself far enough back into this chair that I'd disappear.

Hunar pipes up. "Come on, guys, if she was going to steal the keys, she'd have tried it already. When have you heard of the Arcana being subtle or sitting down with us for dinner?"

I shoot him a thankful smile while Marta clenches her jaw. Hunar and a few others continue eating in silence.

*Who are the Arcana?* is the obvious question the room is far too tense for me to ask.

"The Arcana will try to get in here, like they do every four years, and just like every other time, they won't succeed," Reina says definitively a few moments later.

"But—"

Reina cuts Marta a severe stare. The rest of dinner is silent, and in less than twenty minutes the room empties out. Teal collects the plates and is the only one to offer me a restrained smile before hurrying off. I move to stand but Reina rests a light hand on my sleeve to hold me in place. Once the room is empty, she turns and speaks to me.

"There's something else I should have mentioned. Do you remember when I said only some of the Godspring live here at Malachite?" she asks.

I nod.

"Where we are sent to live depends entirely on who our god-relatives are. As I said, Malachite is the home of Godspring with mixed lineages, but there are also others . . . The children of the gods who created a major pantheon, for example. They call themselves Arcana. We have to be cautious of who leaves the house early in their awakenings, in part, because of them," she says, then moves her hand, rolls down the collar of her shirt to reveal a deep long-healed scar dragging from below her collar bone to the crevice of her armpit.

"One of them did this to me when I was only ten. They tried to get me to give up the location of Malachite before it moved so they could take what little we have inside. I hadn't even had my second awakening. I did not give in," she says soberly.

I try to weigh how scared I should be of this statement, how much capacity my body has for more fear.

"What do they want with Malachite?" I ask, already dreading the answer.

Reina stands and moves quickly. "Come with me," she says, her gray eyes shadowed.


**REINA COMES TO A STOP** before a set of double doors after we've walked through the body of Malachite, past paintings that, as night fell, turn darker than they looked just an hour ago. We walk past statues I didn't notice before: short-bodied ones made of dark stone that remind me of the one I found in Mom's closet. And when we walked past Tiana's bedroom, I hesitate because I could have sworn I hear something like a whisper behind my neck as I look past her head of braids into the large velvet-lined space. But then she shuts the door and Reina moves on, so I rush to keep up.

The double doors are rounded at the top just like the front door, radiating a distinct and odd heat. The feeling is more the presence of an energy than a real temperature shift. It's unusual, but not so much stranger than everything else.

Reina unlocks the door with a subtle press of her finger before pulling it open to reveal a shallow cupboard bearing just one ledge.

The wood of the ledge is black, as if charred. Resting on it is a box the length of my forearm and made from a deep green stone. I take a small step forward when I spot the three intricate keys that hang from hooks above it.

"*These* are the reason we must be cautious with who we allow inside our house. Inside this box is a power not seen on earth in thousands of years," Reina says reverently, stroking its green stone surface. "It's the reason this house has so much power. It keeps our location ever-moving and keeps us safe. It was once part of a god older than time, who gave it up to protect all of us from the darkness in this world. They were one of the first gods to ever exist, so old their name is forgotten." Reina gestures toward the keys above the box. "Each of these keys was made from a piece of the gods who helped create the box, and they are the only way to open it."

I take it all in with wide eyes and pursed lips. The box and keys remind me of items one might find at an antique store. I lean back on my heels while Reina keeps talking, her voice lowering into a whisper.

"All of us understand that, above all else, we protect these keys, and this box. Without them, all Malachites would be doomed to an unimaginably dangerous life. Without the box, *all of this* would go away, our protection, our safe haven, our family." She looks at me then, very intently. "After you sign your name in our Crimson Ledger and vow to protect these objects and this house, and live by our tenets, everyone will understand you're not from the Arcana," she says.

I swallow and look into her eyes, prepared to give her expectant smile what she wants: a single nod up and down, but instead I shake my head. *This is too much. This doesn't make sense. Nana told me about these keys; she said they would go missing. How did she know?*

I open my mouth to tell Reina what I'm thinking, but then pause and hold back. No matter how trustworthy she seems, I only just met her. *What if she secretly feels about me the same way all the others do?* "What exactly happens if these keys go missing?" I ask cautiously.

Reina's eyes darken and her mouth tightens into a frown. "If the keys go missing, we're all in for trouble. It only happens when someone is either inside or near enough to the house to use them for harm. We do have a safety protocol in place, but I've only ever read about it. Apparently, if this happens, the keys would return to the god who blessed them initially and the box would hide itself within the house. We would need to retrieve the keys immediately, before any other being did. Only Godspring are able to get into the house—no gods, no demons. But if anyone else did figure out how to open this box with those keys, the chaotic power inside could wreak havoc on all worlds. And without the box and the power it contains inside this house, Malachite would have no defenses at all." She shakes her head and begins to close the wooden door to the closet while sporting a comforting smile entirely for my benefit.

I watch from where my feet are firmly planted, now three steps back. "What's the likelihood of the Arcana getting in here?" I ask, quietly. A sinking feeling settles into my stomach.

Reina's smile dissolves. "Not high, the door is hidden from them, and only Godspring who belong to this house can enter."

"But if they did?" I insist as an idea begins to form, as an image pulses through my mind of the boy with the strange black-and-white uniform and that eerie symbol on his breast pocket. When I blink, I can still see him watching me across the counter of the Snack Shack—less than an hour before frogs started falling out of the sky. My heart leaps erratically. More than ever, I want my mother to come through that front door. Reina opens her mouth to answer, but I cut her off in my realization. "I think I met one of them. Back home, I was at work and a boy came in just before *everything*." I pause and look away. "It was like he was looking for me," I confess.

Already turning back toward the rest of the house, I have the urge again to run through the front door to find my way home. But no, *there must be a better way to make sure my mother is all right.* I hear Reina shuffle behind me, finally latching the cupboard door closed.

"Can I use your phone?" I nearly shout into the hallway. "I don't have mine. I don't know why I didn't ask earlier, but I've been struggling to take it all in," I start to ramble. The shock I have been floating in is finally wearing off.

I can't believe I fell through a magical door and made chicken! I should have screamed; I should have run. *Why didn't I run? Why isn't my mother here yet?* Suddenly, I can't breathe. My eyes are swimming with little white spots.

Reina turns me by the shoulders to face her and stares directly into my eyes. Everything feels as if it's happening all at once: the fleeing, the drowning, the swimming, the loss. *I just need it to slow down so I can* think. When I look at Reina, for a second it does. Distantly, I feel my chest rise and fall with air—but then it moves from steady to quick and I tremble under her palm.

"Thea," Reina says, calmly squeezing my shoulder.

I squeeze my eyes shut and lean into the buzzing electricity circulating off her.

"I need you to breathe slowly, all right? Can you do that for me?"

I usually hate when someone tells me to breathe during anxiety attacks, but when she does it's not the worst. When she touches me, that emptiness that comes off her drowns out the banging of my heart. I force an inhale through my nostrils and exhale through my mouth, then repeat. Reina nods and releases my shoulders, handing me her cell phone from her back pocket after I finally open my eyes.

With sweaty fingertips, I punch in the number of my mother's cell phone and wait as it rings and rings. With a mix of dread and exasperation I call it again, twice, then the house phone number, then my nana's, then Auden's. No one picks up. My chest squeezes tighter each time it doesn't work, and I keep calling even after a few heads pop out of bedroom doors to gawk at the girl about to have a meltdown in the middle of a magical house in the middle of nowhere.

I finally hand the phone back to Reina when it's clear I won't be reaching anyone, defeated.

Reina smiles compassionately. "Come, tell me more about the boy you saw, and I will tell you more about the Arcana's Quadrennial Hunt. It's like their Easter, if Easter meant stealing other peoples most treasured items for your own personal collection."

# 6

**I** **F I WERE THE TYPE** to write stories or keep notes, my experiences here would certainly make a manuscript. I am sitting inside a bedroom, conjured from the deepest imaginings of my thirteen-year-old self, manifested in a house that exists somehow outside of space yet within time. Outside my window is the sea, but outside the window in the room next to mine is a hilly landscape.

Right now, my knees are tucked under me and I'm sitting on the ground at the foot of this enormous bed, facing the door. The stories Reina told me still ring in my hollow ears, and my stomach sloshes unevenly with the dinner I wolfed down. *How could my mother have known enough about this place to send me here, yet never once mention it? And what does it mean to be the relative of a God?*

I used to imagine my dad all the time growing up. Whenever I'd see one on television holding his daughter, I'd feel a small lost part of myself open and wonder—wonder if a father was what was missing from my life every time I woke up feeling the slightest bit empty. I'd wonder, if I had had a dad, would taking care of

Mom have been easier? Would it have even been necessary? For the past couple of years, I've been telling people my mom is ill when they ask. It's the only explanation for her weird behaviors: the forgetfulness, the never leaving the house, the constant fatigue. Maybe Mom never would have stopped going outside if she'd had a husband to take her places.

The idea that all along my father has been a god "watching over me" is sickening. Even more so when it mixes with the loss in the center of my chest that increases with every passing moment Mom and Nana don't walk through the front door. As time passes, I also grow angrier. To think that all along there *has* been a man, a god, a father, remaining distant for some reason no one here can explain—always watching and never helping—infuriates me. Reina said my father must have been the one who showed my nana and Mom how to get me to this house. She said he must have been looking out for me. I have a hard time believing this mysterious and absent figure is capable of anything selfless. I wonder what he expects of me now that I am here.

Finally, I have the moment of silence I was hoping for, but now that I do, I'm too upset— too furious—to use it properly. I want to hit something and cry. I can manage neither. I'm too exhausted and this place is too unfamiliar.

I lean my head against the side of the bed, trying to focus on something stimulating *other* than my anger to keep me awake. I need to hang on only until Mom and Nana get here.

I close my eyes and remember Reina's tale of the gods creating this place and then tasking us, their descendants, to look after three mysterious keys and an old box that holds the spirit of another even older god within it. Behind my closed eyelids, I remember my grandmother's steely gaze the last time I saw her, her mouth opening to tell me I need to be the one to find those keys *when* they disappear. The *when* echoes. Finally, I let myself remember Reina's description of the group looking for them. The Arcana.

When she walked me back to my bedroom after my meltdown in the hallway, after I explained my encounter with the odd boy, she laid it out plain: There exists a place where only the most powerful Godspring are allowed to train—those descended from a single deity who created their own pantheon of gods—a place that is as much a school as it is a stronghold. While Malachites must sort through the tangled mess of their awakenings before they can uncover their god ancestry and hope to control it, the Arcana hone their power from birth.

My head is spinning and my eyes are heavy. I wish I could believe all this was a trick or a never-ending dream.

Trying to stay awake longer, my heart squeezes tight in my chest with exhaustion and panic over what will happen when I do eventually fall asleep, and what will follow when I wake. *Will everything be the same?* The longer I wait with no sign of my family, the more I remember the veiled warnings each of them gave me before I came, which only leads me to worry that they will never walk through that door at all. I gulp.

Wrapping my hand over my right wrist, I hold it tight to keep myself awake—then, my eyes shoot open—*my bracelet is missing!* The one Mom gave me, the one she told me to never take off. My head sinks down to rest between my knees. *I must have lost it during the swim.* Several exhausted tears escape my tightly squeezed eyes until eventually I collapse on my side and fall asleep.

*AHEAD OF ME the world is a spool of white snow. In the distance I think I see something shining. I pick up my pace until a frozen pond comes into view. I run toward it, noticing while I do that there is someone behind me. It's Auden, asking me to slow down. I will not. I know there is something important in that frozen lake; if I can just get to it, everything will make sense. I run until I notice she's no longer behind me and I'm entirely alone on a snowy hilltop.*

I RECALL MY DREAM as I dress in a fresh set of deep brown knit pants and a white cotton shirt in the bedroom that feels as unfamiliar as it is. I look at my frowning reflection and hate how refreshed I look. I should have bags under my eyes. I should look like I am suffering. Instead, I shine. My hair falls in even ringlets, unlike their usual unruly pattern, and my eyes sparkle. Frowning, I secure the paintbrush Nana gave me back into my curls like a pin. I wipe a hand down the front of my face, over the freckles Mom and I share nearly spot for spot. *What do I do?* I am so far outside my daily routine, so far away from everything I have known.

There is a knot in the bottom of my stomach that tightens when I fix my eyes on the patch of my wrist, empty of the one thing my mother told me to always wear. I am anchorless.

This morning, I have already heard the footsteps of two separate people, going in opposite directions outside my door. Reina told me everyone meets in the library each morning before breakfast to check in for their daily assignments. Still, I think I'm early even for that.

The fear I marinated in last night is slow to pass, but the anger I recognized when I thought of my father still simmers. A deadbeat albeit powerful god who is responsible for my being separated from my mother for the first time in my entire life. My fear is hard to reckon with, but my anger is easy to direct and use. I clench my teeth and walk across the large room, opening the door with a huff—and reveal a familiar face.

"Oh," I exclaim, then take a step back. "Teal, right?" I ask.

They're wearing a low-cut floral shirt, with blue jeans and old Converse. Layers of delicate gold chains hang from their neck and their ears are studded with several sparkling jewels. Teal looks like if Jhené Aiko and Sk8ter Boi–era Avril Lavigne had a sixteen-year-old Victorian-pale child.

"You remembered! Yeah, I'm Teal." They give a small wave, flashing a thick golden signet ring on their right thumb. "Reina told me to give you the upstairs tour. She said you didn't get around to it yesterday?"

"Yeah I—I only saw the downstairs," I say, looking past their shoulders to the hallway, still coated in paintings and soft wallpaper, still wide and cream-colored. Teal moves aside to allow me out of my room, which I gladly shut behind me, as if wood could hold back the ghosts I had been wrestling with in there.

"Do you know if anyone's heard from my family?" I ask.

Teal looks caught off-guard. They frown as they shake their head no. I try to look less lost than I feel.

"This will get easier," Teal promises as we set off down the wide hallway.

"Will it?"

"Yeah, I remember when I first got here, I was terrified. My bedroom, thankfully, looked the same as the one back home—so I hardly left it. I just pretended that's where I was," Teal explains.

"Sorry," I reply. My heart sinks for Teal. They seem gentler than most of the other people here. No one deserves to feel even a hint of the loneliness I'm currently nursing.

Teal shrugs their soft shoulders as we turn left at the end of the hallway, toward a second staircase a few feet opposite the closet holding the three keys and that green box. While we ascend the stairs, I grip the handrail, certain that a strong breeze could knock me over. When the stairs end, the ground ahead of us spreads out in curved glass tiles in different shades of blue, rippling from sapphire, to lapis, to seafoam. Overhead, a webbed glass ceiling is held up by white clay support beams intricately inlaid with pieces of sea glass and shell, threaded with flecks of gold and metal. I feel like I am on the surface of a star, or the bottom of the ocean. Everything here is vivid and highlights the sight beyond the glass ceiling: a wide expanse of soft stars set in a liquid black night sky. It is completely at odds with the lighting downstairs and everything else in this house.

"It's nine a.m." I pause at the top of the stairs. "Isn't it?"

Of course, the sight of the night sky isn't what's pushed me over the edge; this is just the latest thing on a list of about a dozen that makes me feel like I'm struggling for breath. The tile flows into five different hallways equally as grand, equally as wide as each other—*This house is significantly larger on the second level than it is on the first.* I think Teal can tell I'm overwhelmed.

"Yeah, it's about nine. Here, let's sit for a minute. Then we can move on to the armory after." Teal motions to a low stone bench beside one of the clay columns. I try to ignore the impossibility of the star-filled night sky over our heads, instead focusing on Teal's blue eyes. Sitting down, the uneven edges of glass in the support column behind me poke into my back. Teal looks around as if they aren't sure how to start.

"I had my first awakening on this landing," they begin quietly, their hands folded in their lap. "They say it's the awakening that makes a Malachite luckier, but my first power surge hit hard. I had only been in Malachite for six weeks, I think. I was ten and terrified." With Teal sitting beside me, I don't pull into myself like I do with most people. There is a warmth to them that draws me in. Even without touching them, I feel at ease.

After a few seconds, Teal flips up their palms and shows me their surfaces. Where ordinary hands have smooth dark lines, Teal's lines glow golden. They shimmer as light lifts up and off them, becoming projections growing brighter and brighter the longer I look. I gasp as a halo of golden light forms and hovers off their palms.

"In Malachite, everyone is connected to two gods. For me it's my father Baldr, Norse god of light, and on my mom's side my grandmother is Freyja, another Norse goddess of love and war," they say.

"Did you always know who your family was?"

"I knew that my father was important, and that my mother's family was connected to Freyja. I had to figure the rest out for myself." Their light grows larger, pushing upward to create a flashlight effect emanating from their palm. As much as I try to resist, I reach out and run my fingertips through the glow. Teal lets me. It sends shivers up my arm.

"Freyja, Baldr." I round my mouth over the two words. When I think of Norse mythology all I can picture is Thor (the shirtless one from the movies).

"Everyone here is related to two gods but we have to claim just one," they reply, "or else the two lineages intersect inside the Malachite until they go mad."

"What do you mean?" I draw my hands back into my lap.

"First, we have to remember that part of what makes us Malachites is our conflicting mortality. We come from immortal beings but have a human body that can't reliably handle what we are." I watch the beam of light in their hands as they continue. "We have to choose which of our ancestry to draw from, and over time, our connection to the other side diminishes. If we don't choose one, the two energies become too much for our human bodies to handle. We have until our third and final awakening to decide which lineage we claim," they say.

"Which did you choose?"

"Baldr, my father," they say, clenching their hands closed, pressing their fists flat against their pants. I blink at the absence of light as the rest of the room comes back into focus.

"How do you choose?" I begin to wonder not just who my father could be, but also what other deity I'm related to.

"I, I chose the one that was stronger. The one I had more of," they explain with a very serious tone. "Most of us do."

"How do you know you made the right choice?" I ask, wrapping my arms around my chest, suddenly cold.

Teal shrugs. "I have affirmations I tell myself. I repeat: 'In this moment, I am doing my best,' so regardless of what I choose, if I'm consistently trying, I'll always be fine," they say softly.

I nod like I understand, even though I don't. *How could anyone be forced to make such a huge decision?*

"Why do we have to choose though?" I ask, shaking my head. "It doesn't make any sense."

"It's just how it is." Teal shrugs. Whatever darkness I thought I saw on their face disappears into sunshine. "And to be clear, *that* sky is a real view happening right now, somewhere this house has already been," Teal adds, pointing to the sky I gawked at when we first entered the room.

The sick feeling in my stomach doesn't go away, but my willingness to keep moving increases. I picture my family as I stand up. I visualize my grandmother, who immigrated to Canada from China as a young child with parents she hardly ever speaks about. Then I think of my mother, who met my father presumably at least sixteen years ago, only to lose him in the shuffle of her ever-moving life.

I've wondered about my family tree's missing limbs before, whenever I'm in class and someone mentions going to visit relatives, or how many cousins they have. I've always ignored these empty spaces in my tree, but now that I see them as holes for gods to fit into, I feel naked and unsure about the truth of anything. As far back as I can remember, it's just been the three of us: me, Mom, Nana. No more, no less.

Teal shrugs. "I know this is a lot to take in, but try not to worry too much. You probably have weeks until your first awakening. You can sort through it more then."

—————

**THE REST OF THE TOUR** consists of discovering the expansiveness of the Malachite house. We go through a dusty-smelling armory filled with both weapons and a couple of shelves of artifacts. They explain the associated myths of a variety of items Malachite holds: bags made from unicorn hair, a phoenix feather, a piece of sea kelp blessed by Mami Wata, an arrow belonging to Hou Yi, a crossbow—so many pieces of stories I don't know. Then Teal guides me through a temple room filled with air thick with incense and sand that spills out into the hallway. The temple room is where Malachites are encouraged to meditate, hoping to glean messages from their god relatives. Afterward, Teal shows me a music room, an indoor climbing wall, and a wide saltwater pool. The tour ends with us visiting the attic where the Godspring keep old clothes and more knickknacks.

Now, I sit cross-legged on the ground of a large library. Around me, Godspring are trickling in, smiling at one another, and taking their own seats in chairs or on the ground. Around us, the generously curved shelves are filled with storybooks, mythological epics, and fairy tales from all around the world.

Teal is sitting beside me, and on the other side of them, Tiana lounges with her legs stretched out ahead of her. She and Teal lean into one another like two old trees while I'm like a faraway reed in the wind.

Hunar sits across the room in a reading nook with a book pressed open between two of his fingers, hardly looking up as the library fills with bodies. When I first saw him, my stomach tightened. I felt a bolt of fear that he might ignore me because of how rude I was to him yesterday. Instead, Hunar looks up at me just as I walk in and smiles. Blood rushes to my ears when he waves.

Bare, stripped-back wood meets the book-lined walls of the room, and stained glass caps the corner of the magnificently intricate windows peeking between shelves. The deep hues of blue, red, and gold in the glass show scenes of mighty figures standing taller than smaller ones, holding stars or weapons in their hands. I realize as Reina shuffles papers in her lap—where she sits on the other end of the room in a white egg-shaped chair—that these are depictions of gods, the ancestors of the people in this room.

It's not until everyone has filed in and about a dozen of us now take up the room that I realize how long it's been since I was in a space with so many other Black and Brown people. For the first time in a long time, I don't have to worry about standing out so much. I distantly realize that in this room, I could be just Thea—a Malachite. Not the only person of color within a fifty-mile radius.

"Normally, we would be checking in with our daily progress and activities, but as we have a new arrival, we will instead use this morning to officially give Thea Beren the opportunity to sign her name into our Crimson Ledger, our collection of every Malachite who has ever devoted themselves to this house and vowed to protect its inhabitants and our sacred items." Reina gestures toward me. Every head in the room that wasn't already watching me turns in my direction. I raise my palm in a half-wave, then immediately wish I could fold myself up into a tiny square to be tossed away.

"Thea, come up to the front."

My brain stalls. I want to stay seated, think this over, mull my options. But Reina is looking at me expectantly—the whole room is. With clammy palms, I stand up.

I can't imagine how I will do any of this on my own: be this new person, exist in this place that is foreign to me. *How can I accept being a Godspring when I'm not even sure I knew who I was before I arrived here?* I start walking across the room toward Reina's expectant smile. It's clear to me now that Mom and Nana aren't coming just yet. They sent me here for a reason.

Reina smiles encouragingly and pulls a large, wide crimson leather book onto her lap. When she opens it, I see a list of names written in different styles, all in a rust ink. Reina then pulls out a sharp fountain pen and looks up at me with an inviting smile. I notice there is no ink in sight and start to ask her what I am supposed to use to write, when suddenly, the doorway at the end of the oblong library flings open to reveal Marta—eyes all fury.

"The keys are missing," Marta spits.

I blink. The room blinks. Reina tenses. Somewhere in the distance, someone laughs at the notion of my story slowing down, of this tale turning tame. Then, all at once, the room is a flurry of motion: bodies piling over one another to push through the door ahead of us like a flock of confused sheep headed toward a cliff. I follow the surge down the hallway in a daze, the fountain pen still gripped in my hand. We rush to the cupboard, which Teal opens with a press of their thumb. From the back of the increasingly alarmed crowd, I see the shelf—previously full of four items— now sits empty.

Then, several eyes turn to face me where I stand, arms wrapped around my stomach, leaning into the wall behind me for support. I don't know what to say or do, so I glue my eyes to the edge of the carpet and wish my father is a god of invisibility so that I can truly disappear.

# 7

**T**HE BLOOD IN my face has pooled somewhere south of my knees, and everyone is looking at me like I did something wrong. *What do I say?* Reina clears her throat and thankfully draws their attention. Immediately, the Malachites' voices rise in speculation. From where she stands on the edge of the crowd with an unreadable expression, Reina raises her hand up to grasp the river stone hanging at her neck, before holding it up for all to see. Suddenly everyone quiets.

"Back to the library," she says.

The Malachites quickly follow her up the stairs in a rush.

"What's happening?" I ask Ian, the person nearest to me. He keeps walking as though he didn't hear me. For a second, I am transported back to the hallway at school again, where no one would look at me. Shaking my head to dislodge the sensation, I spot Hunar beginning up the stairs behind Teal and Tiana. I pause, worried that he'll ignore me the same way Ian just did. But then he smiles, and I smile back.

"What's happening?" I ask.

Hunar pinches the narrow bridge of his nose for a second and steps onto the bottom stair. "Reina is in charge, so she wears the stone that controls the front door. That stone works a little like a garage door button, but—never mind, that doesn't matter. If she still has it, that means the front door hasn't been opened."

I frown and begin walking with him up the stairs.

"Okay?" I push.

"And if the front door hasn't been opened, that means a couple of things," Hunar says.

Marta chucks my shoulder and races past us up the stairs, tossing a scowl my way as she does. I draw in on myself, and despite wanting to appear strong, I trip on the step ahead of me. Hunar reaches out instinctively. His hand is warm and it catches my sleeve-covered shoulder before I can barrel into the carpeted stairs.

"Like what?" I ask as the rest of the Malachites disappear into the hallway at the top of the staircase.

"I'll let Reina explain," Hunar says. He continues ahead of me, his soft cotton jacket trailing along the handrail as we ascend. I wonder why my heart is still beating so fast.

BACK IN THE LIBRARY, no one is sitting on the ground. Everyone stands at attention, hands at their hips or in tight balls. Reina is the only one who doesn't seem panicked, her posture steady. It's easy to understand why she's the one in charge. The only indication of her nervousness is the way she twists the cord holding the oval gray stone.

*This is not my element.* Back home there was no situation I couldn't interpret: my nana's feet shifting side to side in the kitchen meant something was dirty; my mother making her bed in the morning meant she intended to sit in the living room for the day. Looking around at these people, I realize there is subtext all around me I'm too new to decode.

"It was the Arcana, how isn't that clear to everyone?" Ness says. Teal hushes him gently.

"If it wasn't them, then who was it?" A voice I haven't heard before speaks. I find Tiana's face near the back of the room, standing between Teal and one of the younger children. "It has to be them," she decides, while Reina only watches the room ahead of her, as if she were reading a book and translating it at the same time.

"It wasn't the Arcana, Tiana. The door was unopened," Ian calls back. He folds his arms; all sixteen years of him look indignant at the suggestion, even though he was the one who so confidently accused me of being Arcana just last night.

"But how do we *know*?" Marta speaks up.

My eyes stay on Tiana. Her gaze is positively alight, staring holes into Reina. Beside her, Teal threads their fingers through hers as if to hold her back. *What is going on here?*

Reina finally speaks. "There is only one reason for the keys to be missing, and for the box to have hidden itself inside Malachite. Someone is close to opening it."

"What does that mean, 'close to opening it'?" Hunar presses, his eyes meeting mine in a mutual understanding across the room, like he's asked so I don't have to.

"In order to open the box, someone would need to first combine our three keys using a ritual lost to time. If the keys are missing, someone has found that ritual and intends to use it—and Malachite sensed it," she says.

"So, the Arcana might be just outside the front door?" Tiana asks, stepping closer to the middle of the room.

"The keys have ejected themselves from Malachite already. Whether or not there is someone outside, or if this is a test from the gods, they're safe—for now." Reina taps her lower lip with the tip of her finger. "They have returned to their respective Keepers," she says.

The room murmurs. I notice a few words ringing louder than the others, one in particular: *quest.* I try to follow where the conversation is going but everyone's voices layer atop one another, too fast to keep track.

"Well, what are we waiting for?" Marta says. "There are only three places the keys can be, and we need to get them back home before the Arcana realize they're gone," she says.

"And be back before the winter solstice," Tiana adds.

*Why the winter solstice? And where did the keys go? How is everyone so calm?*

"I'll go!" Tiana declares.

As she steps to stand directly ahead of Reina, I remember what my nana said to me. *When the keys go missing, you must be the one to find them.* How did she know this would happen—and how could I ignore an instruction as specific as that?

"Tiana, I *am* sorry, but you can't. You haven't even had your second awakening. If you have one outside Malachite, the Arcana will track down your magic and find you. It would defeat the purpose of all this." Reina gestures to the house around us. "They would know the keys are missing—if they don't already."

"I can do this. I *need* to do this. You all know how badly." Tiana's voice becomes low at the end of her sentence, and she turns to face the room when she speaks. Her eyes are wet, and when they lock on mine, I sense an intensity in them that mirrors my own. The other Malachites in the library look as though they want to reach out to her, but only Teal does. Tiana quickly looks back at Reina for an answer.

Reina shakes her head. "I said no."

In a huff, Tiana explodes past Teal, who tries to catch her arm but fails, past the crowd, past me.

"*T*," Teal mutters as they hurry after her through the open door behind me.

If I were in a different state of mind, I'd look over my shoulder to see if Teal reaches her. Instead, I know I have to speak up, I have to say something. I can't let this moment pass me by, not after what Nana said.

"Can I go?" I ask Reina, slightly too loud, and from the back of the room, into the void Tiana left. "I can help," I follow up.

Ian laughs at my request and Marta rolls her eyes.

Reina folds her hands across her lap. "I'm sorry, but no, Thea. For the same reason as Tiana—you're far too new here. Besides, don't you want to wait for your family?"

I bite my tongue because that is what I said I would do; it's what I should do. I step back and nod, defeated, but say nothing. Hunar catches my eye curiously, but I look away before I can decipher his expression.

"*I'll* go," Marta announces. Her voice is louder than mine, and it eats up any consideration Reina may have had left for my plea. Then the room continues talking without me, voices folding over one another in a weave of practiced familiarity—like I hadn't said a single word. *I have no place here.* As everyone continues figuring out their next steps, uttering words I don't understand, like *Kunlun* and *Frost Giants*, I edge my way out of the door behind me.

**THE TEMPLE ROOM** is smaller than other chambers I've seen so far in this house. It is a welcome respite from the noise of the library, the pulsing in my head, and the absolute knot in my stomach.

I had thought for a second that maybe, if I could follow my grandmother's instruction and return the missing keys, then she and Mom would be waiting somewhere along the way. I admit to myself, as I sit down on the smooth stone ground in the middle of the aisle, that a small part of me saw finding those keys as an opportunity to prove I *do* belong here—though whether I'm trying to prove it to the Malachites or myself, I still don't know.

I've never had a big group of friends; in fact, I've never had any real friends besides Auden. Even if I've been here only a short while, the way everyone here moves around each other, anticipating each other and knowing each other, I want that. *I want to belong.*

*God, that's so stupid, Thea. Get your shit together.* I shake my head in the dim light of the temple, a rounded room full of four benches and a single empty podium. I inhale the scent of incense and press my hands into the sandy floor. There are no idols in here, no writings, no books. There are so many gods it would be strange to put the likeness of just one in this place.

Looking at the podium ahead of me, the hollow feeling in my chest widens. I wonder if my father is watching me right now as I'm sitting on the ground ready to give up before I've even tried. *Maybe he hasn't contacted me, not because of some rule, but because he is ashamed to call me his daughter.* I decide that's why I never knew about this place and why he never visited. I sigh as my eyes fill with unwanted tears but wipe them away before they have a chance to streak down my cheeks.

"I wish Mom were here. She would know what to do. I even wish Nana were here. I wish I didn't feel so alone," I mutter into the corner of my sleeve in the silence of this room, rubbing the soft fabric of this borrowed shirt into my puffy under-eyes.

Then, a soft warmth starts in the center of my head, distracting me from my emotions. It stays for just a second, long enough for me to open my eyes to find that the platform ahead of me is no longer empty. I'm shocked as I realize what I'm looking at: the idol from my mother's closet, the stone carved woman with large hands. Seeing it sitting there, as if it had always been there, makes the breath I had been struggling to exhale splutter and cough out.

Cautiously, I glance back at the hallway behind me. When I find that I'm truly alone, I push my body off the ground with shaky arms, then walk between the rows of wooden benches across the stone floor. When I reach the small carving, I kneel ahead of it and hesitantly pick the thing up. Its solid weight anchors me in place, and with my breath held, I wait for another prophecy, another string of words to rhyme and wrap around me like ribbon.

I hear nothing but my own breath.

The forearm-length statue is cool in my clammy hands, and the space on its face where eyes should be echoes deep and strong. For a second, I think I see something flicker in the stone's surface and a sharp pain burns over my palm that causes me to release the idol in shock. Stifling a shout, I rush to try and catch the statue as it falls, but fail. I tense in anticipation of hearing a crash when it hits the ground. But, when I look at the floor, it's empty too. I search all across the sandy stone ground for any shard of the fallen statue but find nothing. With my heart racing, I look down at my right hand, which I had clasped tight against my chest in shock. Peeling it away from the fabric of my shirt, I look down at the throbbing pain across its surface. My mouth drops open as I see my wound: a burn left by the disappearing statue that pulses hot in the shape of two crescents, one within the other, topped by one small circle. Lightheadedness takes me over when I look at it. *What does this mean?*

Without knowing where I am going, I back out of the suddenly menacing temple. Its rounded walls look like the arms of the gods reaching overhead, blocking out sunlight. My throat constricts with confused terror—and then I hear it, or rather, *her.*

*"Left,"* the female voice whispers loud enough to shake me just as I reach the edge of the temple. I look over my shoulder, already knowing there will be no one there, and pause for a moment in the threshold of the room, feeling the presence of *something* beside me.

*"Left,"* the voice says again, this time with more urgency.

Looking down at the burn in my palm, I recall the insanity of the past few days in a flash. Then, I turn left.

I follow it: the tug in the air pushing me down the hallway past the library full of Malachite voices.

*"Down,"* the voice says when I reach the top of the stairs. I descend with a light hand on the railing beside me. Somewhere far off I hear Reina's voice like a river running through the chaos of the Malachites' confusion. The farther down the stairs I descend, the less I can hear any of them, and the more I recognize the feeling of my own heart beating steadily.

*"Right,"* the voice says.

I turn right at the base of the stairs past a large iron doorway that looks melted shut. I walk through an ample archway to find myself on the opposite side of a wide room I briefly glimpsed during my tour of Malachite.

The den is rectangular and has the smell of orange peels heavy in the air. There are eye-level bookshelves lining the wall ahead of me. Nestled between them is a large fireplace holding a crackling blaze within the confines of a carved stone inlet. Above the fireplace is a mantle covered in seven smooth stone statues depicting the faces of whom I now assume are deities from myths I've never studied. There are many thick stuffed chairs and a worn pale-mustard couch along the wall. Overhead, an antique chandelier is alight, casting the room in an orange glow.

"What now?" I wonder, still cradling my right hand against my chest although the pain is already fading. The voice does not immediately return, and I wander farther into the den, feeling the dry warmth of the fire in the air around me contrasting the crisp cool of the hallway I left behind. And then, slowly, I hear it. Not a voice, but a sort of creak—the sound of shuffling metal or loosening wood. It is coming from the wall ahead of me. I follow the noise farther into the room, feet sinking into the dense carpet. Only when I'm inches away do I notice that over the fireplace is a groove in the wall, a shallow dent no more out of place than the hundreds of others in the wooden walls around me. But something about this dent, the warmth in my palm, and the flutter in my blood makes me pause.

"*There,*" the voice sighs.

I stiffen a little when I hear that voice again but still reach forward to press my finger into the shallow groove, instinctively pushing it upward, then pulling it toward me.

Out of the wall comes a narrow slice of wood, not broken, but built. It rolls from the wall to reveal a tightly wound scroll of paper wedged inside.

I pull the paper out of the wall with my breath caught in my throat. Ignoring the wince in my burned palm, I unfurl it. The silence of the room is broken only by the snap of this movement and the crackle of the fire to my left.

The square paper is old, but not so old it's too brittle to understand. The paper depicts, in plain black strokes, what look like three maps side by side with crisp writing above them. The first map, showing a jagged landscape of harsh rocks and trees, is titled *Jotunheim.* The next, a fuzzy and dense forest with a pond of water in the center is titled *Ginen.* The third is a mountainscape with winding trails that crisscross over each other in so many patterns it's hard to follow. This one is titled *Kunlun.*

But none of the maps, or the titles, are what really capture my attention—what does are the small initials in the bottom right corner of the piece: *L.B.*

My grandmother's initials, penned in her brushstroke.

I nearly drop the map.

In a rush I realize why the voice in my head sounds so comforting. *It's Nana's voice.* The same way it was her voice warning me to find the keys when they went missing.

*Why is she doing this to me? Where is she trying to lead me?* I stare down at that *L.B.*, with my heart sinking.

*I have to do as she says,* I realize.

I must leave this house and find those three keys, because as I stand here, looking down at this map drawn by a woman I now realize I never knew, I also remember the second thing Nana told me before I left her. She told me not to trust *anyone* in Malachite.

The marking on my palm burns hot as I roll up the map and slide it into my back pocket, clicking the wooden panel back into place a moment later.

# 8

P ACING IN THIS BEDROOM only makes me feel like a rat in a cage. When I get like this, I know that nothing can stop me from moving. Mom always says my single-mindedness is my greatest weakness. I think my constant desire to move forward is natural and useful.

Wearing the loose jeans and shirt from when I arrived, I hastily pack a bag as a way to stall the truth: I have to leave. Mom and Nana planned all this—for me—but why? *They knew the keys would go missing and they know who my father is. It's all a test. It has to be.*

It took me an hour of deliberation and silence to make up my mind. Now, I raise my hand up to the door handles and pause. *I thought I was sure.* A moment ago, I was, but with my hot hand on the cold metal handle, the bag on my shoulders suddenly strains and pulls me back, holding me in place. Of course, this is a mistake. Every move I make seems to become one. *But I must do this.* Isn't that what Nana asked me to do? And when have either she or my mother ever been wrong? I pause, looking down at the door handle in my grip and see the warped reflection of my face, the hint of curled bangs, the rim of my old glasses. For a second I think Mom's face is looking back at me. With that thought, I turn the handle and open the door.

*Where to start?* I don't know how to get to any of the places on the map. I try to put myself in the shoes of a person better suited to this task. I pretend that I'm Reina. *What would she do?* She would research where the places in this map are—but the library is chock-full of Godspring.

I walk through Malachite toward the foyer quietly, pausing when I reach the threshold of the kitchen. I look down at that thin line where tile meets wood, through which the stifling hot of the white painted room turns into the cool oxygen of the foyer. I stare up at the looming front door ahead and to the left of me. It seems to stare back. Balling my hands into fists, I take a step forward, immediately tensing when I notice that I am no longer alone. My hands spread out along the sides of my jeans.

Hunar sits where I first met him, curled up on the half-landing of a staircase I haven't yet been up, with a book on his lap. He's folded lazily into the corner, legs spilling down the stairs. Hunar notices me at the same time I see him. When he looks up, his eyes are almost amber in the morning light. I shift my body slightly to keep the edge of my bag out of sight. I can't tell if he notices.

"Avoiding the crowd?" he asks.

I dip my head and take a step closer, unsure whether to divulge my plans. My mind screams to tell him, to tell anyone what I'm planning. Half of me wants someone to tell me to stop, to stay where it is safe and hold tight, and the other wants someone to light me on fire with passion and force me out that door. Instead of saying anything, I take another step into the room so that only the foyer table laden with a vase of red roses separates the two of us.

"It isn't always so intense." He gestures vaguely with an apologetic smile. "Sorry it was such an abrasive introduction."

"What's it usually like?"

"It's usually Reina yelling ingredients to potions most of us don't have her proclivity for, or Snail burning scones in the kitchen," Hunar says as he closes his book. "Usually we're learning how to use the magic in our blood—less for survival, more for understanding."

"Snail?"

Hunar smiles at the ground, wipes an errant lock of black hair behind his ear. "Teal, everyone calls them Snail. It's sort of a running joke."

"Ah." I incline my head and take a step back, reminded of how much I don't fit in here.

"You'll get used to it though. Most of us have known each other since we were little. Malachite tends to bring Godspring here in waves. Me and Marta arrived in the same week when we were ten," he says.

A weird stab of pain arches up my stomach as I imagine Marta and Hunar arriving here together, learning about themselves and each other at the same time.

"So, this quest," I begin, quickly changing the topic. "I don't understand what it means. Can you explain it to me?"

Hunar nods and straightens up, "A quest is like a test from the gods or from fate. This one seems to be both. When someone is plotting to open the Malachite box, and has the means to do it, the keys eject themselves from the house. What you would have known, if you'd been here for longer than a day, is that it's our job to retrieve those keys and prove that we're still worthy of protecting them now that they're missing. *And* we have to do it all before someone else has the chance to, because if someone manages to open the Malachite box, this whole house will lose its magic—the box is sort of like a battery for this place." He gestures to the tall walls around us.

"But Reina said I can't go," I say.

"That's just because you haven't had all of your awakenings yet. You can't even fully *see* the magical world until your second," he says.

I bite the inside of my cheek. There's so much I don't know.

"And what do awakenings do, exactly?"

"Well, awakening number one basically affects the magic in the world around you—your fate—it draws you into your destiny and reveals your god lineage. Your second one gives you the ability to see the magical world and kick-starts the magic your body is capable of. The third is when you decide which deity lineage you want to pull from for the rest of your life—but that's a lot of information. While we're gone, Reina will talk you through everything," he says.

"Gone?"

"Yeah. Me, Marta, and Ian are going to do the quest. We're the only ones in the house, besides Reina and Snail, who have had all of our awakenings," he says, and shifts his seated position to a higher step, so that we are eye to eye.

"When do you leave?" My heart is beating in my throat.

"A few hours."

A rush of panic makes me take a step closer. "I thought it was bad to leave, that there were dangers outside." I shrink back as I speak, half out of embarrassment at showing so much care to a near-stranger, and half at the actual prospect of bumping into those creatures I saw in the woods behind my house. They flash through my mind while Hunar seems to contemplate my question objectively, weighing the pros and cons.

"Yeah, they'll come for us, but the three of us can manage ourselves. We should be okay, and we *should* finish before the winter solstice deadline too." I can't tell if it's arrogance or confidence I read in his eyes, the glance is so quick.

"There you are," a female voice calls from the top of the stairs.

I jump back, feeling caught, not realizing until then how close I had been leaning in, drawn in by Hunar's too-low tone of voice. I look up and find Marta frowning down at us, leaning over the banister.

Hunar unfolds himself. "All right" is his short response to her.

A sudden surge of panic rises in my chest at seeing him go— strange since that's exactly what I was planning on doing. But Hunar doesn't immediately leave. He turns and walks toward me, stopping only when he's mere inches away—the closest he's been since I met him only twenty-four hours ago. Marta sighs and pushes off the banister, disappearing somewhere above. I struggle to keep myself still as Hunar stands so close. I wedge my bag behind my back and out of view.

"Listen, it's weird, and it's tough, and it's not at all like the movies. But learning to control your powers—whatever they are—is worth it," he says compassionately. "Being here is worth it.

So, just keep your head on straight, listen to Reina, and here—" he extends his hand out, offering me the book he had been reading. "Tell me how this ends when I get back."

"Oh," I say, taking the leather-bound book.

*No one besides Mom gives me gifts when it's not my birthday.* My hand brushes his when I take the book, and a dart of electricity races up from my fingertip to the edge of my earlobe before disappearing across my neck, the sensation paired with a thrilling sort of sweetness. *Was that him or me?*

I bite the inside of my cheek. "Thanks."

I press the book to my chest, and the center of my body hums with warmth. Hunar smiles and says nothing else for a moment before turning to find Marta up the stairs.

A few moments later, I am finally alone, staring at the cover of a blue book with thick black letters: *The Unspoken.* I place the book in the side pocket of my bag and look around the empty foyer, feeling suddenly lost. It's as if the room has doubled in size without Hunar. What once seemed cozy now looks immense. The carpeted road from where I stand to that front door seems endless. Hunar's words echo though my mind: quests, awakenings, and fate. *Am I in over my head?*

"*Not alone.*" It is her again, Nana's voice.

*Does that mean she is with me, guiding me to her, or something else?* Just as I think it, I hear something in the distance, a *tap, tap, tap* and a low humming voice. I realize it is the sound of a song threading its way through the hallway.

Something else Nana said rings through my mind, her guidance to be mindful of who I trust in Malachite, and when I trust them. The contradiction confuses me. *How can it be that I'm both "not alone" and in a position to "trust no one"?* Without really deciding on it, I follow the voice away from the front door and toward the courtyard.

TIANA IS SITTING under the low branches of a thick blossoming tree, tapping her hand into the side of a stone bench with her long-pointed nails while humming softly under her breath. She is wearing a long orange leather jacket and a pair of thick combat boots. Her braids are tied behind her neck and wispy baby hairs are slicked down in smooth waves around the sides of her face. Tiana pauses her song and presses a delicate fingertip to the tree beside her, then to the base of her cheek, clearly unaware of my presence. It's an action she practices with such feeling that I freeze. I've trespassed into an intimate moment. While taking a step back into the dining room of Malachite, my foot creaks a floorboard. Tiana turns to face me immediately. Her eyes are red from crying. I feel caught for a second, but then my heart opens to her. *Is it possible we're feeling the same?*

"What are you doing here?" Her voice is like a knife.

"I—" My confidence buckles.

"Listen, if you're looking for Reina, she's upstairs still. I don't have time to show you where the bathrooms are." Tiana waves me off. I see a carving in the base of the tree beside her where she just touched. *T + Z.* Then I notice the bag at her feet. I briefly wonder who the *Z* must be, when it all clicks together: the bag, her boots, her autumn jacket unnecessary for the balmy temperature of the courtyard, and the voice telling me *I'm not alone.*

"You're going to do the quest, aren't you?" I ask. The words come out unintentionally sounding like an accusation.

Tiana's body stills. Her fingers pause, and her soft shoulders rising and falling with her breath become the only thing about her that moves.

*Shit, I said the wrong thing.*

"What do you care?"

"I want to come with you," I reply boldly before taking a step forward when her face doesn't become more hostile. I recognize a familiar hope in her voice—a hope that she too won't be in this alone.

"Why do *you* even care?"

"It's complicated, but I know I'm supposed to do this. You can trust me," I say, pushing my jaw forward and standing as tall as I can. Trying to look as confident as I wish I felt.

Tiana's mouth sours. "You'd only slow me down."

"I'm much faster than I look." This is a lie. "And you can't do this alone." *No one could*, I say the last part to myself.

Tiana weighs her options. For a full ten seconds she only stares, frowns a little bit, stares again, and finally exhales.

"You're not Arcana, are you?"

"Of course not. I'm Canadian."

She laughs just once, then stills, and looks me over top to tail. "Okay."

"Really?"

"Yep." Tiana stands, picks up her bag, and starts walking toward the door behind me.

"So, where are we going exactly?" I ask. I debate showing her the map but decide it's probably best to keep it to myself for now.

Tiana stops in the threshold beside me, looks at me, and doesn't give an inch of what she thinks. "Ginen, Jotunheim, and Kunlun."

While she rattles off the names of these places, I swallow as I remember those exact words written in my grandmother's handwriting. I try to keep my expression plain and open while Tiana continues. "In the original tale, Malachite's formation took three beings. One from a realm that reflected each of the three aspects of the self, the outer, the physical, and the emotional self. A similar pattern to our three awakenings. In the legends, the outer self was best understood in Ginen, a land of spirits and creatures all once known and forgotten to time, filled with mirrors. In the old tales, adventurers would go there to test what kind of person they were. The physical realm was characterized in Jotunheim, where giants rule and the earth is as direct and alive as any person. It apparently tests your strength." She pauses for just a second to gauge my reaction. I keep as cool as possible. "If the legends are true, our keys are in the hands of their respective keepers, otherworldly beings with a sworn duty to steward them. If you know where to do it, a Godspring can jump from one realm to the other to get the keys back. And I know where to do it ... mostly," Tiana says with a slightly faltering but still proud smile.

"So, Kunlun would be the realm connected to the emotional self?" I ask.

"Yeah, they say that if you spend too much time there, Godspring or not, the place will make your subconscious emotions come to light and switch them with your conscious thought until you lose yourself completely." Tiana looks as if she's going to continue explaining, until her expression suddenly changes. "You haven't even had a single history lesson, have you?" She visibly remembers that I got here yesterday.

I can see her mind taking in the fact of how little I have to offer, how new I am. She knows so much, and I know nothing.

"I have a way to find the keys once we're there," I say, a little too loud. "I swear, take me with you, and we can use it." I say this with all my force. When I look at her, I try to look brave, but I know when she accidentally bumps my exposed wrist with hers that it's not my false bravado making her say yes—it's my tangy desperation that matches her own.

"Okay," Tiana says cautiously. "Meet me by the door. Wait ten seconds to follow."

TIANA HAS ONE HAND on the handle of the front door when I arrive behind her. *This is it. We're really going to leave Malachite.* I scamper to make up the lost time separating us—until a voice shouting for us to stop slices through the still air of the foyer and I freeze. Tiana turns her head over her leather-clad shoulder with surprise, and a little fear, until she relaxes when she sees who is coming through the kitchen doorway.

Teal is wearing a white apron over their layered light pink and soft green outfit. "What are you doing, T?" they ask.

"I'm going on the quest, Teal. I've made up my mind," Tiana says.

Teal's blue eyes widen, look from me to her, and back again.

"You're taking her with you? What are you both thinking?" they ask, arms widespread.

"That we have to do this," Tiana answers for us both.

"There's no way you have enough supplies." Teal puts their hands on their hips, then drops them, becoming far more serious. "You could both die."

I silently feel indignant at the implication. I mean, I *did* swim through a whole bunch of weird water to get here and didn't drown; I *did* escape the demon in the forest. So far, I'm doing a fairly good job of not dying.

Tiana shakes her head. "You don't know that! We spend our whole lives inside this house, doing as we're told, leaving only for a few hours with Reina's permission, while the Arcana stroll around doing whatever they want"—she pauses, her eyes suddenly misty—"to *whoever*," she adds meaningfully.

Teal's voice becomes thick with emotion. For a second I am sure they forgot I am in the room too. "I'm sorry, Tiana. You just haven't spent enough time training yet; you're not fully awakened. You're not ready—neither of you are."

"We don't have time to be cautious, *Snail*," Tiana says pointedly. Teal stiffens but doesn't draw back. "What is it you're always saying, 'I am worthy of what I desire'? This is that! This is our chance to take what *we* need."

To their credit, Teal doesn't shrink when Tiana raises her voice. "What happens if one of you has an awakening out there? The Arcana will be able to track that surge of power and come *running*. And since we have no idea how they do it, or how to block them from finding you, you'll give away that the keys are missing by simply *being*. And when they do come, neither of you will be able to defend yourselves," they say emphatically. "Tiana, bravery isn't always about running straight at danger. Sometimes it means letting other people do what you can't," Teal explains.

Tiana's sorrowful expression turns quickly into a fiery one. Her shoulders push back, her eyes blaze, her mouth opens like she's going to yell even louder, but then she just . . . doesn't.

"What are the chances we get our awakenings that soon?" Her voice comes out rational and even. "I had my first one two weeks ago and she *just* got here. It usually takes a Malachite a month, at least, after getting here to have an awakening. If anything, this is the safest moment for us *to* go. Besides, I'm doing Ginen first," she says. When Teal doesn't speak up again, she continues. "Twenty minutes. That's all we'd need. We can be in and out in twenty minutes earth time."

Teal looks as if they're trying to find fault in her logic but can't. It doesn't matter if they did; all Tiana needed was their momentary hesitation to reach a hand behind and open the door, letting in a gust of warm city air.

"Are you coming, new girl?" she asks quickly as she steps backward.

Her orange jacket flaps in the suddenly warm air. Teal remains still, and I take an involuntary step forward. Then, Tiana glances over her shoulder to look at both of us from outside, a reckless smile already working its way across her face. Teal's eyes light up and my fist tenses. Wordlessly, Teal and I arrive on the threshold side by side.

"At least I managed to grab a snack, I guess," Teal says while lifting their left hand, which is in fact holding a bagel. They take a bite out of it just as I realize that Tiana is already partway down the foreign city street, confident in us following a second later.

"Sorry about her; she's fast," Teal says, stuffing the rest of the half-eaten bagel back into the one long pocket along the front of their apron and closing the door behind us. "Twenty minutes," they repeat to themself, before beginning a light jog to catch up with Tiana.

My heart beats in my throat at the absurdity of what we've just done. I was so caught up in their exchange I hardly had a moment to think on the enormity of leaving. As I follow them down the stairs and onto the sidewalk, the urge to look backward, just once, surges. The urge to tell myself I should have stayed still like everyone said—like I told myself I would—comes with it. But then I hear that voice again, this time slightly fainter than before.

*"Eyes forward, little bird. Destiny doesn't wait."*

So, instead of looking back, I keep one eye fixed on the backs of Tiana and Teal, and the other on the world around me, because ever since stepping out of Malachite—nothing looks the same as it did before.

# 9

**M**Y FOOTSTEPS ARE hesitant at first, but Tiana moves so fast I am forced to keep up. Teal checks over their shoulder every now and then to make sure I'm still following.

I can't help pausing every now and then to look at the world around me. This city is so much fuller than Crofton, or even Salt Spring: not just of people, but stores and activities, smells and sights. It's a startling contrast to anywhere I've lived. Widening my eyes, I try to take in as much as possible. The road names here are sometimes in French, other times in English, and even though it's December, the air is hot, humid, and soft.

Teal and Tiana walk as if they know exactly where we are and where we're going. Together they weave down streets sheltered by narrow second-story balconies fenced over with delicate grates, and with easy familiarity pass worn-looking marble columns flanking boarded-up doorways. I recognize that while some of the bricks on the buildings here are new, a lot are old and somewhat cracked in places. None of the buildings are very tall.

It's only when I see a small café advertising beignets and chicory coffee that I fully take in the license plates of the cars nearby. *We're in New Orleans.* Locking eyes with an American flag jutting off the side of one of the low buildings, I can't believe it: *I left the country without Auden.* We always said that the first trip abroad either of us took would happen together. My throat constricts as Teal turns on the sidewalk ahead to find me lagging several paces behind.

"Thea, come on," Teal says, as Tiana crosses the road with elegant, confident steps. I wipe sweat off my forehead and detangle myself from the winter jacket I put on when I decided to leave the house.

"Where is she going?" I ask.

Outside of Malachite, I notice how much Teal and Tiana glow in comparison to the people on the road. Tiana has an otherworldly air: her high cheekbones could cut glass, and wherever she strides, people turn to stare. Teal looks as if they are lit from within; golden jewels shine out from their neck and ears, and no matter where they stand the light finds a way to catch them.

"One of the keys will have gone to the land of the Lwa—a spirit world only accessible by a descendant of Legba, or the deity of crossroads and necromancy themself. Wait," Teal says after we cross the road, holding an arm out to keep me from smacking into a group of street musicians crowding the corner. We pick around their music and skirt beside an artist painting a galactic landscape on a nearby brick wall. It's hard to focus on anything when so much is happening. Then I see Tiana—several paces ahead of us, only now noticing our absence—paused with her hand impatiently resting on her hip, and I snap back to the present moment.

"And you know where to find this Legba?" I ask.

"Tiana does. Her sister was obsessed with places like this—gateways," Teal says, as we arrive to stand beside Tiana where the busy street has somewhat thinned.

"Come on." Tiana taps her foot against the cobblestone, seemingly unbothered by the heat and noise though sweating as much as me. "We're almost there."

THE STREET HERE isn't deserted, but for some reason it has an air of silence to it, a reverent hush that falls over pedestrians and birds alike. We stand at a crossroads just like Teal mentioned. Ahead of us, three different roads fan out: we can continue straight or turn either left or right.

Directly ahead of us, on a building almost at the very edge of the street, the awning of a small bookstore pulls my attention. It has no clear OPEN or CLOSED sign, but I think I see a light on somewhere inside. I look from Teal to Tiana and back again. *Even without any awakenings, I can clearly tell this is the spot. So why aren't they moving?* Instead, Teal is watching Tiana with a strained expression and Tiana is simply staring at the door for one, two, three seconds longer than normal. Suddenly, she moves, pushing the door open and charging in with the same energy I've seen in bungee jumpers. Overhead, the sky is dimming to a blue moon when Teal follows behind her, holding the door open for me to follow. I pause as well, bracing for a warning from my grandmother's spectral voice. Crickets.

Inside the bookstore, the floor sags downward like the pressure of so many books has made a dent in its floorboards. The walls press tight to my shoulders and Teal walks directly ahead of me down the aisle. Volumes of books, spines facing outward, nearly choke each side of my neck as I follow them to the desk at the very back of the warped room.

Sitting at a table, under a swaying overhead light tinted red, is a girl about our age wearing a hundred layered brass necklaces over a short black shirt. Tiana arrives at the desk first and puts her hands flat on its glass surface. The girl at the desk raises her head up to reveal two bored-looking brown eyes framed by red glasses. She frowns and raises an eyebrow.

Teal stays a few steps back, arms still crossed over their chest, their fists clutching the apron while I peer over their shoulder.

"Three to cross over, Madame Giroux," Tiana says.

"I didn't think I would see you again so soon," the girl says to Tiana.

Tiana stiffens. "You must be remembering wrong," she says. "I've never been inside."

The girl behind the desk inclines her head and looks at Tiana over the rim of her glasses. "The price is a vial each." She has a slight French accent that dips upward. Madame Giroux couldn't be more than a few years older than us, but the way she commands the room tells me she's seen enough to garner our respect.

"I thought it was a tablespoon each," Tiana replies.

"A vial." Madame Giroux shakes her head, folding her arms on the desk between them.

I try to pretend I know exactly what they are talking about, not letting my gaze wander to the books around me, or even to the wall behind the girl, which is made of a mirror that reflects the room in which we're standing, but slanted and odd. Ignoring my pulse beating against the fabric of my shirt, I focus on Tiana's fingertips tapping the glass between them.

"Fine, a vial each," she mutters. Tiana lifts her hands off the table and reaches into the front pocket of her long orange coat. Then Teal steps forward immediately, hand outstretched to stop Tiana, from what, I'm unsure.

"I can do it," they say as they hand her their balled-up apron.

"It's fine," Tiana snaps, "I'll do it."

My jaw clenches when I see the blade Tiana pulls out of her back pocket. *I guess it seems fitting that you'd pay in blood to get to the land of the spirits.*

"Do you have a bowl?" Tiana asks gruffly holding the knife up over her hand.

The girl at the counter looks dispassionately from the knife to Tiana's delicate hand, shrugs, and pushes forward her presumably empty coffee cup. Despite my best efforts, I do look away when Tiana brings the knife down, though I can't avoid hearing the drip of liquid into china.

When it is over and I look back up, the scene has changed. Madame Giroux is holding her cup, sniffing it slightly and nodding her head. I question whether I should run away, but my intrigue overpowers my nervousness. With Teal having moved out of the way, I step closer while Madame Giroux looks up from the cup and tilts her head to the side, assessing all of us. Eventually, she stands from her chair.

For a moment, I wonder where I would be if I weren't here, if I had never fallen through the well behind my house. Before I can think on it too long, Madame Giroux is turning to face the mirror behind her, dipping her fingertips in the cup, and pulling them out, red and wet. My stomach gurgles when she smears the blood across the surface of the mirror, forming a cross. She begins adding more flourishes and details, dots here, waves there, forming an image that could almost belong on an iron gate. I don't realize I'm inching closer until Teal's shoulder collides with mine. I gasp when the image on the mirror shifts. The reflection of the bookstore behind us disappears—the cars on the street too—until the four of us are staring at another store, another row of shelves, another hallway, and another desk at the very far end. As if we were looking into this very store from the doorway, and not the back of the shop.

My eyes widen as Madame Giroux walks through what was once glass but what I now see is an open portal in the wall.

"It's the same room, but different," I whisper to Teal.

"It's an in-between dimension. Same store, different plane," they explain.

This clears up nothing for me, but I accompany them as they walk around the desk and follow behind Tiana, who eagerly ducks inside. At the threshold, I lift my foot several inches to get over the sill—but when it comes down on the other side, the floor creaks and sags, just the same as when I first walked into this bookstore. *Wow, déjà vu.*

After walking the length of the new store, no longer filled with books but shining trinkets of all sizes, our host takes a seat on an identical chair at an identical table. She sets down the cup filled with blood, picks up an identical cup filled with coffee, and takes a steaming sip. I look over my shoulder to find nothing but a wooden wall behind us, except this one is covered in images:

human-shaped figures stretch over the entirety of it, long-limbed and dark red. More blood.

"What are you doing sitting down? Open the next door," Tiana demands.

"Wait, T—look," Teal says, gesturing to the shelf beside them, laden with small objects resembling the contents of a school-child's backpack yet humming with nearly imperceptible life.

Teal picks up two round stones, each with a perfect hole in their centers. "How much?" they ask Madame Giroux.

"For you?" She gives a conniving smile, tilts her head to the side, and says, "I'll take a secret and a hair."

"Done," Teal agrees, and presses past Tiana's chest to fit down the aisle and pay up. I feel newly alone in the strange hallway until Tiana walks up to stand beside me.

"Don't. Touch. Anything," she whispers through her teeth without taking her eyes off the back of Teal's head. I'm sure that Madame Giroux is watching us even as she pulls out a thin leaf of paper and pen and holds them out. Teal takes both and scrib-bles something I can't read from this angle.

"Is she . . . a Malachite?" I whisper, remembering what Teal told me earlier about the Legba.

Tiana shakes her head. "Not a Malachite, a Godspring, yes, but the blood is too faded and too far in the past for it to do much other than activate ours."

Tiana shifts and walks down the aisle to peer closer at a small stone carved bowl. I return to scanning the shelves and try not to gawk as I read some of the stranger labels: DEADMAN'S FIRST LOST TOOTH, HAIRY PEBBLE (POISONOUS WHEN RAW), then simply CINNAMON. Finally, my attention snags on a small brown vial filled with tan powder. SANDMAN'S SAND, it reads in neat typeface.

"*This*," the voice whispers, faint yet audible.

My fingertips itch to move. *But Tiana told me not to touch anything.* I anchor my hand at my side.

"*This.*"

"How much for this sand?" I ask Madame Giroux.

Teal looks over their shoulder at me after they finish handing over the piece of paper they scribbled on to Madame Giroux. When they see what I'm now gesturing toward, they shake their head in warning. Tiana remains very still and circles back to stand beside me, her hands in her pockets.

"I'll take a quart for that . . . or a favor." Madame Giroux's voice reminds me of ripping paper. I stiffen.

Tiana exhales through her nose slowly.

*Maybe that isn't so bad a price?* I open my mouth to reply but Tiana interrupts.

"We don't have time for her to lose a quart of blood. We have to go," Tiana insists.

Madame Giroux frowns and shrugs, looks down at the piece of paper Teal gave her, then back up at Tiana with a slightly more authentic smile.

"Will you let us through now?" Tiana asks after Teal gives Madame Giroux one of their arm hairs.

"Here you go." Madame Giroux ignores Tiana and hands Teal their stones. "Your friend wants some sand. I will complete our exchange before entering a new one," Madame Giroux says to

Teal, while Tiana clearly clenches her hands into fists within her pockets.

"*The sand.*" My grandmother's voice whispers as Tiana turns her blazing eyes on me.

Whether it's out of a decisiveness or panic, I speak, "I'll do the favor."

Tiana's eyes widen; Teal visibly bites their tongue. My stomach sinks at their reactions. *I chose wrong.* Madame Giroux's eyes sparkle.

**WHEN WE FINALLY EMERGE** from the doorway beyond the bookstore's second desk, the world is not at all how I expected—which is to say, it's quite normal. I thought that Ginen, the land of the Lwa, would at least be toned purple and filled with huge mushrooms. Instead, it looks like the gloomy part of the forest your mom warns you to stay away from after dark, threaded through with ribbons of low fog. Here it is wet and warm and looks full of ticks and venomous brown spiders—just like the woods behind my house. I shiver even though the air is hotter here than it was in New Orleans.

"Okay, so we're here. What's your plan?" Teal asks Tiana, who surveys the tree line carefully through the hole in her stone. Stones that, Teal explained, allow humans and Malachites who haven't had their first awakening to see hidden magic. Above our heads, a soft, sunlike, glowing red orb shines through the mist. Tiana turns to me decidedly.

"What?" I draw back with my own stone cold in my hand, only to step in a wet patch of dirt and notice the tinge from my scraped ankle against the sweaty fabric of my sock. I haven't had the chance to change my Band-Aid yet. I hope I don't get tetanus.

"You said you had a way through here, that you could find the keys. Now's your moment, new girl," Tiana says.

My chest flutters as I register an opportunity to prove my worth—even if I don't actually feel capable enough to journey through this enchanted landscape.

Closing my eyes, I visualize the map and remember a collection of rocks similar to the ones we just arrived through, a path of trees, a wide lake. "There's a body of water, completely circular, beyond the trees," I offer. I remember from the way it was outlined in the map, illustrated in thicker lines, that it was important.

"Which way?" Teal asks, looking around the dark woods evenly.

Shrugging, I adjust the bag at my shoulder. "I don't know. North, I think," I say.

Tiana sighs. "Useless."

I balk.

"The information, not you," she explains, then turns her back to us and takes off to her left. Teal whistles low; Tiana adjusts course right.

"She's just tense," Teal says, as we follow Tiana through the forest.

"It's fine—I'm fine," I say, as we pass below the long arm of a tree infected with wide black mold patches that smell like tar.

"Put it to your eye—you'll see everything I can," they encourage, gesturing down to the stone I still clutch in my palm.

I do as they say and press the stone to my eye. When I do, the forest suddenly buzzes to life. The spots of mold take on a deeper violet texture, the ground shifts from being simply shades of brown to having patches of amber and hickory. On the edges of my sight, I think I see shapes moving, but when I turn to look at them properly, they vanish. When I look at Teal, they shine brighter than the surroundings, overlaid with shades of gold. Ahead of me, Tiana is cast in an array of reds: like a molten supernova. Wherever she moves, a hum follows her body, threading through the air like steam.

"How did you know how to get here, and about the bookstore?" I ask Teal when it seems as though the sky has disappeared under layered pink leaves dripping with that same black-tar mold, which, through my stone, I can now see shines silver and reflects the forest around it. *Besides looking like a hall of mirrors, this place doesn't seem so bad.*

"Tiana's sister studied portals and history extensively," Teal says. "She told us about this place last summer," they explain.

"Tiana has a sister?"

"Zola," Teal says.

*T + Z,* I remember the carving in the tree. Ahead of us, Tiana pauses but doesn't look over her shoulder at us. I observe Teal's eyes, the way they measure how tense Tiana is and how slow her steps falter as a gauge for how to continue.

"Zola loved finding hidden information," Tiana says before they can. "At first, it was portals through our world, shortcuts between cities and countries." She stops walking entirely, letting us catch up until we are only a step behind her, before continuing more slowly, so we can stay close. "Zola found the way into Ginen and Jotunheim. She would have found the way into Kunlun too, if she hadn't gotten derailed." Tiana shakes her head.

"Was it just portals, or was she looking for something specific?" I ask.

"Zola started looking for something that belonged to our father, an artifact that connected him to his grandfather: the Egyptian god of magic and medicine, Heka. She found evidence that all Malachites—all Godspring in fact—are meant to have artifacts that connect them to their god relatives," Tiana says.

"And she didn't find it?" I ask, trying to read between the downturned lines of Tiana's face.

"She did." Tiana shakes her head. "And then the Arcana found her."

Tiana pauses momentarily to inspect a tree, gouged through with the long talons of a creature I never want to meet. Teal reaches out a hand to rest on Tiana's shoulder. For a moment Tiana appears relaxed, but then she quickly stiffens and picks up her pace.

"This place is supposed to test your outer self," Tiana muses, looking around at the shiny liquid pouring out of the trees, her own silvery full-length fun house reflection in the nearest one. I avoid looking my reflection in the eye; I don't want to trip myself up so early into our journey. But then I nearly bump into Tiana where she's halted, staring directly into her own mirrored image as though she were seeing a ghost.

"Let's keep moving," Teal says gently.

I swallow and march forward after Tiana robotically sets off again. As we keep walking, the terrain becomes choppier, the dirt more agitated, and the gouges in the trees ever more frequent. The thick slices in the trunks here leak black-silver goo down to the forest floor that reflects a hundred too many angles of myself.

Suddenly, the air heats, growing damper each second, accompanying a bizarre emptiness in my bones: the kind that makes my teeth chatter despite the heat.

Teal lets go of my arm to catch up with Tiana when I realize that I feel like I am being watched. In the same moment, the hairs on the back of my neck stand on edge, Teal's hands light up, the lines on their palms glow, and Tiana's body tenses. They both feel it as much as I do—we are not alone in this forest.

Tiana palms her knife discreetly as she turns in a slow circle. I see the flash of feather only a moment before it descends, melting out of the mist overhead. I shriek as the monster claws downward onto Teal's fragile and exposed head. I brace for the blood, eyes halfway shutting. But there is no need, Tiana is already moving. As fast as the creature, which resembles a sort of prehistoric heron with blade-sharp talons and eyes as red as a setting sun, Tiana slashes upward with her knife, mouth set to the grim task. Teal moves beside her, blinding the creature with bursts of light.

The pair of them move in anticipation of where the other is with the trust of a pair of dancers. The whole exchange lasts only a minute before the bird flies away, up again into the clouds. I gape while Teal and Tiana survey each other for injury. When Teal finds a slash of red along Tiana's upper arm, they look for a moment as if her pain is their own, and the light in their palm flickers.

"It's fine," Tiana mumbles, smearing the blood to the side with the back of her hand. Teal winces. "We're nearly there. Kongamatos live by the water," Tiana says, one eye still on the tree line above our heads.

Only when Teal looks back at me do I realize I haven't moved an inch. *Why didn't you move?*

"What was that?" I ask.

"An animal that no longer exists on earth. It went extinct decades ago. Sometimes animals who pass over get caught here. Come on, let's not wait for it to come back." Tiana's voice is higher than normal though her movements are easy. She's as scared as I am and doing a much better job of hiding it. I gulp and wonder how she can hold all these facts inside her, when I can barely remember my schedule at the Snack Shack without a reminder on my phone.

When we arrive at the edge of a large pool of murky black water, almost flush with the emerald grass ahead of us, the bag at my shoulder sags down, and I remember the map neatly folded within. *What do we do now?* I take a step closer to the watering hole, partially shaded by dipping weeping willows glowing an ethereal mint. Pressing the stone even tighter against my face, I look out at the water, at the trees that move almost as if they can see me watching, waving back with their leaves and smiling from the creases of their bark.

Tiana shuffles behind me as we all look out at the water ahead of us.

"It's here," I say, because that's what the map showed.

*It must be.* Why else would this body of water be so heavily outlined in black? Why else would the map show a pathway through the trees to this exact spot? I remember it so vividly when I close my eyes now—this was the clearest of the three drawings.

*Someone will have to dive in,* I surmise. Pursing my lips, I wrap my hands around my stomach. "I'll go in," I say, recalling Teal and

Tiana's bravery just minutes ago. I don't know who I am, but I want to find out. I want to make myself into a person like Tiana and Teal, who take adventure and magic in stride. I don't want to be the kind of person who doesn't move. *I wish my hands weren't shaking.*

"Um, no. I don't think that's a good idea," Tiana calls.

I frown and turn my back to the still water to face her and Teal.

"I can do it." I try to push my shoulders back from my face in a confident gesture, avoiding the thought of how cold the water must be.

"Okay, hold on, you two." Teal takes a step between us, holds their ringed hands up. "*I'll* go. I can light the water up from underneath. With you two up top, we'll find the key easier."

I frown but internally agree. I *would* be sort of useless under water—even the thought of it reminds me of the last time I swam. I shiver at the memory of that jarring cold, the ends of Mom's curly hair fading above me. *Teal is right.* "Okay, I'll—"

Before I can take a step away from the water's edge to join them, cold flesh grips my ankle. There is only enough time to look down, register the bony and slightly webbed hand wrapped around me, before I am dragged backward. I shout, my chin clips the edge of the grass, I taste blood, and then everything is wet and endlessly dark.

# 10

**M**Y EYES OPEN to the ceiling of a domed room from which deadly mineral points drip like winter icicles, aimed straight at my head. I scramble first to my side, then to my knees, then to my feet. In the space of one inhalation, I register the moisture in the air and the slosh of water lapping at the shore behind me. The only thing I really pay attention to though, or rather *who* I really pay attention to, is her.

The woman's hair hangs in locks of various length, some thumb-width and bellybutton-long, others straw-thin and the length of a hand, all in different shades of seafoam. I shrink at the smell of her: rotting seaweed, iodine, and shell—the scent of low tide. She sits at a table low to the ground on a wooden stool soft and bleached from the water. Her eyes are the same color as the inside of an oyster shell, and she is naked. The table ahead of her has two empty chairs across from her. When her pearly eyes lock on mine, I'm reminded of a dead fish's skull.

The stone cave wall beyond her is carved into the shape of a shelf and holds trinkets and bones of various sizes. I want to retract, but if I move any farther away, I'll fall right back into the water behind me. *How do I get out of here?*

The woman seems to know this or sees the panic in my face because she parts her blue lips into a sharp smile, and I grimace in reaction to her razor-sharp teeth. The water behind me sloshes with movement. I turn in time to watch Teal's head appear out of the dark waves, their eyes searching wildly around, holding a ball of light in the palm of each hand. Their flowy clothes are soaked through and cling to their body as they drag themself onto shore. Teal smiles when they see me, having not noticed the woman yet.

"Thea!" they exclaim.

I shake my head in warning, clutching my bag close to the side of my body, wondering why I didn't think to bring a weapon when I left Malachite.

"You look tired, why don't you sit?"

My spine tenses when I hear the woman's surprisingly smooth voice echo.

I look at Teal as they take in the scene around us, realizing as I do that my stone is long gone in the waves behind me. If there is more to this room than I can see, Teal will need to be the one to tell me.

*Clink*, the sound of metal on wood. I look back over at the woman, whose hand retracts from the silver item on the table between us: one small, intricately woven metal key wrapped into the likeness of a sea creature lies innocently ahead of her. I inhale as Teal steps forward. We approach the seated woman side by side.

"Go on," the woman says again. Her voice is like a song. She blinks up at me, and though her eyes are milky, I sense she sees me just fine. She gestures to the stools ahead of us. I try to keep my expression neutral as I sink down onto the bleached wood. *How am I supposed to act? Should I fight? Run?* I look at Teal for instruction; their gaze is even.

I suppress the urge to gag at the smell wafting off the woman, whose hands remain on the table with long fingernails sharp as knives and tinged red. I glance down at my ankle through the corner of my eye, note the fingernail-size puncture wounds just above my still-healing scrape, and wrinkle my nose.

"So—you're a Keeper?" Teal asks.

"I am La Sirène," the woman says softly.

"Can we have it?" I ask, turning my attention back to the key, remembering our quest.

"Surely, you can. Whenever we are asked for a key by a child of the gods, we must give it away." La Sirène says this like it is amusing, but doesn't laugh. In fact, her face is still while she speaks.

"Okay then," Teal says, reaching toward the key.

Before Teal can touch the key though, La Sirène's head snaps toward them, long hair flicking tiny splatters of water at the side of my face. I wipe at the wetness with my shaking palm.

"I said I would give it. I did not say it would be free," La Sirène cautions, her voice lower now than it was before.

I inhale. *Another bargain.* I don't know if I can stomach the sight of blood again.

"What do you want?" Teal asks. *I'm so glad they came in after me.*

La Sirène tilts her head to the side as if in consideration, though her white eyes remain flat. "When I was young, I was in love with a beautiful god of the waters and waves. We were in harmony for centuries—until we weren't. The sea became too small for us to share, and so he diminished me," she says, and closes her eyes. "Cut me in two." She trails a sharp fingernail down the middle of her face as if to illustrate her point, a weak trail of red leaking from her fingertip like paint.

I squirm as the temperature seems to drop ten degrees. Searching for a clear exit from the room, my gaze snags on something else: a narrow bottle wedged into the shelf behind the white-eyed woman. It is glass and opaque, and it shines even in the dimness of the room almost as brightly as Tiana and Teal do, almost as bright as a star.

*"Get the bottle."*

I try not to show that I have heard something.

La Sirène continues, "I was tricked and told that if I came to this place, I would find a precious gift. But only a piece of me could enter here—a shard of the soul. He cut me in two and chained this piece of me in Ginen forever. While my beauty, love, and unwavering obedience remain in the surface world, *I* am locked away in these stagnant waters," she says, while she spreads her hands out on the table ahead of her.

La Sirène laughs and it is like music, but sharp. Her eyes flutter as she reaches into the folds of her hair, pulling out a hemp bag and emptying it onto her now open palm, revealing a cluster of pearls and very small teeth. Teal and I both tense.

"A fractured soul," she says, shaking them.

I look around the empty space of the room, wondering if there might be other white eyes in the darkness staring back that I can't see.

"To keep a key is a heavy weight, and to give it even more so." La Sirène's tone switches as she releases the teeth and bulbous pearls onto the table between us. A gust of wind rushes through the room, bringing the smell of bones and blood and lake water. The teeth crash onto the wood just as I hear the voice again:

"*The bottle.*"

"I see trouble," La Sirène says, looking away from the pearls directly into my eyes. "You're followed by a great man, a powerful man"—she runs a hand over the teeth—"shrouded in darkness, protected, and looking for what you seek. Shadow is his weapon, but you will have your own—soon enough," she says softly. "Soon enough."

I can feel her looking at me more than I can see it. She is staring into my core. My blood freezes; even *I* don't know what is in there. She doesn't blink. I try not to look away.

"What's that supposed to mean?" I ask.

"You'll see," she warns.

"Is someone else looking for the keys?" Teal's voice breaks the spell, interrupting the energy in the room.

I finally exhale and the woman looks away from me, pointing her head at Teal.

"My payment is feeling. For this and only this, you may have your key."

"What kind of feeling?" I whisper past a dry throat.

"Love," she replies, still looking at Teal. "I do not remember it; I want that feeling back. I want *great* love," she whispers.

I pull back. The only person I love that deeply is my mother and there is nothing in the world worth losing that feeling for. I start to ask for an alternative before Teal interrupts.

"I'll do it," they say.

Teal's fists are tight on their lap, and I open my mouth to interject, but La Sirène is already smiling, already darting her fingers across the table before gripping Teal's smooth head. Her own white eyes close tight as oysters while my heart surges.

*I should have offered; this should be me.*

*"The bottle!"*

I can ignore it no longer; my opportunity is clear.

I look over the woman's wet shoulder at the shelf and see the bottle again. Gleaming with some unseen light, it draws me in like a string to a spool. I stand even though I shouldn't. Moving carefully and skirting around the side of La Sirène like a puppet, in a second I am snatching the bottle with two trembling hands. I hold it out ahead of me as Teal squirms in pain behind me, still seated at the small table. I should stow the mysterious bottle away quickly, but there, on the bottle's smooth surface, is a soberingly familiar symbol. *The same one burned into my hand.* I look from one to the other, palm to bottle, and back. My eyes widen. Teal lets out a low moan. I slide the bottle into my still-wet bag and hurry back to my seat only a moment before Teal and La Sirène finish their exchange.

There is a wet glimmer on Teal's cheek, sparkling and thick. La Sirène's finger darts out, scooping it up. I press my lips together as she slides her nail into her mouth and closes her eyes. Despite the barnacles on her skin, and the pieces of driftwood in her hair, there is joy in her expression so uniquely human it makes me feel almost guilty stealing from her. But then Teal gasps in air, and I remember the price of that expression. I check their face for any damage. Teal only blinks, looking around the room dazed, clutching the gold chain around their neck, and recovering quickly. "The key?" they ask.

La Sirène pulls her finger out of her mouth with a wide smile, spreads her hands out in the air over the small object as if to say, *Be my guest.*

Teal grabs the key and stores it in their front pocket, standing immediately.

"Thanks."

I rise beside them, eager to leave this place—surprised it could be this easy. But when I move, the glass in my bag brushes against my wet book with a *clang.* I inhale. La Sirène's white eyes darken to gray. She looks over her shoulder at the shelf I stole from, then back at me.

Understanding flashes across her face. *She knows what I've done.* A heartbeat later, the room is all movement. La Sirène is sliding over the low table toward me. Her mouth opens, revealing several layers of serrated teeth; one clawing hand hooks out toward me, and the pearls and teeth fall to the floor. On instinct, I raise my palm up to block the woman, grabbing her wrist just before she can dig into the flesh of my forearm. Her skin is warmer than I expect, and rough. La Sirène screeches, rearing back as if burned. She staggers, and I freeze in confusion and fear. But Teal doesn't question her sudden turn or my reaction to it, already dragging me toward the water by my upper arm. I notice they don't feel the same as when I last brushed against their skin. We crash into the waves before I can wonder what my hand did to La Sirène. *They feel lost.*

Teal lights up the water ahead of us, heating it slightly and exposing a narrow tunnel about twenty feet away—the exit I was searching for. The tunnel winds beneath the cave around us and presumably back up to land. I kick my feet and try to keep my eyes open, while they hold my arm tight enough to block out my panic with their determination.

She is there before I can doubt my ability to hold my breath and swim in jeans. La Sirène covers the rounded exit with her whole body. She looks like a jellyfish emerging from a sewer vent: pale skin fanning loosely off her bones, hair floating up from her neck exposing a set of gills on either side of it. I gasp—my lungs fill with water—then I burn with the pain of trying to cough it out. In my fit, I squirm free of Teal's grasp. *I can't believe this is happening again!* Still coughing, my eyes close and I float in nothingness momentarily. Then I notice something strange: there is a warmth in the center of my chest that expands outward, a tingle in my right palm, but Teal isn't touching me anymore. *It's coming from inside of me.*

I open my eyes as the world changes around me. The water folds over itself, creating a ripple that extends toward La Sirène, whose eyes widen while her hands splay open to block the oncoming current. But it's useless. Instead, the water moves as I desire and shoves her aside.

*I did that, I moved her, I created the waves.*

So, I *will* it to carry us to shore as Teal grabs hold of my arm again; they feel as shocked as I do. I might be imagining it, but swimming doesn't feel as hard as it used to. As we move through the current, I watch La Sirène, dragged away on invisible currents, and I think I feel the water propel us forward. As I turn to watch the woman disappear into a dark corner of the watery depths, for just a moment, I see a flash of two things: a red burn on the woman's arm where I touched her—the same mark I have on my palm—and two figures in the water beside her.

One of the apparitions is my smiling mother. In her right hand is a staff as tall as her body that shines with golden light. Beside her is a petite Chinese woman who looks like a painting come to life, wearing long robes in shades of blue and yellow. She holds a familiar paintbrush in her hand, outstretched toward me.

Then Teal is pulling me up, up, up by my arm, and the two images stay locked behind my eyes, like an impression of the sun after staring too long into its brightness. In a heartbeat, we are well past the exit and I can see the sunlight overhead cracking through rippled water.

We heave one another onto the bank. Once on flat earth, I gasp, filling my lungs.

*What did I just see? What just happened?* I cling to the grass under my knees, pushing myself as far as I can from the water's edge, pressing my hand belatedly on the bag at my side, and registering the clink of glass. *I still have the bottle.*

"Thank the gods you're both safe," Tiana says, pulling my arm so I can get farther away from the waves.

Even with my eyes closed, I can still see the outline of the two women, fainter than before, but still close to me. Sinking my head backward against the trunk of an unfamiliar tree, the world is upside down. I pull the paintbrush my nana gave me out of the tangled mess of my hair and hold it in my left hand like a lifeline. *What's going on?*

"What happened in there?" Tiana asks us. Teal is folded in half, pressed against a log beside me and eyeing the waterline with suspicion, but it is as still as when we first arrived.

"I—I don't know what happened," I begin. "There was a woman who looked like she was made of the sea, with so many teeth. But we did it, we got—Teal got—the key." Every time I blink, I see that woman and my mother again, closer again and half-transparent.

Tiana's face lights up with excitement. I smile too and then gasp. My heart pounds and the light becomes too bright. Distantly, I think I hear a song playing.

"What?" Tiana asks.

"I—I feel like I'm falling. It's a rush of something—more than adrenaline. Were there drugs or a poison in the water?" I splutter as I try to give voice to this incredible, albeit confusing, sensation.

"Is everything brighter? Are you seeing anyone or hearing anything?" Tiana takes a hurried step forward and sinks to her knees.

"Yes!" I shout. There is a chant. The music that was at first faint now grows and I can hear words, hums, and shouts. It's like stepping into the middle of a welcoming crowd.

Tiana rocks back on her heels, hastily picking up her discarded backpack. Her fingers move too quick.

"What is it?" I blink past my exhilaration.

Tiana pushes her bag over her shoulder, scanning the tree line just the same as when that prehistoric bird flew overhead.

"It's your first awakening," she says steadily for my benefit. "You're being introduced to each god in your lineage. The ticking clock to decide which lineage you will claim begins," she says.

I shake my head and close my eyes against the blinding lights. I focus now and realize that the chant is saying just two words over and over again. *Amina,* my mother's name, and another: *Chang'e.* When I focus on the latter, the woman holding the paintbrush appears behind my closed eyes. She is fainter than before but smiling and holding out my paintbrush toward me. Silver light shines off it. When I focus on the sound of my mother's name, the other woman disappears, and Mom is there. My heart leaps. I try to reach out to her. I notice this ethereal version of Mom is dressed in green, still holding a tall staff glowing gold. When I reach for her, she disappears—they both do. The humming stops though the lights continue to gleam.

"Mom! Where are you?" I shout, opening my eyes and trying to force myself to stand up despite my shaking body. *She was right there!*

"Teal come on, we have to go." Tiana nudges Teal with the tip of her shoe.

Teal shakes their head, as if broken out of a trance. They push themself to stand, but when they look at Tiana, whatever clarity they gained seems to slip away. Teal looks perplexed and asks Tiana what's going on, says something is missing and grabs at the center of their chest.

My eyes fill with water, and I try to resummon the image of my mother's face. *Why didn't I reach out for her sooner?* Now she's gone, *again.* I have so much to talk to her about.

When my eyes refocus, I find Teal and Tiana staring at each other with equally confused expressions. *La Sirène meant what she said literally,* I realize. *She must have taken Teal's love for Tiana.* I open my mouth to explain this to both as the elation humming through me dims—and then we all hear it. An out-of-place noise emanates from behind the trees to our right. It is the sound of coals sinking into water, fire sizzling in waves, crashes of thunder.

It does not belong to this forest.

Tiana curses. "It's the Arcana, they're here. They've found us."

# 11

A MINA, CHANG'E. When I told Tiana the two names my
first awakening brought, while we raced through the forest
back toward the stone wall we came through, she could tell me
only that Chang'e is the Chinese goddess of the moon. When she
heard *Amina*, my mother's name, Tiana had no explanation for it,
or any explanation for why I saw my mother's face instead of my
father's.

"Unless—" Tiana shakes her head. "No, impossible," she continues as we race past mirrored trees.

"What?" I ask.

"I mean, it's rare—unheard of—but, Thea, what if your mom is
a god?" she says.

"My mom?" I scoff even as my mind whirs.

"Gods don't raise their kids," Teal inserts.

"But what if they did?" Tiana insists.

I shake my head and my steps falter. *My mother, a goddess, all
this time?*

"If a god spends too much time on earth, they lose their power," Teal says.

My mind is whirling with this new information, so much so that when I see a familiar face across a clearing in the gloomy forest ahead, for a second, I think it's my imagination.

Amid the shining leaves and misty treetops—in a jungle full of noises as familiar as they are menacing—is a pair of hazel eyes and auburn hair I would recognize anywhere. *Auden?* I stop in my tracks at the same moment Teal and Tiana do.

"Malachites," a voice calls from my right.

My mouth is still hanging open when four figures walk out of the trees, all wearing identical black-and-white uniforms. I am only half-surprised to find the voice belongs to the boy from the Snack Shack, from the night when this all began. His dark hair is tucked behind either ear, and even in a forest full of tall trees, his stature is imposing. I close my mouth as I stare between him and Auden. *Why doesn't she seem surprised to be here? What is she doing here?*

"You," I exhale, as I realize that this boy from the café, this *Arcana*, must have kidnapped her.

"You can call me Zero, son of Zeus," he says with a slight British accent. Folding one hand over the other, resting his wrists atop a black cane, he smiles at me like we're old friends. "You've already met Auden, daughter of the Morrígan." He gestures to my best friend, who now stares directly over my shoulder, like she can't even see me. *What?*

Zero continues introductions like we're meeting under normal circumstances, pointing to another Arcana coming out of the woods beside him. "This is Ophelia, daughter of Hera." A red-haired girl with a firm scowl stands at his right. "Stone, son of Olorun." A tall boy with catlike hazel eyes holds a crossbow in his arms and frowns at us across the forest floor. "And Basil, son of Isis." Only slightly shorter than Stone but as beautiful as a dewdrop, Basil looks the least like a villain.

"Auden, what's going on?" I shout.

Tiana looks at me for an explanation, but my eyes are glued to my friend's. Auden still isn't meeting my eyes.

"Thea, right?" Zero takes a step forward. "I'm sure Auden would love to talk to you, but right now she's under strict orders to do the opposite. So, why don't we get to it. Tell me, what are *you* doing here?" He nods for me to speak.

I ignore him and start walking toward Auden. Tiana holds me back and I sense a spike of rigid anger in her grip.

"Thea," she whispers.

I try to pull free. The whole world is shining, my heartbeat is as loud as ever—I'm having my first awakening—but that is my *best friend* and the Arcana have her.

"Thea, look at her," Tiana says.

I pause just long enough to see the uniform Tiana is pointing at: a black-and-white shirt and blazer. I stop struggling. *Auden is Arcana.* The truth settles in.

"What the hell," I shout. "Auden, look at me. What is going on?" I ask her.

"Auden was keeping an eye on you, for us," Zero says patiently. "What your mother was doing was . . . unorthodox. We thought it best to put one of our best on the matter," he says.

*No. My* best friend *is not a spy.* I open my mouth to contradict him, but my words lodge in my throat when Auden still won't look at me.

"You have something that belongs to us," Zero says finally.

I shake my head. *She wouldn't do this to me.* Auden wouldn't have kept this a secret from me. I've known her since I moved to BC. Since that first day of school. Auden was one of the most popular girls in our grade and she *saw* me like no one else could. She befriended me, she—*she used me?* I shake my head. *This can't be happening.*

"We don't have anything of yours," Teal says, while my arm tightens around my bag. "Why don't you just let us past. I'm sure this is a misunderstanding," they say pragmatically.

Everything becomes sharper as I integrate the truth of what's going on. I stop looking at Auden, who won't meet my gaze, and turn my attention to Zero. I remember the last time I saw him, the way the café convulsed as a premonition of what was to come at home. Tightening my jaw, my mind whirs with the possibilities of what he could be after: the bottle in my bag, the map, or the key. I will part with none of them.

*He must be the man La Sirène warned me about,* I realize. *And the one from the first prophecy! The one chasing me and looking for the Malachite keys.* I see it now, so clearly. This boy standing at the café, sending frogs and shadows after my family.

Zero is the reason for *all* of it. I tighten my fists.

When I first saw him, I ran. In moments since, when things have gotten scary, I've frozen. *I won't freeze now.* I act without knowing what I'm doing and take a step forward. My whole body is still tingling with heat; my right palm is blazing. When I close my eyes, it's as if the entirety of my being is pressing against the spirit of the forest around me; my awakening spreads so wide that I can feel the power of this place like a blanket I could pull toward me with an inhale. So I do. I draw my breath in and feel it connect in the palm of my right hand. Distantly, someone shouts something I can't make out. And then I open my eyes, poised to let it all out in a focused wave aimed directly at Zero—but then my eyes lock on Auden's—and I remember everything.

In a flash, I remember walking in on her and my mother arguing a few months ago. It was the middle of the night and I had gotten up from our sleepover to find Auden missing. When I got to the kitchen of my house, whatever fight they were having simmered down, but the result of it lingered in the air.

I remember never meeting her parents, her kindness toward me when everyone else at school treated me like an outsider, the way she always seemed to have a secret. *It was all a lie.* My control over the energy around and inside of me disappears.

It takes everything in me not to direct this power back on myself after the clarity of these buried truths comes to light. Instead, knowing I'm about to lose control of the energy I hold, I direct it at the ground between us, and the Arcana, in an explosion of light and sound, throwing everyone back in different directions in the process.

*DID I JUST DO THAT?* My ears are ringing, and instead of finding any familiar faces, the red-haired girl named Ophelia stands and faces me from about forty yards away.

She smiles when she sees me and holds up a hand covered in a golden glove. When I spot that slanted smile, I scramble out of the way immediately, sure that whatever she has planned won't be good. I manage to get behind the trunk of a tree as she lashes out with a shatter of energy. It slams into the base of the tree, causing wood chips to fall around my shoulders.

Remembering what Tiana told me about artifacts and her sister's hypothesis, I dig around in the front pocket of my bag, taking out my paintbrush. *This paintbrush that Nana gave me is what the moon goddess tried to show me. Maybe it can help.* I clutch the brush in my hand. With my breath held, I curl forward, waiting for some amazing feat of energy to come out of it. Already my first awakening is fading, the connection I had to the power around me is barely half of what it was moments ago.

Another crash booms into the tree behind me while the paintbrush lays dormant in my hand. Panicked, I squeeze the brush tighter and shake it a little bit. Nothing happens. The tree absorbs another bolt of energy from Ophelia and I bite the inside of my cheek.

Nearby, Tiana and Teal are battling other Arcana. Their grunts pair with the crash of heavy objects into bark. When Teal shouts somewhere behind me, my whole body tightens more. *Why can't I summon that same energy I did moments ago?* The lights are dim now; my eyes can see normally. My awakening is moments from over.

The air ahead of me shines bright with a single wide bolt of electricity. When the light fades, a tall figure stares down at me: Zero. I grimace and try to back away but am already pressed tight to the tree behind me. I squeeze the paintbrush tighter in defiance, but nothing happens.

Zero kneels with a patient expression. "I know you have something of ours," he says.

The paintbrush? The bottle? The map? The key? Doesn't matter. He can't have it.

"Nope." I shake my head while subtly pulling my bag behind my back.

Zero frowns like he's disappointed. "Come on, just give it to me and we'll leave," he says.

I narrow my eyes. "What do you even want?" I ask.

Zero falters. *He doesn't know what he's looking for.*

"If *you* don't know what you're looking for, just leave us alone."

"Listen, I have my orders and I won't leave without an artifact level nine or higher—so that's either whatever you have in that bag—or you." He says this softly.

My eyes widen and I instinctively hold up a hand to keep him back, like he might lunge at me. He doesn't; instead Zero looks down at my palm. When he sees the image burned there, his brow furrows. "Where did you get that?"

"Leave us alone," I say.

He stares at the mark, then at my face for a few seconds. I remember when I first saw him on that dark street, I felt as though he could truly see me. I recognize that same feeling now—for a second—before his eyes flick over my shoulder and he's joined by the red-haired girl who tried to split me in half only moments ago.

"Do you have it?" Ophelia asks. Her accent matches his, clipping words to come out shorter than they're spelled.

"Not quite, Fee," Zero says, and stands up.

*If I try to run, they'll catch me. And if I try to fight, then what?*

Ophelia sneers down at me, then raises her golden glove at my chest. *Okay, no fighting.* Zero quickly puts a hand on her arm.

"It's fine, she's going to give it to us," Zero explains.

Ophelia seems confused at his interruption but lowers her arm anyway. Somewhere behind me I hear Tiana shout my name.

"Why do you even want it?" I snap up at them, trying to stall. Maybe if I can wait long enough, I'll be able to muster that same energy I had before. Ophelia looks at him with a haughty expression and taps her wrist where a watch would be.

Zero rolls his eyes, suddenly much colder than he was a few moments before. "Because in this game, of magic and gods, it's important for Arcana to control the board," he says to me.

"This isn't a game, and the world isn't full of winners and losers," I spit.

Zero's mouth tightens for a second. "Fine, kings and pawns— whatever metaphor will get you to understand the gravity." Zero lifts his staff forward and touches the center of my chest. I open my mouth to respond, but the electricity racing out of his staff paralyzes me. I try to move my arms, fight off the energy, but I simply can't. I remember when I touched his bare skin in the café by accident; this reminds me of that feeling—but much stronger— and much more uncomfortable.

Ophelia bends down and picks up my bag and holds it out over her shoulder to Zero, who takes it without looking me in the eye. He lets his staff drop from my chest, but the paralysis continues. My heart beats quicker with every passing second.

Zero pulls the edge of my bottle out first, then places it back inside. A moment later he's pulling out the book Hunar gave me. My body strains against his power. I want to rip that book out of his hands, but I cannot move. My heart stops completely when he spots the yellowing pages of my nana's map out of the top corner and slides it out without hesitation. When it comes completely unfurled in his palm, he can't resist releasing a slow and satisfied smile.

"The keys are missing from Malachite," Ophelia surmises.

Zero's smile fades as he looks from the map to me. Pensively, he holds it ahead of him and Ophelia.

"And you three are the team Reina sent out to retrieve them?" Zero mutters.

I still can't speak.

"Well." Zero raises his eyebrows. "This isn't too much of a loss, huh?" he asks. "You wouldn't have gotten them all anyway."

"Do you have La Sirène's key already?" he asks while Ophelia takes the map, turning it over in her hands. Its ink is slightly faded after its dip in the water.

Even if I wanted to say something, my mouth is stuck still. Zero seems to realize this. "That should only last a few minutes," he says, almost apologetically. "And when it's over, you all need to leave this place. It is full of monsters you cannot handle." He casts a weary look at the forest around us.

The only monsters I see are standing right in front of me.

I mentally strip the skin off his bones, flay them, and let rats peck at his eye sockets. I remember every other privileged boy I have ever met, who took things without asking, without caring whether they had permission or not. Then I feel it, my hand is twitching, my marking is hot. I don't know if the power comes from me or the symbol, but it arrives with a strength I didn't realize was possible. My right hand raises up while the rest of my body remains still.

The forest around us rustles to life with air and fury, then it pushes toward Zero and Ophelia in a focused wave. I remember my anger from before, when I realized Zero must have led the demons of darkness to my mother and Nana. With that fury building, I *push*. Zero's eyebrows raise, as does his staff. When he plunges his staff down, it causes a clear stillness in the air around him and holds him up, while Ophelia is knocked off her feet.

In one brief moment, Zero looks at me directly and the arrogant air fades away. For a moment, he looks like he is in awe, but then he blinks, and I blink, and the moment changes. He's closing his eyes in concentration and lifting his staff from the ground. When he does, a bright light shines where he once stood and in four other places throughout the forest.

When the lights fade, he is gone, and so are the other Arcana. A second later, my energy dies down too. My ears ring and my skull vibrates with everything that just happened. I slump backward into the tree behind me.

"Thea! That was amazing!" Tiana jogs up to me looking winded and bruised.

Teal is bloody but smiling at our turn of luck.

We escaped with our lives. I try to smile back, but I can't manage it because I know—even if they don't yet—what I have done.

*I let Zero know the keys are missing, and I gave the Arcana the map that will lead them to the other two.*

# 12

TIANA, TEAL, AND I stumble out of the bookshop significantly worse for wear than when we went in. Madame Giroux hardly looked up from her small hand-width novel when we crashed through, and now we pile out onto the sidewalk while the sun slips below the horizon.

"That was—" Teal begins.

"Horrible," I agree.

"Successful," Teal says at the same time.

I notice the smile across their face as they look down at their open right palm, which holds a single silver key. *At least I didn't manage to lose that.*

"Guys," Tiana says from my right. I notice that the sun is casting a peach glow over the city street at the same moment that I finally register the chill of air through my wet clothes. It is not night, but early morning. I shiver. *How long were we in there?*

"Three days," Tiana answers my unasked question with stunned reverence, holding up a newspaper from the rack beside the open bookstore.

"It's the tenth," Teal mutters, their expression darkening significantly as they pocket the key, taking a step closer to Tiana to peer at the printed date. Their clothes are as wet as mine. I bite the inside of my cheek when I notice Teal reach for the paper and take it out of Tiana's hands without asking.

"That means we have a week and a half to get the keys back—and the door to Malachite has moved," Tiana says.

"*Twenty minutes.*" Teal shakes their head.

"And we can't call it to us?" I ask.

Tiana frowns. "The door moves every twenty-four hours. Whenever we leave Malachite, we know to be back there before it changes location. I could call Reina, but now that your awakening is over, I don't know what good it would do to go back. She'd only try and stop us from leaving again. I, for one, want to keep going."

Teal discards the newspaper on the stand behind us.

Tiana notices their abrupt movement and looks at them as she continues. "And now that we have the first key—and the Arcana know they're all missing—we don't really have any time to waste, right? Hunar, Ian, and Marta are probably figuring a way into Kunlun right now; our next move should be getting to Jotunheim."

Teal shakes their head. Folding their arms over their damp chest, they take a deep breath: in, then out. "We'd have to get to Northern Europe to reach the entrance of Jotunheim. Without

Malachite, we can't get there any faster than the Arcana." They shake their head.

Tiana raises a soft hand toward their arm. Her leather jacket looks only slightly scuffled from our journey.

"We have each other though, right? We can figure it out," Tiana says with a gentleness I haven't heard from her. When her hand comes down on their arm, Teal stiffens. Frowning, Tiana removes her fingers.

"We should get something to eat," I insert. "I am starving, are you?" I ask to change the subject. *Teal might remember who Tiana is, but La Sirène clearly did take their love for her away.*

**I AM BEYOND THANKFUL** that Teal could control their power enough to dry our clothes. The breakfast restaurant is fuller than I'd expect for 6 a.m. in New Orleans, with wide seats ringing glass tables on a covered outdoor patio overlooking a wide cobblestone road. This is the exact type of place I planned to go with Auden during our gap year. Sitting here now, nursing a hot mug of green tea after the waitress leaves to put in our orders, I don't feel half as glamorous as I imagined. Just thinking about my former best friend sends a shot of anger and shame down to the pit of my stomach. *Do I even know who she is anymore? Did I ever?* Zero introduced her as daughter of the Morrígan. My mouth tastes suddenly sour.

"I'm going to use the restroom," Teal says, excusing themself after Tiana's second attempt to start a conversation.

I wish I could ignore what's happening in front of me, but when I see Tiana's crestfallen expression, I know I have to tell her what I suspect.

"Back there, in the land of the Lwa, when we were underwater, Teal made an exchange with La Sirène. She took a piece of them in exchange for the first key," I say.

Tiana's fingers, which had been tapping the tablecloth a moment before, suddenly still. She leans forward with an encouraging expression.

"She asked me first," I confess. "It's my fault. She asked for the feeling of a great love, and I hesitated. Teal stepped in, and now, well, it's clear they don't feel the same way about you as they used to—at least they don't seem to."

Tiana's eyebrows furrow, and she shakes her head, looking away. "That's impossible." She bites her thumb. I don't know if she's doubting Teal's love or the deal they made.

"If there was any deep love between you two, it was clearly taken from them. I—I'm sorry," I say. I wish I was more comforting. "It's *my* fault," I repeat.

"It's not your fault," she says. "Snail is always like this. Always holding everything for everyone even when their plate is full." Tiana shakes her head. Her eyes are full, but they don't spill. "It's fine," she decides. "We'll fix it later."

Her response feels as impulsive as it is intentional. Instinctively, I reach forward and wrap my hand around hers. When our skin meets, a wave of salty disappointment, musky anger, and sweet longing slides through my whole body. Only now, this feeling—this empathy—is more intense than it's ever been. For a second, her emotions are so palpable I can almost bite down on them. Even after I've taken my hand away from hers, I can taste them in the back of my throat.

Teal returns a moment later, crashing down into their seat with a tense smile. The café hums with the noise of plates clinking together and voices rising in conversation.

"Okay, so, you have some special way of finding the keys, right? Now would be a good time to show us," Teal says this to me.

The moment I was dreading.

"I—I lost it. I had a map, but the Arcana—*Zero*—stole it."

Tiana closes her eyes and palms her face with both hands. The server comes and lays our breakfast out ahead of us. Our stomachs grumble audibly, but none of us eat.

"Damn," Teal finally breaks our silence.

I exhale in agreement.

"You had the only map—in existence—of Kunlun, and now the *Arcana* have it," Tiana says from behind her hands.

"I mean, to be fair, I didn't know it was the *only* one."

"But you knew enough not to tell us about it, right?" Tiana adds.

Her words sting.

"Sometimes the negative things in our life put us on the path toward the positive," Teal suggests.

Tiana shakes her head again, very slowly. "I don't want any of your affirmations, Teal." She stares at the food below her, then back up at us. "We should go. We can't leave this to chance. We need to *act*, now." Tiana slams her hands down on the table like she's going to try and run after the Arcana this very second.

I have the urge to reach out to her again, but hold my hand in my lap. "Hey, we will figure this out, okay?" I don't know what else to say.

She seems unconvinced.

Teal begins eating.

My eyes flash with the memory of meeting Zero in that café, how the walls trembled the same way they did when the frogs came. I grit my teeth. "We're going to find the next key before they do. You said it's hard to get into Kunlun and Jotunheim, right? Well, those maps aren't simple to understand. The lines are harsh and jagged and unclear. I only knew that this key was in the lake because I—I think my grandmother drew that map. I remembered her specific strokes, thicker lines for importance. Even when I had it, the map didn't show us how to get in, just where to go once we were. And the Arcana couldn't get there before us—could they?" I ask.

Tiana purses her lips. "Well, Jotunheim does have a few door-ways. Most of them are in Europe, as far as I know. But they have limitations. You can't teleport into them, for one. So, for the Arcana to get in, they would have to trek through the mountains, through a cave." She continues, "Kunlun is the real tricky one. It's been said the last entrance was lost, or destroyed, hundreds of years ago." Tiana's fingers continue to beat against the tablecloth. *At least she isn't running away.* "And even if you find the Kunlun entrance, you'd need to know how to use it in the first place. They definitely don't know about that."

"Okay, then good. We'll find out how to get there, and we'll get the keys before them," I insist. "We can get a flight to Europe, can't we? I have a credit card." I start to rummage in my bag. "My mom put me on hers for emergencies. I'm sure this counts."

Tiana nods and Teal does too, their eyes lighting up under the warm overhead glow. In silence, the three of us look around the table at each other. We know without saying that in this moment we are *seeing* each other; and what we are seeing isn't strangers with the same goal, but *friends*.

I didn't expect this, this warm feeling in the center of my chest that can come only from knowing I am not alone. I look from Teal to Tiana with a fluttering heart. Maybe I *should* tell Teal about the exchange, what they're missing. *No, that's not for me to interfere.*

"What's in your bag?" Teal asks.

"What?" I ask, stunned by the change in topic.

"I see something—it's glowing yellow," they say.

"I—" I turn to look at my bag. There is no glow, as far as I can see, just a regular black bag.

"*Open.*"

I reach into its slightly damp pocket, rifling past my book and clothes, and pull out the glass bottle. In the cave, it was a regular shade of clear foggy gray; now the glass has changed. Teal is right, the bottle is as yellow as a daffodil. *How did they see it through my bag?*

"This?" I ask.

Teal puts their egg-filled fork down and reaches out.

My heart rate spikes at the thought of handing it over, but I do anyway. The curved neck of the bottle settles into their ring-clad hand like a lock and a key.

"Where did you get that?" Tiana asks.

"I stole it from La Sirène," I mutter.

Teal pulls out the cork from the definitely magical bottle and I brace myself for a blast of wind or a jolt of electricity. Neither comes. In fact, besides the *pop* of it opening, nothing incredible happens other than the bottle's liquid changes color from yellow to a watery clear, and before our eyes the cork regrows.

WHY WE PLAY WITH FIRE + 141

"Whoa," I say.

Teal frowns a little, tips the bottle upside down. The new cork stays still.

"Teal," Tiana exhales, pointing just over their shoulder.

If I had been holding my tea, I'd have dropped it.

There, beyond the glass walls of the outdoor café, parked on the sidewalk and nestled between a Vespa and a tiny car, is a golden ship. The boat is huge, curved, and wide in the middle but narrow toward each tip. It has rows of holes along the top of the sides where thick wooden paddles stick through. Along with complex overhead rigging, a white sail flutters in the breeze. I shake my head in disbelief. While the boat is longer than a tour bus, not a single person walking along the sidewalk looks up at it even once.

"*Hringhorni*," Teal exhales, turning back to face the bottle sitting innocently on the table beside their breakfast plate. "What is this thing?" They gape.

"You know that boat?" I ask.

"It was the boat my father was burned on when he died as a god a long time ago."

"Died?" I ask.

"Gods die, but they can always come back—unless they're killed properly," Teal explains, looking back over their shoulder as if to make sure their eyes hadn't deceived them, a wide smile blooming across their face.

"What do you mean *properly*?" I ask.

Tiana waves for the waitress.

"Depends on the god, the year, the weather, their mood." Teal shrugs, grinning as the waitress arrives and Tiana asks her for to-go boxes.

OUTSIDE ON THE CURB, *Hringhorni* curves up over our heads by at least three body lengths. Teal begins boarding the ship using a rope ladder without hesitation. Tiana follows behind them. I hesitate for a second, looking over my shoulder back at the café. An errant panicked feeling spreads over me, like I forgot something, like I left something behind. But my bag is on my shoulder and Teal and Tiana are ahead of me.

"How come they can't see us?" I ask, as I mount the narrow ladder, moving to look over the prow of the ship. There is a man fastening his helmet on the seat of his Vespa behind us. He doesn't look up at the magnificent vessel ahead of him. I can now see the ship is inlaid with intricate carvings of people holding long swords, wearing clothes that remind me of movies set during the Dark Ages, with wolves at their heels and fire under their feet.

"Mortals see what they want to see," Teal says, running their hand across the interior of the boat. "They see what they believe. So do you. It's not until your second awakening that you can see anything other than the magic you believe to be true."

I nod, although it doesn't quite make sense. Tiana sits down on one of the benches, looking out into the bustling city street.

"How does this thing work?" I ask, looking around at all the empty seats. "Can it get us to Jotunheim?"

"What's happening?" Tiana asks, looking over her shoulder when she notices a change in lighting.

Teal looks over at us. Their whole body simmers a burning yellow.

When Teal speaks, their voice is louder than I've ever heard it. "I can see—everything. Whatever the light touches, I can see," Teal gasps.

"Do you see the way into Kunlun?" Tiana asks.

"No, it's not somewhere I can find. But there, Jotunheim, I see it," Teal says. As they speak, the blue of their eyes starts to fade into gold entirely, glowing from within.

I wonder, for the first time, what I will discover about myself—about the world—when I have my second and third awakenings. Even now, while the first one is fading, something inside of me feels different, something I can't quite put a finger on. Sitting down beside Tiana, I hold my paintbrush in my right hand and remember what she told me about Godspring and our artifacts. I know that this brush connects me to the goddess of the moon because I saw her holding it. Looking at this boat, I know it connects Teal to their father. But why—how?

*Why do Teal and I have artifacts when the other Malachites don't? And why now?*

Just then, Teal casts their glowing eyes away from us and puts both hands on the front of the boat, turning to face the world beyond.

I forget about everything except for us and this vessel as our surroundings fade away. The roads melt, the sky disintegrates, even the wind dies. There is nothing but blackness and the sensation of us being pulled forward, through it.

As my eyes adjust, I see that "endless darkness" isn't fully accurate. In the blackness there is something familiar, a look of wet and the shine of sparkles. It mirrors the night sky overhead to the point that I cannot tell where one ends and the other begins. This is the water I swam through to get to Malachite—and I am no longer struggling against it; we are gliding.

Tiana looks impressed despite herself. Teal keeps their eyes fixed forward, casting two far-reaching spotlights from their eyes like lighthouse beams into the starry water. Teal has the posture of someone who can't hear anything but the voices in their own head, their floral shirt flutters around their shoulders. Tiana looks at them for a long moment, then sits back down on the bench beside me. We both lapse into a deafening silence.

*"Let her in."*

The voice is fainter than before. A chill races up my arm.

*Let her in?* I never let anyone in. My entire life I've operated with a mask on, except when I was at home with Mom. I've never felt close enough to anyone else. If I'm honest, I never even let Auden completely in.

Looking at Tiana, I falter. There is so much behind the girl's dark eyes, hidden in the folds of her braids or the corners of her pursed mouth. I wonder what it must be like, to know that Teal had loved her, and now any essence of it has evaporated. It's clear that the affection the two shared for each other was deep and layered. But now when Teal looks at her, they seem to know only who she is and no more.

"I'm sorry," I say as the boat turns slightly right, then continues straight in the endless starry night.

Tiana looks up at me, bewildered, like she didn't notice me sitting beside her.

"For what, losing the map? No, I'm sorry for snapping. It's not your fault. It's the Arcana's fault for taking it and, am I wrong, but did you know one of them?"

I bite the inside of my cheek and tuck my chin against my chest. "My whole life I have felt alone—even though I had my mom and my grandmother—until I met Auden. She was so kind to me when no one else was—and so generous. We were best friends for three years back home. Now I know it was all a lie. She works for the Arcana." I pause. "Auden *is* the Arcana." I shake my head. "I don't know how I didn't feel it sooner."

"Feel it?" Tiana asks.

I purse my lips, then hold out my right hand between us. "For as long as I can remember, when I touch someone, I can *feel* what they feel," I whisper. "I *always* thought I was imagining it, until now. Nothing seems crazy anymore. I mean, is the tooth fairy real? Are ghosts?" I try to joke, but Tiana only raises her eyebrows.

"Ghosts are, yeah. Far before they get their first awakening, most Godspring can see, hear, or even sense them," she says.

I shake my head. "Oh, that's news to me."

"I know. Look, we have one key, and soon we'll have two," she says decisively. "Once we get the one in Jotunheim, we can go back to Malachite, meet up with the others, and help them figure out a way to Kunlun—if they haven't found a way already. When we are back in Malachite for good, we can read about your mother, Amina, and Chang'e, and see which of them you've gotten this sensitivity from. I'll even *personally* give you a lesson about which fairy tales are real." She nudges my shoulder.

I smile, relieved to have someone to confide in. Then my eyes widen when I remember something else.

"When we were in the forest, I felt this marking, this burn." I raise up my palm so she can see. "And when one of the Arcana saw it, he looked, like—worried? Do you know what it means?" I ask.

Tiana frowns and reaches out. Running her finger through the air over my skin, her warmth radiates over me in waves even though we don't touch.

"No," she mutters, "I haven't seen this before—but it's not uncommon for Gods to mark their children. How long have you had it?"

"A couple of days, I guess. I got it in Malachite when I was in the temple. After the keys went missing, I picked up a statue that came out of nowhere. It burned me with this marking before it disappeared. Then, when I was underwater with Teal, I think I used it somehow, to escape," I confess.

"Well, do you feel like its power comes from inside? Like, from one of the gods you're related to?" Tiana asks.

I shrug. "Sometimes yes, sometimes no—I have no idea."

She bites her lip. "Well, be careful how often you use it then, at least until you understand it better."

I smile even though the knot in my stomach tightens. Before, I was so hell-bent on doing all this alone, keeping my life a secret from these people. Now, Tiana knows everything, and if Teal can hear though their golden haze, they do too. I have a familiar urge to wrap myself up tight and hide in a corner of myself. For a moment, I want to disappear. Then I realize: I don't really want that, it's just my instinct. I purposely move closer to Tiana until our arms press against one another through the fabric of my shirt. I can't feel her feelings through fabric, but I can feel her warmth.

"My sister was an adventurer her whole life. I wish she was here with us now," Tiana confesses. "When she died, Teal was there." She gestures toward Teal's glowing body ahead of us. "Teal has always been there, and now, they're still here—but it doesn't feel the same."

I nod my head, and Tiana goes on, confessing into the darkness ahead of us rather than directly at me.

"And I have been having these dreams lately, of her—Zola. She keeps trying to tell me something, but then she's cut short." She shakes her head at the mystery of this message.

"I'm sorry she's gone," I say.

Tiana doesn't say anything else. I close my eyes as the boat pushes forward.

I have never had people in my life, my age, who I could be myself around. Honestly, I haven't ever known who I was enough to try and be her. But with Teal and Tiana, I think I could give it a try. Even though Nana's warning still rings through my head, I want to trust them. I don't want to disappear anymore. *I don't want to be alone.*

The boat shudders around us, and the momentum I sensed under our feet tapers. In three blinks, the darkness around us shifts to a soft and pale watery green. An unfamiliar landscape is opening ahead of us full of jagged rock and spindly dry trees.

"We're here," Tiana exhales.

# 13

**A**S THE SHIP SLOWS, a whisper from the voice shifts over my shoulder—only this time it's farther away—so faint I can't hear it at all over the sound of wind and the pounding of my own heartbeat.

I expect to come up on shore, or at least a wooden dock—what we find is something entirely different.

Overhead, the green sky is stained peach with early morning light, but beyond the ship hardly anything is visible except for a distant horizon full of jagged rocks. Most notably, the air just beyond the ship is a mess of swirling vermilion dust. It's like looking into a campfire, or a vortex. I can't see anything past it, not even the ground below the boat. *What do we do?* According to Teal, Jotunheim is a lawless place, half man-eating forest, half marauding tribes of vicious giants. I hesitate at the edge of the boat while Teal and Tiana appear more resolute than ever. They both stand on the edge of it, prepared to disembark.

"Come on," Tiana says, turning back and reaching an arm toward me.

I frown, looking at her palm and remembering how intense it was to touch her the last time. Tiana rolls her eyes and pulls down her sleeve.

"What if we jump and fall forever?" I ask, taking her covered hand and rising to stand between her and Teal.

"We won't," Teal says.

"Are you sure?"

They don't answer and instead take the first step off the ship, into the swirling air ahead of us. I jerk forward and peer over the edge but can't be sure that they ever reach the ground.

"There is no room for hesitation, Thea. When you're on a quest you don't really have time. Teal knows we're in Jotunheim; we have to trust that," Tiana says.

Time. The one thing I took for granted back home: time to grow up, time to be anxious, time to spend with my family. Now, I don't have time to stand here and cry, I don't have time to hesitate. I resolutely grip her hand and we jump off the boat together.

Breath is sucked out of my lungs as I fall through swirling plumes of bright red and electric blue dust. Then I see my nana. Her thin, straight salt-and-pepper hair is tucked behind both ears. She's wearing her classic white high-waisted pants and cotton button-down shirt combo.

*She's right there,* and she's smiling—which is odd—Nana rarely smiles. Then her mouth parts to whisper something I can't make out and the rest of a scene materializes behind her.

In this flash, Nana is standing in the parking lot of the Walmart near our house—the one we walked through three weeks ago when we went shopping and she ranted that blenders shouldn't be so expensive or so breakable. I realize how much I took her for granted. Nana smiles at me again as though she can hear my thoughts, and a rush of satisfaction floods through me at finally seeing my eternally angry grandmother peaceful. Everything is still while I smile back, and the scene shifts again—the world rushes into a streaky mess of color—then comes the smell of smoke. A second later, the jagged edges of rock are under my hands.

I know as I arrive in Jotunheim that she is gone, and this has been her goodbye. *Nana's spirit was the voice in my head.*

I'm consumed by smoke all around me. Blinking past it, I cough through thickness coating my tongue and register the emptiness in the middle of my chest again. My limbs sink into numbness, and even though the world is returning to stillness, I still feel like I'm falling. *It's like I lost a piece of me I didn't even know was connected.*

I can't believe how much time I wasted hating Nana for being aloof, all the hours I'll never spend with her again. I don't have time to dwell on the loss and grief that are crashing into my core because the ground is shifting beneath my feet. Everything comes into focus: I am crouching in the center of a fire pit, flanked by Teal and Tiana, in the middle of a camp. A sea of tall white tents sprawls out ahead of us. We are not alone.

Surrounding the pit where we stand are women of all ages and shades towering at least eight feet tall, wearing combative expressions and soft linen clothing harnessed with strips of leather.

Behind them, the maze of tents spreads out over thick green grass. The same jagged mountains I saw from the side of the boat rise beyond.

My throat is dry from seeing Nana during our descent into Jotunheim, and our boat is not behind us anymore. In fact, I can't see any water around us at all. Before I can formulate a sentence, the three women nearest to us raise medieval-style swords from holsters at their hips and point them at our chests as Tiana helps me stand.

A second later I'm knocked flat on my back, neck pressing against cold coals before any of us can wonder what to do next. I blink and everything happens quickly: Teal and Tiana try to fight, but strangely, when Teal moves their hands to activate their light—nothing happens. Instead, all three of us are easily bound by the women's skillful fingers.

"Who are you people, we just want to talk," Tiana says before all three of us are gagged.

The women take the knives Teal and Tiana carried concealed in their clothes. They rifle through my bag, finding nothing but a now dry book, a few articles of clothing, and my thin wallet. The women push us up and start walking. Even if they hadn't been giants, I wouldn't have known how to fight back. As they push us through the web of tents and speak to each other in a language I don't understand, I try to memorize our surroundings.

Teal, Tiana, and I walk shoulder to shoulder, arms restrained behind our backs. We pass through cramped passageways between tents filled with low down pallet beds and baskets of cloth. Occasionally, a small child peeks their head around a corner ahead of us, before a larger female hand snakes around their shoulder to hold them back. The air here tastes different from what we left behind; it's not as hot, not as wet. Crisp.

The structures we pass are three-walled, held together by a large pole in the middle, and secured into the earth at the corners with stakes and twine. Every time I try to look over my shoulders at the fierce women who lead us, I feel the tip of a sword press into my spine and I'm forced to look forward again. I feel as if I have fallen back several hundred years in time.

Finally, we come to a halt at the base of a tent four times the size of those surrounding it. We are positioned in the middle of a wide expanse of grass. While the other canvas tents we've passed looked homey and lived in, this one is clearly more of a statement. It is set upon an elevated platform with four torches burning at the perimeter.

Outside of the closed tent are three women sitting on low chairs, speaking to each other softly with wide smiles and hands full of fruit. Their features and ages are different, but their hair, clothing, and overall aesthetic are nearly identical. They wear long robes of various shades of blue; their hair is the same shade of red as clay from a riverbank. It falls around their faces in intricate thick braids.

"Your Highness, these three have just arrived," a woman says in English behind us. I wonder which one is the "Highness." Not one of the women appears to be more in control than the others.

The woman in the middle stands.

I hear Tiana gasp beside me, whisper a name under her breath. "Penthesilea," she says through the muffle of her gag.

"Your Highness" picks up half of an orange, peeling it as she surveys us from five steps above. Her height is breathtaking. I'm pretty sure she could crush my head between her two muscled hands. With one motion of her index finger, luring us closer, the three of us take a step forward. She pops an orange wedge in her mouth and descends the stairs.

When she arrives to stand ahead of us, I see her arms are covered in a crisscross of small dark tattoos, which she folds over her muscled chest as she looks each of us over.

"Three Malachites on my island, uninvited no less," she mutters.

The women behind us laugh slightly.

Tiana struggles to speak, so the "Highness" makes a motion, and immediately all of our gags are untied.

"We've come for a missing item," Teal says.

The woman looks at Teal and sneers. "Your father owes me a debt. Have you come to pay it?" she asks.

Jotunheim is the alternate world belonging to both sides of Teal's lineage. I didn't expect they would be met with this level of contempt. Teal doesn't seem to know what to say, so remains quiet.

"You," the giant queen says to Tiana, taking a step closer, "may speak."

"We have come for a key to our long-sealed box. We believe it is hidden somewhere on your island, Your Majesty."

The woman raises her eyebrows. "A key—*hidden?*" she says over her shoulder. The women on the platform incline their heads as if in silent communication, both standing a moment later, then disappearing into the thick folds of the tent ahead of us. As they step in, a waft of spiced scent drifts out.

"Yes, and we need to find it quickly," Tiana insists.

The giant woman observes her for a long time before inclining her head and taking a step backward onto the lowest step of the platform. She then pulls a long curtain of her braids to the side and reveals a delicate metal cord hanging at her throat. After reaching under the front of her blue dress, she pulls out a brilliant silver key. It is intricate and midsize, with two interlocking squares of metal topping its hilt. I remember it from Malachite. *There it is, the thing Nana wanted me to get.* I take an involuntary step forward, but Tiana shifts to block me in place at the same moment someone yanks at the ropes tied around my wrists.

"This key was given to me a very long time ago," the woman says, as she pulls it off her neck to admire it in the morning light. The strength of Tiana's torso and the burn of the rope keep me very still. *I have to have it. I have to get it for Nana.*

"Frigg said that this key would be sought after by many, foes of dark and light. And that in exchange for a life here, I must both protect it from the gods *and* give it to any Godspring who finds me here first," she says. "But I do have a price. I am allowed a price."

I swallow and wait for the caveat as she places the cord back around her neck, tucking the key out of sight.

"What is it?" Tiana asks when no elaboration comes.

The queen smiles. "In the forest, there is a blossom that grows only by moonlight called Auroria. Deadly to touch in sunlight, and cousin to the plant Moly, this flower contains specific qualities I require." She pauses, puts a piece of orange in her mouth. "Do you know it?"

I shake my head, while both Teal and Tiana nod.

The queen continues, still casually eating her orange, "Bring me its nectar by this time tomorrow and the key is yours, paired with safe passage back home."

I turn to look at the woods beyond the narrow field filled with horses. Even from here my arm hairs stand on end from the chill spilling out of it.

"Our group will meet you on the other side. We are due for a change in camp. If you go straight, and leave now, you might just make it," the woman says as she turns her back to us, beginning to ascend the stairs. My mind is already racing. *Isn't the forest of Jotunheim deadly?*

"Wait, has anyone else come looking for the key yet?" Tiana asks.

The queen looks over her shoulder with a casual shrug. "No one but you three. Are you lucky or stupid? Only time will tell," she mutters, continuing up the stairs one at a time, leisurely popping the rest of her orange into her mouth. I feel a measure of relief at knowing that although Zero has the map, he hasn't been able to use it yet.

She leaves the three of us wired, gaping, and with a whole new task ahead of us. One I didn't ask for and am not sure I'm up to now that I know my nana is dead and her spirit has moved on. *When will I get a second to just process, to just think?*

The sword presses into my back again, so I remind myself that there is no turning back. I already dove in. From here on out it's sink or swim. Besides, if I'm moving, maybe I can outrun this feeling in the pit of my stomach, the sensation that I made a terrible mistake in wanting to leave home in the first place. *When I find all these keys, when I bring them back to Malachite, then I'll be able to process*, I decide.

Then I will be able to think about the other question that's been rattling around in my head too: *If Nana is dead, is Mom gone too? Or is she actually an immortal god, waiting somewhere for me to find her?*

**ON THE EDGE OF THE FOREST** we find a table holding a spear, a sword, an axe, a bow and arrow, our confiscated knives, plus a few daggers. All of them are appropriately sized for human hands, much too small for the giants guiding us, making me think this isn't the first time a band of travelers has been sent on a deadly quest here.

Tiana, Teal, and I all look at each other over the table, wondering what this forest is going to bring, realizing as we peer into its depths and recall what happened in Ginen that just because the Arcana aren't here yet doesn't mean they won't be. With the warrior women watching us carefully, Tiana and Teal each grab their knives back.

"What do I pick?" I ask.

"What can you use?" Tiana whispers, as the giants behind us supervise through heavy gazes, their swords still drawn.

"None of it," I admit, as Teal gingerly picks up a sword of their own.

"Then, dude, I don't know—but we have to get moving," Tiana whispers. "Just pick anything."

For some reason I pause, wait for that voice—Nana's voice—to tell me what to do. When nothing comes, my adrenaline spikes, so I pick up the remaining daggers on the table, holding one in each hand.

When we've finished our selection, the three of us turn to the deadly forest rising up ahead of us. We walk in together, eager to put distance between us and the giants.

My mind races with thoughts of what I'll do once we have the second key: *Will the door to Malachite appear and help us get out of here? Will the casual queen stay true to her word and let us out?* I follow Teal and Tiana as the trees shade away most traces of sunlight and the sounds of an active camp full of people fades behind us, replaced with the screech of foreign birds and the smell of wet earth.

This forest is different from those of cedars, firs, and ferns back home. The trees here are narrower, with leaves like jagged knives. And unlike the mirrored forest of Ginen, the forest of Jotunheim is bright and vividly green.

The edges of my shirt occasionally catch on branches that slightly tear at my skin. Every step I take into the loamy earth is sticky, as if it doesn't want to let me go. A chill races up the back of my spine and doesn't disappear even after twenty minutes have passed. The route back toward camp is as unclear as the one ahead.

"The Amazons," Tiana says, breaking our silence with a loud exhale.

"What?" I ask.

"That's who they are," she says. "Warrior women from across what is now known as the Asian-European continent. A society of god-touched women who fought against everyone and won."

"Until they didn't," Teal fills in.

Tiana rolls her eyes. "Until they didn't," she says.

"How did they lose?" I ask.

"The Amazons were wiped out after the Trojan War over the infamous Helen. One of the many wars that Greek gods had a direct hand in and one of the last battles deities ever waged against each other through human proxies," she says, turning to look over her shoulder at me when she realizes I've stumbled several feet behind. "Thea, keep up," Tiana says.

"Sorry," I mutter, and pick up the pace.

"So, the Trojan war, it's a Greek myth?" I ask.

Tiana nods. "And Penthesilea was the queen of the Amazons. *The best fighter in the world.* They say she was a Godspring. I don't know why she's here though."

"Jotunheim is from Norse history," Teal adds.

"And Penthesilea was supposed to have been killed by Achilles," Tiana says.

"Apparently not," Teal says.

We continue in relative silence for another few minutes, with Tiana leading, Teal in the middle, and myself dragging behind. Every song the forest makes is a potential threat, every movement I detect out of the corner of my eye leaves me gasping. My heart rate climbs high, and for a little while I fear I won't hear anything through the rush of blood in my ears. *Deep breath, Thea, you said you'd focus until you didn't have to anymore.*

"I remember when Reina taught magical botany, I thought it would be so useless. Now, look at us, looking for *Auroria majoris* on Jotunheim," Teal suddenly says. "I never pictured that when I came here my powers wouldn't work . . . I wonder what my father did."

"Do you remember the story Reina would always share about the Malachites who came here last?" Tiana asks hopefully. She is testing how much they remember.

Teal shakes their head and Tiana's shoulders tense, but she continues.

"In the story, there was a group of Godspring who left Malachite to find the cave at the center of the world, where the eternal grandmother keeps a seed for every plant that has ever existed. Along the way, in the dark, they found a huge river running where one shouldn't have been," Tiana says somewhat theatrically.

I find myself fixating on the tone of her voice to ignore the tension in my stomach.

"The ground didn't give any indication of water, and there were no animals nearby. Then the river began to speak to them and offer things the Malachites had lost and never thought they could get back. So, each of them forgot themselves and walked in. The river swept them away and none of them were ever seen again," she says.

"If they were never seen again, how do we know the story?" I ask, taking a deep breath in, the heady and calming scent of flowers filling my nostrils.

"Good question," Tiana replies. Her pace slows down.

"I remember now," Teal says, inclining their head. "It wasn't something they had lost, it was something they hoped for," they say. "The Malachites saw their greatest hope in the water and when they went toward it, nothing could break them out of their trance, and in their hope, they drowned."

"Still, someone must have survived to tell the tale," I say, while stretching my arms over my head.

"True." Tiana blinks past suddenly glossy eyes.

Taking in another deep breath of the sweet floral scent in the air, I finally notice how the forest around us has changed: the way the trees arch upward with abnormally large leaves turned toward the sunlight; how everything is softer here than it was before. Slowly the pleasant smell intensifies, but no matter where I look, I can't find the flower making it. As far as I can see, it is only us and these luxurious, thick trees in this small clearing in the forest. No flowers, no buds, no fruit, and no noise. Our feet press into sawdust-soft ground and the air is temperate. Something about the hazy warm glow around us makes me want to lay down and go to sleep—*wait*.

"Guys?" I look around suspiciously. "I think—"

I notice the trap of the clearing too late and my ankles are wrapped up in what I first took for an innocent exposed root system. Now snaking around my bare skin like a vise, I'm pulled off my feet in the same instant that Tiana and Teal both come to a crashing fall. *Not again.*

I shout as the root tightens its grip on my ankle, reopening the wound I got when I first saw Zero down the street from my house and the grip marks from La Sirène. My eyes pinprick with tears from the immediate pain. As I flail, attempting to use my two daggers, the roots pull me toward the tree I so foolishly labeled "innocent."

The previously soft ground scrapes against the bare skin of my legs like broken glass while the root pulls me closer to the base of the tree to my left. From this lower angle, I can now see a large hole at the base of it, similar to the hollows in trees around my house, except darker and sloshing with malevolent black liquid. This is where the sweet smell wafts out, steady and comforting even as I shout, thrash, and pull—even as I try to dig my fingers into the earth to prevent myself from being pulled in. The smell makes me want to close my eyes and go limp.

*I won't.*

After a moment of scrambling, I go back to trying to use my weapons to hack at the root around my ankle, wriggling into a crescent position. I succeed only at glancing off the root's rough exterior and stabbing myself in the soft meaty palm of my left hand. The bite of metal on skin is a shock that leads me to drop my daggers. I look on in horror while the root wrapped around me opens a penny-size disgusting round mouth to lap up the blood lying on its surface. In a second, there are hundreds of them; like the suckers on an octopus, the roots show their little wooden teeth and velvet-soft tongues. They all open and close onto the skin of my hand, burrowing and suckling like newborns.

The sweet smell encourages me to fall asleep as, now half-bent and completely prone, I am pulled closer to the gaping mouth of the tree. *It's going to eat me.* Part of me wishes I could just close my eyes and finish this seemingly endless struggle.

While I limply pull against the root, I realize that this dampened feeling is a familiar one. I remember being in class and wishing it would be over, being with my friends and wishing I was asleep. It is a depressive wet blanket that pulls me deeper than ever right now, practically whispering the words: *Just give up. There's no point in fighting anymore. There is no hope.* The clincher is when I picture Auden's face in my mind's eye. The moment when she avoided eye contact with me in the clearing in Ginen is overlaid with her standing beside Dom at that party, and it turns my insides to fuzzy weakness. My arms go slack, the root grips tighter, and I stop fighting its pull.

My eyes completely shut now while I remember the look on Mom's face the second before she pushed me into the well. Tiana's words ring through my mind: *"Malachites can see and hear ghosts."* I allow the truth to consume me: when I stepped off Teal's boat to get here, Nana's ghost was *really* saying goodbye to me.

Whatever time she had to spend guiding me is over. And if Nana is dead, then that could mean my mother is too. She isn't coming even if seeing her in my first awakening might have meant she was a god, even if she is alive. Either because she can't or doesn't want to.

I realize then that if I do give up, maybe I'll finally see them again, this could all be over.

*But no, that's not me.*

Then I hear it, Tiana's voice in the real world, her whimper of terror and anger. Eyes fluttering open, my heart strains for her though I can't see her from this angle. As my head partially clears, my hands register something flowing through them, a distant pulse similar to when I've felt people's emotions in the past, but so much stronger. I hold on to that feeling, paired with the sound of Tiana, and now Teal, struggling against this octopus root. I latch on to the energy, and it brings life.

Something inside me stirs. Something that makes me want to really *see* again, makes me want to listen harder to that far-off heartbeat. So, I do. I hold on to the pulse of the world around me as it spreads up my arms toward my scalp. The grip from the root at my ankle loosens. Instinctively, I place my fingertips onto the dirt below me and then press while the root keeps dragging. Inhaling with my eyes wide open, I focus and exhale. When I do, I instinctively picture the root around my skin relaxing its grip, gently retreating, letting me free. It's strange; I've never pushed my own feelings *onto* something before, it's only ever been a wave that crashes into me.

The root releases me and, in what feels like a second later, someone is pulling me away from the base of the tree trunk that was only inches away from swallowing me whole. Blinking dazedly, I look behind me to find one of Teal's hands under my right shoulder, and Tiana's under my left.

In the clearing, the roots are settled back down into the earth, covered again in loamy brown earth. The trees around us shudder as if breathing out a sleepy sigh, and the sunlight is just where it was minutes ago. *I did that.* The whole ordeal must have lasted only a few minutes, yet the moment felt like it spanned a lifetime.

"Are you okay?" Tiana asks as she helps me to stand. I wobble when I do, but Teal is there to keep me up with a hand on my upper arm.

"I'm fine?"

"How did you do that?" Teal asks.

"I don't know," I say, wrapping my left hand around my right while the tingle over my entire body recedes. "I just—breathed?"

"Thank you," Teal says seriously. "I haven't felt that powerless in a long time." Teal visibly shivers, and I put a comforting hand on their upper arm.

"Of course," I say.

"Come on, we should keep going," Tiana says, eyes skeptically looking at the roots around us. And sure enough, as soon as I spoke, I felt my concentration break. The sweet smell is beginning again, faint, but present. We all recover our fallen weapons and leave the grove of people-eating trees behind, embarking forward through the rest of the carnivorous forest.

## 14

I WISH THERE WAS more comfort in this forest, but every step I take brings an edge of danger. It's been hours since our encounter with those roots, hours of silence punctuated by brief stints of conversation, mostly spearheaded by Teal. I'm both annoyed and thankful for the nearly endless slew of positive affirmations they drip as we walk.

Finally, I am the one to break our latest decided silence. "So, what does this flower look like?"

We snake down a deep path while the sunlight fades to a sliver of orange in the sky.

"It's supposed to be big and white. It grows on live tree trunks," Tiana replies. "It's used in a myriad of different spells when harvested in the dark. But, if you touch it during the few moments of daylight it stays alive, it becomes incredibly toxic. We'll be able to see it only once the sun has faded." Tiana gently pushes a few hanging vines to the side. I register how dark it's getting when her braids melt significantly into the blackness of her shadow.

"So, who can actually do magic, like spells? Do you need to be a child of a god of magic?" I ask.

Tiana uses her sleeve to move more branches out of our way.

Teal cuts in, "Most Malachites can do a light amount of basic magic because most gods can. But it would be more heightened if you were related to a god of magic." They continue, "Though the style or methodology would change depending on who you were related to. The Mother of the West deals in potions, while Isis uses spells."

*If my mother is a goddess, like my first awakening suggested, what kind of god could she be? Nothing too major, or else I would have noticed, right? Perhaps Mom was a goddess of rain.*

"Guys." Tiana stops in her tracks.

Peering over her shoulder, I recognize the wide breadth of a churning river. It shines silver as the last of the sun sets. Around it, the forest takes on a very different hue: the brown bark of nearby trees deepens and brightens from within. The ground, which had been moss covered, now sparks with static electricity wherever I move, and there across the river blooms a head-size flower clinging to the base of a thick tree. Its iridescent white petals fold like a lotus. There is no mistaking it for the flower we have come for. *Auroria.*

"How do we get across?" I ask, as Tiana approaches the water with her feet precariously close to the edge.

"I don't know, I can't see." Tiana looks in either direction, presumably for a bridge or a footpath over the deadly river.

"It doesn't seem too deep," Teal says over the churning waves, coming to stand beside me, their sword still drawn.

I frown, because something about the water, the bend of it, reminds me of a dream I had what feels like forever ago—before we left Malachite.

Our words fall short when we see what I feared: something beneath the water's surface. The bottom of the river glows with the same light as the flower across from us, illuminating the story Teal and Tiana told about the Malachites who came to Jotunheim. Pressing my lips together, I draw myself straight as I look down and find my mother's face below the surface of the rushing waves.

Mom's black hair fans out around her smooth freckled face. She smiles serenely with her eyes closed. *She's right there*—just feet away and below choppy waves. *If I reach out, I could touch her.* Mom lies flat in what looks like a white stone casket fit to her shoulders. The water continues rushing over and around her. She is wearing a flowing white gown that reminds me of that Millais painting of Ophelia just before she drowns. I take an involuntary step forward when her eyes open and lock onto mine. Tiana does too. My mother's brown fingers reach out toward me, just below the tension of the water's surface. The tips of my shoes are already wet. It would take only a few steps to touch her hand. I could finally have the calm of my mother's embrace. My eyes water and I hear a small gasp escape from beside me. Turning, I find that Teal's expression is one of equal joy. Tiana, on my other side, is stone-still with tears running down both of her oval cheeks.

"What do you both see?" I ask.

"It's her," she says simply.

Tiana doesn't need to continue for me to understand; Tiana sees her sister in this river. Teal takes a step forward, farther than me; I reach out to hold them back. Lacing my fingers over theirs, I feel their hope as wide and deep as the river ahead of us mirroring my own, but I push it away. I try to clear the sensation inside of them until I can feel Teal again. They blink and take a step back as the illusion dissipates.

"It's not real," I remind them.

Teal looks from me to the water and nods, though their throat swallows and their lips part. Whatever Teal sees, they don't want to believe it isn't real. Neither do I.

"It's not her," I say out loud. "It is not my mother because she is gone, probably dead with Nana." With this sentence, the clarity of the image flickers, fades slightly. Panic rises in my throat, and I say no more.

*I don't want her to leave.* The image becomes stronger, her hands reach toward me again; this time she's just a few inches closer, her fingertips *almost* breaking the tension of the water's surface. I can smell her in the air around us: roses and rain. Even knowing the truth, I want to dive in after her. Tiana is the one to stop me this time when I move slightly forward, grabbing my upper arm.

"My sister is dead!" Tiana says. "The Arcana killed Zola while she was out of Malachite having her third awakening, and I will never get over it," she says bitterly. "That isn't my sister."

I take her cue, turning back to the image in the water. "You're not real," I whisper, and bite my tongue after the words escape. The image does not fade.

"It's not working," I whisper half to myself, half to Tiana, who still holds my shoulder the same way I hold Teal's arm.

"You have to tell the truth," Tiana says.

I swallow. "I lost you already. I am lost now, but you are lost in a different way," I begin.

"You aren't real," Teal mutters to the water ahead of them. "My father does not speak to me, and he never will."

I widen my eyes at this confession, but still have more to say to the half-transparent image of my mother: "I don't know how you kept this whole world from me. I trusted you to always tell me the truth, I *needed* you to be there with me these past few days, but you weren't, and you haven't been. Why didn't you prepare me better? I don't know why I am asking this picture? It isn't you." The image fades away. I am left staring at nothing but empty waves.

I grasp Teal's hand on one side and Tiana's on the other. Out of Teal, a mix of emotions flows at once: panic, optimism, and tangy intimidation. From Tiana, fury, hurt, and dazzling hope crashes through my shoulder. Inside of me, all these emotions swirl, until I finally choose to focus on Tiana's hope, Teal's optimism, and my own trust.

Our words ring true and clear across the water ahead of us. We remain standing, holding each other long after our apparitions have faded and our hearts have sunk. We stay standing for minutes as the water brushes away any of the hope we've had for our greatest wishes and our greatest lies.

I CURSED MYSELF for losing the map several times as we walked down the length of the river—losing hours to our pursuit of a safe way to cross the treacherous water. With the map I might have known roughly how far through the forest we are.

Eventually we find a narrow bridge that allows us to cross over. As we walk, I try to remember what the map showed, continuously drawing a blank. I surmise that the bridge must have been how the Godspring from the story survived.

Finally, we stand on the other side of the riverbank intact. Ahead of us, the black stain of night is interrupted with glowing shades of white and green lights crackling to life under our feet when we step. We walk until we reach the base of the large tree harboring a single iridescent bloom growing from its side. Teal reaches a hand for one of my slim daggers, which I secured into the side of my pants. It's sharper than theirs, so I hand it over gladly—only to realize the sun is rising when I do. It's *just* turning the dark sky to muted shades of peach and yellow. We have to hurry and get back to the Amazons in time, and we have to cut this flower quickly.

Teal gets to work methodically, slicing across the base of white petals, peeling until they find the stamen of the flower. Liquid sloshes around on the inside of the thumb-length piece of plant material when they dislodge it. I sigh with relief when the flower doesn't attack us for taking its nectar, then watch as one of its petals falls to the ground beside me. Teal places the nectar-filled stamen into a bag they produce from their pants, while Tiana taps her foot in excitement.

"We did it," Tiana says.

Smiling, I look down at the discarded flower petals underfoot and hear *something*. "Do you guys hear that?"

"Hmm?" Teal asks.

Crouching, I listen to that sound spilling off the petal. Its potent magic reaches my ears just as the sun climbs into the sky.

*Incredible.* The sound sticks to the middle of my chest like a hook in a fish. At the same time, the forest starts to hum as well. New voices crash into my ears, lights flood my eyes, all while my heart soars. Startled, I jerk away, from what I can't place.

My ears are ringing and I am trying not to fall down the slight hill into the water of the river we just crossed while Teal and Tiana discuss which way to walk next to get out of the forest. Then, as I struggle to regain my balance, my palm crashes down on the fallen Auroria petal. I hiss in pain at the spark of energy that trails up my arm.

The trees in the forest begin to shake when I do, though there is no wind to stir them.

"Thea?" Teal asks.

I look down at my hand, realizing that where it touched the Auroria petal it's now slightly green, and burning. I wipe the burn onto the moss beside me and it immediately disintegrates, just like the petal does as the risen sun turns it from a luminous white to a puckered puddle of brown.

"What's happening to me?" I ask, rushing to stand back up, blinking past the suddenly too-bright forest. "Is the flower killing me?"

"Did you touch it?" Tiana shouts.

"What are you feeling?" Teal asks.

I shake my head, uncertain and overwhelmed by the rising sounds in the forest around us. "Do you hear them? So many voices." I shake my head, clenching my eyes shut. It doesn't help. It's like I am a waterfall, an earthquake, a storm: not unpleasant, but enormous. Even with my eyes shut I know Teal and Tiana are looking at each other.

"Could it be?" Tiana asks.

"I mean, given her track record," Teal replies.

"Is this my second awakening?" I cut in, opening my eyes.

There is a pause as the three of us look at each other—before bursting into movement as one, running toward the edge of the forest.

The Arcana have a way of tracking our awakenings, so if they didn't know we were in Jotunheim before, they do now.

"What if we don't make it back in time?" I ask.

Tiana hooks an arm through my right arm, while Teal does the same on my left. My body tenses but then relaxes when I realize: *I don't need to try to do this alone the way my instincts insist. I am not alone. I have them.* Warmth stirs in my chest as I cling to each of their arms, and we leave the forest of Jotunheim behind. I do not look back at that rushing river even once.

# 15

WE PAUSE ON the edge of the tree line, knowing that in the twenty minutes it took to get here, we are too late. We spot the Arcana as tiny black-and-white dots across the sea of canvas tents. Looking away before I can pick out Auden's features within them, I turn to my friends.

"Wait," I say, letting go of them to reach into my hair and pull out my paintbrush. In the time it took us to reach the edge of the forest, I realized that while the voices rising around me aren't in a language I understand, their sentiment is clear: power.

Tiana's eyes dart out to look at where the Arcana stand, on a strip of rock edging a great chasm in the earth beyond the Amazon's camp, which falls downward into an inky black cloud. Beyond the crevice, the grass disappears into jagged rocks, and in the distance, massive mountains rise to scrape the clouds.

"Maybe I can use it to help," I say, staring down at the brush.

"So, do it!" Tiana shouts just as the three of us spot the queen astride a magnificent and huge horse only a hundred feet away.

Would the queen of the Amazons greet the Arcana standing at the edge of camp as enemies, or would she give them the key we fought so hard to retrieve? As I stare down at the brush in my hand, the weight of an energy I don't understand rushes through me. My scuffle with the Auroria will have to wait until later to unpack; for now, my second awakening is bringing so many new sensations: bursts of color in the corners of my eyes, the sound of voices coming from every direction. But when I look down at this paintbrush, everything quiets the slightest bit and sharpens. This brush has something bright inside that matches the energy coming off me. I'm sure that if I can just figure out how to reach it—this brush will do something powerful. I shut my eyes and try to focus like I did in Ginen. I try to pour myself into this brush as I did with Teal by the river. Nothing happens except a few more wasted seconds. When I open my eyes, Tiana is stepping out of the tree line toward the giants and the Arcana. Teal is tugging on my sleeve. I am out of time.

As we leave behind the forest, the sounds crashing inside my head gently fade, but the bursts of color only intensify. Teal is so bright I can hardly look at them, and Tiana is a swirling vortex of energy to herself—but it's not just them. The very ground is alight. The giants walking ahead of us, and especially the queen, have a brilliance about them. From across the camp, I spot the blazing light coming off the key secured around her neck. It flashes against the rising sun.

"We have it—the nectar—will you give us the key?" Teal asks when we intercept her advance on the Arcana. They thrust the bag containing the piece of Auroria we gathered toward her. Around us, the Amazons appear to be rushing toward the Arcana on the cliff—not greeting them with open arms. At least we can rest assured they won't be trading with them.

The queen looks from them to the pouch, sneers, and begins to set off immediately when she hears the cry of one of the first Amazons to reach the cliff. The crash of metal and energy fill my ears. *The Amazons are fighting the Arcana.*

Tiana intercepts again. "You promised," she presses.

The queen glances down at us, her hands tightening on the reigns of her horse, which is equally larger than a regular horse as the queen is larger than us. "The Arcana have come here without taking the required pilgrimage or a vessel connected to these lands—for that they are trespassing. Will you stand with us against them?"

Tiana nods immediately; I make the same movement. The queen reaches down and takes the pouch out of Teal's hand, shoving it into a pocket hanging off the side of her loose pants. Then, in one swift movement, she sheds the key necklace and holds it out toward us. The voices in my mind briefly grow quiet again when I see the key, as if they're giving me a break to notice the change in tone in the air beside us. Like they are warning me. But it's too late. In a flash, he arrives.

Zero intercepts the exchange, flashing into existence beside us like a bolt of lightning. The air smells of coal. Before any of us can stop him, Zero wraps one black-gloved hand around the key, pulling it out of the queen's hand and against his chest. For a moment Zero turns, looks at me with two dark eyes, and seems surprised. He pauses just a second—before pounding his staff into the earth and disappearing. The queen sets off immediately toward where the other Arcana stand, and we follow behind her. I frantically scan the landscape around me until I spot Zero across the rocky cliffside coming back into appearance beside the other Arcana boy, Stone, who holds a crossbow level at a giant's torso. When I look at the Arcana, I see in them an energy similar to Tiana and Teal's. It trails slightly behind their bodies when they move, like a dazzling scarf in the wind, or a watercolor of an aura.

I grip Tiana's forearm as we arrive at the stretch of rock behind the queen and realize what she is looking at: all the Amazon giants who had been fighting the Arcana are now incapacitated, either halfway buried in the rocky landscape, stuck to stone with golden arrows (presumably from Stone's bow), or frozen motionless in place, the same way I was. I swallow a dry lump down my throat. The only thing between us and the Arcana is a length of pebbly rock.

More than anything, I want to tear across this clearing and take the key Zero has stolen before they can get away, but then I see her: Auden, standing beside that awful Arcana girl, Ophelia. When our eyes meet, Auden's expression is one she'd have when she tried to solve a hard question in class.

"Okay, stay together," Teal says, as we look out at the scene, five Arcana, one Amazon queen—and us. Tiana makes a statement of agreement, but I don't know what to say, because Auden is finally looking at me. From across the twenty feet separating us, I think I see her mouth my name. But then a noise comes, a familiar one—a howl; like wind through an abandoned tunnel, it brings with it an icy gust. With eyes still wide, I turn at the shoulder to stare at the rows of tents we ran through to get here. Their billowy bleached-canvas openings flutter in the wind, casting long shadows against the rising sun.

My blood runs cold when one of the shadows pieces itself together. Darkness lengthens out as tall as the giants here, stepping forward accompanied by the same screech. Before, when I looked into one of these demons' eyes, I saw nothing. But now that I'm having my second awakening, I see it's much more than an emptiness; it's an absence of life, a sensation of falling backward forever.

"Thea, move." Tiana is pulling me away as the demon advances from between the tents.

I blink and take in the fact that this demon is not the only one; there are others, gathering themselves up like nightmares so dark they swallow the light around them. Just then, an arch of gold sails through the air from behind us, landing in the center of one of their chests. When it does, the demon concaves in on itself, then disintegrates into a wet smoke. I turn in time to see a golden javelin reappear in the queen's hand.

Tiana is still pulling me away while the Arcana burst into action, turning their arrows on the approaching demons, instead of at us. That's when I see the demons interact with the frozen Amazons, pulling frozen heads into their black shadowy bodies. After they drop one woman, all that is left is a corpse that appears as black as the monster who touched her. In a heartbeat, we are side by side with the Arcana, facing the approaching creatures. None of us look at each other. Teal and Tiana are quick as always, using their weapons and their speed to fight off the nearest demon when it arrives. I pause and look down at the paintbrush in my hands again. If there were ever a moment for this to work, I squeeze it tight and imagine my nana's face, Chang'e's face. I focus, and I push, and I *will* the paintbrush to help me. When I look up, I am staring directly into familiar hazel eyes, my grimace only deepens.

"What are you doing here?" Auden asks me.

"What am *I* doing here? What are *you* doing here?"

"It's not safe, Thea. You should be inside Malachite."

Any thread of doubt I had that Auden was hypnotized or kidnapped fades.

"So, you did know, all along," I spit.

"Thea, listen to me, this isn't what you think." She shakes her head.

"No, you listen. You were supposed to be my friend. I didn't keep any secrets from you—any. And you hid all of this?" I ask.

Auden looks over her shoulder at the demons and Godspring fighting around us; for this moment, the two of us aren't missed.

"It's not like that; I had to," she says. "Thea, it's you and me, remember?"

I shake my head, heels dipping dangerously close to the dark chasm behind us. Of course I remember. Long drives after school to stare at the ocean, secret confessions of all the ways we wanted to be different from our parents when we grew up, looking at each other as if we were the only ones in the world who understood. Just thinking about those treasured moments makes me nauseous now.

"You didn't have to, Auden, you decided to." I shake my head; a demon is fast approaching and all I have is a dagger. I hold the hilt of it in my palm to fight the darkness off, but before it can come any closer, Auden is turning, whirling into action, and fighting it away with the practiced accuracy I now understand comes from years of training as Arcana. I need to get away from her. I push past the sting in my eyes and look across the clearing at Zero. He fights off two demons with his long staff, shrouded in silver light. The cord he stole is now wrapped in his fist.

I move as quickly as possible, leaving Auden to fight alone, threading below Arcana and slow-waking Amazons, demons, and bits of sand, until I'm close enough to touch Zero. He's nearly dispatched the two demons he was fighting. I see an opportunity when his back is turned in combat and I reach out to wrap my hand around the key that hangs from his wrist. He jerks it out of the way at the last second.

"Not quite," Zero says, looking over at me as the last of the demon ahead of him fades to silky smoke. He tightens his grip on the key at the same time. "You made it here without your map."

"Give me back the key. We earned it," I say.

Zero looks over my shoulder as the fighting continues. *Why would he be fighting these monsters if he's the one La Sirène warned me could summon them? It doesn't make any sense.*

"I was thinking about what you said: that there is no such thing as winners and losers," he says, eyes still scanning the fight.

I don't answer him but continue to wonder if I might be able to muster the energy I had before. I want to blast him backward. My hand itches.

"I think you're right, sometimes there can be allies instead," he says, folding his hands over the tip of his staff. Behind him, the queen is single-handedly fighting three demons and nearly winning. Zero doesn't seem to care. "If you give me the key you already have, I can give you what you're *really* looking for," he continues.

"And what's that?" I ask. If I can keep him talking, it will give me enough time to gather my strength and attack.

"Answers about your past, your future, and that marking on your hand. It's all more connected than you think, Thea. If you come with us, I can tell you everything," he says. "You won't have to be confused or alone anymore."

I falter.

While I pause, he lifts his staff. I realize in a flash that if it touches me, I'll be stuck in place. I've been so stupid. But he doesn't use it to touch me; instead he juts it forward over my shoulder, moving so close I can see the hairs on his cheek when he does. I shout in panic but turn just in time to see a towering demon go up in a plume of smoke. I swallow. For a second, as the smoke from the vanquished demon rises in the air over my shoulders, Zero looks down at me, and I forget why we were fighting.

But then he takes a step back and holds his stolen key out between us and I remember.

Zero clears his throat before he speaks. *Am I imagining the flush on his neck?*

"If the Arcana obtain all three keys, we won't use them to open the Malachite box; hell, we don't even know where it is. We will keep the keys safer than the Malachite ever could." His voice is smooth and deliberate. "That's what Arcana does, we get everything too powerful for everyone else to handle and take care of it."

I frown, and Zero's eyes widen like he genuinely wants me to agree with him. But instead, I take my opportunity, darting out a hand and grabbing the key from him. Big mistake. The second my fingers coil around its metal exterior, the voices in my head get so loud it hurts. My eyes squeeze shut, and no matter how hard I try, I can't let go. Stumbling backward through the demon smoke, I can't get away from this feeling and this sound: like an enormous gong being hit directly between my temples. I stumble on a couple of rocks, hitting my hip into the ground after I lose my balance and fall. Everything is noise and chaos. I can't hear my own heartbeat through the force of the key in my fist. My hand cramps from the force of holding it. My muscles are screaming to release.

When my eyes open, Zero is towering over me with an expression that might be concern, but then I remember him as he was in Ginen. I remember how terrified and helpless I was then and raise a hand to hold him away. Except it's the hand with the key, and when I move that quickly, my previously tight grip suddenly loosens, and the key finally flies out.

Zero and I both lunge for it as it falls to the ground and starts to roll down the slanted rock and toward the edge of the cliff and the dark abyss pooled beyond it. I am so close to catching it, and it is so close to the edge—and then nothing.

The ringing in my ears is gone, the overwhelming cacophony silenced.

# 16

THE WORLD AROUND ME *has changed. Ahead sprawls a stony landscape of thick chalk-white rocks and boulders. The starry sky presses too low overhead, like a blanket fort held up by a child's arm. I swear that if I were a couple of feet taller, I could touch those blinking stars. My feet are bare, and the air is warm and still.*

*When I turn around, the landscape stretches out into forever—but it is not empty. There, in the distance, sitting on a boulder larger than all the others, is a woman with her back turned toward me. Her hair is curly and wild, and her spine is straight. She seems familiar but I can't place where I've seen her before. I'm overcome by the urge to get closer to her. I start running, bare feet pushing over pebbles. I climb up the eight-foot-tall rock she sits on to meet her. Fistfuls of its chalky substance come off in little clumps of luminescent white under my nails. Looking down as I ascend, I realize this white powder covers a very dark textured surface. This boulder is pocked and puckered, rough and thick beneath me. It dries out the skin of my hands. While I climb up the rock, I think I see something flicker in the corner of my vision. For a moment the white landscape changes.*

*There is a figure standing in the distance wearing a dress the shade of moonlight and a soft smile. I blink and she flickers, fades. I throw this out of my mind and climb again. Despite my determination, every time I get slightly higher on the rock, the flickers become more permanent. Until I am standing at the top of the boulder looking out at the world around me, finding it full. Not of just one woman in one white dress, but of dozens. All of them staring up at me from where they ring the wide expanse of white rock at a distance equal to the width of a house. Their bodies are half-translucent.*

*The woman on the boulder ahead of me turns to face me with a serene expression. I recognize her finally: Heather. She's nearly the same as she was outside of Matthew's house what feels like forever ago.* What is she doing here? What am I?

*Heather holds a string of white pearls in her hands and casually pushes one from one finger to the next along the length of its string.*

*"Thea," she exhales my name.*

*"What is this?" I ask, gesturing to the women on the ground around us, to herself, to this place.*

*"I will be honest with you, my love. I am not what I first appeared to be." Heather shifts on the ground ahead of me and I narrow my eyes.*

*"What are you then?" I already have my suspicion.*

*"I am a goddess, and while I have been called different names in my lifetime, most think of me as Hathor," she says.*

*I frown slightly, so she continues.*

*"Egyptian goddess of fertility, love, and beauty, among other dominions." She tilts her head to the side. "Have you heard of me?"*

*"No," I answer honestly.*

*"I was worshiped for thousands of years, and still am to this day,"* she says, as if this would convince me.

*I start to shake my head; I don't have time to be convinced. The longer I stand here, the clearer the circumstance of my arrival becomes.* I was in Jotunheim with Zero and the key. *My face falls.* I dropped it.

*"We don't have much time, Thea," she says, sensing my shift.*

*"What is this?" I ask again.*

*"This is a space in between," Hathor explains. "Difficult to get to for a Malachite," she says. "But you are here now, and that is all that matters."*

*I take a step backward as she continues to move the pearls from one finger to the other. When she speaks, so do the women circling us, their voices rising like steam, uniting into one harmony, one familiar voice.*

*"Do you remember what you heard when you found that statue in your mother's closet?" Hathor suddenly asks.*

*I freeze. Of course. I remember this layered voice, this tangle of tones. The marking on my palm tingles.*

*"Yes," I say quietly. "I remember."*

*Hathor opens her mouth, and those same words spill out again:*

"There are tales of foes and fate, with heroes never asked to wait.

A chance to come and sweep the stars aside at night with wanting arms.

But when a hero is born to earth, chased by a villain of shadow and mirth,

To steal and thwart a girl of age, to seal a tale of oppression and rage,

There will come a point in this young life when waiting could bring forth the knife.

A journey is long, and some will desire more, but she should not forget the key came before," *she echoes.*

I hate poems. *"Are you calling me a hero?" I ask.*

*Framed by angelic curly brown hair, Hathor smiles, undercutting the bite to her words, "Are you rising to the occasion?"*

*"What do you want from me?"*

*"The Malachite box going missing at the same time of your arrival, a quest to three lands that you already have a map for—doesn't it all feel like too much of a coincidence for it not to be fate?" Hathor asks me, her fingers slowing down in her pearl counting as I don't reply. "I have seen ages come and go, empires rise and fall, and through it all I've seen heroes trying to prevent the inevitability of their destinies. And here you are in the middle of one such era without a clue," she chuckles.*

*"So, tell me," I insist, stepping forward.*

*"Very well." Hathor inclines her head and places her pearls on the rock beside her.*

*"There was once a time when gods and the creatures we created could live in harmony on earth. But as time passed, and the divide between the magical and physical world became wider and wider, different lands were born to contain different types of magic. This is an example of one such place: Jotunheim, Ginen, and Kunlun are as well. Earth too became a middle place, where a being with too much or too little energy could not exist for very long. Sprits would fade on earth the same way a god's power would leak out of them," she said.*

*I nod along to her story but fail to understand how it applies to my situation.*

*"What that meant is that we gods could come to earth only for brief visitations, lest our energy spill out of our spirit, or worse yet, we begin*

*to upset the balance of the cosmos," she says. "Just like our children, we are made up of three pieces: our celestial body, which can only exist in higher realms; our physical body, which may move in between dimensions, existing on earth for a time; and our inner spirit, which would die if left too long exposed in a corporeal land and which also gives us the ability to move in thought." She waves in the air ahead of her to illustrate her point.*

*When she sees that I still don't comprehend entirely, she only sighs.*

*"This meant we could not be with our children, those we had with mortals: Godspring. So, we built for them homes where they could be safe. Imbuing them with the gifted celestial body of one of the Unspoken gods; beings with names and stories forgotten to time," she says.*

*I begin to piece together what she is saying. "You put a body inside the Malachite box, the box that someone is trying to open?"*

*"Not just any body," Hathor says softly. "Your mother's."*

*I am speechless. Hathor continues. "Your mother offered her celestial body to the service of protecting Malachites from the creatures who could slip between worlds and hunt them down. It has been held there for centuries, inside the Malachite box. Until now it has been entirely safe," she says.*

*I start to speak, "Are you saying my mother really is a god, so she isn't dead?"*

*Hathor's eyes darken. "When a god spends too much time on earth, their inner spirit fades away, until all that is left is the physical, nearly mortal vessel. Your mother's spirit faded months ago. All that was left was her body, but now . . ." She frowns. I shake my head and take a step backward.*

She can't be saying what I think she's saying.

"*What?*"

"*Your mother is as dead as a god can be. But you have the chance to recover what remains of her and help that piece of her spirit do what she always wanted: protect Malachite—protect our children—from what is coming,*" she says.

"*I can't.*" *I don't know where my voice comes from, but it arrives strong. How am I supposed to do anything if what she's saying is true? Because if what she's saying is true, it means that even if I do complete this quest and protect that box, I will never see my mother again.*

*Hathor sighs and raises a hand, wiping it across the air ahead of us. Beyond the rock, the women on the ground below raise theirs to do the same; the air ahead of me ripples and shifts.*

*The image the goddess shows me is both felt and heard, the crackle of fire is electric orange, the heat of it on my face is scorching. But more than anything is the wrenching sound: the screams. It takes a moment for my eyes to adjust, but when they do, the scene is clear. It is a city, completely engulfed in flames, people running out of buildings on fire, lava raining from the sky, the ground bubbling with heat, sizzling flesh, falling metal rods, breaking glass, and a darkness thick and velvety that hangs low around the buildings like a cloud. The image shifts like a hologram; at the same time, the fiery scene is also a forest full of beasts with grotesque arms and legs, rows upon rows of teeth; and again, on top of that, it is a field of electric blue grass, and one of barren rock. My head hurts. The images dissolve.*

"*This is what happens if the box is opened by he who pursues it,*" Hathor says. "*Whoever opens the box can repurpose what the box powers. Whether that is a house to protect our children, or themselves. If you are not the one to recover those keys, your mother's sacrifice will have been for nothing,*" she says gravely.

*I don't realize I am crying until I put a hot palm against my cheek and wipe away the water with numb fingertips. I shake my head and can't help but repeat the same sentence soundlessly: Mom is really dead. I can barely hear Hathor speaking over the rush of blood in my ears.*

*"Why me?" I manage.*

*"Because you are the only person with a claim to any of her energy, and without her energy still living, still flowing, the box will become obsolete. The celestial body within will die," she says.*

*My mother risked all the Malachites, all the world, to be with me while I grew up? She did all this knowing that if she died a mortal death instead of staying in a celestial realm, so much terror would follow.*

*"What do I do?" I croak.*

*"I have already said too much. We're not supposed to interfere as much as I have," she says. I think I detect a hint of terror in her voice. Hathor's eyes are wide, watery bronze, and focused.*

*"Fine. What can you tell me?" It's easier to fixate on what I can do than to start down the spiral of thoughts currently unspooling in my mind. I could run a mile right now, if only it would take me out of my own head.*

*"Remember that your friends are your strength, and your palm is important. Find your people, find the keys, finish what your grandmother started," she says. "And use your power to do it. It's not sitting there for nothing, you know."*

*Hathor picks up her pearls the next moment and methodically begins to count them again.*

*"Wait, I have so many more questions—" I start until something wet hits my face.*

I groan and sit up. The world around me has shifted and I take in the new palette of colors: deep tans, reds, and thick orange, and a woman's face staring down at me, her right hand holding an empty cup. The queen of the Amazons smiles when I come to.

"Good, you're awake. I thought you might have died," she chuckles.

Part of me feels like I did.

**17**

**T**HE QUEEN HAS been gone for hours now, leaving me to rest in this wide room filled with beds holding the wounded Amazon women, the air smelling of blood and bitter herbs. I am still reeling over the news: *Teal and Tiana are gone.* They, along with the key we got from Ginen, were taken by the Arcana. I dropped the second key over the side of the great chasm here in Jotunheim.

I finally have a moment of stillness, the very thing I've been begging for for days, but I can't enjoy it. How could I? Hathor told me in no uncertain terms that my mother is dead, and it is up to me to save the world from someone unleashing her power. My head is spinning; my stomach is in knots. I stand up violently from my cot, which is pressed up against the canvas wall of the medical tent, and tear out of it.

A light breeze hits the top of my head when I exit the tent. Outside, I remember what Teal told me when we were walking through Ginen, about the changes I can expect after a second awakening: brighter colors and louder sensations. It's all there with or without my somehow-still-intact glasses. The wind rustles in shades of shivering light, and the ground vibrates with life. Ahead of me, in the forest, it's like *I can feel it breathing*. I even hear the voices of the trees who speak, not just in words, but also in emotions, caressing each other with leaves and roots; looking at me as much as I am looking at them. It's not a scary feeling to be watched back, but it does make me wrap my arms around my torso and wonder what they think of me.

I start walking aimlessly in the field bordering the Amazon camp, unable to ignore the jumble of thoughts running through my head. My body seizes when I think of my mother. I can't walk any more. I want to lie down on the dirt below me and never stand up again. So, I don't think about her. Instead, I fixate on the other major problem in my life. *How do I get Teal and Tiana back if the Arcana have them?*

The ground shifts beside me and I turn to find the queen, Pen (as she asked me to call her in our brief conversation after I woke up) approaching. When she's not astride a horse, or looking down at me from a raised dais, she seems much more real. Her giant form covers the distance between us easily. As she does, her arms ripple with muscle beneath a short indigo shirt layered over a long-sleeved grass-colored dress. Despite the fighting, she is relatively unharmed.

"You're able to walk?" Pen asks me from her great height. Instead of the necklace she wore earlier that held the key, she now wears several thin strands of gold wrapped around her throat. My eyeline meets the center of her chest as she stands ahead of me.

"We have a few hours until the fire is ready," Pen says, tilting her head of reddish braids to the side.

The Amazon's bonfire is the only accessible portal out of Jotunheim, and can only be used at sunset. Teal told me they recognized the sigils on the stones surrounding it when we first arrived; Pen explained that the Amazons have a bonfire pit in every camp across Jotunheim that can be activated to get back to earth.

"Thank you," I say after an unnecessary pause. I want to show my sincerity, but at this point it honestly hurts to smile.

Pen waves me off. "The Arcana should not have come here, especially not with that forbidden magic," she says. "There will be retribution," she continues, as if that was what was bothering me.

I nod woodenly. *How is a person supposed to continue forward with so much on their shoulders?* I'm sure that I'll burst if I don't speak. So after a single look into Pen's patient expression, I explain what I saw in my vision with Hathor in a torrent, leaving out the revelation about my mother.

When I'm finished, Pen tilts her head as if she completely understands. "I once led an army with the backing of a god who I thought cherished me above all else: my father. The weight of that toll was insurmountable," Pen says, while motioning with her chin for me to follow her. I do so automatically, and we begin to cross the field and get back to camp.

"Back then, my half-brother and I were used frequently as pawns by the gods of my people, to battle each other when they themselves were isolated in varying celestial planes," she says. "They sent me and my bother to war against one another, in a battle whose infamy lasts to this day."

"And you killed him?" I know where stories like this lead and am suddenly grateful to not have any siblings, no more family to lose.

"No, I couldn't. I wouldn't." She shakes her head resolutely. "I was on the battlefield— with my sisters in arms behind me, and my brother ahead of me—and I finally realized what it meant to be a Godspring, to wield the artifact of your lineage." She pulls her javelin off her back and extends its length for me to see. The golden rod shines so bright I might have mistaken it for a ray of pure fire.

"When you have their power inside of you, it's easy to mistake it for yours. It's hard to tell where you end and they begin. This was true for Achilles, as it was true for me. But on that day in Troy, I swore I would not let this lust for power—for pleasing my father— rule my life. I prayed to a different god instead, a goddess who answered my prayer and sent me and the Amazons here," she says.

I look at the javelin in her hand, tug against the weight of the paintbrush in my hair, and bite inside my cheek. A tingle runs along the skin of my right hand, and without thinking about it, I raise it up to show the queen, cutting through the silence that lay between us after her confession.

"I don't know what it is, but it helps me when I need it," I say, remembering what Hathor said to me about my palm in my vision, deciding this will be where I start. "Do you know what it means?"

Pen looks at the marking on my hand, then back up at my face. She stops walking. "May I touch you?" she asks.

I extend my arm farther and she takes it between her two large, smooth, warm hands, running a fingertip down the length of the symbol. Her emotions are stronger than I'm used to; her sharp curiosity makes the hairs on my arm stand on edge. When she reaches the top of my wrist, her finger stills.

"I know someone who might be able to help." She finally releases me, and I exhale, clutching my palm against my chest.

**WHEN WE REACH** the wide tent on the outskirts of camp, I recognize the two giant women sitting at the fire beside it as those we first encountered when we got to the island. One of them appears older than Pen, the other younger. Both have thick, coily hair arranged in elaborate braids and Pen's wide, thick lips.

"Mother," Pen says, as she stoops to sit beside the woman with gray hair on the log beside the fire.

The sky overhead is darkening. *I will be leaving soon.*

"Penthesilea." The old woman smiles at her daughter.

"This is Thea. She has a marking she'd like to show you," Pen says to her mother a little louder than she speaks to me. I step forward on cue, ignoring the scowling younger girl beside them, holding out my arm.

"Hello," the old woman says. "My name is Otrera."

I should smile at the older woman, but with everything going on, all I can muster is a soft grimace. Otrera looks down at my palm with gentle eyes. When she sees my marking, she only sighs, then motions for me to lower my arm back down.

"You remember when you agreed to be a Keeper?" Otrera asks her daughter. "And I told you it would bring more trouble than glory?"

Pen looks down at the ground, suddenly appearing much younger. "Yes, Mother," she says.

"I was right." Otrera tips her nose into the air.

"What does it mean?" I ask, an uncomfortable tickle sitting in my throat.

The younger girl, poking at the embers in the fire, visibly rolls her eyes. I begin coughing.

Otrera patiently waits for me to finish. When I'm done, she hands me a cotton handkerchief large enough for her, but comically big between my hands.

"This is the marking of one of the Unspoken," she says.

A shiver runs down my spine as my suspicion is confirmed.

"The gods dead for so long their names are no longer known nor spoken. They are from long before our time, which has, admittedly, been longer than most."

*Of course, this marking has to do with my mother.*

"Why would an Unspoken mark her?" Finally, the youngest of the three women speaks. Her voice is high-pitched.

I straighten under her scrutiny.

Otrera shrugs her shoulders, then smiles gently when my face falls. "Don't fret, Thea. I know someone useful who can offer you more information about your marking and the destiny surrounding you and your friends. I have been too long out of the loop of what transpires on earth," Otrera says. "But to find him, you'll have to leave this place."

I frown. "Of course I'm leaving," I say.

The younger girl scoffs.

My face heats. "It's not that I don't like it here," I stammer. No matter how cozy it seems, as dusk descends and the smell of cooking meat wafts toward me from the bonfire, I will find my friends. I *will* save the piece of my mother locked in the Malachite's box.

I awkwardly shift the weight in my hips from left to right on my seat beside Otrera. I want to tell her about the vision I saw. I want to confess to her as if she were my own grandmother. But when I try to press the words out of my throat, my cough starts again. Turning away from the women, I cough into the handkerchief. When I face them, any words I had are interrupted.

"For you. Here," Otrera says. In the time I spent turned she had scribbled on a small piece of paper and hands it to me now. "Toss it into the flame before you leave, and our fire will bring you there." While I reach out and take it, she tucks a long and very modern pencil into the folds of her dress. I wonder if these women ever leave this place.

"But I want to find my friends," I protest.

"Do you know where they are? Can you write down the address, a description? Have you been there before?" Otrera asks.

I shake my head.

"Then it won't work," she says.

I nod and try to look less ungrateful. "Thank you," I say, and stand mechanically. I turn over my shoulder to show the paper to Tiana instinctively, but of course, she isn't there. My heart sinks.

"Our camp is home to many forsaken souls," Penthesilea says from where she still sits. "In these lands, I found home. You could too."

"I have to find my friends," I say.

Pen inclines her head as if she already knew I would say that, then stands as well.

Otrera promptly chimes in. "One more thing," she says. "You channeled enough energy to drain most of those Arcana leeches and momentarily light up that chasm when you touched that key that fell over the edge—a key forged from the bones of an immortal being—and you survived."

I breathe deeply.

"You are strong, Thea. Strong enough to battle this illness, strong enough to survive the Auroria poison," she says perceptively, looking down at the handkerchief in my hands.

"You touched the plant in daylight?" Penthesilea exclaims.

My mouth parts. In everything that happened after, I forgot.

"It's lethal," the younger girl chimes in with a barely hidden smirk.

I gape while Otrera chides her, and Pen smiles at me observantly.

"What's going to happen to me?" I ask with a carefully restrained tone.

"You're still standing," Pen says, without answering my question.

I open my mouth, close it, then open it again. "I have to get the keys," I decide. If my time is limited, I must spend it wisely. I decide here and now that when I leave this land, I will not bring *any* of the fear I have sat in this whole day. I will leave it behind like dust.

Otrera inclines her head; this was the point she was hoping I'd walk into.

"Can you help me get them back?" I ask both women. "Can you help me get to Kunlun?"

"Sorry, no, I stay here with my family, always," Pen says definitively. "And if you want to find yours, the sun is about to set. We should head to the flames."

I let her turn me away from the two women, though my legs struggle to walk normally. Pen begins leading me back to the middle of camp and I start to follow, until suddenly a hand wraps around my wrist. With this contact comes a jolt of energy, the bitterness of a lifetime of past betrayals, the tang of a warrior's spirit, and a spring-fresh whiff of determined hope. I turn to face Otrera, who is closer than before and sitting on the edge of the log farthest from the fire and the younger girl. She is looking up at me with ferocity as she pulls me slightly down toward her large head. With Pen's back turned, and the young girl absorbed in her fire-tending once again, Otrera whispers in my ear so fast and so soft I think I might have imagined it.

*"You have to believe in real miracles, and surrender your disbelief, even when it would be prudent not to."*

"What do you mean by—"

Otrera turns back to the fire suddenly, as if nothing happened. I have no choice but to follow Pen away from her mother, reeling, and still clutching her handkerchief.

**BEHIND PEN,** the flames of the Amazons' bonfire—a portal to the outside world—is licking the stars. For some reason, I hesitate. My head is finally clear after a whole day spent in fog. I shake it to cast aside any remaining confusion, or overwhelm, and steel myself in a way I've never been able to before.

Ringed around us are other women, speaking in loud voices, playing music on wooden instruments, celebrating life and victory, seated and happy.

"Poison like that can be as slow as it is fatal," Pen says. "You should move while you can." She steps aside to reveal the flames dancing with tendrils of magic I wouldn't have been able to see before, threads of white and blue and green. I look briefly down at the stones ringing the fire. They are engraved with symbols I don't yet understand and glow with a potent power of their own. My right palm itches.

"Thank you, Pen," I say earnestly, turning to face the giant queen.

"No gratitude necessary, child," she replies softly, then pauses for a moment. "This place is for people like you. Whenever you need it, we will be here," she says. Her words carry the weight of fate, as if she is calling in a future where I return, maybe even with my friends.

I hold that in the center of my being, a small candle set against a sea of darkness. "Okay," I inhale, and toss the scrap of paper Otrera gave me into the flames. It bursts into a lavender plume. "Goodbye," I say.

Pen doesn't reply, just takes a step back as I move forward into the fire.

# PART
# Two

## 18

**T**HREE DAYS. I have three days left before the solstice, before all three keys need to be back inside Malachite, and so far, I have none. In traveling between earth and Jotunheim, we lost more time than ever. The pedestrian I just talked to, who was kind enough to tell me the date, was also loud enough to showcase their thick English accent and contextually tell me that I have traveled to the United Kingdom through the Amazons' portal. Since I fell through that well, I've traveled more than I ever have in my entire life.

Across a quiet suburban street is a beige-bodied building with thin front shutters. Above its overgrown front garden, the address Otrera wrote down for me, 742 Rixem Road, is clear as day.

This isn't where I'd expect to find the man with answers to the mystery of the marking on my hand, *if* I were the type to still have expectations—after everything. I cough into the handkerchief Otrera gave me, which is already sticky with watery blood. I know that this cough, paired with an ever-constant headache between my temples, signals the poison is spreading through me. Even though Otrera seemed confident I could beat it, I'm not so sure.

I swallow. *I'll have time to think about this later.*

I have *one single lead* about the marking on my palm that I hope will somehow lead me to understanding my place in this journey, complete the quest, and find my friends. This hope runs through my blood while I cross the road, passing over an empty street filled with cars parked on the wrong side, cast in the water-gray light of the late December sun.

The voices of the trees haven't gone away. But since my second awakening ended, they have grown quieter. And even if they weren't, the plants here feel restrained. Their noise is more of a whisper than a scream. Looking at the perfectly manicured hedges lining the road, I can see why.

When I reach the front door, I raise my hand and knock, ignoring the new burning sensation in my chest. I don't have time to waste. There is a shuffle inside the building, a creak of old floorboards, and then the large panel of wood swings inward, releasing with it the smell of old tobacco, shaved ice, and leather. Standing ahead of me, two inches shorter with a salt-and-pepper beard, is a soft old man. His eyes wrinkle at the corners even when he says nothing, and he wears a sweater vest that looks as handmade as it does ratty.

"Hello," he says.

I imagine what he sees: a dirty girl with a thin smile wearing bloodied and torn clothes. I try to stand taller than I am.

"I was told to come here by Otrera." I raise my eyebrows, waiting to see if this piques his memory. It doesn't; I continue: "Well, she said I should come to you to speak about a marking I have," I explain, glancing over his shoulder, spotting a dark and windy hallway leading to a wider room with more light.

"What sort of marking?" the man asks, suddenly less friendly. He looks over my shoulder, his hand tightening around the door handle.

"Penthesilea and Otrera said I could find you for help!" I say this in a rush before he can close the door. Pressing my palm ahead of the frame, I make sure he can't slam it in my face.

The man looks at me, the marking on my outstretched palm, and then glances once more over my shoulder before ushering me inside his house. When I step in, I notice the neglect of his space. It's not so much dirty, just forgotten. The stairs sag from being walked on over a long period, the wallpaper is chipped, fading, and the paintings on the walls are so dusty and fogged up from tobacco smoke I can hardly make them out. The man locks the door behind me, and on instinct, I raise a hand to my concealed dagger. When I turn to look at him though, I notice a series of intricate locks spread out over his door in spirals and lines of thin energy. This is not just a home, it's a safe house.

"They can't find us in here," he says.

"Who?" I whisper, while noticing a dark room to my left, filled with unused furniture and old bookshelves. *Did I really just follow a stranger into a locked house?*

"The Arcana, of course," he says.

I exhale at his response.

The low ceilings grow slightly taller in the kitchen, the only room in the house so far that I can tell is in constant use. The dishes are neatly done, but the small table occupying the right side of the room is covered in placemats burned through from cigarettes. The ground is smooth linoleum in wavy designs, and the light fixtures overhead flicker occasionally in a quaint kind of way. Out the window beside the lone table with its two chairs is a narrow garden brimming with life. The plants here aren't refined like the ones outside. They have a mark of wildness that I have a feeling is quite rare.

"My name is Arthur. Would you like some tea?"

"No, thank you."

"Take a seat." He motions to the chair nearest to me and sits in his own, clearly well-loved, small armchair.

I press my lips together and sit. "So, Arthur, do you know what this symbol means? I'm hoping once I know, it'll give me enough information to move forward in my quest and find my friends— which is a whole other story."

He looks across the table at me in such a way that it feels like he knows me. "I *have* seen it before, though slightly lighter. A girl I used to know was obsessed with it. She was there, actually, when I met Penthesilea in Jotunheim," he chuckles. "Otrera went by *Reyelle* back then." He shakes his head.

"You knew someone else who had this marking? Who was she? What does it mean?" I ask before I lean in closer. "Are you a Malachite too?"

"Yes, I used that name—Malachite—once, a long time ago," he fades off, amber eyes unfocused. After a moment of thought he brings a pair of glasses down from the top of his head and peers through them at the garden outside.

"So, your friend, did she tell you what this marking means?" I ask, straining to know why it was given to me.

"When I met her, I was an explorer. Always on a mission to unravel the mysteries of my own father: Kssa, the Lakota god of wisdom. He would visit me in dreams, and my friend taught me a method to capture those visions so I would remember them upon waking," he says fondly. "Back then, I was sure my father was trying to warn me of something, some great evil that never came. There was no prophecy for it in Malachite, and no one else foresaw it. But my friend, Lily, she believed me. She had been having strange dreams of her own, of a marking just like that," Arthur says.

"My nana's name was Lily," I say, quite sure by now that in my life coincidences don't happen.

Arthur's eyes light up and he looks at me anew. Through the lenses of his freshly donned glasses, he squints and tilts his head. "Yes," he says, standing up, as if this isn't a surprise.

Arthur goes to the fridge in the small kitchen and pulls down a cookie tin from above it. Walking back to the table he places it between us. Opening the lid, he reveals a neat stack of square pictures, faded and black and white. He looks from one at the top, then to me, before handing it over.

In the picture is a young girl with narrow shoulders and a pair of eyes I've known my entire life. Her hair is feathered below her chin. She stands beside a truck, wearing casual cutoff jeans, a simple tank top, and a smile.

"That's her," I say. *Arthur's Lily is my nana.*

Pausing, I press my hands down onto the table ahead of the picture, peering at it for another few seconds. "She really was a Malachite." The unanswered question I had been poking at ever since I found that map with her initials.

Arthur smiles. "Lily was many things, a descendant of the Chinese goddess of the moon, and another god, one far older," he says. "That's where she figured the dreams were coming from." He trails off for a second, as if lost in the past. "Did she ever have her third awakening? Some Malachites don't, you know. In those cases, both lines of their power fades. I knew a woman who used to call those who didn't 'false starts.' She was a menace. Anyway, Lily was always a late bloomer." He trails off as my eyes fill with water. "I didn't mean to upset you," he says, curling backward into his chair as if he were the upset one.

"I'm not upset," I lie. "What more did she know about the marking, the god who gave it to her?"

"Well, she said that if only she could strengthen her connection with that older god, then maybe she would not have to forsake it during her third awakening. She thought that if she could connect with both energies in her bloodline equally, she could find a way to balance them and carry on living a sane existence, instead of making the choice of one over the other. She was *so* determined that we wouldn't have to diminish ourselves to survive any longer," he says. "Her quest led her to mapping out the known realms."

"Lily's ancestor was an Unspoken god?" I ask.

"You know about them?" Arthur asks.

I shrug. "A little."

"In the oldest texts—the few that remain, that is—the Unspoken gods were said to have had immense power, the kind that could create or end worlds," he said. "Lily found a way to get that same marking you now have, though hers was fainter. And through that connection, I think she did manage to communicate, or at least initiated near communications, when I last spoke with her. Gods, it's been years. How is she now?" he asks, his eyes alight with memories.

"She's dead," I admit.

Arthur's jaw tightens and his eyes shine. "I don't know which of the Unspoken she was related to for absolute sure, but that symbol led me down a rabbit hole, long after Lily and I parted ways. I discovered it was related to the Unspoken mother goddess. This same image was also discovered in an aerial view of the Atlantic ocean by several Godspring on a quest some-odd years ago; they all claimed to have seen it in the ocean's waves. They came to me for help with a particularly difficult bit of prophecy and mentioned it in passing." Arthur starts speaking on a roll, as if he's more used to giving lectures than having conversations. "I could hardly understand it at the time, but reflecting on it later, it stands to reason that an Unspoken god would have made their mark on this earth in peculiar ways," he says. "Perhaps that's where you could start. I'll find you their contact information."

I frown down at the marking as he shifts to rearrange the items in his box. The idea that my mother could have been a goddess of motherhood makes me laugh slightly. It's so fitting, her being a goddess of the thing she did best. But how does that help me now? And how does this marking tie into the quest for these damned missing keys? *Maybe Otrera didn't know what she was doing when she sent me here.*

I begin asking Arthur another one of my thousand questions when a faint whistle pierces toward us from the front of the house. It's high-pitched and airy. Arthur quickly stands from his seat.

When he does, I notice a shine to the palm of his hand a moment before a short field of energy pulses out of the lines on it. The color is close to the one Teal has, but less bright and more focused. Without my second awakening, I wouldn't be able to see it. Arthur quickly strides across the length of his house to the front door, flipping open his peephole and peeking through, with me hot on his heels. Cursing under his breath, he retracts.

"They're here," he says.

"The Arcana?" I ask, pushing past him to press my face against the door.

Sure enough, there they are. Stone and Ophelia, clad in black-and-white uniforms. They stand on the opposite side of the street, looking in either direction—searching. *Where is Auden, and where*—my breath catches at the back of my throat—*is Zero?*

"We have to go." Arthur begins backing away.

Then I see him, Zero standing cocky as always with one hand lazily topping his staff, which presses into the cement sidewalk. My knuckles tighten into a fist.

"No," I say. It springs out of me; I barely decide I'm going to speak before I am refusing.

"Girl, they will take your hand and study it. The Arcana collect powerful things, and that marking is a powerful thing—they followed you here," Arthur concludes.

I shake my head and step away from the peephole, remembering that the last time I saw Zero was just before I found out for sure that my mother was dead, before he stole Tiana and Teal away from me.

"I'll draw them away," I decide. "I'm sorry for the trouble."

Arthur shakes his head. "That's a very bad—"

I have already opened the front door of Arthur's house, and I step out onto the cement beyond with a fire lit in my stomach.

"So, you found me!" I shout at Zero. Widening my arms apart, for the first time, I can clearly see the palpable light coming off each of the Arcana, hues of silver and white. I see the Arcana as they are: powerful. But I also feel the marking on my palm, the one Arthur had such a huge reaction to, the one I've been trying not to look at too directly—the light pulsing off it is so intense. *I can do this.* When Zero sees me, he smiles, and my heart skips a beat, *in anger,* I tell myself.

# 19

I BEGIN TO STEADY my shaking hands, but I realize, as I step down from Arthur's front porch, they aren't shaking at all. My body is still, though my mind whirs. As I look at Zero, smiling and casual, walking across the street toward me, I remember what Hathor said to me—that there was someone specific coming after the box, after the keys, after me. At the time, I barely heard her over the rushing in my ears. Now, I harden my jaw. Zero was there when the demons first attacked my family; he was there again when they reappeared and I lost the first key. *He must have been the one to summon them; he must be the one Hathor warned me against.* The front door of Arthur's house slams shut behind me.

"Where are my friends?" I demand.

Zero raises his right eyebrow, crossing his arms over his chest. His staff has vanished, and I spot a thick streak of black ink around his wrist when he moves. I hadn't noticed it before, and somehow it shines silver when he flexes his muscles.

"They're safe," he says, slowly.

"I see there are less of you this time." I gesture at the other two Arcana, Ophelia and Stone, each with a glow of power beaming around their shoulders.

"Auden and Basil are home taking care of our . . . guests." Zero smiles, though his jaw ticks. I don't know him well, but I get the sense he is lying when I look into his eyes. *The blast I made on the floating island must have done more damage than I realized.*

As soon as he's finished speaking, Ophelia takes a step forward, her Arcana blazer whipping in sudden wind. "We will return your friends in exchange for the key you found in Ginen."

Ophelia's accent matches both Zero's and the man whom I passed on the road minutes ago. I realize, as she stops to stand just behind him, they are *from* here. The Arcana are based in England. Which means I'm closer to Tiana and Teal than I realized. *They really meant it when they said that luck gets stronger after your first awakening.*

"Ophelia is right." Zero inclines his head. "If you give us the key, we will return your friends."

*He doesn't know I lost the Jotunheim key down the dark chasm; he must not have seen it fall.* I might have more of an advantage against him than I thought.

I make sure my expression remains controlled and scowl. "You think I'd sacrifice the one key I have left after *you* stole *my* map, *and* our other key?"

"You seem like the type to care what happens to her friends— so, yes," Zero says simply.

Stone scoffs out laughter, crossing his wide arms over his chest like there are a hundred places he'd rather be than here. They are treating me like I didn't just burn a hole through them in Jotunheim, like I didn't banish them from Ginen. I grit my teeth and fold my arms over my chest. Out of the inner pocket of my jacket, the dagger I brought back with me from Jotunheim slides into my palm.

I have power, I am *sure* of it. Though I've never been one for violence, I think I could stab Zero if I needed to. An energy starts to build at the base of my skull, new but not unfamiliar.

"We didn't come here to fight. Just give us the key and we'll bring you your friends, simple," Zero says, noticing my defensive posture.

Ophelia clears her throat to hurry him along.

When I don't make another move, Zero takes a step forward onto Arthur's lawn. When he does, I hesitate as I recognize a wave of energy rush through me. The dagger in my palm falls to the ground, but it doesn't matter—because I now realize I have a far greater weapon at my disposal.

As Zero's foot connects with the grass ahead of him, I shiver and understand the feeling I have been holding at the edges of my consciousness ever since my second awakening. It comes through in startling clarity along with a deeper awareness and intuition about everything around me. When I inhale, I can sense the vibration of the earth under my feet, the air in the space between us, and when I look at each of the Arcana, I think I can *almost* feel the flickers of their emotions—even from here—even without touching them. When Zero touches the grass at our feet, that feeling intensifies. Without a thought, I push toward him through everything around me and exhale. When I do, the grass below him changes from solid to liquid. Quicksand pulling him under, the boy begins to sink. Panicked, his eyes look up at me in audacious alarm.

"Stone! Fee! A little help here?" he calls to his friends as my eyes flutter shut.

Now that I've begun to let this feeling in, I expand into *so much more*. I am no longer limited by the edges of my skin; now it seems that the atoms that make up who I am spread out into forever. It's overwhelming, the crush of emotions, sounds, smells, tastes—they all rest in an almost unbearable weight within me.

The Arcana struggle to free Zero while my awareness turns inward. I see myself as a series of overlaid thoughts and feelings, experiences, and denials. When I look at myself on the inside, I see myself like a knotted piece of string without an ending or a beginning, just a circle of rounded curves, folding over itself and in some parts fraying. Looking at it, I smell the scent of rainwater, which reminds me of my mother, then I notice the scent of my grandmother, and something else. Before I can focus on any of it, something hard hits my head and I am falling backward, my concentration broken.

I blink dazedly and look back at the scene ahead of me. The Arcana are so bright now I can hardly make them out. I think they're speaking to me, but I can't hear them over the rushing in my ears. Another blow of energy hits me in the stomach and pushes me back into the brick behind me. I look behind me briefly at Arthur's front door, and when I do, I find no stairs, no porch, no front door, just a smooth wall of brick and mortar. I taste metal in the back of my throat and slowly the world returns to focus.

Ophelia is standing in the center of the lawn. Zero is free and standing again on the sidewalk with Stone helping him. Ophelia's hands are outstretched toward me, and I can see the energy looping off her, the golden glove on her hand humming with a power similar to her inner energy.

My hearing returns in time to catch Zero saying, "This isn't supposed to be violent, Fee," as he brushes dirt off his trousers. I notice his staff is again in his hands and the black band at his wrist is missing. *What just happened?* Distantly, the edge of that energy is still all around me.

"Thea, just give us the key and we'll give you your friends. Everything can go back to normal. Isn't that what you want?" Zero pleads.

I shake my head. *Why does he sound so sincere?* I turn my head to the side to spit blood out of my mouth, eyeing Ophelia's still raised hand. When I do, I notice that in my scuffle backward, my paintbrush fell free.

I remember the last time I tried to use it, how it hadn't worked. It is gleaming and gold with energy shrouding its wooden exterior. Seeing it now gives me pause, because where my blood touches it, the gold hums a little different. My breath catches and I reach out. When my fingers wrap around the paintbrush, I remember the patient expression of the woman who handed it to me during my first awakening, Chang'e, the Chinese goddess of the moon I still have so much to learn about. When my hand covers the paintbrush's wooden length, I feel the pulse of her, of a celestial body existing almost in a world of its own. And then I register something else, like the beating of a drum in my bloodstream. It travels up my arm into the middle of my chest, through the marking in my hand, connecting with my heart and the bottom of my stomach. My mouth dries because I am no longer looking at a paintbrush anymore. What I am looking at is a golden staff, laid out across my lap, gleaming and covered in interlocking images. *This is the staff my mother was holding toward me in my first awakening.*

Zero inhales sharply. "Impossible," he says.

I remember what Tiana said about Godspring needing an artifact that connects them with their deity relative. But she didn't say that one item could connect you to two, the way this staff is doing now. Nothing could have prepared me for the feeling that washes over me as I hold it for the first time. I can feel both goddesses inside of me when I have it in my hands. A serene mix of mischief and calm from the goddess of the moon, and a deep reverberating power from my mother. They swim around each other like fish in water, and when I look up at Ophelia, her face is pale.

Before anyone can react, I press the staff down into the grass below me and use it to stand. It is like plugging into a live wire; the whole world rushes around me, but instead of being overwhelming, the staff makes it easier to manage. Like using a magnifying glass to direct the sun's rays, I funnel all that energy through the staff, using it to focus my power. Zero is the only one fast enough to react, digging his own black staff into the ground as I lift mine. For a moment, the entire street flashes white. With a startling *pop*, Ophelia, Stone, the leaves on the trees, and the old paint on the buildings are blown backward.

I pant with exhilaration, looking at the fallen Arcana and the trembling Zero while my ears ring. If I do what I just did again, Zero will be knocked over as well. I begin to smile as I lock eyes with him, pressing my staff into the ground—and then I hear it.

Over my right shoulder, the plants go quiet, the birds stop chirping, the wind stills. Zero and I both look down the ordinary street and see something very out of the ordinary: a shadow in the distance. Except it's not a shadow, because it is moving toward us—no, limping toward us. My face goes cold, my hands numb. The energy in my staff dissipates. *Those are the creatures that killed my family.* I look back at Zero, terrified. *He summoned them, he must have.*

"What have you done?" I whisper.

Zero's stance doesn't relax as he grips his staff like a flagpole in the wind; his eyebrows draw together. "What are you talking about?"

"You're the one who brought *them* here!" I look once more over my shoulder, suddenly wishing I had never left Arthur's warm albeit messy house. There is only a wall where his front door once was.

"Me?" Zero asks, squinting as the figures continue approaching from down the street, genuinely confused. "We fought against them together. Why would I—how could I?" he trails off.

Ophelia and Stone don't stir on the sidewalk behind him. While the shadow beings approach from a few blocks away, the world becomes quieter, and around them the light dims. Zero raises his own staff, probably to teleport out of here in a way I wish I could. But nothing happens. I realize, as I blink at him and the other Arcana, their energy looks different than before, slightly less bright, and more huddled into the center of their bodies versus radiating outward. *Did I do that?*

My stomach cramps and I briefly try to connect with the power I just held so easily in the palm of my hand. But my heart is beating too fast, I am sweating too much, and when I register how quickly the monsters are advancing, I see Mom's and Nana's faces

WHY WE PLAY WITH FIRE  ✦  217

in my mind's eye. I'm unwillingly picturing their dead bodies as I start walking, without realizing what I'm doing. Only when Zero catches me by the shoulder do I realize I am fleeing.

"Where are you going?" he asks.

"As far away from those as possible!" I say, yanking my arm out of his grip.

"I'm coming with you," he says, as he releases me.

*Why would he run from creatures he summoned? Why did he fight them in Jotunheim—unless, unless he really didn't bring these things here.* I swallow over this newfound certainty, because when he touched my shoulder, I felt him more acutely than I ever have before. His fear was unexpected, and it affirmed what he claimed: he couldn't have done this. But there was also another, stranger undercurrent in his touch too, a protectiveness that makes me eye him wearily.

"Followers of Kek don't give up once they've locked on their prey—and it's not me those abyss eyes are staring at," he says gravely.

My mouth falls open, and I take a step away. Zero takes a step forward. His eyes don't leave mine. We don't have time to argue.

"Fine," I say, taking off down the street.


LOOKING OVER MY SHOULDER, I see them in the distance, following, seemingly walking slowly yet always moving closer and closer. What's worse than seeing them there, clinging to the sides of buildings like black slugs, is when I don't see them at all.

"You know what they are?" I ask, as we crash out of the quiet house-lined streets and onto the sidewalk of a road with cars and storefronts, people wearing parkas being led down the cement by dogs wearing shoes.

"They are followers of Kek, an Egyptian god of primordial chaos—we thought he was one of the faded ones, a dead god, but if these creatures are powerful enough to exist on this plane, that must not be true," Zero explains.

*That* must be who Hathor warned me about.

Behind us a woman screams. When I look back again, the shadows are closer, moving fast as smoke. Although they don't have eyes, I sense those gaping holes in their heads focused on me. The screaming woman is looking down at a young girl lying face down in the snow. The shadow creature hovers over her, half-submerging her in its darkness. Even the few trees lining the sidewalk of the now much busier section of the city curl away from the shadows. And although no one seems to be able to see the demons, their presence is felt.

I don't realize I've stopped walking until Zero grabs the side of my shirt and pulls me down a side street painted with a mural of the ocean.

"When I got back home after Jotunheim, I researched them immediately," he says. His hand is still wrapped in the fabric of my thin shirt, knuckles pressing through it into the side of my torso. "How long have they been chasing you?" he asks.

"Since I was home, a week maybe—no, the time changed—I don't know, a couple of weeks ago," I say.

He nods like this confirms something he had been thinking but didn't want to share. Suddenly, he points at the large open doors of an old cathedral ahead of us. It's complete with white spires and gargoyles lining its roof. It looks empty, though the street is not.

"We'll hide," he explains, pulling me toward the building.

We hurry across the street—sticking to the space under awnings and between cars so the demons can't see us—slipping through the large wooden doors of the cathedral when a bus passes by the road. If the demons are following us by sight alone, they could not have seen us slide in.

When we step inside, I exhale and scan for a back door. There isn't one. Zero releases my shirt and closes the doors. The building seems empty, with white marble archways over our heads and rows of empty benches. There aren't a whole lot of places to hide.

"What now?" I ask.

"Why are they tracking you?" Zero asks.

"I have no idea," I say, looking down at my body, as if the answer might lie in the folds of my jacket or the pockets of my jeans. The staff in my hand shakes. My breath is coming out short and fast. *How long can we hide in here; how long can we put off being found?*

"Hey, Thea," Zero says, stepping forward. He reaches out as if to touch my shaking hand, and I draw back. It was one thing to get a sense of his feeling through the air or through fabric, but if he touched his skin to mine it might be just as overwhelming as when I first accessed my new power. He retracts patiently. "Are you hurt badly, from Ophelia?" he asks. "Can you use your powers again, against them?"

I swallow and shake my head to both questions. "I—I don't know how to focus," I admit.

He seems to understand what I am talking about. "That staff, it's like mine, a godly artifact paired to your essence. It shouldn't be possible that it is also Chang'e's paintbrush, but that's a conversation for another time. It interacts with your energy as much as you interact with it. Let it guide you," he says simply.

I look back up at him with an uncertain expression, prepared to try, when a coolness slides up the back of my neck. I turn around, stifling a scream upon seeing a single black head poking through the gaps in the wood of the closed cathedral door, eyeless, terrifying, and only a foot away. I scramble away from the door as another head appears, poking through the gaps in the wood, confirming my idea that the creatures really are made of shadow. When they see me—or sense me—they push the rest of their bodes through. They are all joints and long limbs, like a terrifying approximation of a figure; just human-shaped enough to be unsettling. They move like animated Jell-O. When the three monsters arrive inside the building, they stand at least three heads taller than me with sharply pointed fingers hovering like talons. We have nowhere to run.

My hands tingle cold and stiff, but I clutch the staff between them for dear life. Zero's shoulder presses against mine as we face them, and in a few seconds, I notice the brightness of his energy returning.

"How do we kill them?" I whisper, as we back down the aisle slowly while the demons advance.

They step toward us at an odd angle, hands outstretched. The candles lit on the other side of the cathedral flicker, fade a little. Zero raises up his staff; whatever light I knocked out of him is nearly back. "I don't remember. I—we haven't covered it yet."

He looks over at me, and I look at him. And although I shouldn't trust him, for a second I want to. Then, before the creatures can get any closer, he bangs his black stone staff into the ground. Out of it a ripple of electricity frays across the tile in the same pattern I imagine lightning would. That lightning crawls up and into each of the creatures and disappears in their darkness. It looks disturbingly like *flashes* of a storm in a dark sky. The demons are unaffected. A little whimper escapes my lips, and Zero looks over at me instinctively—at exactly the wrong moment.

One of the monsters reaches out toward him with an arm that stretches to twice its length with fingers hooked like claws, only to land and burrow in his shoulder. Zero's body goes limp, the staff in his hand clatters to the ground, and the candles at the back of the room go dark. Zero's eyes roll into the back of his head as he falls onto the tiled floor with a moan of pain. *He's still breathing*, I note after he crashes.

The monsters pay him no mind, stepping over him as if he weren't there at all. I keep backing away, shrinking as I do, willing myself to be smaller than my height. But then I feel it, or maybe just remember it. The marking on my palm tingles as if reminding me of its existence. The staff in my hand hums with power, far away and faint, but there. I realize the energy is trying to guide me. The whole room smells like a cold night, and the space in the air around the creatures folds into them, as if they are walking black holes.

I recall the other times I've seen them, when I've felt trapped and terrified, and I falter. But then, as if in an answered prayer, the staff in my hand heats and I remember my rage. My rage over loosing Nana and Mom, my rage over letting down the Malachites by losing those keys—by losing Teal and Tiana.

I hold on to my rage enough that my despair dissipates, and when I manage to lift my staff again, it is nowhere near as magnificent as the first time I did it, but it is *something*. It is enough to knock the nearest monster back and cause a strange scream to come out of one, high-pitched like a kettle. They wail and I cringe. Then, no longer docile, and deadly curious, the creatures move quickly, bodies pressing toward me from where I jolted them a few paces back. I scramble away instantly as two of them flank me on either side, halfway submerged in the pews. Smoke through wood. I begin to raise my staff up again, when one reaches out an arm, which grows longer by the second, nearing my cheek. I dodge it only to come directly against the chest of another one who snuck up on me.

Suddenly, my rage is gone. In fact—everything is gone. There is no pain at all when the monster touches me. The darkness is cold and wet and desolate. Sticky like a swamp, I am sinking painlessly, and in the darkness, I hear a deep voice whispering to me. *Thea, relaaaax.*

The voice is soothing. My shoulders soften, my mind becomes blank.

Then I am jolted. A bolt of electricity to my stomach forces my eyes awake and my body into action. Pulling away from the shadows and back into the dim warm light of the cathedral, I turn to witness the scene ahead of me.

Zero is standing now, clutching his shoulder with one hand, and lashing out with electricity with the other. When he sends the electric charges at the monsters this time, they flicker slightly from the force of it. I can smell the effect of the charge he sent in the air beside my face.

With the creature shocked into stillness, I use this as my opportunity to move. I turn and use my staff to push it away, a surge of my own energy crashing through my staff and me. Then, like water on a hot rock, the monster disintegrates; tendrils of gauzy black float toward the ceiling a second later. My whole self feels incredibly weak, nearly ready to fall over, but there is more to do. I turn back to Zero.

Now, though, grunting from the effort, Zero uses his staff to direct all of his energy at one monster at a time the way he did in Jotunheim, instead of splitting his lightning. It works enough to stun them. Newly recovered, I swoop in, pressing my staff into the monster ahead of him, turning it incorporeal. We work in tandem, striking down creature after creature, an unstoppable duo I could never have anticipated.

Zero and I turn to the final demon left in triumph—until three more slink through the closed cathedral door. We are outnumbered yet again. I pant from the effort I've just exerted and look over at Zero. He smiles like this is an engaging game of tennis and not a fight to the death. His confident smile makes me feel like I can handle this.

There is no moment to catch our breath again; the other creatures don't hesitate, and two of them lash out immediately. These monsters are harder to disintegrate; they are sturdier and taller. It takes almost everything I have in me to knock out the one standing near me. Slightly lodged in the pews, it sprouts more arms than an octopus, looking for a way to touch my skin with its serrated fingernails. I dodge and weave and push when I can, and finally, it too evaporates in a thin mist.

I hear Zero shout as the monster grabs him by the same shoulder as before; his knees sag, his body folds forward, and I notice a dark gray spread across his skin. When his face connects with the ground, I am sure he's dead. I don't have time to check though, because now it is just me and one last demon. *A follower of Kek*, I repeat. *The god who murdered my family.* My blood is boiling, and I harden into three words: *I can't fail.* I let go of everything but that thought and direct it in a rush at the demon ahead of me. When I push this blast of power, my shoulders tighten with a held cough. Blinking against a sudden wave of dizziness I remember Hathor's warnings, Tiana and Teal's expressions the last time I saw them, and Nana's face when she said goodbye.

Both she and Mom knew what was coming for me when they pushed me down that well. They believed I could face it all. My power lashes through the air in tendrils of vibration, and when they reach the final demon, holding it in place, I keep it alive. Long enough to walk closer to its wide, unseeing, cold black eyes.

"I don't know what you want from me," I say, not to the creature but to the man, the god who I know is watching behind those non-eyes. The one who whispered for me to *let go*. "But I will make you pay for what you have done."

I exhale and the demon disintegrates, the energy in the air falling away as it turns to tendrils of smoke. Under my palm, my staff retracts into a paintbrush once again.

I pant hard and finally cough out a spray of blood. For a moment, the church is silent.

"Are we dead?" Zero groans.

# 20

STICK MY PAINTBRUSH in my hair as Zero raises himself off the floor to lean against a church pew across from me.

"I thought you died," I say hoarsely.

"We're hard to kill," he says, looking at me, strangely open.

"Godspring?" I ask.

He inclines his head and winces at the movement. His eyes go clear as he scans the space around us. "They're gone?" he asks.

"Yep," I say, folding my arms over my chest and feeling conflicted as I watch him struggle to stand. On one hand, this boy is my enemy; he stole Nana's map and my friends. But on the other, he didn't leave me to face the demons alone. I remember what Tiana said about the Arcana being untrustworthy and terrible.

Zero gives up on standing and instead slides down the pew, settling onto the ground. His face is pale, and black veins are crawling up the length of his neck where the demon touched him. I take an involuntary step forward and kneel in front of him. I don't know what to say; my cough stops me from having to decide. I catch the spray in the corner of my shirt.

"You're hurt," he says.

I back up so that I am pressed into the pew opposite him. Our feet meet in the middle of the aisle. "You too," I say, then go on, "I touched Auroria in daylight."

He exhales through his teeth. "You know, at Arcana we have medicines that could help with that, if you came and—"

My nostrils flare with annoyance. "Are you seriously still trying to take a key from me?" By now I know what his pitching voice sounds like. "After we both nearly died, after I saved your life?" I ask.

"Mm, I'm pretty sure you saved *your* life and left me for dead," he says, pulling the collar of his shirt open to peer down at the dark webbed veins there. "But we can call it even and say we saved each other's lives," he mutters.

My eyes widen as another wince of pain hits me. I cough again, deeper.

This time when he speaks, most of the flippant ease is gone, replaced with concern. "If you come back with me to Arcana, we truly can help."

I don't know what to do with this strange expression in his eyes, so I try to sound unconcerned when I answer, "I'm not sure we agree on the same definition of 'help.'"

Zero rolls his eyes. "Come back with me, give me the key. We'll heal you up and give you your friends."

*He doesn't look in a state to help anyone right now.* I shake my head and close my eyes, wincing at the wave of nausea that follows.

"Auden will be there. She could be the one to help you," he says gently.

Those are the wrong words. My eyes shoot open. "Goodbye, Zero." I begin to stand. *I need to get out of here.*

"If it's any comfort, Auden wasn't meant to be your friend. She was just supposed to watch you. Everything else that happened was because she wanted it to," he says.

I shake my head and blink back sudden tears. Auden and I were closer than friends, closer than sisters. The idea that it was all a lie has been eating me up more than I want to admit. Hearing Zero say that maybe I didn't lose as much as I thought makes hope rise in my chest, only to be replaced quickly by shame. *I wish I could stop caring about her completely.* I have too much else on my mind.

I hate how gentle his voice is when he speaks next. "Thea, I haven't ever met someone with power like yours. If you wanted to come to Arcana, to be with Auden, you wouldn't have to leave," he says.

I scoff. "Are you asking me to join you?" I look down at Zero. His eyes are steady and even, though his mouth curves in a flippant smile. Under my scrutiny he reaches into the inner folds of his blazer. I stiffen. *Will I have to fight him next?*

"I meant to give this to you," he says, producing a white envelope, slightly crumpled from the fight. I eye it mistrustfully but reach down to take it from him.

When I take the paper in my hand though, my fingers skate over the black wax seal and accidentally graze Zero's outstretched fingers. Despite myself, a shiver runs up the length of my arm, scattering through my whole body. I inhale. Everything tingles like the carbonation from champagne. I exhale quickly and pull the letter out of his hand, blinking a few times because I'm unsure if what I just felt came from Zero—or me. I swallow and look down at it to avoid his fixed gaze.

"It's an invitation, to the Arcana end-of-term ball. Go home, get dressed up, and bring the key to the enclosed address at seven p.m.—we can make our trade then," he says slowly.

*Am I imagining the shake in his usually steady voice?*

I don't know what to do with this feeling that's scattered over me. It reminds me of something I've tasted before. Though we aren't touching anymore, the feeling still lingers, growing in intensity the longer his gaze rests on me. I want to throw the envelope, and all it symbolizes, away. Instead, I swallow and take a step back.

"I mean it, Thea. If you come to Arcana, we'll do our best to help you," he continues.

I open my mouth with the sudden urge to tell him where he can shove this letter when something shimmers in the air ahead of me. A bubbling energy spreads into the familiar lines of a wide and imposing door along the cream wall. I'm so excited I forget to breathe. Zero just keeps talking.

"I mean, the theme is Olympus, but don't be too on-the-nose, okay? No togas," he says, as if my apprehension was surrounding the dress code.

I raise my eyebrows as if what he's said is incredibly relevant, then begin to slowly move away from him. He doesn't turn to watch me go when I slip between two rows of benches.

"You need all three keys to open that box, Thea," he adds casually. "Without the one we have you'll have no chance—even if you do get to Kunlun."

"Who says we're trying to open the box?" I ask, partly to humor him, partly to distract.

"Whoever opens it controls it," he explains. "The Arcana have no need for what's inside. If you bring us the key and the box, we'll take care of them. We have the facilities to handle them safely. No one will ever get into it, not even us."

I am within a few feet of the door, which breathes out a soft warm draft, the smell of citrus and spice.

"I don't believe you," I say, eyes stuck to the door handle.

Then comes a rush of movement in the air beside me. I turn in time to find Zero leaning beside the door to Malachite with a half-smile across his face and his staff in his hand. *He recovered more than I realized.* He doesn't move to stop me.

"You don't have to believe me," Zero says. "In fact, in this world, Thea, you shouldn't believe *anyone* but yourself. Trust your gut." He shrugs and takes a step away. "But just remember, the people in *there* won't have an antidote to the poison you've got," he says, nodding to the blood staining my sleeve.

"Thanks for saving my life," I say for some reason.

"We can call it even," he replies, without losing my gaze.

I narrow my eyes at his seemingly open expression, and he still doesn't move to stop me from leaving. A second later, I throw myself into Malachite, breathless, letting the door shut behind me with a thud.

# 21

SITTING IN THE living room of Malachite feels like a dream. I remember Tiana said that the door appears to Godspring who need to get home, but only when it chooses. *Why did it choose me?*

"So, the Arcana have the two keys you found?" Aiko asks me. Her heavy-lidded dark eyes stare straight into me.

I clear my throat. "Uh, no." I say, "One is lost in a chasm in Jotunheim. But I wouldn't put it past them to figure that out and find it themselves. Although, if they ever do try to go back to Jotunheim, the queen there will surely fight them. So, there's that."

Aiko frowns and nods her head, stepping back to sit on the couch with the other young Godspring. She presses her hands flat down the length of her pale purple dress. On her left is the slightly built Emilio, whose looks at me as if I might try and make a run for it. Omari is beside him and smiles at me kindly. They are all staring at me. I try and smile back while Ani blinks at me from where she sits tucked into the corner of the couch holding her knees against her chest. Looking at her, I remember she was the first to ask me where Teal was when I returned.

Behind the couch, in the living room of Malachite, Reina holds Ani's shoulders and stands beside Ness. They are the two remaining oldest Godspring. Hunar, Marta, and Ian haven't returned. That knowledge makes my knees shake with anxiety. *Tiana, Teal, and I were counting on them finding the Kunlun key.*

"Well, go on, tell us what happened next," Ness says. Ness wears a loose-fitting black shirt tucked into the waist of trim orange trousers. The mole over his lip twitches in impatience. *He looks so much lonelier without Ian standing beside him.* I realize I had only ever seen the two of them together the couple of times we interacted.

I shift in my seat, self-conscious from all the attention. The fireplace beside me crackles with life, and the sweet smell of wood wafts through the air of the living room. I press my hands into the upholstered couch and push myself backward, farther in. Repeating the story so far has been surreal.

"I came back through the portal to find a man the Amazon queen thought I should talk to. But when I did, the Arcana were there. We fought, and then those dark monsters we battled in Jotunheim came again. The Arcana gave me this afterward, but I barely escaped with my life—and then the door appeared," I say, holding the invitation on my lap. *Why am I ashamed to tell them that Zero is the reason I am still alive?*

I look at Reina where she stands, observantly silent, covered in the red glow of her power. Her blonde hair is pulled into a low

232 ✦ GISELLE VRIESEN

bun at the base of her neck. She hasn't spoken a word since I arrived and she collected me from the foyer.

"Nothing is ever truly lost," Reina mutters. She lets go of Ani's shoulder and walks to stand in front of the fireplace. Then, she turns toward me and hands over a glass of water I didn't realize she had collected. *What is she thinking?*

I take the cup.

Finally, Reina continues, framed by the fire's glow. The chandelier overhead reflects its shades of gold and amber. "Ian, Marta, and Hunar—they should have been back already, and you shouldn't have left," Reina says.

Emilio raises his eyebrows at me, satisfied with my chastisement.

Reina continues, "But you did, and now you're back here, safe, at the very least."

Ani smiles in agreement. Ness rolls his eyes and takes a step backward until he leans into the bookshelf. *I had forgotten how hostile this place was.* I frown and clutch the glass between my hands. *Should I tell them I touched the Auroria? Should I tell Reina about Hathor's warning?* My interaction with Hathor and the convergence of worlds is another piece of the story I couldn't utter after I looked into Ani's wide dark eyes.

"All right. We've all got the story now," Reina says, clasping her hands together. "Everyone go back to your lessons so Thea and I can finish up." Her tone is sweet, and she gives Omari a quick rub on his shoulders as he stands. In a couple of seconds, the room clears out and it's only Reina, Ness, and me.

Reina inclines her head. "You too," she says.

"What?" Ness asks.

"Go with the others," Reina nudges.

"I'm not a kid!" Ness insists. Reina doesn't reply, just stares until he blushes with frustration, turns around, and walks out, leaving the door ajar.

Reina closes the door completely, then pauses for a moment with her back turned. I take another sip of my water, listening to the sound of the crackling fire, my heart beating hard in my chest.

"When you left, I was terrified," Reina finally says, turning to face me. Her eyes are wide and earnest. "I was terrified that you would get an awakening and that the three of you would never be seen again. I am supposed to *protect* you, Thea, *all* of you. I thought I had failed. But here you are, and mostly unharmed. Defying logic." Reina puts her chin in her hands, elbows pressed into her gut. She walks around the side of the couch and sits where Aiko just did, leaning forward. "I have no idea how you did it, but we don't have time for that conversation, do we? We have two and a half days until the solstice, and none of the keys."

I swallow at this reality. "I—maybe Hunar got the third one?"

Reina wrinkles her nose, shaking her head. "Even if he, Ian, and Marta got the final key—they aren't back yet. We have nothing." She pauses and looks away. "Well, I did find *something*. I already talked to Ness, but I wanted to tell you as well, of course," Reina says.

"What?"

"I did more research. I went and visited some old friends, and I managed to scrounge up a *very* old text, with a ritual that I think could be of interest to us."

I dip my head, the glass of water in my hands growing warmer by the second.

"*If* we can get just two of the keys here, there is a way to destroy one of them. But in order for it to work, everyone in Malachite would need to help, including those missing: Hunar, Ian, Tiana, and Teal. We need at least twelve."

I encourage her to go on. She smiles and continues, "Together we can finally be rid of the possibility of someone opening the box; we could all *finally* have peace," she says softly. "The keys can only be used together; destroying one of them would mean that none of them could ever open the box."

"Fantastic," I say. If no one can open the box, then the vision Hathor showed me can't happen. "I'm in," I add.

"But again, we need *at least two* of the keys. We'd need to channel the power of one of the keys, through all of us, to destroy the other, and so far, we have neither," she explains, spreading her hands out wide through the air ahead of us.

I frown, unsure why she's repeating this, then my eyes widen with realization.

"You want me to go to the ball."

"Pretend you have the other key—that you're willing to exchange it. We'll find the key the Arcana have *and* Teal and Tiana," Reina says, her gray-blue eyes sparkling. "I can make sure the door opens for us to take us back here." She looks down at the necklace hanging at her throat, an ordinary river stone hanging off a leather cord. I remember Hunar comparing it to the button of a garage door. My blood sings; I allow hope to convince me that this might truly work.

Reina continues, "Hopefully by the time we're back, the others will be as well. If they aren't, we will need to find a way to Kunlun ourselves, retrieve a second key there, and destroy it."

"Okay, yes!" *This is it.* For the first time in what feels like months, I have a reason to hope. With clammy fingers, I fumble as I hold the letter out toward her, making sure not to touch her skin. I let Reina take it and crack it open.

"It's tomorrow," she says.

"It is."

She smiles in a short burst, exhales, and hands the letter back to me. When her eyes meet mine, they are shining.

"We'd better get ready. No time to lose." She smooths her hands down the front of her trousers, then unexpectedly places her hand on my own. When her skin touches mine, I brace for a torrent of feeling. Instead, all I sense is wind through an open tunnel, a nothingness that gapes. I frown as she retracts her hand, all smiles.

"Now, I want to know more about the old man—Arthur, you said—you went to him about that marking? What did he say precisely about it and your grandmother?"

I am ready to respond despite my unwarranted apprehension when a dry tickle brushes down the back of my throat. I can't hold my cough in any longer. Thankfully, there is a knock at the door the same moment I cough.

Reina looks over her shoulder. "*Who is it?*" she snaps.

"It's Ness," the voice replies.

"Come in."

Ness pokes his head inside the room looking far less upset than he did a few moments ago. "Can I speak with you?" he asks. "It's important."

Reina purses her lips but nods. I cough a little and a light spray of blood falls over the tops of my legs. Reina glances back at me just as I fold the letter down over my lap, hiding the spray.

"Do you mind?" She arches an eyebrow.

"Not at all," I exhale, relieved.


MY BEDROOM IS exactly *where* I left it, down the long-carpeted hallway with the strange paintings and drippy chandelier. But when I opened the door seconds ago, I faltered. The room is no longer *how* I left it.

The space that had been frilly and soft before is now hard lines. The ground is smooth marble, the bed is mounted into the wall, and the colors are in shades of sober brown, the same arrangement you'd find on the bottom of a forest floor. As my eyes scan over it, it feels as though my mind can finally still. Without so much pomp to focus on, I can breathe. I am thankful to step into the room, dropping my bag by the door with a clunk. The blue book I have been carrying all this time tumbles out.

Reina said we should meet later so I can show her my staff and recount my conversation with Arthur, but upon seeing the bed, all I want to do is lie down. I remember Tiana and Teal, and my stomach twists at the idea of relaxing when they are still missing. Biting the inside of my cheek, I walk over to the newly appeared bathroom on the other side of the room.

Moving with new purpose, I peel off layer after layer of clothing as I step forward. The water hasn't fully warmed when I push my head under the spray of the shower and stand in silence, letting it run down my back.

In the stillness of the shower, I slowly lather fennel-scented soap in my hands, smoothing it over my arms, legs, face, and tangled hair. I clean until all the dirt and blood melts away and I am just me, shivering in a towel, in an unfamiliar bathroom, staring at my reflection.

My eyes are in the same place, my mouth is the same shape, yet they are so different. When I look into my brown eyes, I recognize something I didn't before: a kind of piercing expression I've seen only in animals. A wild focus that shocks me, but not enough to look away. My cheeks appear gaunt as well. I look older and more like my mother. *Beautiful*, I realize dispassionately. I walk out of the bathroom, into the main room, and turn toward the closet, which still sits where it did before. I pick up the first pair of pants and shirt I see. Stretchy, long-sleeved dark fabric passes over my wet hair, and then corduroy brown pants over cotton underwear and my strong legs.

I sit down on the floor at the foot of the bed next to the discarded blue book. I do my best to ignore the tantalizing call of the pillows behind me as I pull the volume onto my lap. *The Unspoken.* A title that had meant next to nothing to me before but now potentially holds so much. I flip through it for a couple of seconds but stop when my eyes snag on a page showcasing a familiar outline. It is the body of the statue that burned my hand. My eyes widen. Next to it are a few lines of text: *The Unspoken goddess of motherhood and fertility was one of the first I discovered in my research, but also the one with the least amount of information to uncover. Did she transform, as some gods have over the ages, going by a different name? Or did the same phenomena I have discovered in the other Unspoken occur with her as well, a splitting of energy, and a fading of essence?*

I frown and run my fingertips over the page. *What does this mean?*

I want to keep looking through the book and dive in deeper. It dawns on me that this is less a book and more a well-titled journal when I realize some of the lines are smudged with ink. I am hooking my fingertip beneath the next page when suddenly the wall shakes ahead of me. A tremor fans out through the body of Malachite, and I startle from my task. It sounds like something very large is hitting the front of the building—as if a large door is being flung open with great force against the wall in the foyer.

I don't think, I just move. Throwing open the door to my bedroom, I rush through the hallway. I enter the foyer where I stood not even three hours ago, notice the collection of dark blue flowers dripping stamens of brilliant gold with stems of deep red on the table, then stare past them to the open door.

The wood of it presses into the wall. Beyond the door, instead of a cathedral interior, or a city street, the familiar white walls and blue overhead lights of a mall shine. What I notice ultimately, though, is the heap of dark fabric on the ground, the groaning bodies.

Around me, the foyer fills with everyone in the house who heard the same tremor that I did. Reina and Ness appear through a door behind the staircase. Reina's hands are at her sides prepared to defend herself, and Ness looks angrier than the last time I saw him. The younger kids crowd the pile on the ground as it begins to move. Differentiating pieces of clothing from the bodies wearing them, I take a step forward, reaching for Ani's small shoulder to hold her back, unsure what is happening. Then my grip relaxes as I smile for the first time since the forest of Jotunheim.

"Hunar," I exhale, as he looks around the room, jaunty despite his odd position.

Ani yelps with delight and runs forward to wrap her arms around him as he rises to kneel.

"Hey," he says. To her or to me I am not sure.

I shake my head, unsure what to do or how to move.

The rest of the mass reveals itself to be Marta, peeling herself off a third form who lies crumpled under her weight, shocked and a little shaky.

"Where's Ian?" Ness asks.

I look over Marta's shoulder, at the empty space between her feet and the door. There is no trace of the red-haired boy who so thoroughly scowled at me the last time I saw him. Marta's expression darkens. My stomach clenches. Ness walks to her and helps her stand. Hunar stands as well. Ani sandwiches herself between him and Marta. *They look like a sweet little family*, I think with a slight frown. The third body behind them stands as well. It is shorter than Hunar, who obscures my view, and from a brief glimpse of dark brown hair I can easily tell they are not Ian. They shift and my breath catches in my throat. The smile I had fades.

"We were coming," Marta begins, "back from where we *thought* the entrance to Kunlun was, when everything went wrong."

I distantly register that both she and Hunar look far worse for wear than when they left.

"We ended up in the middle of nowhere, in a shopping mall, and the door was just there. So, we ran for it," Hunar says.

"Except it wasn't opening for us," Marta continues, stepping aside, revealing the small face of the third person more fully.

I stay as still as I can, not on purpose, but because my body won't move.

"Thea?" She says my name gravely. The weight of everything we've been through hangs between us like a literal chain.

"Auden," I finally exhale, as Aiko shuts the door to Malachite behind her.

**22**

**I** **SHUT MY MOUTH** and look at the people in the room around me. *What do I say?* Is there anything *to* say? Auden's expression is guarded; mine is frozen. I already told everyone all about her when I recounted the quest so far. Just now when I said Auden's name, Reina bristled. Before I can decide what to do, my best friend, my newfound enemy, walks up to me and wraps her arms around my neck. Breathing into me she says, "I have missed you so much."

I stay frozen, meeting Reina's eyes over Auden's shoulder, trying to convey to her both my disbelief and confusion. Then my jaw constricts, because Auden's feelings are the same tastes as I've always experienced when I touched her, only heightened now: tart trepidation, briny guilt, and sugary love. This sweet-bitter combination is the hardest to swallow.

Oblivious, Hunar and Marta continue recounting their story. The younger kids wearily eye Auden but can't look away from the two of them after Reina doesn't rush to kick her out.

"Can I talk to you?" Auden asks, finally releasing me only enough to look into my eyes.

Instantly, I am back in her bedroom, painting our nails bright yellow, talking about homework on the floor of her room. I remember the hours I have spent beside her, how many moments we've shared. But then I remember the last time I saw her too, the rocks in Jotunheim, and the time before in the forests of Ginen. Suddenly, I can't look past the yellow haze of power surrounding my best friend, the bright light gleaming off the medallion at her neck differentiating this Auden from the girl I trusted so completely. I tighten my jaw and pull back.

"Thea, the courtyard is unoccupied," Reina cuts in, softly. I didn't even notice her walk up to us.

THE SCENE IS PEACEFUL; a trellis over our heads hangs full of thick vines, heavy with grapes that weren't here when Tiana and I last stood beneath them. Auden and I sit on a stone bench; beyond us, a lush garden grows with low-to-the-ground herbs and bushes. They tingle with life, whispering to each other when I look over at them. The cobble warms the soles of my feet through my cotton socks. I try to look anywhere but at her.

"I guess you're wondering what I'm doing here," she begins at the same time I do.

"If you're going to try and get me to go with you to the Arcana, you can forget it," I say.

After a pause we look at each other, and if this were a few weeks ago, we'd both have laughed. Instead, I just feel alone.

"That's not why I came here," she says.

"Why are you here then?" I ask, wrapping my arms around my legs and stifling a cough.

"What you said to me, in Jotunheim—I, I didn't mean to hurt you like that," she says. I narrow my eyes, and she scrambles to continue. "I didn't mean to. I—Thea, you are *the* most important person in my life. Not everything on Salt Spring was a lie. You know me better than anyone—just not the details," she says, reaching out to take my hand, but I flinch away.

She frowns down at my hands. "Has that gotten more intense?" she asks quietly.

"You knew I could feel through touch?" I ask.

"Your mom told me," she explains. Now *she* is the one avoiding *my* gaze.

My stomach churns. *Of course my mom knew about her. Of course.*

"She didn't tell you because it wasn't time. Your mother was powerful enough to see fate, Thea, and she trusted me to be your friend—despite who I was," Auden says.

I shake my head, half at her, and half at the fact that I want, more than anything, to have *my* Auden back again. Of all the moments since everything changed, *this* is when I would want my best friend most. But I can't get over the wave of hate bubbling in my stomach; the stabbing feeling in my gut caused not only by her lies, but by my mother, who kept so much from me. None of it is easy to let go of.

"Why should I believe you?" I ask.

"Because I'm here. When the Arcana wanted me to stay away from you, *I* came to help you. Whatever you need, Thee," she says. "I'm here now, and I never should have let you go."

She reaches out and deliberately presses her hands on top of mine. Her sincerity washes over me, and something else too. Something complex and soft. Auden pulls her hands onto her lap and looks away, eyes suddenly full. I study her profile, small jaw, tall forehead, thick hair. Then I look over her shoulder at the tree carved with $T + Z$. In a flash, I remember Tiana's pain over losing her sister, how alone she felt. My own eyes are full of wetness that refuses to fall.

"Knock, knock," a voice calls from the glass-paned door to our right.

"Hunar," I say quickly to cover up my shock.

"Hey." He looks from me to Auden. As if in response to the tension, he holds his hands up in a peaceful gesture, stepping forward slowly. "Reina told me to check if you were ready to meet her in the training room? I'll stay here with Auden." He speaks with a firm tone confirming that he now knows Auden is with the Arcana.

My eyes widen. "Yes, I am. But, hey, did you find a door while you were out there? Did you get a way in to Kunlun?" I ask, remembering the larger reason for all of this.

Hunar frowns and shakes his head. "We were *really* close, but it was more than we could handle." A shadow passes over his brown eyes and I remind myself that he came back without Ian.

I smile softly, not wanting to press him any more than I would want to be pressed. "I'll go," I say after a too-long beat of silence.

In the time since we last saw each other we have both lost people precious to us. Hunar also lost Teal and Tiana, on top of Ian. I lost my friends and my family. When I look into his eyes as

I rise, I recognize a mirrored expression of my grief, masked by an affable smile.

"Yeah," Hunar says. "But I should have mentioned, the whole thing wasn't a total bust," he continues as I walk across the courtyard to meet him at the halfway point.

My heart spikes. "What else did you find?" I ask, reaching out and briefly grasping his forearm in excitement. Before I can register his emotions, I let him go like a scalding potato. *Why did you just do that?*

"We reached an elder creature who told us that even if we did find a doorway to Kunlun, we'd need a passcode to get in," he says.

"What is it?" I lean forward with my arms now crossed.

Hunar looks over my shoulder at Auden, then leans forward and whispers the rest to me. Auden shifts as if to look in a different direction, like she doesn't notice the hostility.

"Between the caves, the time loss, and coming up in a Walmart in Western Canada at the exact moment that *your* friend was opening the door to Malachite, no"—he shakes his head—"we didn't find out." His breath tickles the side of my cheek and my stomach flutters, but then I frown. We're no closer than we were before. In fact, if anything, we're farther away than ever.

But then I realize that something about this feels familiar. Between Hunar and Marta coming up in the Walmart I saw in my vision with Nana, Auden coming through the door at that moment, and the mention of a *passcode* . . . the migraine between my eyes blossoms just as my mouth drops open.

"I know what it is," I exhale, looking up at Hunar at the very moment he begins to turn away.

I step forward in excitement, anticipating him taking a step away from me. But instead, he turns to face me in the blink of an eye; for a second we're almost nose to nose.

"What?" he asks, equally breathless.

I remember Otrera in Jotunheim, saying it to me like a secret: *"You have to believe in real miracles, and surrender your disbelief, even when it would be prudent not to."*

**"YOU ARE SURE OF THIS?"** Reina's eyes remain neutral, but her mouth can't help but slowly crawl into a smile. The mirrored walls of the training room rise around us. Hunar followed when he heard that I have a theory, so Auden was towed behind us like luggage that no one feels safe leaving unattended.

Reina looks at me with so much intensity that my breath hitches in my throat, her smile continuing to spread, becoming infectious until I too am grinning.

"I—yes."

Reina presses her lips together tightly, suppressing a noise of delightful glee. "Well, in that case, there *is* another way into Kunlun, but it isn't safe or easy."

"The Arcana have it, don't they?" I can see it flicker behind her eyes.

Reina nods. "I thought of it as a last resort, if Hunar, Marta, and Ian didn't get back in time—but I knew it was nearly impossible to use. There is a place *under* Arcana, where they keep the stolen artifacts not on display. If—and this is a *large* if—we can get access to their gateway into Kunlun, then Thea, with your passcode, we could still get the final key, bring it back here, and do the spell in time for the solstice," she whispers, eyebrows rising with anticipation.

Two days until solstice, two days to finish this quest. I begin to nod before hearing Auden clearing her throat behind us. Suddenly I freeze.

Reina spoke our entire plan in her excitement. Now our enemy knows almost everything we do. I look over my shoulder suspiciously to where Auden stands just behind Hunar.

She steps out bravely. "I can help you," she declares.

I frown and watch her, remembering her sincerity, but also the trust she broke when I first found her in that clearing in Ginen.

Auden presses forward. "Let me show you how to get into the archives and lead you to your friends. I know Arcana like the back of my hand. Let me do this for you, Thea."

I swallow and look back at Reina, who considers Auden's proposal before slowly nodding. "If Thea trusts you?" she says, eyes flicking to me.

I don't correct her, so Reina continues. "If Thea trusts you, then yes. We accept your help, Auden, daughter of the Morrígan."

# 23

**T**HE BUILDING IS HUGE: half brick, half glass. The Arcana's self-named monstrosity reminds me of an opera house, or a secret society's evil lair—which feels fitting. Beyond the castle are the wide rolling waves of the Atlantic Ocean. I never imagined the sea in England would look so similar to the ocean back home.

Reina, Auden, Hunar, Marta, and I all stand above the entrance atop a grassy hill with various degrees of apprehension. We all wear finery picked from Malachite's attic: I have on a sky blue dress, Auden wears a silver, thin-strapped number, Reina dons a cascading floor-length white and gold dress contrasting her crimson lipstick, Marta wears a peony-pink mess of fluff, and Hunar has on a thin, off-gray suit. Ahead of us, down the slope of grass, the Arcana's front doors are wide open. Inside them people are milling around, and the sound of laughter rings up at us. My heart is in my throat.

"Are we sure about this?" Marta asks.

"What other choice do we have?" Reina replies.

Auden has been holding my arm ever since we finished getting ready inside Malachite, like one of us might disappear at any moment. When we stepped out of the door of the house, Auden's grip tightened. I look down at her painted nails against my skin, our touch outlined by the light fabric of my dress. I wonder how often she came to this stronghold while we were friends. Did Zero pick her up whenever school ended and take her back? I think back to her home, the one that was always mysteriously absent of her parents when I visited on the weekend. Was it always empty when I wasn't there? I have so many more questions to ask Auden, but as it stands, we have no time.

Reina begins down the hill while holding either side of her gown in white-gloved hands. I take her lead and follow tightly behind.

The building itself is only half the marvel. We cross a classic drawbridge set above water so still it reflects the deep black of the night sky, shining with an energy I haven't seen before. My spine stiffens and I repeat what Auden told us before we came: that a single invitation extends to an entire group, and that not all of Arcana knows we're coming, and they likely do not care. As far as the Hunt is concerned, each group of graduating students is responsible for how they obtain whichever artifact they decided on, alone. Auden tried not to offend us when she explained that most don't feel threatened by Malachites enough to monitor if we're coming, but the sting was evident in Reina's clenched fist.

When we arrive at the front door there are two young girls wearing identical sour expressions and black dresses. Around their shoulder-length black curls crackle matching turquoise auras; they stand behind a carved wooden booth already stacked high with invitations identical to the one in Reina's hand. I try to look like I belong, and one of the girls seems to recognize Auden, because her face turns up in a bemused smile.

"Why are you coming in through the front? Everyone else is in the lounge," she says to Auden, who stiffens beside me as she accepts the invitation from Reina's outstretched hand.

"I just came to dance, Magdalene. I don't want to see everyone right now," Auden says.

Both of the young girls shrug while a car pulls up behind us with more invitees.

"Go ahead," Magdalene says quietly in response.

*How could that have been so simple?* I think to myself as the five of us walk into Arcana effortlessly, but with guarded caution. Just inside the room, a group of milling teenagers all giggle in matching long sequined dresses as they secretly drink from a small metal flask, casting glances in our direction. Flickers of curiosity trickle off them and I notice that, despite their giddiness and effortless ease, like Auden and Zero, each has another source of power on their person that mimics the energy haloing their bodies. For some it's a bracelet or a tattoo, for others it's a cloak or a crown. Each glows in a way similar to Auden's necklace, the Celtic knot I never paid attention to until I became aware of its bright yellow aura.

Only in comparison to the people here do I understand how much less energy the Malachites have. Only when I see those artifacts amplifying the Arcana's power does the "why" click. My stomach turns upon realizing the reason is theft. I force my fist to unclench. *Why do Malachites have to live in constant vigilance and fear, while the Arcana can stroll around doing whatever they want,* taking *whatever they want?* It's clear they don't even know what to do with all the power they have.

As we walk across a checkered black-and-white marble floor, Auden reaches over and gives my hand a tight squeeze. I can feel her attempt to soothe my suddenly tense muscles. I realize, as we walk through a set of wide double doors, that throughout my life, my sensation of other people's emotions has been one-dimensional compared to what I feel now. I used to recognize happy, sad, reproachful, afraid—now those emotions are blended with complexity and reasoning. With Auden near me, I can feel her desire to comfort me as well as her guilt over her secrets, and her need to make up for it. The emotional tastes are more complex, not just a binary of sweet or sour.

**AS WE CONTINUE** down the hallway, all of us gaping at the portrait-covered walls and gilded doorframes, I notice the Arcana's year-long party is open to the magical public. Other creatures mingle about: androgynous fae-like beings in capes the color of the rainbow, small furry creatures wearing suits, and tall, lanky beings of preternatural beauty who remind me of a praying mantis, and *so* many more. I wonder how many of them I wouldn't have seen prior to my awakenings.

A few hours ago, as we were getting dressed, I offhandedly asked Auden if she had experienced all of her awakenings. She looked at me guiltily and explained that all non-Malachite Godspring only experience one awakening. The reason Malachites experience more is to allow time for us to choose which god's energy we'll follow for life. Arcana don't have to go through them

WHY WE PLAY WITH FIRE + 253

since they only have one option. Yet another thing that's easier for them.

"But when I did have mine, I spoke with my mother," Auden said, sitting down on the bed in my room and pulling out her necklace. "She apologized because she knew all of her children were cursed with the weight of her power inside of them."

"And that is?" I asked, still a little hesitant to talk openly about all she hid from me for so long.

"The ability to move between worlds," Auden said.

My eyebrows raised, thinking that sounded convenient, especially for the quest we're currently on. But then her gaze darkened, and she shook her head.

"It's not as convenient as it sounds, Thea. It means that I could take a step and end up in the underworld, in space, in—somewhere I can't exist—where oxygen doesn't exist. This necklace is the only thing that keeps me here," she had said, clinging to it as if it were a life raft and she were at sea.

I looked down at the knot and pursed my lips. "So, if you took it off, you would just—vanish?" I asked.

She shrugged and finished pulling her hair back from her face. "I've trained to use it my whole life; visiting the realms that the Arcana can't reach has been the goal, but so far I can only manage to *see* them safely."

I return to the present from this memory and look over at her as the hall opens, spreading into a large ballroom. It is gilded and extravagant with an enormous staircase at the far end. Golden tables line the room's edges, with dancing figures in the center. Aerial performers swoop and dive above the crowd. I take it all in: the people, the creatures, the dancing, the gold. For a second, my mind stutters at the image. Then it kicks into high gear. I remember what I am here for and focus on the black-and-white floor to ignore the glamour of the room.

*Somewhere in this enormous building, my friends are waiting.* Occasionally, lining the room between tables, raised cylindrical objects laden with items I can't make out shine. The little figurines, bowls, busts, and other items glow with power. I frown, realizing *those are the stolen artifacts the Arcana puts on display.*

On one side of me is Auden; on the other Reina now stands surveying the room, her lips mouthing words we can't hear. When Reina doesn't speak, I finally look up past the tall ceiling of the ballroom, noticing as I do that it is made of stained glass in vibrant hues depicting striking scenes: smooth-skinned beings hurtling the elements at monstrous creatures, women wrapped in gauzy fabrics wailing beside nude corpses. They all strike me as familiar.

*If I were a key, where would I be?* I don't see it on any of the display platforms.

"The only one who might know where the key is, or where your friends are, is Zero. He's the leader of his group," Auden chimes in. "And the door to the archives is across the hall, over there."

I follow her fingertip to a slice of smooth wall between two pillars across the dance floor. I squint.

"I don't see a door." Marta takes the words out of my mouth.

"It can only be unlocked by the handprint of a head teacher," Auden continues.

*Great, another obstacle.* My eyes run over the opulence of the room. *This whole place is a monument to stolen wealth; it may as well be a mausoleum.*

"We should disperse," Reina says definitively. "Hunar, Auden, and Marta, you look for a head teacher. Thea and I will try to find the others." Turning to face me now, Reina meets my eyes levelly. "I don't think it's a good idea for you to talk to Zero alone. After we retrieve Tiana and Teal, we'll approach Zero as a group to get the Ginen key."

Nodding, I tear my eyes away from the scene ahead. No one has any objection to her plan except Auden, whose hand tightens on my arm. I sense her vivid apprehension.

"I'll see you after," I reassure her.

Auden looks at me with doe eyes and smiles. In her touch and gaze I sense both fear and trust, and I accept completely that she is still my best friend. This is the moment I decide to forgive her. I hadn't realized I was working up to this point the last few hours. I'm surprised by how easily it's happening. She seems to see this in my eyes and releases my arm to branch off with Hunar and Marta as we descend the few steps between us and the dance floor. For a second, I feel secure in the fact that I'm not actively losing someone, I'm regaining a friend. The feeling is brief, because the moment we split off I'm faced again with our impossible task.

*Okay, find Tiana and Teal, then get out of here.*

Reina and I stand on the edge of a crowd full of strangers, and the mass of people surges around us. Like the ocean, a wave of bodies crashes toward me, caught up in the music streaming through the air and the bass vibrating the ground.

As the bodies collide into me, a familiar sensation even stronger than the mess of their joyful, self-conscious, wild emotions crashes over me. My dress and the glitter of the room take me back to the day I swam through the night sky and arrived at Malachite. My breath is stolen from my lungs as I'm overcome with remembering it, paired with the elation of the crowd. Everything is terrifyingly endless.

My heart rate is rising to my throat when someone's hand steadies my shaking elbow. Slowly, balance returns and my eyes focus. I look around the crowd and spot Reina across the room nearing a door, looking for me to join her. Our eyes lock and I realize I'm in the middle of the dance floor thirty feet away. Her confused expression widens and then sours when she looks over my shoulder.

Zero stands at my side, holding my elbow, while the crowd of people rock back toward the center of the dance floor, all of them moving in sync with the music.

When I first see him standing there, holding me, I feel a little guilty at how much I don't want him to let go. Zero smiles like he can read this hidden thought. His hair is pushed back and sleek, and he's adorned in a black satin suit pressed flat. There's a glimmer in his eye that reminds me of the North Star.

*I came here for a reason. I have something to do.* Ordinarily I would push him away and start negotiating, look for a way to find my friends and those damn keys. But, before we came here, when I was standing in front of a mirror in Malachite looking at the fabric of my long dress, I realized how much of my life I've spent not-living. How many hours I've spent pining over boys and dreams or anxious about the future. All the time I spent not realizing that the future is found in the present: always happening *to* me. No matter where I've been, I have always been directed by other people: my mom and our moves, how I ended up at Malachite, and even my friendship with Auden was decided *for* me. So, I have wasted most of my life worrying about what *might* happen in a day, a year, a decade from now, and it's always led to more indecision, more letting other people's desires lead me around.

But as I sat at Malachite preparing for this dance, a part of me looked at my reflection and wished for the courage to make my own choices. This contemplation was only reinforced by my need to cough into a handkerchief like a woman in a period drama with tuberculosis.

I bite the inside of my cheek now, wondering if I manifested this. When I look into Zero's dark eyes, staring at me like I'm something to be studied, I know that if I started dancing, he would too. Registering his hand at my waist and the rush in my blood, I can't tell if what I'm feeling is coming from me or from him. I frown a little, and Zero looks away like he's surprised with himself, or me, I can't tell.

"Where are my friends?" I ask, returning to the task at hand, uncomfortable with the fact that Zero and I have history now. We've been through an almost-death together and it wasn't by each other's hands. The only other people I can say that about are somewhere locked away in this castle. Zero still holds my waist.

Behind him, I notice the stairs are filling with polished young people ascending them. Each holds an object that glows with energy, and all wear black just as Zero does. A tall older woman wearing all red is at the very top. Her piercing eyes search through the crowd. Basil, who has a bandage on his head, stands beside Ophelia, whose arm is in a cast. *Zero is supposed to be up there too.* This must be when they display their newly stolen artifacts.

"I brought the Jotunheim key," I say, pulling a black velvet bag out of the folds of my dress and letting it sway side to side in the air between us. Zero's hands tighten at my sides and his eyes follow the fabric like a cat.

"Take me to my friends and you can have it." I palm the bag. Somewhere in the distance a soft bell rings. Zero notices it but doesn't look away. I worry he'll call my bluff and grab the bag, but I remain steady. Instead, Zero's face relaxes into the hard-to-read mask I've become accustomed to. "Okay, Thea," he says evenly.

It's strange, but I notice the absence of his hands when he lets go of my waist, the cold air that replaces them, but not the absence of the rush they brought on. I frown and follow behind him as he turns to exit the rushing crowd.

**24**

AS WE WALK, I notice a few heads turn. Their gazes brush over Zero's face first as he leads me away from the crowd, then land on mine. *Do they know who I am? Is this part of the trap? Do I have any choice but to follow him?* The Arcana sparkle in shades of the rainbow. Zero is silver light. No one moves to stop us.

I no longer see Reina or the others anywhere. I hope they've found a way to open that door. I hope that our plan comes together without anyone noticing. Zero leads me past raised platforms with glass cases over them protecting various small objects dripping with bright energy, through a discreet doorway beside the grand staircase, and into a round-walled corridor. Shrouded in a layer of quiet, Zero and I start leaving behind the sound of classical instruments. I try not to appear nervous as we also leave behind the commanding voice of that woman in red addressing the crowd while the music dies down.

"Welcome, all, to the Quadrennial—"

The rounded hallway is a light sand color, lit with candles fastened under thin glass shell-ribbed sconces along the walls. It opens into a wider set of corridors that gently slopes downward. Zero does not look over his shoulder once to check that I am following him. As I follow, I discover that some of the doorways lining the walls lead to shallow ends, some seem to branch backward and fold in on themselves, and others turn into stairs going up or down. Different smells waft through the doors: earth, sage, smoke, and candy. When we pass by the different branches of the Arcana, the air changes temperature beside the different doorways too. It goes from hot to ice cold in seconds, wet warm to simmering tepid. *Like the temperature changes in Malachite.* Through it all we stick to one path, the same unadorned sand-colored hallway that cuts through all the others. When we've been walking long enough that I don't hear music at all anymore, I stop walking.

"How much farther?" I ask. My paintbrush is fastened in my hair; if I have to defend myself, I will. Zero doesn't look threatening in the soft underground light of the Arcana's hallway system as he turns to face me; in fact, he looks softer the farther we get from the main hall. I remind myself of how I met him, the chaos that followed, the theft of my map, until the butterflies in my stomach ebb.

"Not far," he says. With his hands in his pockets, his expression opens like he wants to say something but stops himself soon after.

"What?" I snap, discomfort making my voice harsher than I mean it to.

"You should know—the Arcana—we aren't villains." He continues, "We protect things: artifacts, creatures, people. Without us, it's probable that humans would have hunted every magical being out of existence. We keep things hidden, safe, and protected," he says.

I raise my eyebrows. "Is it protection or are you hoarding magic for yourselves?" I ask, looking around at the quiet hallways, each of them presumably leading to another gold-lined appendage of this obscenely large building.

He frowns a little, like I'm missing the point. "Every institution has its flaws. That doesn't make what we do less important."

I roll my eyes. We drift into silence and keep walking.

"Given what I've seen of your abilities, there could be a place for you here as well." Zero pauses meaningfully. "If you wanted, we could finish this quest together."

I furrow my eyebrows and hold my arms down on either side of my body as if I couldn't care less, as if I don't even consider it.

"Just bring me to my friends," I say, purposefully slow.

Zero obliges and our silent walk continues until we finally arrive at a smooth wall. Zero presses his hand against the wall and suddenly the surface becomes an open door. It reminds me of how Reina opened the closet the keys were in. Except, this time, I can see the magic working. The pulse of energy he exuded from his palm fans out and interacts with intricate silver links of energy under the wall's surface, before dissipating into its edges and revealing the entrance. Suddenly, I see them.

"Thea!" Tiana says.

Teal jumps from her side, against the wall within the shallow, windowless room. They're both wearing the same clothes as they were the last time I saw them, only clean. Teal's head has a new shine of light blond peach fuzz, and Tiana's braids are pulled into one larger braid down her back.

I run to them and the three of us embrace at the threshold of their prison. I don't even flinch when their bare skin wraps around my neck. Tiana's excitement and desire to pick up our quest are a mix of spices, and Teal's relief and care are a honeyed mint.

"You found us," Teal exhales.

Zero shifts to the right of me. Tiana notices him over my shoulder, and her body tenses until I shake my head slightly. She then looks at me intently, brown eyes squinting like she's trying to read my mind. But there's no need. In one exhale, I move just the way Reina and I talked about before we left Malachite.

I turn on my heel and pull out the velvet pouch from my pocket, heavy and swaying. Zero sees it and his pupils dilate. He thinks he's getting what he wants. But then, right as his posture relaxes, I open the drawstring, reach in my thumb and forefinger, pull out a pinch of sand, and blow it in his face. It falls out in a shimmering haze, dusting over Zero's face before he has a chance to speak, striking his nose and mouth as he inhales.

*Sandman's sand.*

Reina wanted me to do this while she was nearby, but I think I did fine on my own. Zero's light eyes flutter closed, and he sways backward, unconscious. I instinctively reach out and grab the front of his shirt, softening his fall backward as his grip loosens off the large wooden door. Without him to hold them open, the doors begin to close. Teal and Tiana scatter out.

"Well, well, well," Tiana says. "Looks like that came in handy."

"It did," I say, perplexed at why I'm still holding the front of Zero's shirt. He hovers a foot over the ground. *When did I get so strong?* With my free hand, I search Zero's pockets, enacting the next point in Reina's and my plan. Then, I curse under my breath. *The key isn't here.*

Letting go of his shirt, Zero hits the ground with a gentle thud, snoring. I turn to find Teal and Tiana rummaging in a cubbyhole across the hall. Tiana pulls their bags out of the shallow depths while I pocket my pouch.

"Yes! They didn't take it," Tiana says, pulling her backpack onto her shoulder gratefully. Teal puts on their jacket, and I exhale because *finally*, we can pick up where we left off.

THIS TIME WHEN I trace my way back through the maze of corridors I am flanked by Teal and Tiana. I try to push past my disappointment at not finding the key and stay optimistic about the next part of our plan: join Reina, Marta, Hunar, and Auden, who hopefully found someone to open the door into the Arcana's archives. Then we can all leave this dimension behind without anyone realizing.

It's strange, but as we walk away, I'm aware of how I left Zero sprawled out on the floor, and guilt pangs in my stomach. I force myself to remember that he's the villain, not me, and I try to tuck that feeling away.

While we walk, Teal and Tiana tell me about their stay in Arcana. They briefly explain how they had been sent through a questioning sequence by a couple of angry older men trying to find out where the door to Malachite stood. Of course, neither of them knew. Then they were asked about me.

"Why?" I ask, as we arrive at the entrance to the ballroom.

"I don't know, something about your ancestry?" Tiana's words die on her lips when we realize—the ballroom is in chaos.

On the far end across from us, at the base of the hall I walked through to get here, Reina is standing with a web of red mist sprayed out ahead of her, bleeding down the lengths of her bare arms, pouring into the air. Auden is standing over her shoulder with a drawn expression. Ahead of both is a wall of about twenty Arcana dressed in finery. Beyond Reina and Auden, Marta and Hunar stand beside the opened door to the Arcana archives.

Between us and them, the crowd of Arcana have different devices in their hands, swords of light, knives like stars, a whip. Everyone is poised in the moment before an attack, gleaming with energy so bright it's hard to keep my eyes on them. I don't immediately know where the rest of the Arcana went. Did they run? Or had the party moved to a different room when Marta and Hunar were caught? *At least they managed to get the door open.*

I pull the paintbrush from my hair immediately. As it lengthens under my touch, I step forward on shaky legs. *Why do I feel so unsteady?* I cough a spray of blood, which none of the Arcana notice as they charge toward Reina. The closer they get to her though and the farther they wade into her red mist, the slower they move. It's like they're suspended in molasses. *How is she doing that?* Is it her innate ability or a spell? And how is it so powerful? I haven't actually seen Reina use her power.

No time to ponder. Hunar spots the three of us and waves us toward him from across the room, toward the open door. *I suppose we won't be leaving as quietly as I hoped.* I take a shaky breath in after my cough passes. Blinking past suddenly blurry vision, I raise my staff just as a few Arcana finally notice the three of us standing behind them.

Tightening my hand around my golden staff, my power simmers below the surface just the same as it did when I fought those demons. It's in the world around me, the ground beneath my feet. With all the energy I have, I lower my staff down. But at the last moment Tiana reaches out with a hand on my forearm, to block me.

"Save it." Her eyes are ablaze as she looks at the Arcana who imprisoned her.

I blink, looking over to find that her other hand is holding the glass bottle I got from La Sirène. *I forgot she had that in her backpack.* Except now, the bottle's color has changed. Instead of foggy and transparent, it shines a glowing burgundy, similar to the hazy light haloing Tiana herself. My eyes widen, and I let my grip soften on the golden staff in my hands. Tiana lets go of my arm and uncorks the bottle completely while a few more Arcana turn to face us.

In a single heartbeat, a *zing* slices through the air like a firework has gone off. Just as the dark red in the bottle empties out as if drained from the bottom, everyone turns to look at us.

Wincing, Tiana releases the glass, which returns to its normal color as it tumbles to the ground and doesn't crack. Teal quickly picks it up while I look around, expecting another golden boat, or some item equally as unlikely. A few Arcana are coming toward us now and Teal's hands are lighting up. Tiana screams. When she doubles over, Teal's light flickers.

"Tiana? What's happening?" I ask.

"She's having an awakening?" Teal's eyes are wide. They are as confused as I feel to see the telltale arcs of energy racing through our friend.

"Then why is she in pain?" I ask, just as Tiana stands back up straight, eyes watering. She holds out her hand. Wordlessly, she is showing us that the soft brown of her skin is changing, her light palms are darkening while her usually long nails are growing longer, curving to a point.

Tiana takes a halting step forward and the Arcana ahead of us hesitate. My eyes struggle to catch up with what I'm seeing as Tiana's arms and legs lengthen, becoming hairy before our eyes. Her braids loosen into a mane, and she thrusts herself out onto the tiled marble floor ahead of us with a ferocity that steals my breath.

In the span of only a few terrifying heartbeats, Tiana has disappeared, her clothes in ribbons on the ground. In her place roars a mighty lion.

Tiana is larger than I imagine most lions grow to be, towering overhead. Her claws are so sharp they shred into the tile. When the Arcana rushing toward us finally see her, they skid to a halt. Tiana lets out a thunderous *roar*.

*What on earth?*

Teal is the one to jolt me into action, pulling me forward as Tiana charges ahead, carving a line through the Arcana like they are strands of grass; tossing them side to side while I gape.

Many of the Arcana recover quickly and launch into action. A golden lasso is sent toward Tiana's enormous fur and a flurry of arrows fall onto her left flank, but none of them penetrate her coat or slow her down. Teal blasts a couple of Arcana with bolts of light as they drag me behind them. While we're running behind Lion-Tiana, I'm not steady enough to use my staff. An alarm is rung somewhere far off, and Reina notices our movement. As we run and the room is in an uproar, Reina backs up toward Hunar, still struggling with the effort of holding off the Arcana in place.

I block out the blood we pass, the sound of Tiana's claws sinking into soft flesh. Instead, I keep my eyes glued to Hunar and Marta, standing beyond the red mist that Reina is already parting, holding open the door for us. *I just have to make it a few steps.* Already, other Arcana are answering the alarm, rushing in through the open doors in a flood, holding weapons they didn't have when we first arrived. *So, that's where they went.* I can't help but feel a little self-satisfied that we, Malachites, were so underestimated.

In less time than anticipated, we're through the crowd and slamming through the open door after Auden and Reina. Hunar and Marta stand beyond us, panting on a metal landing before a staircase that descends into pitch black. My heartbeat is in my ears. Tiana is still a lion and not yet through the threshold of the door where I stand.

I turn back toward the crowd and see her immediately where we passed her by. She's in the middle of the dance floor with every Arcana pointed straight at her, their weapons either raised or firing. The power they throw at her now does more damage, and with every hit she grows smaller. Now, she looks the height of a regular lion. My hand tingles against the staff under my hand. *I need to help.*

Closing my eyes against the pounding in my ears and the slickness under my feet that smells like iron, I focus. With my eyes closed, I can still feel the room. Holding the staff in this state, I register the energies inside. Instinctively, I take a breath in and picture the Arcana members like the flames of candles behind my eyelids. Distantly, someone is tugging at my arm. I block them out until I am only the feeling of air in my lungs and the staff in my hands. Focusing through my staff on the Arcana nearest Tiana, I steady my heartbeat. When I lower it, I exhale and imagine the flame of those candles being snuffed out. My artifact hits the ground with a *clang*.

When my eyes open, the halo of marigold from a nearby Arcana member flickers, just for a moment, before it disappears in a flush. They blink and look down at their now useless artifact: a long broadsword no longer alight with yellow energy. The other Arcana beside them reacts the same way when their connection to their power, and their artifacts, has also dissipated. *I did that. I don't know what I did, but I did it.* I don't have much time to be excited because Lion-Tiana has now noticed the absence of magic all around her and is bounding toward us, pushing through the confused crowd easily. In a few leaps she's crashing toward the door where we all stand.

Stumbling away from the opening, my now-snapped concentration turns into a volley of coughs. My ears ring as someone pulls me the rest of the way out of the doorframe, just as a lion the size of a girl falls forward, past the threshold. When Tiana hits the ground, she's more skin than fur. When she looks up at me, her face is back to normal, though stained red. I blink past a bout of nausea, and Marta and Reina close the door behind her quickly.

Teal kneels and probes her shoulder softly. "Tiana?" they ask, "Are you all right?"

I wonder what it was like for the two of them in that prison cell before I got there; if she finally explained their forgotten feelings and the cause. Tiana grimaces in pain; she has several cuts across her face and a bleeding wound on her left shoulder that oozes dark red when she tries to sit up. Hunar looks away from her naked body and Teal takes off their jacket, wrapping it around Tiana's shoulders as she pulls herself to stand on the quiet metal platform.

"I'm fine." Tiana coughs up a clump of human hair. "I ruined my coat," she says. Not a single sliver of the orange-red leather coat she wore remains.

"We should go," Reina declares, stepping away from the door. "This won't hold forever."

As she speaks, the Arcana begin beating on the metal door, which is sealed shut and vibrating with the same red magic Reina was using to hold everyone off. *How powerful is she if that's able to last even when she isn't focused on it?*

"That was an awesome second awakening, Ti. One for the ages, huh?" Marta asks gently after Reina turns to descend the functional metal staircase. Marta's pink dress is torn in a couple of spots, but otherwise she looks the least wrecked of us all. Tiana nods her head, still disoriented. I look to where Teal stands beside me, the glass bottle clutched in their left hand; now it shimmers a peach-gold. Tiana leans into their arm and suppresses a groan.

"Thea," Auden whispers, "are *you* okay?"

"I'm okay, I'm fine," I say.

Marta descends the stairs after Reina, and I face Tiana and Teal, who eye the new addition to our group warily.

"This is Auden, my friend from back home. She's Arcana, but she helped us find you," I explain.

Teal's eyebrows raise and Tiana shakes her head.

"Guys!" Reina snaps from farther down the stairs.

Behind us, the sound of the Arcana beating on the door reminds us of our limited time. Wordlessly, we all scramble to follow Reina into the archives.

# 25

**B**ENEATH ARCANA are rows and rows of industrial-strength shelves, all of them full. Some hold crates plastered with ordinary stickers and stamps showing dates, locations, and symbols I don't understand. Others display their keepings bare. As we walk, I spot small objects giving off hues as varied as the people surrounding me. I inhale the scent of metal and plastic.

"Wow," Marta says, as she raises a hand and touches one of the shelves we pass by. Her fingertips come off dusty. The shelf reads INCAN RITUAL BOWL in neat typeface. "This is incredible," she mutters in a mix of longing and repugnance.

In these halls are the missing links every Malachite never got the chance to connect with, possibly even their missing ancestral artifacts too. This knowledge makes it feel less like I am walking through a storage room, and more like I am walking through a temple.

Reina shakes her head. "Come. We don't have time to browse. This place is organized by region. Find China, and the gateway to Kunlun *might* be there." Reina casts an even glance over the whole warehouse, completely focused.

We fan out in groups: me with Auden, Tiana leaning against Teal, Marta with Reina, and Hunar walking ahead on his own. Fluorescent lights beam down in slices of pale blue. *This place reminds me of the locker room in the basement at school.*

"I've never been down here before," Auden says soberly.

"You'd think if you steal something, you'd at least label it," I say, realizing just how many of the shelves are unmarked.

Auden exhales. I look over at her necklace, which glints chartreuse as we continue forward, searching for a shelf that will get us out of this basement.

"Did you never wonder where all of the artifacts went, after they were taken?" I ask.

"I—I guess I never really thought about it."

Neither of us needs me to point out how messed up that is, so we continue our search in silence. Squinting through their light, I peer at artifacts to read the labels that do exist. Auden searches the shelves with an unreadable expression across her face. Looking at her, I remember all the wishes and plans we made together, all the dreams we had beyond this mess. For a second, it occurs to me that we can still have that future we planned. We can travel the world. We can finally tell each other *all* of our secrets. Auden and I can be better friends now than we were before. Of course, after we get a chance to talk—after things settle down. She tucks a lock of shiny auburn hair behind her ear while she reads the labels off the shelves with the same tone she had when she read the board in class. Even in this odd circumstance, she is so familiar.

"I'm really glad I'm here with you," Auden says suddenly, as if picking up my train of thought.

I pause, suddenly full of feeling. Before I can reply though, I cough. Back at Malachite, Marta quickly picked up on the poison in my energy. She crafted a tincture to help slow the spread, but it's clearly wearing off.

"Hey!" Hunar's voice reaches our ears from beyond the shelves to our right. I try to peek at him through the rows of boxes and vases, pieces of chipped pottery, and large mirrors. It's impossible.

"What!" Tiana calls back from the left. Her voice is hoarse.

"I think I found something!"

When we find Hunar, he is standing at the very end of the long room, where the shelves stop and bare brick walls rise to hold the lofty ceiling. Ahead of him, with a sheet crumpled at its base, is a cluster of head-size stones with familiar symbols written across their length. *They look like the rocks that surrounded the campfire in Jotunheim.* Except these rocks aren't just covered in strange symbols, they are also flecked with vibrant living green moss. The aura of all of it is white gold and piercing.

"It says 'gateway, K' and it has a marking on it." Reina crouches beside them, picking up a placard wedged beneath. "But it looks like most of it is missing." She gestures at the four pieces of disconnected stone, no door, no archway, no clear method of using them.

"Do you know what the markings mean?" Teal asks.

"No," Reina answers slowly.

Tiana steps forward. "How are we supposed to figure out how to work it?" She toes the ground as if pondering whether kicking them will do the trick.

Teal shrugs while Reina turns the placard over in her hands. Then, somewhere far behind her, a door opens. Voices filter toward us. Locking eyes with Reina, my jaw clenches. *Our time is up, the Arcana got through her magic. They're coming.*

"What now?" Marta asks, not panicked but alert. Her magic, which is a swirl of lapis blue, trembles in the air around her.

"Hush," Reina snaps. Eyes wide, she peers down the long rows of shelves. It took us nearly ten minutes to get to this end. *We have a little time*, I can practically hear her think. "I need to think," she says out loud.

While Teal and Marta turn toward the aisle behind us, both alight with their own magic, I remember what Otrera said to me on the floating island about believing in magic. I repeat the sentence over and over in my head. *How do I believe in magic even when it would be prudent not to?* Distantly, I remember something Teal told me, about humans only being able to see the magic they already believe in. It's like the answer is on the tip of my tongue. *If I could just understand.*

From the pack of Arcana descending the metal stairs and arriving at the base of the archive shelves to search, I register Zero's familiar voice rising. My blood starts rushing in my ears when I hear him, my stomach cramping. For whatever reasons, I am equally pulled to both apologize for leaving him in the hallway and use my staff to find him and knock him out again. Instead, I stay still.

*You have to believe in real miracles, and surrender your disbelief, even when it would be prudent not to.* Those were the exact words Otrera said to me.

I whisper it to myself again as I look at the archway and the moss, trying to block everything else out. *Mom and Nana wouldn't have brought me this far without believing I could do this, without* knowing *I could make it.*

"This is the gateway," I announce.

"What?" Reina asks.

"Right here." I nod my chin toward the collection of crumbling stones, the empty wall. "*This* is the gateway."

"How?" Teal asks over their shoulder. I can practically feel the thundering weight of the approaching Arcana. I sense about ten.

"We must walk through and *believe* that this wall isn't there. We have to *believe* in magic that we can't see, that these stones will take us to Kunlun. That's the way in," I say, looking at the plain, unassuming brick wall. It doesn't rustle with any hint of magic.

"You want us to run at the wall?" Marta repeats, not in a rude way.

"We have to believe. And I do," I decide. "Do you believe me?" Auden is already nodding.

"But we all have to go at the same time—we can't have proof it works—we have to have faith," I say.

Reina stands up and folds her arms behind her back, light hair falling down the sides of her face. She is like a beam of discerning light, completely unbothered by the approaching enemy.

"They're coming," Hunar reminds us, eyeing the shelves behind us, stepping closer to the rest of us.

"We don't have time to waste!" Reina decides, and reaches out toward Hunar.

I quickly grab Marta's sleeve where she stands beside me, and with Auden still holding my arm, I walk up to the base of the stones. The closer I get to them, the more noticeable the gentle hum emanating off them becomes, settling under my skin. It cancels out Marta's terrified curiosity and Auden's complete trust in me, until all I feel is a serenity unlike anything else washing through me. Teal and Tiana quickly follow to stand beside Auden and link hands while Hunar holds Reina's arm and stands beside Marta. All of us are connected now and facing the brick wall.

"How do we do it?" Marta asks when all of us are standing in line.

I can practically feel the Arcana's breath on the back of my neck. They are getting close, and their voices are becoming clearer.

"Just empty your mind, be still and calm, and imagine that calm opening for you, leading you into Kunlun. Let it be as real as we are," I say, instinctively, feeling the weight of these stones in a way I didn't feel from the ones in Jotunheim.

As the Arcana come closer, I sense without looking that Zero has spotted me. The hairs on the back of my neck stand up, but I force my body to relax as I take a deep breath in and let the power of these stones flow through me. They bring peace and a serenity I didn't think I would ever have again. I let it fill me up until it is all I can focus on. Then I raise my right foot and know the others are doing the same. My calm radiates out through my fingertips into theirs, down the line of our linked palms. Together, with our eyes closed, we step forward.

# 26

**M**Y FOOT LANDS on something soft on the other side of the portal. The air tastes as sweet as melted honey, and I open my eyes. A gasp escapes my lips as my eyes adjust to the scene ahead. The world in front of me is displayed with saturation set to max: the greens are electric and the blues are shocking. The ground is covered in the same thick green moss that the engraved stones in the Arcana basement bore, except here it's draped over more stones, boulders, and pebbles that reach miles forward.

In the distance, twisted vines as thick and tall as trees wrap around rocks and reach into the air weightlessly. They resemble beanstalks from fairy tales with leaves the size of my head glistening with magic the color of the rainbow. I fill my lungs with sweet earth, rain, and fresh mountain air. When I exhale, my anxiety over the Arcana being just behind me floods out. I'm so stunned by the scenery that for a second I forget—I shouldn't be alone. My skin touches nothing but balmy air, and the only sound I hear is my own heavy breathing.

Then comes the first footfall. Where there had been nothing but air beside me before, Auden appears, then Marta, followed by Teal, Tiana, Hunar, and finally Reina. Each of them takes in the landscape the same way I did, with a deep breath and eyes full of awe. There is no door and no engraved stones behind us, and better yet, no Arcana. Everyone whoops in excitement, but then reality sets in. We are in a foreign place that operates by different laws than ours, and we have very little time to find our way through it. And, even if we did find the key hidden here, it would be the only one we have.

Reina takes control immediately. "Everyone, remember what I said before we left Malachite: Kunlun is one of the most beautiful realms a Godspring can visit, but it is not safe for us for long. We are not mortal nor god, so the longer we spend here, the less our bodies will be able to tolerate it. The magic of this place strives for symmetry, and we are not symmetrical. Our conscious selves will, over time, be overcome by our subconscious selves until we forget who we are, much less that we should leave. Afterward, our power will leak into this world."

Reina then begins ripping the hem of her long pale gown until she can move easily. Auden and I do the same.

"Where do we go?" Hunar asks, looking up at the pillowy white clouds with his arms crossed, probably thinking what we all are, *How can a place this beautiful be so dangerous?*

I remember my cue and pull out the book Hunar gave me from the deep pockets of my dress. He notices it but says nothing as I flip it open to a middle page with a smile.

"The map Zero stole from me was written with thick black ink," I explain. "Me and Teal went into the water in Ginen with it and, well—" I turn the page over to show everyone.

Back at Malachite, before we left, I made this discovery: the pages of this book somehow absorbed the wet ink of my nana's map. The images were transferred—in part—*into* the book.

"Wow," Teal says, walking to stand beside me. "Those mountains must be the ones right ahead," they say, and gesture at the blue-tinged slopes in front of us.

"Yeah, so then this"—I point at the shadow on the page, blotted over a couple of words of notes—"must be where the key is," I say.

"How can you tell?" Teal asks.

"It's darker, look. All the other strokes are faint, or wispy, but this is intentional and bold. It doesn't fit the style," I say.

I remember my nana's focused expression when she would stand in the living room and paint; for hours it looked like she was transported to the landscapes she brought alive through her paintbrush.

Reina looks at the map and nods once. "Excellent."

Tiana lets go of Teal's arm and peers forward as well. The wound on the side of her shoulder pusses green beneath her borrowed jacked. I want to ask her how she's feeling, but she speaks before I can.

"That tree over there has a star on it," Tiana says, jutting her chin out toward the base of the twisted tree ahead of us. "So that is the path, here." She gestures from the map to the tree and back.

I peer at the spot she's gesturing to and see it, barely visible with the amount of bush gathered near its base, but visible enough: a five-pointed star.

"That's great, let's go!" Auden exclaims.

Tiana shoots her a guarded look.

The seven of us walk toward the river, where the mossy rocks turn into fields of rolling hilly grass. *We'll need to cross it to get to where the map directs.*

I look from right to left at my friends; the water rises only to about mid-thigh. Rationally, I know we could just walk across the choppy, clear waves, over those white stones at its bottom. But at this point, I understand that rivers and tests are never as easy as they look—especially when you're not on earth. No one takes a step forward.

"I think I can do this," Reina says, pushing her hand out.

"What?" Marta asks.

"I can make a way. I'll just need a little power boost. Will you all grab on to me? What I did at the Arcana—it took everything." Reina juts her right hand out, expecting our agreement. *I didn't realize we could share our power in this way. There's so much I'm still learning.*

"Of course," Hunar says, and grabs onto her wrist immediately, then Marta onto her upper arm, Teal and Tiana onto her pinky and middle finger, Auden onto her forearm, and lastly me.

"Of course," I say, holding onto her thumb. When I take Reina's hand this time, it's different than it has been before. Instead of a faint buzz wafting from her, I feel myself pool into her. It's like something is hollowing out my bones.

I exhale in relief when Reina finally relaxes her grip on all of us and we each let go. After we do, I see trails of our power join into the red pool dripping down from the hand we held on to, shining ever deeper as she turns to the stream ahead. Before our eyes, the water ripples and the current stops, as the red leaking from Reina's hands dams the water so effectively the river bottom becomes as dry as the shore, revealing a pathway between the waves. We step forward only after she does, cautiously. As we cross through the bottom of the stream, I notice that the white stones I saw at the bottom of the river were not stones at all but worn-down pieces of bone. My eyes widen and I keep my pace steady. When we all make it to the other side of the river, I cough, and Reina lowers her hand. The water returns to flowing, and a soft ringing between my ears ebbs into a migraine, but I continue forward.

The mountain range seems to spread out into forever, with rolling green hills spread between the mountains like blankets. Overhead, the sun shines bright, yet the air never warms above a comfortable temperature. Every now and then Tiana shoots a look over her shoulder at Auden and me but doesn't say anything.

As we walk, I occasionally hear wings flapping above us. Each time I hear it, I remember the creature that attacked us in Ginen and tense up—but when I look skyward, I find only clear blue skies and billowing white clouds.

Hunar is the one holding the book now. After a long while of walking in anticipatory silence, he speaks, almost as if he can't help it. "So, Tiana, guess you can turn into a lion now? I didn't know Malachites could do that. Can you do it again?"

"I'm not sure," Tiana answers, blinking slowly.

"Are you feeling all right, Tiana?" I ask, noticing that a slight green hue is tingeing her neck and cheeks now.

Tiana waves me off, holding Teal's arm tighter to stay upright. "I'm fine, Thea—it's you who should be cautious. Allying with an Arcana is like getting in the ring with an alligator and then trying to feed it," she says, her dark eyes fixed on Auden's profile. She turns to me and finishes her sentence, "It's as stupid as it sounds."

Auden stiffens, and I clench my jaw.

If it were anyone else, I might have defended myself, but even without my abilities I could sense the sting of betrayal in my friend's voice. I can also practically hear the words she doesn't say: *After everything they did to me, to my sister?* I don't know how to respond.

"You still have the bottle, right?" I ask Teal instead.

They pull it from a pocket in their bag and hold it up for me to see. Just as it was before we last emptied it, the bottle holds a peach-gold color.

"A part of me hopes that if I open it again, it will bring me *Hringhorni* so that I can travel back to Jotunheim and find my father," they say, then pause pensively. "I don't even know what I would say though, if I did. I think I want to punch him in the face."

I frown at the abrupt change in conversation, but then Hunar piles on.

"Sometimes I'm so scared to be alone I'm worried there's nothing I wouldn't do to make sure I have someone beside me," he says, looking confused by his own confession. He frowns deeply. "Is anyone else having an overwhelming desire to tell the truth?" he asks the group. His mouth opens and more confessions spill out, one after the other. "Like the desire to say that I'm not sure I would care so much about finding these keys if it didn't directly affect *my* house and *my* bedroom? Or that Tiana looks super green, like on the verge of death, but I also don't know if there's anyone who *could* help her now, and how weird it is that Snail hasn't said that already, because they've been in love with her for like seven years." Hunar blurts it all.

Marta jabs him in the arm to stop talking and Hunar's eyes bulge as though he wishes he could physically put the words back in his mouth. The silence that follows is overwhelming.

Teal frowns pensively for a moment, then clears their throat. "I don't love Tiana anymore, Hunar, she's—she doesn't feel the same way, so why should I bother? Also, turns out I willingly gave La Sirène any feelings I had for her. So, aside from knowing I *should* feel close to her, all I feel when I look at Tiana is a near emptiness, and a sort of hunger. And right now, that feeling is reminding me it's been ages since I last ate, and even then, it was only a ham sandwich." Teal shrugs.

Tiana shrinks away from the words coming out of Teal's mouth. I hate seeing how hurt she looks. Before I can think better of it, my mouth is opening again, uncomfortable with how far away Auden is standing since Tiana's outburst. "I'm going to die."

Everyone turns to face me; our walk stops.

"I touched an Auroria when we were in Jotunheim and I've been sick ever since," I explain. No one says anything, so I start walking ahead of them. "Marta gave me a tincture for it when we were back at Malachite, but it isn't working. I've mostly ignored it. I guess like everything else, I'll deal with my impending death later."

"Thea," Auden says.

I turn back to face her. "What?"

"I didn't know that. I—" she falters.

Suddenly I have the pressing urge to tell her how much I needed her all this time, and how glad I am she's here now, and how angry I still am at her for being Arcana, for lying to me about who I am, for Dom. I am about to say this when I notice our group is one member short. "Where is Reina?" I interrupt my own train of thought.

Everyone looks at the empty green grass and sloping hills around us. Reina is nowhere to be found.

"Reina!" I shout into the blue sky before running back in the direction we came from.

"Reina?" Marta shouts.

The whole group looks everywhere, but Reina is gone.

I lock panicked eyes with Teal. The only option we have then is to run forward, thinking that maybe Reina had somehow ended up just over the next hill while we weren't paying attention. We rush up, only to find a landscape of twisting tress peppered over mossy ground, framed by taller mountains.

"Where could she have gone?" I ask, turning back to face my group, finding only three pairs of eyes staring back at me.

"Guys!" I shout. They pause their search. "Where is Tiana? Where is Marta?"

Hunar's, Teal's, and Auden's mouths gape open as we look all around us for our now three missing members. There is nothing but grass and a soft murmur of crickets in the distance.

I shake my head while Hunar jogs ahead of us. The three of us follow him as he races up the next hill, this one taller than the last. Though, with every step I take, the less the world around me makes sense. By the time we crest the next hill, I can't differentiate between the sounds outside of my body and those inside. I forget why I am running, or why my blood is pumping so loud in my ears. All I notice is that the grass is too green, the air is too sweet, the sun is *too bright*. Hunar lets out a grunt of frustration when all we find at the top of this hill is more grass—*not what we were looking for? What were we looking for?* Hunar charges forward and I follow him over the next hill.

We walk, and run, and walk again until eventually I can't walk anymore. I fall to the ground and find myself hugging the side of a very steep hill speckled through with white star-shaped flowers. The grass here is not bright green but deep and rich as pure chlorophyll. When my eyes catch on the flowers, I giggle, turn onto my side, and find just one person staring back at me. Hunar's eyes are red-rimmed, still pleasing to look at.

"I can't feel my heartbeat," Hunar slurs.

The two of us are all that's left, but this doesn't alarm me. We are lying beside a great big tree, flowering with tiny pink blossoms that rain down over our faces in the wind. As the pink petals fall, they streak like paint across my eyesight. I don't feel a trace of panic as I lean backward into the grass of the hill, but wonder if I should. I wrap my hand in Hunar's so he doesn't disappear, but don't remember why that is something to be concerned about. When I touch his skin, I'm aware he feels different than I distantly assumed. Hunar's energy is not as stable as I pictured. It spikes and dips like a bird in the wind as he skates over thoughts. I stare out at the scene ahead of us, beautiful, bright, familiar.

"I think I've seen this before," I whisper, still holding his wrist tightly. Hunar entwines his fingers into mine, simultaneously trying to sit up. Failing, he lays back down with a moan. My eyes are fixed on the grassy slope and how it evens out below us into a grove of more cherry blossom trees in shades ranging from pale pink to rosy red.

"ARE WE ON DRUGS?" Hunar shouts, unaware of his volume.

I sit up. The image ahead of me flickers, once, twice—*yes, I have seen this before.*

"My grandmother used to paint scenes of this place. She hung them all around our house," I gasp.

Then I remember the brush in my pocket and pull it out. Moving it, I imagine it dipped in streaks of paint.

"Your grandmother went to Kunlun?" Hunar asks, as he finally manages to sit upright beside me.

"I guess so." I shrug, remembering the beautiful paintings, the green grass, blue water, pink cherry blossoms. "She was very hard to know and could be extremely awkward in public. I always thought she was a mean person—greedy—and not as loving as she should have been to my mother. It made her a hard woman to love, and there's so much she didn't tell me. Why didn't she just *tell* me?"

"I have a confession," Hunar says, staring at the beautiful glowing view with me.

"Another one?"

"When I was very little I lived with *my* mother," he says confidentially, rubbing his eyes with the back of his free hand.

I raise my eyebrows. Hunar's mother is a goddess, this I remember distantly. "I thought that didn't happen," I say, as I slide off my shoes and blink up at the bright blue sky, relishing the feeling of grass between my toes. I feel pulled to glance up at the wispy clouds. *I wish I could put my hands in those clouds and feel their cool wet on my fingertips.*

Hunar shrugs beside me. "I barely remember it. I know that she kept me a secret, then one day she was gone and the door to

Malachite was there, and I just went through. I was so young, I don't know where I was before, but sometimes—sometimes I still think I can hear her, in the dark," he says, and looks over at me. "Why are you crying?"

I notice that my cheeks are wet only when Hunar mentions it. Looking over at him, the smooth expanse of his skin, the thin bridge of his nose that widens out in the middle, I realize he looks like a sculpture.

"Because I lost my mother and my nana *forever*." I press my free hand into the middle of my chest. "What happens when I can't remember them outside of paintings?" I slur, then place my paintbrush inside the pocket of my dress.

"Everything leaves an impression, even when it seems to have gone," Hunar says, putting the blue leather-bound book with the map on his lap. "Like the map inside this book, like your family inside of you."

I read the title again: *The Unspoken*. It feels hard in my mouth, like a name given to a flower by a colonizer who never bothered to ask what it would like to be called, who couldn't hear it even if the plant answered.

Hunar lets go of my hand to pat me softly on my upper back. My eyesight is blurry as I gaze at the smears of pink ahead of us. The rhythm of his emotions soothes my own heartbeat into a slow and even rhythm. *I feel like I am here for a reason, but I can't remember what it is.*

"Do you remember when we first met?" he suddenly asks. "You came up behind me when I was on the stairs, and I turned around. It was because I thought you were her, something about your presence, your energy, reminded me of her."

I wipe my cheeks with the back of my hand.

"I reminded you of your mom?"

"That's sort of a weird thing to say, isn't it?" Hunar says.

I shrug and look back out at the world, still streaking with pink and green and blue, like everything is a painting and someone just splashed it with water. I lean back so I'm lying flat in the grass again.

"I remember now, I thought that because I found a prophecy by myself, at home, that this quest was meant for me." I realize distantly why I am here. "I thought that because of this mark, and the voice in my head, and my nana, that it was up to me to fix everything. But I was wrong." Some small amount of clarity returns to me, sharpened by the pain in my throat after I cough to the left of us. "It's not just for me, because this isn't only about me, it's about all of us, every Malachite." I turn to see if he understands my meaning. Hunar smiles back pleasantly and lies down too.

"You're very pretty," I remark, my cheek pressed into the grass now. It hums with the same calm happiness that the air does and sings unintelligible words into my ears.

"You're very pretty too," he says.

I smile and roll back to stare at the clouds, breathing in a delirious breath of air as the sky shimmers above me. Then I notice something, something white and falling, slow as snow. I reach up with my left hand and catch it. It is one long flat and brilliantly white feather, tipped with sky blue. I sit up so quick my head rushes and I register the beating of a bird's wing flap somewhere above me again. Peering from the feather up at the sky, I'm suddenly determined to find the creature who shed it.

It occurs to me that the white thing I had taken for a cloud, languidly floating through the sky, is no cloud at all, but an enormous bird with a tail and piercing jade eyes; eyes that are only noticeable when someone takes the time to look. My lips part in shock. The bird opens its mouth in response, and a piercing noise fills the air around us clear as a bell. I jerk on Hunar's arm beside me and he murmurs something about not wanting any more "SLD."

"Hunar, *look.*" I point the feather at the enormous creature hovering only about fifteen feet away. The bird flaps its feathered wings over our heads, stretches out long as a car. It looks like a cross between a flying albino peacock and a dream. I can smell its plumage from here, a soft and alive animal smell—a break from Kunlun's constant sweet haze. The bird looks down at us like we are the peculiar ones. My head begins to clear in earnest now.

"Is that a bird?" Hunar mutters.

Nodding, I pull him to stand with me. Though the ground shimmers and shakes, if I keep my eyes on the bird, I can keep myself centered.

"It's leading us somewhere!" I shout. Hunar makes a noise of agreement and stands with the movement of someone with their eye on true north.

I keep my eyes fixed firmly on the smooth white underbelly of the most magical bird I've ever seen with wings like ribbons in the wind. As we walk away, my head clears. The bird leaves behind the soft noise of flapping feathers, though its wings don't flap; it glides like a cloud and ripples with streaks of blue. There are a few times I look down and away from the creature, but when I do, my delirium begins to sneak in and I get the urge to lie back down. Each time I start to lose myself, the bird caws sharp enough to draw my attention. Then when I look back at it, within a few seconds everything steadies.

I register Hunar's warmth through the sleeve of my dress as we cross from grass onto rocky terrain, and then back onto grass. We pass over three hills and under one thin canopy of flowering trees, until I finally see where the bird was leading us. My head becomes as clear as glass.

Up ahead, a hill topped with an enormous flat slice of smooth ground raises up, level and buffed shiny. On top of the flat space are my missing friends, all seated in a semicircle around a woman who towers above them all. Taller than Penthesilea and the other Amazons on Jotunheim, this woman rises at least fifteen feet into the air and resembles a moving statue. When I blink, I think I can see power radiating off her, but it doesn't act the way I have ever seen power act before; it is farther-reaching and wide. It also doesn't resemble the hazy cloud auras I've grown accustomed to seeing. Her energy stretches like petals, hands, or long strings she has total control over. Trying to understand it gives me a headache. My steps falter when I register her serene smile, which is visible even from here.

"That is the Mother of the West," Hunar breathes just loud enough that I can hear. The large woman's black hair is folded around an intricate golden and jeweled headdress, but those few pieces left out flow in an invisible wind mirroring the breeze carrying the bird toward her.

"Who is the Mother of the West?" I ask, keeping my eyes steady on hers.

"Her name is Xiwangmu. The goddess and queen of Kunlun," he says. "This whole place is her domain."

Hunar and I walk forward hesitantly. As we approach, I see the folds of her light dress fall artfully around her hands, which fold in her lap. The white bird now perches on a stand behind the goddess.

Once Hunar and I arrive at the edge of the apparent picnic, I gulp, registering Xiwangmu's enormous size. Everyone is seated on comfortable cushions over a tiled ground. They don't look hurt. Ahead of them is a feast of meats and vegetables, soft-as-silk dumplings, rice, and small empty cups waiting to be filled. Reina locks eyes with me, nodding her head slowly for me to relax.

Then, the goddess smiles at Hunar and me and gestures to the two empty cushions across from her.

"Take a seat, Thea, Hunar, we have been waiting for you." Xiwangmu's voice is like the toll of a bell, and it strikes me in the center of my body. We have no choice but to obey.

# 27

THE GODDESS IS so beautiful it aches to look at her. Her square face is so proportionate it could probably fold in half exactly; it holds two eyes that shine as green as those of the bird over her left shoulder. Crowning her towering height, her hair is as black and shiny as slick oil where it sits folded atop her head decorated with an intricate glittering headpiece. As I take my seat across from her, the goddess parts crimson lips to reveal two rows of straight white teeth. Her golden-peach skin shimmers against energy in a thousand shades of jade. *She doesn't look much older than my mom.* My face heats when I notice how intently I have been staring at her.

All of us are here, sitting on cushions arranged in a half-moon around the goddess and her magnificent bird. Hunar and I take the two empty cushions across from her and beside each other. The second I sit, whatever was left of my brain fog evaporates and I breathe in the smell of cooked food. Laid out ahead of us is a feast contained by small wooden bowls. Some of the bowls are filled with dumplings moist with steam, others with bouncy rice cakes, and steaming fish sits wrapped in lotus leaves. There is porridge, meats with whole peppercorns and scallions, and so much more. My eyes snag on the empty teacup sitting on the mat ahead of me. I remember Teal cautioning me to never eat the food when you're in a realm that isn't your own. My mouth waters regardless.

"Thank you for bringing them, Qingniao," the Mother of the West says to the bird over her shoulder. It makes a purring noise and nestles into the side of her neck, still artfully balanced on the single metal beam behind her.

"What is this?" Hunar asks softly.

I'm not sure if he's talking to me or the Mother of the West.

"This is lunch," the goddess replies.

I peel my eyes off the food, swallowing down the water in my mouth. "Do you have the third key?" I remember to ask.

"Tiana, will you tell Thea what I told you?" The goddess dips her head to the side with a small and tolerant smile. It's hard to focus on anything but the size of the goddess's body; her head is as tall as my torso. But I do manage to look over at Tiana, who sits stock-still with her palms flat on her knees.

"She said she'd give it to us after we listened to what she has to say—and once we all arrived," Tiana says. She seems queasy from blood loss, and a little green, but overall better than she could be.

When I truly look at Tiana, I realize that none of the people around me are looking the goddess completely in the eye. All of them keep their gaze fixed somewhere beside her, or on the ground. Curious, I turn and look into the deep jade eyes of the

Mother of the West. I understand why my friends avoid her intense stare immediately. As soon as I lock onto those two green spheres for longer than a few seconds, I start to lose my sense of self just the same as when Hunar and I were wandering the hills of Kunlun. That same feeling of calm radiates off her as potent as it does the air around us, making me want to melt away. The longer I look into the goddess's gaze, my body becomes more of a concept than a constant. *She is as much this place as it is her.* I tear my eyes away, heart pounding.

"I did, and I will," the Mother of the West promises.

Her voice is stranger than I first noticed. Every tone she speaks seems to have several more layers than an ordinary flat vocal tract. She sounds like a harmony, like the women I saw when I talked to Heather—Hathor—in my dream. Balling my hands into fists, I focus on my friends around me instead. Auden flashes me a reassuring smile where she sits tucked beside the goddess.

"I am Xiwangmu, and these are the fields of Kunlun," the goddess continues, gesturing to the landscape around us. "This is the milder portion of my domain, and the only place in which a Godspring is permitted to exist," she adds. I look over her shoulder and see that this world continues fanning outward into the horizon, as large as any landscape on earth, if not larger.

"Now, Teal, you have brought me something," Xiwangmu says, turning her attention to my right. Looking over at Teal while they shakily pull the glass bottle out of their bag yet again, I tense. The bottle's peachy glow lights up the palm of their hand almost as bright as their power would. They hand it to her hesitantly.

I hold my breath and watch the exchange. Xiwangmu's hands are unadorned, and her nails are bare. She takes the bottle into her large hands. When she does, I notice the bottle change shape, lengthening until it is proportionately large enough for her to hold. Then, without missing a beat, she uncorks it. My breath hitches in my chest as I wait for something incredible to happen, but nothing does. The goddess of Kunlun reaches forward and begins to pour the golden liquid inside of the bottle into the cups ahead of each of us.

"I have been known to make elixirs, like this one, for thousands of years," she says with a faint smile. "This was the bottle from which I unintentionally granted Chang'e her immortality. It was passed down through her lineage for years afterward. I did not think I would see it in Kunlun again," she says, tipping the bottle back upward, now empty.

"Will this make us immortal?" Reina begins. The word hangs in the air ahead of her. We all look wide-eyed at the cups ahead of us.

Xiwangmu's interrupting laugh is like the toll of a bell. "No," she answers. "That magic has long since faded, what is left is something like a wish. The wish I have given today is for you all to stay here a little bit longer, without losing yourselves, or your mind," she says. When no one replies, her tone becomes sharper. "Now, you drink," she commands.

I remember what Hunar said, this place is her domain. On her shoulder, the great bird blinks at me. I reach out and pick up the cup. *If she wanted to kill us, I don't think she'd make it this elaborate.*

Hunar sniffs his cup and takes the first sip. He drinks and I remember how I found this bottle in the first place—*Nana's voice behind my ear.* What I wouldn't give to have her voice here with me now, guiding me when everything feels like a test, or at its worst, a punishment. I am the third to drink, after Auden. The goddess watches each of us take in her potion with a serene smile. I expect a strong or otherworldly taste from the drink but receive nothing but a light flavor of peaches. After it passes down my throat, I recognize the potion doing *something*.

Xiwangmu continues, "Now that you have consumed this, you may all stay long enough to hear what I have to say." The goddess sets the glass bottle down.

When she does, I notice it shine, lighting up with its telltale marking that matches the one on my hand. *How does this make sense? How could a bottle belonging to the Mother of the West have my own mother's Unspoken symbol etched onto it?* I remember something Heather said to me, that she and some of the other gods helped my mother sacrifice her celestial body to protect Malachite. I wonder if Xiwangmu was one of them. I want to ask her, but I stop myself. I might be hardheaded, but I know not to interrupt a goddess in her own domain.

"I know of a quest to retrieve three keys issued to three travelers, and yet I find myself serving six wanderers instead. One destined to die a hero's death," she says, her eyes directed at Teal, who stares steadily at the space between her eyes. "One in love too late." She shifts to look at Tiana, who instantly looks away.

"Another whose loves are cursed to die," she says to Hunar, who gulps and looks down.

"One destined to lead," she says to Marta, who remains completely still.

Then she looks at me. I gulp down the rest of the liquid in my throat and wait for her verdict.

Instead, she swerves her neck right and speaks to Reina. "One whose lack of a decision leads to one being made for her," she says.

Then, to Auden, "One with a uniquely blessed curse." This Xiwangmu says very gently and reaches out to wipe her fingertip across Auden's cheek.

My arms tense. I place my cup down on the ground. The goddess turns to face me again, locking her eyes on mine before I can avert my gaze.

As she speaks, my body loosens. "And one with an opportunity to find a lost mother."

My eyes widen and I lean forward instinctively. "What?"

"I have a way you can see her again, forever, if you wish; but it will come at a cost," Xiwangmu says, green and blue jewels glittering at her throat.

The words spring out of me. "Whatever it is, I'll do it."

*I should have given that sentence more thought,* but even as I think this, I know I don't regret the declaration.

Xiwangmu smiles, her face spreading apart to reveal her teeth, which have now become sharp, like those of La Sirène. I try not to recoil, and the goddess reaches her palm toward me. Looking down at her soft skin, my mouth gapes as I witness the flesh in the palm of her hand opening up, like it is being unzipped from the inside, revealing a slim trail of ruby-red blood. My stomach clenches and then winces when I notice a pain in my right palm. When I look at my own hand, I find an identical slice of red directly over my marking. My mouth dries. I know what she wants me to do—it seems so simple—press my hand against hers and this goddess will give me my mother back to me. *But how?*

"You swear, I'll see her again—alive?" I ask.

The goddess nods graciously, her hand still raised out to me. "This is no trick, it is a call to destiny, Thea," she says. "You found my bottle, and you found me. Your time has come."

I take a deep breath and avoid Tiana's head shaking an emphatic no.

Before I can think more on it, I press my hand against the goddess's.

My palm is dwarfed by the size of hers, and I note her nails are as pointed as her teeth, something I didn't notice when I first looked at her; or maybe it wasn't true then the way it is true now. When our blood mingles, there is a familiarity to it; a sigh escapes my lips, and I remember something like this, in a dream maybe? The goddess wraps her fingers around mine tight for a moment, before releasing me.

Just like that, it's over.

Xiwangmu is pulling her already-healed palm onto her lap and holds a soft smile on her serene face. Finding that my palm is unscarred, my heart hammering against the back of my breast-bone, I cradle my hand against my chest. I wish I could say that this was a decision I made in the heat of the moment, but the truth is that ever since we got here, I've felt my sickness ebb slightly. With that change has come a desperate urge to make the most out of my life. With this poison rushing through my body, I recognize an insistent need to live as I have never lived before— *fully*. If I can do that, *and* have my mother, maybe all this will have been worth it. *Besides, why would she lie—what could the goddess of Kunlun possibly want from me?*

"So, what now?" I ask, wiping my hand nervously on the surface of my dress while Reina's gaze rakes over me. Probably looking for evidence of poison or trickery, finding none.

Xiwangmu sips from her cup slowly. "Your mother is here, in Kunlun, grazing in a field with the Gods Who Remain. She has been waiting for you, but you can go to her, past the gates, only if you change," the Mother of the West says, smiling wider now.

"Change how?" Hunar speaks up.

"How does any hero change? Through acts of service, great feats of bravery, and enough luck to survive a dance with death." The goddess laughs softly. "But none of that right now; you have all come for a key, you've been so anxious, and so you all shall have it," she says, setting her small white cup down. I want to ask more questions but clamp my lips tight as the goddess reaches up one of the sleeves of her robe and pulls forth—an empty cord.

"Where's the key?" Tiana asks.

"All of you should know by now, these keys come with a price," the goddess says and lays the cord down. "And the price I seek is invaluable to me—hard to come by—a way to leave this realm safely—if used by the correct hands." She says this as she turns to her left, looking at Auden. My brow wrinkles.

"What do you mean?" I ask.

"I mean that there is a medallion at your throat"—she says this to Auden—"that I will take in exchange for the final key to the Malachite box."

"No," I say immediately.

Auden fingers the Celtic knot at her throat and pulls it out from under her shirt. It shines between her fingers, and she frowns. "I need this," she protests softly.

I remember her explanation of why: without it, Auden would fall through dimensions ceaselessly.

"It is a crutch, given to you by an organization that would rather see you stationary than free," Xiwangmu whispers.

"If you take that from her, she'll be lost. She could die," I insist.

"It is her choice to make, Thea. Will you, Auden, give me this necklace and finally break free from your captors? Finally find your mother, and speak with her in bare honesty, or will you let your friends' sacrifices be for nothing, and have them return home empty-handed?" she asks.

I am about to interject again, but the Mother of the West's hand flicks up in my direction, then when I try to speak no sound comes out of my mouth. Auden is still looking down at the medallion at her neck. I have never once seen her take it off, but she's fingering the clasp now.

"What do you want with it?" Auden asks.

"It is as much an anchor as a sail," Xiwangmu says vaguely, her large hand outstretched in the same position as when she reached for my palm.

I try to wave my hands to get Auden's attention, to stop her from giving the necklace, but there's no need because she's looking at me now. Her soft hazel eyes reach over the feast between us—over the people between us— and I feel it all: a rushing apology for lying, her hope of seeing her mother, and her love. I nearly choke on the feeling of her love. I widen my eyes and begin to mouth any words that might stop her. "*I'm sorry*," Auden mouths back, then she's dropping her tiny medallion in Xiwangmu's large hand, and as if erased from this earth, Auden is gone.

I wildly search around the picnic, but my friend is missing. Xiwangmu tucks the necklace into the folds of her dress. Suddenly, I can speak again. "Bring her back! I take back our bargain!" I shout.

The goddess arches an eyebrow at my outburst, then reaches forward to adjust a few of the plates ahead of us like I hadn't spoken. *What have I done?* I remember a dream I had once: I was in the snow and Auden was behind me, and then suddenly she wasn't.

"Our bargain cannot be taken back, and it has nothing to do with the decision your friend just made," Xiwangmu says. "Now, the key." She reaches forward into the middle of the picnic, lifting the tray off what I assumed was a saucer for sugar to reveal a shallow bowl holding a gleaming key inlaid with delicate vines and leaves. My eyes are wide as I look between the final key and the cushion Auden used to sit on. Silently, Xiwangmu pulls out the key and holds it in the air over her palm in that same gesture she's made twice now. I can't move to take it; Reina is the one who does.

"Well, that is all then," Xiwangmu declares. "You have what you came for." The goddess picks up one of the dumplings with a pair of very long chopsticks and eats it slowly, smiling in satisfaction.

"Wait, do you know where the other key went?" Tiana asks as Xiwangmu chews. "The one that we lost in Jotunheim?"

The goddess looks at me instead of Tiana when she replies, smiling with a patient expression. "Some things are better left unrevealed," she says.

Swallowing back my rage, I try to convince myself I shouldn't hurl a bolt of energy at her. I remind myself that there is nothing I can do against this goddess, especially not while we're sitting in her realm, and I made a blood pact with her. Xiwangmu turns to face the rest of us with a hidden smile in the corner of her mouth. "Your drinks must be wearing off by now; any more time here, and when you get home, you'll have gone mad," she warns with a cheeky grin.

*I've been played for a fool.*

"Wait, what else do you know about the quest we're on? Why are we doing this, what is it all for?" Marta asks, her eyes lighting up with the possibility of an answer to these elusive questions. "What triggered the keys going missing? *Who* is trying to open the Malachite box?"

Xiwangmu raises her chin up and seems to draw herself even taller.

I can practically see the questions we all leave hanging in the air: Hunar wants to know where his mother went, Tiana wants to know how to destroy the Arcana, Marta wants to know the answer to the question she asked, and Reina wants to know— well, I'm not sure what Reina wants to know, but her mouth is open with a question. Xiwangmu blinks once more. Distantly, something occurs to me.

"Why does Kek want my mother's spirit?"

Xiwangmu's eyes harden as she glances up at me over the rim of a bowl of soup now held between both hands. Zero said that it was followers of Kek who have been after us, after me; those shadow monsters who killed my family.

*He must be the reason this quest began, the reason the Malachite box is threatened. But why?*

"What do you know of Kek?" Xiwangmu asks me. Her eyes are suddenly metal, her grip tightening on the bowl she's holding.

"I know that he killed my mother—an Unspoken god—the one whose celestial body is inside the Malachite box. I know that he intends to open it," I declare.

Xiwangmu's mouth tightens into a red line, and she looks around the bunch of us. "I have been away too long," she mutters, and glances to the place in her robe where she placed Auden's necklace.

"Tell us what to do," I insist. My terror at seeing Auden leave briefly hardens into determination.

"Get back to your quest, little bird," she says, her jade-green eyes scanning the horizon behind us.

I balk when I hear the nickname my grandmother used for me when I was little. In that moment of instability, Xiwangmu raises her hand up into the air with a hard expression, then pulls it down in one smooth moment. When she does, the world of Kunlun is erased like paint smeared off a canvas. For a flash, everything is blinding white, the next it's inky black and sparkling with stars. I think I see the big dipper in the distance. Then, for just a second, I see a familiar sight, the shopping plaza with the Walmart close to home, the one with the McDonald's play-place that smells like lice remover. *What?*

**WHEN MY EYES ADJUST,** the world is sideways—or no, I am. I heave myself up to a sitting position while my skull pounds maliciously. Someone groans beside me. When I turn, I find Tiana sitting up on a dark green hillside. Overhead, the gray sky holds its breath in the moments before rain. My stomach sloshes with nausea. *Where are we?* The Arcana headquarters is nowhere in sight.

"It's like I'm coming down from every drug *all at once*," Hunar moans, as he sits up across from me. Teal is at his side and Reina at his back. Marta is a few feet down the grassy hill from me. We all clutch our temples. Reina heaves, but no vomit comes up, just a long string of peachy-golden bile. My own stomach rumbles when I see it.

We sit on the side of a large sloping hill. There is a field below us, and the sky is the silver of public pool water. The air no longer smells sweet, and the light here is pallid compared to the vibrant yellow of Kunlun. *We're back on earth.* Below us, dewy grass soaks through the fabric of my dress. My entire body aches, though none of the physical pain compares to the absolute hole in the center of my chest, which deepens when I remember that Auden is not here. *Auden. Is. Not. Here.* I press a hand to my mouth as the realization sinks in.

"Where are we?" Tiana rasps.

"Probably China," Reina says. "Legends say Kunlun exists in a mountain range with the same name. It must be true—just on a different plane of existence," she observes while pulling her phone out of her dress pocket, then wiping her mouth with the back of her arm.

Suddenly my breathing becomes quick and shallow, my eyes filling with black spots. *Auden and I—we were going to face this future together, forever.* I forgave her and she trusted me. *Why would she do that? Why would she leave?* My eyes widen and I suck in a gasp that quickly becomes a sob. I try to stop the cries as I press my head into the cold wet grass, ceaselessly repeating the same four words over and over again: *What have I done?*

Tiana softly pats my upper back while tears pool into the ground beneath me. My paintbrush falls to the grass. Listlessly, I reach out and wrap a clammy palm over it. When I raise my head up, I find that the group has gone silent. There's a snot bubble in my right nostril that pops on an exhale.

"I—"

I don't know what to say, but it doesn't matter because now I'm coughing, and my despair is turning into giddy uncontrollable laughter. The laughter becomes a cackle, which turns into a howl. My eyes are streaming with water and my body is wracked with pain, but *I can't stop laughing*. Not just at losing Auden, but at the pain of my mother and Nana being gone, the fact that I am so much more lost than I have ever been. Everything is weighing on me and I don't know if I can stand up again. I cough a spray of blood and then remember that on top of all of that, I'm also slowly dying from a magical plant poisoning. The laughter only gets louder.

"Thea?" Tiana softly interrupts after a couple of minutes. "Do you think you can stand?"

I blink and realize everyone else has stood up. Tiana is reaching a hand down toward me. *Were her nails always that long?* I don't know if I can move at all. I look at her hand dispassionately, unsure if my joints work anymore—until a familiar sound arrives—a crash and crunch, paired with an electric hum.

*The Arcana are here.*

They arrive the same as always, dramatic and clad in black head to toe. When they appear at the top of the hill, I giggle. Everyone else moves. Hunar tries to hook his arms underneath mine to stand me up, but I struggle against it in my laughing. I can't stop laughing even after I break free from his grasp. Instead, I trip on a thick rock and start rolling down the hill.

Landing on my side as my friends continue down the hill after me, my paintbrush falls innocently at my side, humming with power. Suddenly, my laughter stops, my eyes dry, and my insides turn to fire. I reach out and grab the paintbrush as if by instinct. It transforms into a staff that I clutch proudly as I whirl to face the approaching Arcana and my friends join me down the side of the hill. When I see the Arcana, I am filled with hysterical fury. I push myself up and the bottom of the staff settles into the ground. *They will pay for making this quest so much harder on us, as if our lives aren't already hard enough.* With all the energy I have, I lift my staff into the air.

Nothing happens. Only a soft shudder of power, weak and thin, attached like broken baby roots into the ground below, dissipating energy ahead of me like bats scurrying from light. *Whatever magic affected me in Kunlun must have taken more of a toll than I realized.* I think this in the instant before a bolt of energy hits me square in the chest from the approaching Arcana. The power knocks me back and down the rest of the hill, tumbling in a ball of sky blue tulle. The last thing I register is sharp pain when my head hits the side of a rock before my vision cuts to black.

# 28

**M**Y HEAD IS SPINNING and I'm in a room more luxurious than the first one I had at Malachite. There are high arched ceilings with crown molding inlaid with vines and flowers, a hardwood floor dominated by an extreme wooden four-poster bed, and matching armoire and side tables. This room looks straight out of the pages of a fairy tale. Every corner is gilded with accents of a subtle gold. Pearl drapes cascade down the windows, made of a fabric the same texture as the duvet I lay on.

But when I sit up on the bed, the fairy tale is ruined. My hands and ankles are bound. As I look around the gilded room, memories of the past day come trickling back: the Arcana ball, our escape to Kunlun, and finally *Auden*. I choke back a startled sort of noise and wiggle so I can try to sit all the way up. I know that she won't be here, but the urge to check remains. As I look around me, I also remember the very last encounter I had before I crashed to the ground behind my friends, the Arcana drawing in. I steal a breath through my nose and search for my paintbrush, but I don't sense it anywhere. Instead, I find that I'm still wearing my tattered dress, but a throw blanket conceals it. Wriggling like a caught fish, I manage to shed the blanket and press my bound feet to the ground beside the bed. I try to stand, but exhaustion weighs me down. I realize I must be in a room lining one of the corridors Zero and I walked past at the ball. *Are they watching me? Are there cameras in the corners of the room or a form of monitoring magic?* I search for a glimmer of magic on the walls around me, finding nothing save the early dawn rising through the curtains across from me. With a sinking in my stomach, I know then that today is the winter solstice. And as far as I can hope, if Reina escaped, we have only one key. One short of what we'll need to destroy any chance of Kek opening the Malachite box. I bite the inside of my cheek and wish I had contained myself better when we were ejected from Kunlun.

Even now, that same pain is just behind my eyes, heavy alongside the exhaustion that begs me to lie back down. *I wish my mom was here to guide me.* The thought causes an ache in my chest just as the door beside me creaks open.

"Knock, knock," a familiar voice calls cautiously.

I hold my breath as Zero walks into the room. He is holding a glass of water in one hand, my book in the other. The blue leather-bound volume seems small in his hands and must have fallen out of Hunar's bag when we were running. I muster my energy, hoping to finally stand. My power is there, no matter how tired and defeated I feel. *I could call it to me. Even without my staff, I could still use it.*

Zero quickly sets down the glass of water and takes a step back. The door hangs open between us and he makes a motion as if to say, *I come in peace.* I exhale but still eye him warily. He's wearing an outfit more casual than I've ever seen on him: a hoodie with the Arcana emblem slightly raised over matching black sweatpants. He could be any boy, from any school, in any place.

"How am I supposed to drink if my hands are tied?" I ask.

"I can help, if you'll let me," he says.

I frown and lift my arms begrudgingly, noticing now that the knot isn't so tight that I couldn't figure it out with my teeth and half an hour of effort. Zero walks toward me and sets the book down beside the glass of water, then tentatively reaches out and removes my bindings. I notice that he is careful not to touch me when he does. When my hands are free, I rub my wrists and find them raw.

He explains before I ask, "When we brought you here, you were convulsing. Whenever anyone touched your skin, it seemed to get worse. So, someone tied you with these ropes, which are spelled to make you too tired to move. It's only been a night and I've been here the whole time."

I frown and look over to the tall-backed chair beside the bed where his eyes flicked when he spoke. A crumpled blanket lies wrinkled over the armrest. *Did he stay at my bedside?* For a second my disdain melts, but just as quickly it toughens again when I realize the reason I'm here at all is because the Arcana kidnapped me.

"What do you want from me?" I ask.

"Your friends escaped the Arcana team who were assigned to check on the disturbance in the Kunlun Mountains. You were the only one we managed to intercept," he says vaguely, before kneeling on the ground at my feet.

I tense. "Your ankles." He looks up at me through a feathering of his dark hair where he kneels below me.

*Why is my mouth so dry?* I lift my ankles into the air and hold my breath while he unties my bindings, noticing a faint shimmer of magic over the ropes that I didn't see before.

"By 'intercept,' do you mean kidnap?"

Zero doesn't reply, just keeps untying until both my legs are free. Once they are, lightness returns to my body, so I spring up from the bed and walk toward the open door. I don't remember anything of the time I spent asleep, and I hardly feel rested, but Zero doesn't look as if he has any reason to lie. *I don't have any of the keys and he must already know it.*

"If you leave that way, the others might try and throw you in a cell again." He says it not as a threat, but as a matter of fact. I pause and fold my arms over my chest at the threshold of the room. Beyond this room is a wooden hallway framed with a banister, below which appears to be a common area full of couches, chairs, and desks.

"I have to get back to my friends," I say, turning back to face him. Zero is leaning against one of the four posters of the bed with his arms crossed over his chest in consideration.

"The only way out of here is through our portal room, which is heavily guarded. *Or . . .*" he trails off.

I frown, and with crossed arms, tap my finger against my elbow. "What?"

"I could get you out of here," he says, while outstretching his hand. I watch carefully as the black tattoo at his wrist flows downward into a familiar long black staff, clinking into the hardwood.

"In exchange for what?" I ask.

"Just an answer. Where did you get this?" He points at the blue book at my bedside. The one I almost left behind in my attempt to get away from him. I snap it up, folding it between my arms.

"You've seen it before, remember? You took my grandmother's map right from its pages," I say. Zero frowns a little. *Does he look remorseful? Am I being tricked?*

"I remember it looked powerful then. I assumed that was because of the map it held," he explains.

*Why do I get the sense he's not telling me the entire truth?* I look down at the book and notice a faint shimmer of energy. *Was that always there?*

"Why does it matter?" I ask.

"Because it's about the Unspoken gods, something we're not taught about here. And I am a curious man," he says.

I scoff. "If I tell you where I got it, you'll take me out of here?" I ask.

Zero nods soberly, his eyes never leaving mine. I furrow my brows. I wish I could take another step backward without placing myself in the hallway.

"Fine," I decide. "Hunar, my friend, gave it to me when we first met. That's it. I don't know where he got it from."

Zero's expression stills for a second. "Okay," he says.

"That's all?"

"If you want to leave, there's no point in me keeping you," he says as he starts to reach into his hoodie pocket, "but you should take this." He tosses something my way and I reach up reflexively, noticing the outline of my paintbrush as it arcs through the air. When the wood meets the palm of my hand, I let out a small

314 + GISELLE VRIESEN

breath—one I've been holding since I sensed its absence. *I was sure they'd have put this in the archives.*

"What do you really want from me?" I ask, suddenly aware of the strangeness of the situation—an Arcana giving back something they took.

"What do you mean?"

"I mean, you could have left me to die in that cathedral, you could have imprisoned me when I came to the ball, you could have stolen my artifact. And even now, instead of shoving me into a cell or something, you're here, having a conversation with me. Why?" I don't hide the accusation in my tone.

The slight smile that had been spreading across Zero's face stills. "Is that what you think of us?"

"It's what I think of you," I say easily, not necessarily intending to wound. When a slice of pain crosses his face, I wish I could take the words back.

"I—" he starts, but then stops. "I'll take you wherever you want to go." He exhales and reaches his arm out toward me.

"Fine, but for once, give me a straight answer. Why am I here?"

Zero doesn't say anything at all, just clenches his jaw and stares. Under the weight of those dark eyes, part of me falters, and another part of me realizes that while we've been talking, the room has gotten hotter and hotter. The neckline of my dress is damp with sweat. I reach over and pick up the glass of water, downing it in one go. I wish I could maintain my line of questioning, but my heart is beating too fast. There is a rush of energy rolling toward me with increasing strength, rising through the soles of my feet, the bare skin of my arms, through every pore of my skin. The energy intensifies when I look at Zero, so I avoid eyeing him. The feeling must have been building since I woke up, but my heaviness and exhaustion hid it until now.

Zero takes a tentative step forward. "Are you all right? How do you feel?"

I shake my head, intent on projecting power and intimidation. Instead, I cough a little and catch my blood in the elbow of my gown.

"I—" I shake my head to clear it, holding out a hand to keep Zero away. "I'm fine," I mutter, even as the energy rolls toward me stronger.

Suddenly, the room is full of emotion: the whisper of the cut-down trees that make up the wood of the floorboards and bedframe, the Arcana next door worried about their finals and the carnage at the ball, the people below and above us, the creatures in the surrounding area, the magic in the walls. But most of all, I feel Zero.

He is a wave of conflicting emotions, so much stronger than those of the other people in Arcana. *Is it because he's closer to me or because what he's feeling is more intense?* Even in the shock of this onslaught, there is no mistaking the energy rolling off him. On one hand, when he looks at me, I register a gentle care, the same urge I'd have to water a plant back to life. On the other hand, I notice wafts of desire. It's not a desire to have me like an object, but a desire to reach out, to be had by me and me by him—like universes imploding. It's a feeling mirrored in his eyes as he restrains himself only a few steps away. I wish I could say it was one-sided. My morals say it should be—but it isn't. I realize that as undeniable as his feelings are, so are mine. *I should hate him.*

*I thought we hated each other,* I think softly, realizing that the room is completely silent except for the sound of both of our breaths.

The same way I forgave Auden for spying on me all those years, a part of me yearns to forgive Zero for everything he's done, to absolve him of it completely. It's terrifying, to feel something so deeply for someone who hasn't earned it, who I should stay away from, and who I decided *many* times to hate. Pressing my lips together, I tear my eyes away from him and try to stare anywhere else—all while recognizing a connection between us as strong as a tangible rope—a thick thread I could pull until we were nose to nose. Then I step forward and finally look back into his eyes.

Zero's pupils dilate. "You're having an awakening."

I nod. My eyes are glossy and everything inside of me wants to reach up and touch the side of his face. *My feelings are heightened,* I realize distantly. My fingers strain at my sides. Looking at Zero where we now stand a foot apart reminds me of how I used to feel when I was a kid at the fall fair, looking at the candied apples we couldn't afford—hungry.

He's the one who reaches out first, putting a hand on my upper arm as if I am swaying, though I think it might have been for his benefit. As soon as he touches me, our pull becomes as undeniable as gravity. I reach up and brush my left hand along the side of his face. It's as smooth and warm as I imagined. Then, as time stills, he leans down and presses his lips against mine more gently than I expect. For a second everything is melting bliss. Then the ground opens beneath me and I am falling in a very different way.

**29**

**G**ONE IS THE interior of the opulent bedroom, gone is the boy who for a second became my whole world. I am somewhere else entirely. Overhead and around me rise the earthen walls of a cave, covered in familiar symbols glowing with a soft energy the color of light filtering through water. Each looks like a rendition of the marking on my hand. The light in the room is viridian and appears to be coming through those inscriptions. A watery scent enters my nostrils and I realize I am not alone here.

Across the pristine earthen floor covered in those same repetitive symbols is a raised mound of rectangular stone, smooth and gleaming white. Sitting on it are two women. I recognize the first to be Chang'e, from my first awakening. She has a broad smile and wears robes of pale rose and green. Her black hair falls simply around her face in two velvet curtains, and when she looks at me, I remember dreams from my childhood I thought I had forgotten. Beside her, on the other side of the slice of stone is—

"Mom?" I exclaim, rushing forward.

My mom is wearing a pair of loose jeans and a T-shirt. On her feet is the pair of leather shoes I tried to find what feels like a lifetime ago. Her arms are open to receive me when I barrel into them. Mom smells like the cave does: sweet and like fresh-fallen rain. My cheeks are wet before she speaks.

"Thea," she says.

"I missed you—oh my god. I thought I wouldn't see you again. I guess the Mother of the West didn't lie—are you okay?" I look up at her through hanging swirls of her curly black hair and feel like a child again.

Mom smiles and I realize how much I have missed her smile, the crinkle of her freckles along her cheeks, the tilt of her eyes, the warm hue of her dark skin.

"I love you," is all she says in response, and when she says it, I feel it. Like the resonance of a perfect chord, I feel her love fill me, so I sob and clutch her tighter. Mom lets me but continues speaking. "Thea, my love, this is a time for information, not tears."

"What—what information? I made a deal with Xiwangmu, she said I could see you again. Is this that?"

"This is a time to make a decision," Chang'e says. Her voice is like a still lake churning with life below the surface, and when I look over into her wide eyes, I find something familiar in their dark depths. I wipe my cheeks with the palm of my left hand and sniffle.

"What do you mean?" I ask.

"Thea, can you listen to me, can you try to be calm?" my mother asks.

I look up at her and nod mutely, allowing her tranquility to seep into me over the ringing in my ears.

"This awakening is the last visitation you will have from either of us, so we must make it count," my mom says.

I incline my head slowly. "I have to choose one of you, or else I can't have a connection with either," I remember, looking from my mother, who I cling to, and Chang'e, a mysterious goddess I feel connected to but don't really know. Of course, I know who to choose. My hands are knotted in her T-shirt for god's sake. So why aren't I declaring it, and why do I recognize that look in her eye?

"I'm not supposed to choose, am I?" I ask. Mom is giving me the same patient expression she gave me two months ago, when I held up two options for leather jackets I wanted to wear in November. It's the look that made me roll my eyes and pick my parka instead.

My mother smiles. "Unspoken is a hilarious term, don't you think? My name is Amara, and it always has been. The power of gods as old as I am can be tricky for modern Godspring to understand. They believe themselves, and the gods they are descended from, to be finite pools of energy to draw from in one specific way, pools of power that cannot be mixed. Our power is not quite so simple. If you think of it as water, you can imagine that mine is one carried through the life force of many different gods—like separate bodies of water connected through rain and rivers. Though other mother goddesses belong to their own people, there is a thread among us that I have existed in far beyond what you can imagine," she says.

"But you're not that way anymore," I say up at her, remembering all that I have learned. "Your mortal body is dead and the other parts, well, what about the other parts?"

"A god is made up of three parts. They go by different names and can be divided further, but at their center they are three: the head, the heart, and the spirit. The spirit exists eternally, and a very large piece of mine is inside the Malachite box. My head, my rational reasoning, existed on earth as a mortal body. While I was your mother, I forgot most of the reasons I chose to incarnate; I did my best—but I am sorry, Thea, I could have done better. Disconnected from my entire spirit, it was difficult to remember," she said.

I nod for her to continue, but Chang'e is the one to pick up the explanation.

"The final piece of a god is their heart," she says. "And that is something Amara has carried and gifted wisely."

"I don't understand." I look from one goddess to the other. "If I'm not supposed to choose one of you, what am I supposed to do? Is this a kind of test?" I ask.

"Not a test," my mom says. "A farewell. This is the last time we will meet—for a long time. I am sorry."

I shake my head. "But what about this part of you, the part that I'm talking to now—can't you come back with me as this?" I ask.

"This presence is only a reflection. A piece that Xiwangmu can connect you to, left over from Amara's celestial body. A fragment of what they couldn't trap inside that box," Chang'e says.

"Trap? Hathor said you volunteered to power the Malachite house," I say to my mom, who smooths down my hair, gazing at me like I am the sunrise and sunset all in one.

She shakes her head. "I was tricked, as some goddesses can be, so you've found out. Blinded by my own idealistic intentions for the world and for the other goddesses," she says. "They could not understand a power without end."

Chang'e stands up from where she sat on the marble and walks around to stand behind my mother. Her dress and energy are a halo of light behind Mom's dark hair, like they are meant to be side by side. Something strikes me as familiar in the scene, but I can't place where the feeling comes from.

"I will always be watching you. When you look up at the stars, my eyes will gaze back at you," Mom says, her cheeks as wet as mine.

My eyes widen as I look at the two women and realize that they both somehow remind me of the night sky: the stars and the moon set in it, dark and light and ever watchful, each of them a constellation.

It strikes me then that I don't think I will ever be afraid of the dark again, not when I know in darkness I can find their love shining down on me.

"So, what am I supposed to do?" I ask.

Chang'e reaches forward and puts a comforting hand on my upper back alongside my mother's arm.

"You have to finish what you started," Mom says.

"Recover the box and fulfill your role for Malachite," Chang'e continues.

"But don't you hate them for what they did to you, imprisoning your essence to fuel Malachite?" I ask.

"How could I hate a parent for wanting to keep their child safe?" my mom says, her eyes overflowing just as the ground begins to shake.

Chang'e squeezes my shoulder and straightens back up. "It's time," she says.

*Why does it always have to be so short? I have so much to tell her and endless questions.*

My mom holds me tighter for a second, like she doesn't want us to part again—and neither do I—I hold her tighter too.

"No," I say. "Don't leave me again."

"I love you," Mom says.

**WHEN MY EYES OPEN,** I am staring at the ceiling of the room in Arcana and Zero is bent over me with concern etched into his features. I look around wildly for my mother, for Chang'e, for the mysterious cavernous room. I find nothing but useless gold, lace, and Arcana finery.

"How do I get back?" I gasp, noticing that the energy that was swallowing me up before is trickling down, becoming no more than a whisper. *No, no, that can't be it. I'm still so lost! This can't be my final awakening.*

Then I lock eyes with Zero where we both crouch on the ground, his staff discarded at our feet, and I remember how we got so close in the first place. Then Zero moves to reassure me, and I flinch on instinct. When I do, he draws back, lips pursing.

"Are you okay?" he asks, leaning back on his palms while I sit up and lean into the bed behind me.

"Just take me out of here. Get me home, please," I add, softening my tone.

# 30

THE FLOWERS ON the entryway table are poinsettias now: blood red and velvet green, bushy but browning at the edges. Malachite is in a flurry of movement.

"Thea!" Teal spots me first as they pass behind Marta and Aiko on their way down the hall. They drop what they're holding, the restaurant-size bag of salt crashes into the oriental carpet in a spray of white. They have finally changed out of the clothes they were wearing when we left Malachite so many days ago. Their shorn light hair matches a strappy shirt layered over a long sky blue skirt.

"What's going on?" I ask as Teal wraps me in a one-armed hug. In the part of their skin that brushes over mine, a sense of flowery relief simmers over a much wider impending dread.

"We're getting ready for the key-destruction ceremony—Reina got a second one when she was trying to break you out," Marta explains as she attempts to return the dropped salt to the bag alongside a kneeling Aiko. "How *did* you get out?" Marta asks as

Teal lets go of me with a complicated expression across their face that I'm sure is unrelated to the dropped salt, or even my arrival.

I'm saved from having to answer Marta's question when Reina suddenly appears in the doorway of the kitchen. Her light hair is pulled away from her face, which is bright and shining, her clothes slightly askew, revealing the scar the Arcana gave her as a child.

"Thea, you're back," she breathes out.

I nod and look past her shoulder at Omari, who is carrying two handfuls of candles out the back door.

"You got the other key from Arcana?" I can't believe it. *We have two! We can follow through on what we planned; we can destroy one of the keys.* Finally, some good news.

Reina smiles gleefully. When she does, I notice she's uncharacteristically frazzled, like she's been awake for a full twenty-four hours. I realize she probably has been.

"I am so sorry I could not find you when I returned to Arcana, I barely escaped with this when I did." She holds up the second key, the medium-size one crafted with the face of a sea creature we got in Ginen. I gasp as it glints in the light of the foyer, thrust in the air over the plant that matches Reina's red lipstick and separates us.

"It's okay," I say, turning back to Teal's drawn expression. "Where's Tiana?" I finally ask. Their frown deepens, confirming my suspicion.

"She's this way." They begin to lead me toward the living room when Reina calls out.

"Remember, we need to hurry and complete the ritual before sunrise, before anyone has a chance to steal the key and use it to open the box!"

I nod over my shoulder; of course she's right. The Malachite box can be opened only on the winter solstice—today. But I find it hard to focus on that task when I haven't seen Tiana's face since it was pinched and drawn green, and even harder when I can sense Teal's dread.

I follow them across the entryway until Teal opens the double doors separating it from the living room. Everything is as I left it the last time I was here: the warm-toned furniture and crackling fire, the smell of citrus, but then I spot the small lump on the couch. Tucked under a pile of blankets with nothing but a strip of forehead peeking out and a trail of box braids is Tiana's sleeping face. My stomach hardens.

"Tiana?" I ask as I sink to my knees beside her. Teal closes the door behind us and the noise of people moving through the house dims.

"She's been getting worse since we got out of Kunlun. I would have gone with Reina to Arcana last night to search for you and the keys, but I couldn't risk leaving her for too long," they explain.

Tiana's forehead is damp, cold to the touch, and greener than it was before. I move the blanket slightly down to find a bandage over the wound at her shoulder, already leaking through at the edges in a shade of yellow so vivid it could only mean the worst.

"What do we do?" My voice shakes when I speak. Tiana's skin gives off only a pale fraction of her usual energy. She's fading fast.

Teal shakes their head. "Marta has tried everything she can think of," they say.

I draw in a slow breath as my gaze skates over Tiana's closed eyes, which move below her eyelids as if she's caught in a chase. Her always pristine braids are matted down against her scalp, and out of her barely parted lips comes the smell of potent medicines and sickness while she pants for air.

Just then, the door we came through bursts open. I turn to find Hunar standing with wide eyes, searching over the room until they lock on mine.

"How did you get out?" he asks, relieved and lowering himself to sit beside me on the ground near Tiana.

I shake my head. "It doesn't matter, I'm here now."

"Reina knew you would get out—but it was hard to believe," Hunar says.

I press my eyes together and cough loudly into the sleeve of my shirt. "How did Reina know?" I ask.

"I don't know," Hunar says softly now, realizing he's intruded on a somber moment. He looks at Tiana out of the corner of his eye, as though he has a hard time seeing death in slow motion. I remind myself that he has recently lost Ian.

"Can you do anything?" Hunar asks me suddenly.

My eyebrows raise, so he goes on.

"Your energy, it's changed. It looks like you had your third awakening. Now you'll have full access to the god you chose to be your ancestor, and if you chose your mother, a god of mother-hood, you've chosen a god of life as well," he says.

Teal brightens from where they stand behind the couch.

It didn't even occur to me. Without giving it any more thought, I reach out and press my hand against the skin of Tiana's neck. I swallow, my throat too dry to respond. I remember how vibrant her energy used to be. In the past, Tiana's fire and inexhaustible focus were as bright and distinct as her orange leather coat; now everything is a pallid shade of watered-down maroon. I blink past my fear of making a mistake. I need to get out of my own way to see what I'm capable of doing.

At first, Tiana's emotions are faint, simple, and far away. But the longer I sit with her, the less simple they seem. Each emotion is linked to an experience and a quality of her spirit. With my eyes closed, I sense that her cardamom-sweet strength is a result of hardship and pain but also determination for things to be better. I keep sorting through Tiana until I find that at the very core of her is a beacon of hope so strong it lights away most of her fears: strong enough that it can keep her going. It's a hope innate to her but brightened by the proof of magic's existence, her experiences at Malachite, her relationship with Teal and me—and this quest. Connecting with her like this, it doesn't feel the same as it did before. Something has changed since I talked to my mother. Something I don't completely understand yet.

"She wants to live," I mutter into the stillness of the living room, then reach back with one hand to slide out my paintbrush from the folds of my dress. Since my third awakening, when I touch it, the brush feels alive in a way I haven't experienced. It feels ready to be wielded. Holding the paintbrush in one hand, I instinctively run the tip of it over Tiana's face as my eyes flutter open. When I do, I see that wherever the tip of my brush lands, the green tinge to her skin dissipates. In the back of my head, I sense that Tiana is lost in some deep dream, a dream close to death. I pull at the energy of her hope and draw it to the surface of her consciousness with the tip of my paintbrush. I paint over her skin, and as I do, I can feel myself pulling her out of a dream and into the waking world—back to us. I keep moving the brush over her face, her neck, her shoulders, again and again until the green soaks away and the gauze over her wound fills with the poison fluid escaping from her body. When there is nothing more to do, I hold my breath, and Tiana's eyes open.

"Thea?" she says, then looks up to find Teal. With my hand still resting on her collarbone, I feel what she does for Teal. When she looks at them, Tiana is as hopeful as someone seeing light for the first time.

"Hey," Teal says gently, leaning over the lip of the couch to stare down into Tiana's eyes.

I am overcome with the awareness that I should not be in this room anymore, so I disentangle myself from Tiana and her blankets, still clutching my hot-to-the-touch paintbrush.

Hunar and I stand to give them some space just as Tiana lifts herself to sit. She pulls the full bandage off her shoulder, revealing an almost-healed wound that is no longer bleeding. I exhale in relief, then notice her watering eyes. Before Hunar and I reach the threshold of the living room, I catch a glimpse of Teal wiping one of her tears away. When they do, their fingertip shines with a gold like the glitter of the tear La Sirène took before it sinks into the skin of their finger. Hunar closes the door between us and them. The last image I have of my friends is of the two of them gazing at each other as if they were the only people in the world.

"You did it," Hunar says, while I stare at the closed wooden door.

I exhale and turn to face him. "I'm so glad," I say, half to him and half to myself. I saved Tiana. *I should have saved Auden.* The thought intrudes and I frown.

"Did you get that while you were escaping Arcana?" Hunar asks, gesturing to my right palm. When I look down, I notice the marking is no longer a dark brown, but a watery, agitated red. I open my palm wide in the quiet hallway and find that the two curves are leaking blood. I inhale through my teeth. "It hurts."

This pain runs deeper than the skin; it reaches all the way to the bone. Hunar watches me with concern as I shake my wrist. As he does, I realize what everyone must think: that I violently fought my way out of Arcana. My cheeks heat as I recall that my escape was the exact opposite of a fight.

"Here." Hunar hands me a crumpled napkin from his pocket and I take it gladly without meeting his gaze.

"Thanks."

After our conversation in Kunlun, I have trouble meeting Hunar's eyes. There was something so intimate about the moments we spent together in the cherry blossom grove. If he had asked me any question, I would have answered honestly. I don't usually feel that open with people. The remnants of the exchange leave a sour-sweet taste in my mouth.

"We should get going," I say, noticing Omari and Emilio skirting down the hallway, each holding a beeswax candle that towers as tall as them. "It's going to start soon."

THE MIRRORED TRAINING ROOM looks smaller with everyone stuffed into it. Shoulder to shoulder I stand with all eleven Godspring in Malachite. Tiana and Teal are on my left, leaning into each other, and Hunar is on my right. *I thought Reina said we needed twelve.*

"At this very moment, an old god named Kek and the Arcana are probably scoping out a way into Malachite to take the keys and use them to open this box," Reina says, gesturing down to the shining box at her feet. Hunar told me that Ani found it hiding under her bed when we were in Ginen. The stone's green gleams in the dim candlelit room.

The idea of my mother's essence being used to power this house pales in comparison to the idea of her murderer using it for whatever he is planning. The threat is as heavy as the mood.

Around us, the room is bedecked for a ceremony, with salt thinly dusting the ground, candles lining the walls, and all the mirrors covered in long draping fabric. In the middle of the floor is a design made of wood, small glittering stones, and something red and thick, like wax but softer, holding the odd structure together. The air smells of incense and sweat. I squirm nervously until little Ani smiles at me from across the circle. Then I force myself to stay still.

"I know we don't all agree with destroying the keys, but this is our final option," Reina says. Her blonde hair now hangs around her ears like a cloak. "But we must protect the box from all who hope to open it—and our enemies are only moments away. The spells cast on the front door won't last forever. The Arcana will get in. They most likely only let Thea go to figure out where we are," she says pointedly. My cheeks heat, and everyone in the room turns their attention on me. Remembering the animosity that simmered when I first got here makes me fold my arms over my chest.

"But why destroy a key we're supposed to protect?" Marta speaks up. "Why not hide it?"

"For someone to just find it again in a year?" Reina shakes her head. "No, this must end now," she declares. "We have lost too much," she says meaningfully, until Marta lowers her chin into her chest. "No more hiding, no more fear. Today we take control of our destiny, we take our power back once and for all!"

The room simmers with the fire Reina's sparked. Everyone is ready for what comes next. I am sweating through my shirt.

"To destroy a key, we'll need to pool all of our power together," she says quickly, interrupting the cheer. "We must all remain focused while we work."

The Malachites quiet down completely.

Reina holds both keys in the palm of her left hand as she walks into the middle of the circle. Her bare feet make neat prints in the spray of salt. As she does, I eye the key we got from Kunlun while biting the inside of my cheek. *That's the key that meant us losing Auden and her losing any chance at a semi-normal future.* Swallowing, I tear my eyes away and try to focus like Reina said.

"Aside from saying the spell, I'll need an anchor for it to work, someone who'll serve as a channel for all our energy and the power of the keys to flow through." She pauses, her right hand hanging off her hip. "I'll be honest: being the anchor is dangerous, potentially fatal." She raises her light eyebrows.

The knot in my stomach cramps tighter, and instinctively, I take a step forward before anyone else can. My eyes are locked on Reina's. *It has to be me. Auden can't have given so much for someone other than me to give even more. If I hadn't stolen the map and left with my friends in the first place, I wouldn't have lost the second key. If not for me, the Arcana would never have had the map with a path through Jotunheim, and they wouldn't have figured out the keys were missing.*

"I'll do it," I say, raising my hand up. *This is my mess to fix.*

Reina smiles and the rest of the room remains quiet, though I can feel the weight of my friends' gazes on my back. I ignore all of them.

"What do I do?"

Reina smiles compassionately. "You kneel, and everyone else join hands," she instructs. No one makes a noise while they do as they are told. Once I break away from the outside of the circle, I can more fully appreciate the energy flowing in this room, pulsing from the wooden structure beside Reina, the Malachite box ahead of her, and the keys in her hand. It feels a little like standing in the eye of a hurricane; the power of all the Malachites swirling around me overhead. I can hear my heartbeat louder than anything else, air vacuums over my ears.

I stand opposite Reina now and she looks down at me for a single moment before beginning. Barely taking a breath in, words start to pour out of her mouth in a language I don't understand. I gasp as the energy in the room folds over itself and the power of the Malachites rises overhead to create a swirl of power with no one color or shape, detaching from their bodies into one bright cloud. Reina sinks down ahead of me and motions for me to follow her onto the ground. I mirror her position as she takes it. We kneel with both hands lying palms up upon our knees.

In each of her hands is a key. They glow bright, even next to her pale palms. The wood-and-gem structure she built hums a little louder beside us like a vacuum. I inhale slowly when I realize that between the two of us, the keys in her hands, and the box between us, a sort of circuit starts to build. A rising tension of energy tightens behind my skin.

WHY WE PLAY WITH FIRE  ✦  333

Reina moves her hand a little, drawing my gaze back up into hers. As I look into her eyes, her energy reaches toward me. I expect to feel the same way I always do when I connect to her internal quiet, but frown because now when I stare into her light eyes, I don't find it comforting at all—it reminds me of a gaping endless void. An empty space inside of her so vast it reminds me of falling forever. I try to jerk my head back, but find my body is stuck in place with my eyes staring into hers. My energy is flowing out of me like water pouring into a limitless vessel and I am like a bug caught in a spider's web. *Something is wrong.*

The words continue out of her mouth like a waterfall, spreading ripples of power into the air around us, and using my peripheral view I take in the Malachites' energy ringing us. I realize, that as the power pulls out of them to collect in the air above our heads like a storm cloud, the little lights inside of each Malachite dim with every passing second. My eyes widen in alarm to see Omari buckle down to his knees first, followed by Ani. I focus again on Reina as the *wrong* feeling continues to spread out over my body and she starts to move, still speaking in seamless rhythm.

Before my eyes, I watch Reina set down the two keys on the lid of the Malachite box. She reaches forward to take one of my hands in hers. I try to pull away from her, but my arm won't budge. It's like when the Mother of the West held me in place and stole my voice—I am stone-still. *What is happening?* Reina's eyes flutter shut, and hot pain shoots up my right arm, like someone is slicing it open. As the pain races through me, I let myself see something I think I was too desperate, too needy, too naïve to see. Looking into Reina's energy further than the usual surface-level calm and

334 ✦ GISELLE VRIESEN

emptiness, I find something much worse. Inside the woman ahead of me is a dissonance that grates the base of my neck and makes my already wide eyes water. Inside of her body, her spirit, her soul, are two pieces of energy that refuse to mix; like oil and water they repel each other, creating discord. *Each time they collide, they eat up at the space inside of Reina where a soul should be.* I realize with an internal gasp what I'm looking at. *Reina never chose one of her god ancestors over the other,* and unlike me, that wasn't an option for her. *Reina has gone mad.* I can hardly believe it, even as the other Malachites fall to the ground in heaps of powerless flesh. As Reina's fingers press into the skin of my hand, the energy accumulated over our heads starts to pour down into me.

Just as when I first accessed my own power, this is overwhelming, but contrastingly, this power doesn't feel good at all. So much energy, so many different flavors of fear and pain—it's nearly unbearable. I want to scream; I *have* to scream—but my body won't move, and my mouth won't open. Reina doesn't react to what's happening around us, or in me, she just pushes her hands past the now open skin of my palm, which she's cut open with the tip of a previously concealed long blade.

I don't have to look to know that I am bleeding. I can feel the warmth soaking through the fabric of my dress, leaking into the ridge between my thighs. What I don't expect is for the pain to change the way it does. *It's like she's pulling something out.* I don't have to wonder what for long, because a moment later, Reina raises her hand up, triumphant. Clasped between her thumb and index finger is a familiar object I am aghast to see: a gleaming key with a head like two pieces of metal knit together. A scream tears out of me, disrupting my paralysis and filling the muffled room. Reina doesn't react to me, and my body doesn't move as quickly as I want while I scramble backward, streaking through the salt. Everyone is on the ground now; across from me, Reina is kneeling with the widest grin I've ever seen on her face. My already-sunken heart hits absolute rock bottom when I realize the truth.

"It's you," I pant, not looking away from where Reina still kneels, holding in her hands all three of the keys, with the Malachite box on the ground ahead of her. I still feel as connected to her and them as I did before, in the circuit of energy, only now I feel as if I'm completely draining through it, flowing into Reina and the objects she holds. I want to be able to rush her, but it's taking everything I have in me to keep my head upright. "You're the reason the keys ejected themselves from the house," I say.

Reina looks up at me with her true face for the first time; her usually wide brow is pinched, her red lips are smudged and pursed in a scowl, and her light eyes are stormy. "You feel it, don't you?" she whispers.

"What?"

"I've relieved you," she says with a jut of her chin. "But don't worry, I'm leaving. This isn't where I want to do it," she says.

I look around at the room full of fallen Malachites. They're breathing, barely, and my own head pounds with the worst buzzing I've ever experienced, yet it somehow rings familiar. My eyes land on the structure in the room between us and I realize, for the first time, it doesn't look like Reina *just* built it. The wood is old and the red wax holding it together is faded and cracked in some places. I stare from it back to her, about to ask what it is, when my breath stills in my chest, registering what she just said. With a dry mouth, I look from her pale fingertips stained red with my blood to my own palm, and find that my marking is gone.

When I look up, Reina is standing.

"What have you done?" I ask. *I'm going to be sick.*

"What I was *born* to do," Reina says with a smirk. In her right hand where she holds the three keys is *my* marking—dark, and vivid, and shining, etched into her skin. Reina frowns a little when my expression changes. She continues her incomprehensible chant and I am wracked again with pain, locked in place. I watch helplessly as the energy vibrating through me siphons toward her and her task.

The air smells of sulfur, old nails, and wet animals, and then there is a bright light emanating between Reina's fingers from my marking. When the light fades, I am left with ringing ears and lying almost completely on my back. I turn over to watch Reina open her hand again to reveal a single key, shining and pointed where three used to sit. The back of my throat tastes of metal.

"Opening the Malachite box is only possible with the help of an Unspoken god, so thank you, Thea, for being *so* helpful," she says. "I have been waiting a lifetime for a marking like this to walk through that door." She's practically salivating as she looks at the newly formed single key in her hand. Overhead, the power begins to dissipate. The air returns to normal slowly, but every time I try to move and stand up, my body refuses to obey—not because of her magic holding me in place, but from complete exhaustion.

"What are you waiting for," I say to Reina who is standing there, gazing down at the Malachite box almost lovingly, stroking its surface with the combined key, making a loud scraping noise. Every time the two touch, the vibration of their power rings in my teeth.

"Oh, I won't complete the ritual here," she murmurs.

"Where then?" I try to reach toward her energy again, hoping that if I can keep her talking, I'll be able to figure out a way to stand back up.

"Nice try," Reina sneers, nudging aside Ness's limp leg in her attempt to leave the room. The salt around us is slightly charred after she created the single key, the air smells of it.

"Reina!" I shout hoarsely as she begins walking away. "We need the box to power the house. Please don't do this; whatever you think you'll get from opening it, I promise it won't be worth it," I say, as spots of black dance over my half-lidded eyes.

Reina smiles at me from the doorway. It's the same smile she gave me the day we first met. The one that, even if I didn't admit it at the time, made me feel like I could really belong here.

"Thea, I don't care. This house is a prison. The world I'm going to make is one where we don't need walls to protect us. It will be as it used to be—as it *should* be."

I want to try to keep her talking, but even as I start to sit up, I fall backward onto the ground.

"Why?" I ask, as darkness floods my eyesight. Reina, who is already halfway out of the room, surprisingly replies.

"We deserve better, Thea. I meant it when I said that before. I know you want better too," she says gently.

For a second I believe her as my vision fails further, but then I spot Ani's crumpled face across the ground from me, and see only a slight shimmer of her light, a light that I now recognize as being wrapped around that single key in Reina's hand along with everyone else's power.

*How long has Reina been planning this? How long has she been planning to betray all of us?* I don't see when Reina leaves, all I know is that I *can't* fall asleep. *I have to move.* Crawling with my elbows, using the salt-covered ground as leverage, I manage to make it to the edge of the wooden structure still standing in the middle of the room. With the last dredge of energy I have, I trust the only instinct I have, which is telling me to break it. So, I do. In a single push, I topple it. I think I hear it crash, but my own eyes are shut when it does.

As I drift in and out of consciousness, I watch a few things happen over the course of what I distantly assume must be minutes: I am sunken in darkness, then there is a pair of familiar concerned eyes staring down at me, hands on my shoulders, a swaying ceiling as I am carried away.

"Don't worry, you're going to be fine," Zero says.

**31**

**M**Y DREAM IS A STILL IMAGE. In it, I see a picture of myself, my mother, and my grandmother all in a line one above the other, like we're all different-size versions of each other. The image and the sight of my family comforts me, until I wake up with my head pounding and I remember what Reina did.

When I recall the pain of her cutting into my palm, I gasp and jerk up from the soft surface I had been lying on. The warm tones of the living room rise around me, and a stifling heat covers my whole body. Unlike the last time I was in here, and Tiana was lying on this very couch nearly dead, the room is completely full. From the hearth to my right, to the bookshelf-lined wall to my left, every soft surface is covered in the fallen forms of the Malachites Reina betrayed. But standing up ahead of me, in the space behind the second-largest couch in the room upon which Omari is laying, are Teal, Tiana, and Hunar. The three of them lean against one another while facing another group of familiar faces. I swallow down my surprise when I notice Zero, Basil,

Stone, and Ophelia taking up the entryway door beyond my friends. Seeing them in here feels about as wrong as everything else that's happened today.

"Thea," Hunar says when he notices I'm awake.

"Are you all right?" Teal asks.

I look down over my body to find that my aching palm is wrapped in a soft white bandage. My legs burn with effort as I pull them off the couch and onto the plush carpet below.

"I'm fine," I say, unsure if that's true. Hunar comes to my side and helps me stand, which I can barely accomplish.

"What happened?" I ask as I walk with Hunar to stand between him and Teal, looking back over at the room. Ness is on the settee beside Omari's feet. Emilio and Ani are each in reclining chairs, and the fainting couch at the back of the room is covered in medical supplies. Marta is propped up on a stuffed chair beside the fire. My blood boils at the idea that Reina could have looked at all the faces in this room and planned for days—if not weeks, or years—to betray them like this.

"We woke up a few minutes ago. Good job, by the way, on destroying Reina's spell," Teal says gently.

"And now we're deciding who is going to track down Reina—who, it turns out, was working with *them*." Tiana spits toward the Arcana.

I frown and finally allow myself to look at Zero, whose gaze I have been avoiding since I woke up. He looks like his normal self, unruffled. He meets my eyes evenly.

There's no hint of guilt in his voice as he explains, for my benefit, "Reina was supposed to bring us the Malachite box and the keys once they had been retrieved. In exchange, she was going to have her pick from her ancestor's artifacts," he says. "As a sign of good faith, we gave her the Ginen key."

My stomach cramps like he's punched me in the stomach. "You *knew* what she was going to do this whole time, and you didn't say anything?"

Zero clenches his jaw but doesn't say anything.

Ophelia speaks for him. "We weren't obligated to tell anyone about our deal, but when Reina didn't show up at the rendezvous point a few hours ago, we decided to come here."

"You knew where the door was?" Teal asks. "How?"

Now Zero is the one not meeting my eyes. *He brought them here. Of course, he did. I could kill him.*

Tiana taps her fingers against the side of her arm and a part of me is glad, at the very least, to see that she's looking much better.

"Fine. You know no more than we do. Get out," she declares. When no one moves, she repeats herself, "Did. You. Hear. Me? I said, get out."

"Look, we understand that you're upset, but right now we're on the same side," Basil answers quietly, tucking an errant strand of hair behind his ear. "We don't want to open the box. It was never about opening it—this has *all* been about protecting it. Reina, though, she *will* open it if she hasn't already. We're wasting time not going after her. And we would probably have better chances defeating her together." Basil pauses. "It's our fault for giving her the Ginen key, let us help."

I want to shove Zero out of Malachite with my own two hands, both for leading the Arcana to our doorstep, and for knowing about Reina's betrayal and keeping it from me.

*What did you expect?* I ball my hands into fists behind my back and feel the wound on my palm sting. *He has always shown you who he is.* I step forward with my jaw clenched.

"He's right," I say.

Tiana whips over to face me. We haven't had a chance to speak since she woke up—there's so much I want to ask her, like if her holding Teal's hand right now is to hold herself up or if there's finally something more between them.

"Thea." Tiana shakes her head. The last time she was this furious she turned into a lion. The nails on her right hand are beginning to lengthen.

I force myself not to stand down.

"Working with the Arcana is insane. It's like playing with fire and expecting not to get burned," Tiana says. In such close quarters she doesn't have to raise her voice for everyone to hear her, but she does anyway.

It's cold in the middle of the living room where an invisible line divides the Arcana and the Malachites—right where I stand.

"When Reina was stealing the keys, she used my marking to combine them into one. She said that she wants to 'remake the world.' We don't have time to argue." I say this with Tiana in mind but trail my eyes over everyone. "Reina is going to open that box. And there's something you all should know. She never chose a god ancestor. She's—gone."

Teal swallows and Hunar shakes his head.

"How did we not notice?" Marta asks as she sits up from where she had been lying.

"She's been here longer than any of us. From the moment I got here she said she'd had all of her awakenings." Hunar shakes his head in confusion.

Tiana makes a frustrated noise but stays where she is, looking at me instead of the Arcana over my shoulder. "We don't need them," Tiana insists through gritted teeth.

I shake my head. "Actually, we do." I sound much braver than I feel. "They can get us to her."

Now, I look over my shoulder at Zero until he nods once and the staff in his hand seems to shine a little darker. And as much as I don't want to, I end up staring a few seconds too long at him.

"Do you know where she is?" Stone asks, stepping slightly out from where he was tucked behind Ophelia.

"I do," I say, knowing with complete certainty that I'm not lying.

I have always known where this would end.


THE WALMART PLAZA near my old house is empty at this hour of night. The only cars in the airplane hangar–size parking lot look either abandoned or slept in. On the edges of the smooth black cement rolls out the forested backs of residential yards. Beyond them is the city of Duncan. If it weren't for the large pile of cement loaded up on the ground, and the hole in the earth beside it, I might have second-guessed my assumption based on how normal everything else looks. But it is there, a set of stairs descending into earth so black it dares you to be afraid of the dark. *How much of this did Nana know about? Did she show me this place, knowing it would all lead me here?*

"How did you know it would be here?" Tiana asks over my shoulder.

The Malachites who were strong enough to come mirror almost the same group who went to Kunlun: Tiana, Teal, myself, Hunar, and Marta, with the addition of Ness. Behind us stand the Arcana: Zero, Ophelia, Basil, and Stone.

Staring down at the opening in the ground sends a shiver up my spine. The opening is the shape of an oblong raindrop with curved folded edges of earth and cement on each side. The energy that comes off it is unlike anything I've experienced. Looking down into it, I distantly wonder if our group is going to be enough.

"My grandmother showed me," I reply.

"What is it?" Ophelia asks. Before we left, she hardly said anything at all, deferring to what the others in her group decided with pursed lips. I trust her as far as I can throw her.

"It's a cave, obviously," I say walking forward, annoyed that we need the Arcana's help at all. *I have to be the first one in. I brought everyone here.*

I know Reina is in there the same way I know she knew my mother and grandmother were dead from the moment she met me. And I know I should be feeling only pure rage, but for some reason, I falter at the top of the stairs. In my single moment of apprehension, I recognize that overhead stars glitter down on me. I remember what my mother said to me when I had my third awakening, that as long as the stars are shining, she would be watching over me. A wave of warmth passes over my heart. The small but powerful comfort gives me what I need to descend the stairs, into the dark. As my sneakers press over worn earth, I let my paintbrush lengthen into a staff below my right hand, from which I tore my Band-Aid off only a few minutes ago. I want to feel everything.

"Everyone, stay behind me," Hunar says.

I think I hear Zero make an indignant noise, but I don't look over my shoulder at either of them to check.

The fluorescent lights of the Walmart behind us wink away as we walk down the seemingly endless flight of stairs. In the silence of our downward climb, I let my mind rest on details Reina never filled in. *Why is she the oldest one at Malachite, as young as she is? Why is she the only one with the key that controls the front door? Why does she seem to know so much more than anyone else—and what else was she lying about?*

The air suddenly strains heavier with moisture. Every breath I take in is so heavy with water it practically slides down my throat. On the West Coast, everything is always damp, but this is on another level. I peel my shirt away from my chest, which sticks tighter the farther we descend. Just then, the stairs finally end and even out into a wide expanse of earthen cave. My eyes adjust to the darkness quickly thanks to a dim green light pooling out from between motes of earth on the walls. Illuminated ahead of us is one long tunnel that presses overhead at odd angles, dipping and rising and flattening. Even though I can feel my friends and the Arcana fill up the space behind me, for a second, when I look out into the hallway ahead, I feel completely alone.

"Hey." Tiana puts a hand on my elbow gently, careful not to meet my skin. I look over at her.

"Do you hear that?" I whisper.

From the distance comes a scraping sound like metal on stone that disturbs the somber peace of the mysterious and energetically charged cave. We begin toward the noise, having no alternative. The Arcana hold their artifacts out ahead of them, and the Malachites' magic is alive in the air beside them. With every step I take, a sensation of being covered up and waterlogged grows stronger.

I reach out and press a hand to the wall of the cave. A sigh escapes my mouth when I move some of the dirt to the side and find small symbols covering the walls—well, just one symbol repeated over and over again. It is the marking I've been carrying on the palm of my hand since it was burned there. Some of these markings are identical to it, others are longer, shorter, wider, or curvier. The second the dirt is pushed off the wall, a tingle runs down the back of my spine, and the green light of the cave grows brighter. As we walk, I continue to push the dirt covering the drawings away and the light they shine hums brighter and brighter. I stop only when the hallway ends, opening into a larger space through a passageway wide enough for only one person to enter through at a time.

"What is this?" Teal asks, looking from the walls to my trailing hand, and finally to the scene beyond the door.

In the midsize room, the walls and its markings are uncovered and glow a bright chartreuse. On the far end of the room is a large piece of stone covered in thick moss, matching the lighting of the room.

*I have been here before. I remember it from my third awakening.*

This is the place where I spoke with Mom and Chang'e, except now neither of them is here. Instead, Reina's small body takes up the space at the foot of the stone slab. She is hunched over the ground with a thin gleaming key in her right hand, poking down into the earth below, creating that awful scraping sound. Reina doesn't seem to notice us with how preoccupied she is with her work.

*What is she doing?* I peer closer and find that she is using the edge of the powerful key in her grasp to carve lines into my mother's symbol. My body tenses when I notice that with each symbol on the ground she disfigured, the green light they emit fades before blinking out completely.

"There's a barrier over the door," Zero says from behind me.

I see what he means as we all pause at the threshold of the cavernous room. The barrier shimmers red and green-silver and stretches like cling wrap over the opening between us and Reina.

"We shouldn't touch it," I say, after noticing a sort of glint to its shine, a deadly spike in the air around it. *Reina put it here.* I know this the same way I know that what she's doing to the ground is changing the chemistry of this entire space.

"What are you doing?" I call into the small chamber. The Malachite box is set atop the moss-covered stone, still unopened. I breathe a sigh of relief.

"There is an old story my mother used to tell me." Reina smiles without looking at us as she responds across the small room. *Of course she knew we were here.* Reina moves from kneeling to sitting with crossed legs on the ground she's dimmed to darkness.

"A story about a little rabbit who jumped so high it touched God's sandal. In response, God killed it because rabbits are not allowed in heaven—or something like that, more Catholic though," she explains with a wave of her wrist. The key makes a trail of light through the air like a sparkler.

Zero moves to stand beside me and stares through the barrier at her with a vivid gaze. I can practically hear him wonder if it is as deadly as it seems.

"The tenacity of small beings, huh?" Reina asks, finally looking at all of us standing shoulder to shoulder ahead of her. She smiles like we're paparazzi. Wiping a lock of blonde hair behind her ear, something shines silver at her wrist. "I will say, I actually *am* glad you are all here to witness me . . ." She trails off a little bit. The stolen marking on her hand flashes momentarily while she shifts. *It doesn't look right.* On her, the marking is a smudge leaking into her bloodstream, sending dark red lines up her arm.

"Reina, whatever this is, let us help you," I say, retracting my staff into a paintbrush and stowing it away. *There's nothing I can do if there's a barrier between us.*

"I don't *need* help," Reina says as she rises to stand. I notice her feet are bare and her white pants are still stained with flecks of my blood from earlier this evening. She walks around the side of the raised slab of stone, and I finally realize why the dimensions of the stone seem so familiar. It's the size of a coffin. My stomach sinks.

"You recognize it?" Reina asks, leaning forward to place her elbows on the coffin.

"Who's in there?" I ask, now tense.

"We all understand that a god is made up of three parts, yes?" she asks over my shoulder, as if she were giving a lesson, as if we were all back in the library at home. "The same is true for an Unspoken, for your mother, Thea. There is the celestial body." She gestures to the Malachite box. "Unusual to find one on earth outside of boxes like this." Then, Reina dances away from the box with a smile on her face. "Next is the physical body." She looks down at the casket with too-wide eyes, digging her nails into the moss. "And although it is a mortal thing in many ways, the physical body of a deity cannot decompose as quickly as a human one would. Often, it returns to the nexus of the god's power on earth for the possibility of resurrection," she says.

My heart stops. "You want to bring her back to life?" I ask, unable to tear my eyes away from my mother's alleged grave.

"I want to bring *the world* back to life. And the last ingredient is right here," she says, holding up her palm. "The symbol of the goddess, a piece of her inner spirit—the *final* piece."

I shake my head while she shakes her wrist and a bracelet finally becomes visible. It's the one I "lost" when I got to Malachite. I can see a slight shimmer of power over it, similar to the energy of the marking, but less vivid. *She took that too.*

"You can't do this, Reina, come on," Tiana pleads.

"This world needs remaking," Reina replies with a bite.

*She's been planning all of this from the beginning.* The anger I had been toggling with a few minutes ago comes back, hardening my resolve.

I close my eyes and, with an instinctive breath, follow the energy of the cave around us. I finally understand why it feels so familiar. It's my mom. Her energy spreads out like veins through the walls. I flinch when Reina gets back to work, digging her key into the ground trying to gouge out another one of my mother's symbols. I keep looking until I find it: the pulse of the barrier separating us.

*What do I do with it?* In so many situations like this, I've hesitated, or run. But right now there's no space for either of those options. Without giving it any more thought, I shove my body into the barrier between us, braced to absorb the impact, and hoping that I might distract Reina enough for it to drop completely. Something different happens though.

When I step through the barrier she made with my mother's power—my power—the energy of the cave grows stronger, vibrating through my blood. It's like stepping into a warm bath. Immediately, everything smells like my mother. As I come to stand inside the room Reina intended to lock herself in, we both realize her mistake was trying to use any of this against me. It *is* me. The barrier falls away.

There is a pause when Reina stares at me; her red-painted lips hang open. Then, at once, the Arcana and Malachites flood into the room. Even tired, we are formidable.

Hunar reaches out a hand and Reina's arm starts to bleed as it comes apart, her eyes go red with blood, and then Teal blinds her with light. Zero is behind her in a flash of lightning ready to immobilize her, and for a second, I am triumphant. But then Reina clutches her hand around the key and shouts. The next moment, there is a blast of light and energy so intense it fills the room with the smell of char. The ends of my hair sizzle and we're all thrown backward. The wind is knocked out of me as I strike the wall. Little balls of light start dancing ahead of my eyes immediately.

"That was cute, seriously, it was," Reina says, tossing the key from one hand to the other while we all groan, pressed against the edges of the room. She kneels again to gouge the last of the lights on the ground nearest her while I try to sit up, but it's too late. The moment Reina plunges that key into the final symbol on the floor still lit with green, the energy seeping out of the walls turns red. Suddenly, I don't feel at home anymore.

In a heartbeat, the air tightens, becoming freezing cold and dry as ice. I can feel Reina taking something from me through the very air of the room we are standing in, through the earth, through this red light—just the same as when she stole my marking. The same is true for my friends. Out of them pours the energy that makes up who they are, as if Reina were slurping their inner candles through a straw. Tiana's eyes are the first to flutter shut.

I defiantly grip my staff and press it into the earth, searching for connection to that source of energy I felt when I broke the barrier. I can't afford to gasp in relief the way I want to when I finally connect to it. When the exhaustion Reina brought on me lifts, I'm able to focus just enough on *her* inner light: a mess of red and blue, green, purples—some hers and some stolen from the Malachites. Grinding my teeth, I try to find the part of it that is *her*, and with all the strength I can muster, I shove all the energy I hold in a rush toward her.

Reina's smile slips as does her footing when she's knocked back several feet. Digging her right hand into the wall beside her, she recovers from the hit, beginning to mutter words just low enough that I can't make them out as she thrusts out her left hand. Dark red magic inks through the air toward me. For a second, the entire world is made of oil. I am moving slowly, and in that moment, the concentration I held with my staff disappears, and the wave of energy I held on to fizzles and then fades. My hand unclenches from the golden shaft of my staff, and it clatters to the ground, returned to the shape of a paintbrush yet again. The exhaustion I had been fighting off earlier hits harder than before and I fall onto my stomach.

Newly balanced, Reina steps closer. The force of her red power flowing off her hand rocks me into the wall along with everyone else, scraping my exposed arms on the cave floor as I go. Only when I am posted still, swathed in a crimson glow, does Reina stalk toward me. A cough bubbles up in my throat, but I force it down.

"You mother tried to give you the power she had," Reina says. "You rejected it, and her." She raises her right arm, displaying the bracelet I thought I lost, that *she* stole when I got to Malachite. "Your grandmother tried to help you survive, and you failed. Why are you even trying anymore?" she whispers. "You have had every opportunity, even a key inside of your hand, and still you lost *everything* and *everyone.*"

Against my will, Auden's face flashes through my mind's eye, then Nana's, then Mom's, and my heart sinks. Blinking back unwanted tears, I don't reply. Instead, I remind myself of what I know to be true: *There is still power in this room, waiting for me to grab on to it. It is here for me.*

Reina smirks only a few inches away from me. *She thinks she's won.*

Out of the corner of my eye, I look at Tiana, pushed up against the wall so hard she struggles to get air into her lungs. I look at Hunar, upside down with a head wound leaking and his eyes closed—then I see Zero. His face is hard, and his hands are working behind his back where he watches Reina and me from across the room. Out of his flat palms arc little tremors of power into the fabric of the cave. Reina can't see him from this angle, and I hope she's too focused on herself to notice the shift in the room around us. I look away from him immediately, trusting that Zero is working toward getting the key out of Reina's hand. I keep her talking to buy him time.

"Reina," I say, as I notice her about to walk away. She looks over her shoulder curiously, satisfied that I will not move to stop her.

"I can't beat you," I say, sure that in this moment, that's true.

Reina smiles slightly and allows me to continue.

"But please, let everyone else go. If all you want to do is open the box, leave us out of it," I say.

"I like an audience." She pouts thoughtfully.

"I'll stay," I promise. "I'll throw away my staff, and I'll stay."

Reina's red mouth widens into a soft, almost kind smile, and after a second of tense silence, she lowers her hands.

## 32

THE FEELING OF being emptied out from the inside ebbs after Reina lowers her red-stained hands; and all of us who came, so ready to destroy her, are forced to reckon with the fact that she currently wields the power of a god.

"You can all wait in the hall," Reina says to everyone else, but her eyes are stuck to mine.

I take stock of what is around me: my friends and the Arcana begrudgingly standing, my staff on the ground beside me. Reina watches me with those wide light eyes while everyone else hesitates to leave the room. I stay still, knowing that my time is about to come.

I gasp as Reina's power draws back and the ceiling over our heads vibrates with lightning from Zero's hand. As the ceiling cracks down, Reina shouts and jumps back. I tense. Only when the dust settles do I see what Zero has accomplished. His energy has pulled down the middlemost chunk of the ceiling, and in doing so, he's buried the back half of the room under fallen clay, including the Malachite box and half of the stone casket.

As I glance up, I realize the markings that cover the walls run much deeper than I thought. With the ceiling taken off, I can see them now. It's as if they are burned all the way through the earth.

Awash in the red glow of the room, Reina spits out a mouthful of dirt and stands back up. She was knocked several paces away, tucked behind the casket. I scramble to pick up my staff and stand as well. None of the ceiling fell anywhere near me. I look over at Zero where we now stand divided by rubble. His eyes scan the wreckage and then lock on to mine. Am I imagining it or does he look relieved to see me upright?

I silently curse when I find Reina still grasping the key in her right hand. She's barely wounded. I turn completely away from Zero to focus on her, distantly attempting to connect to the energy of the room, despite the pounding in my chest. Reina and I face each other while everyone else moves toward us through the rubble. Without hesitation, Reina raises her hand holding the key, and a new filmy-red barrier divides the room in half. Tiana's voice, calling my name, is cut off when the barrier goes up. The only noises in the entire world are the sounds of my heart pounding in my chest and Reina's dry laughter.

"Clever," she says, smiling with metal disappointment.

When I first saw Reina, even though I didn't know her, I trusted her. She reminded me of how a kind person was supposed to look, and because of that, I thought I could be safe with her. I even thought her beauty was refreshing. Now, all I notice in her features are the dark shadows clinging to their corners.

"Did you know what that marking was from the moment you saw it?" I ask, motioning to the marking on her hand. Reina frowns and looks down as she approaches.

"Of course," she says softly, stopping a couple of feet away from me to lean her hip against the side of the half-buried coffin. "I had been praying for its arrival for so long. It's the mark of the Unspoken goddess of life—but you know that—you chose her."

I shake my head and Reina's eyes light, suddenly more interested than malevolent.

"You didn't choose?" She takes an involuntary half-step forward.

"I didn't have to," I say, still struggling to calm down enough to connect with the power of this place. *How do I talk my way out of this? I* must *play my cards right.* I don't think I can take another blast of Reina's energy; already I'm relying on my staff to hold me upright.

"Because you had that." She gestures to the staff in my hand with her chin. "I always wondered if—when the Arcana took our artifacts—it did more than limit our power. The longer I searched for my own, I wondered if lacking one stopped me from being able to balance the energies within me." Her hand twitches like she wishes she could write this down.

I grip my staff below me and feel a slight connection spread out. I try to hide my excitement.

"If you try that, the sigils I've carved will only send your own energy back to you," Reina says definitively.

I recognize what she means as I inhale and feel deep into the power I am almost touching through my staff. *It's true.* The power of this place is simmering just below a film like the one separating me from my friends. I don't feel any of myself, or my mother, in that energy. I want to move away from it as if burned, but I will myself to stay still and find another way to stop Reina. As I think this, she begins casually moving chunks of fallen earth off the coffin beside us. *Is my mother really in there?* I can't help but wonder.

"What are you going to do with it?" I step forward, not sure if I'm talking about the body or the power.

The hairs on my arm stand on end. Being so close to Reina, the key in her hand, the box still resting atop the coffin, I now feel the same circuit of energy I did in the training room in Malachite.

"I am going to put it all back together. Here, I have your mother's two corpses and enough of her spirit in my palm," she explains, still moving the stone aside. "But it won't be *her* that I bring back. It will be whatever I want it to be, with that energy repurposed." Her eyes light up as she looks at me, like she's seeing through me into her own fantasy. "When the other mother goddesses repurposed her body to power Malachite, they were thinking *too* small. *I* don't think small. I can see *everything*," she whispers.

As she speaks, I can tell that she's barely talking to me anymore. Reina is repeating something to herself she's probably been thinking for longer than I've known her. Her energy moves like a fish below the surface of water. It reminds me of the way Tiana felt when she was asleep, nearly dead, when she was dreaming. *I am seeing Reina's dream,* her hope, and her delusion of the future. My eyes widen and I take another step forward, slow and delicately. "What do you see, Reina?" I ask.

Her eyes flutter closed. "I see freedom for all Malachites. I see retribution," she says, smiling deliciously wide.

In this moment, when Reina is completely in her reverie, I wonder if I should try and use my staff. *Maybe she's lying, maybe I can burn through the barrier she put up again. Maybe I can end this now.* I internally shake my head. *I have to try something else.* Following my instinct, I raise my left hand and wrap it around her wrist instead. When my skin touches hers, Reina's chaos is apparent all over again, but there's also something subtle, a magic contained in the cool metal of my mother's gifted bracelet. Reina's eyes slowly open and they are full of blind excitement. I don't know if she knows I am touching her, so I keep very still. Her hand still grips the coffin ahead of her.

"Can you see it?" she asks me.

I gasp a little because, with my hand on hers—"I can," I say.

Reina's desire for a better world seems fueled by an open light. But behind that light are smaller motivations that pushed her to hurt the people who love her as thoroughly as she did. As I take in the full scope of Reina's dream, I see it as clearly as she does. The list of ends justifying means—choices—the perceived sacrifices she has made. I also see the utopia she dreams of in bright technicolor: Malachites presiding over Arcana, over humans, over everyone in peaceful dominance. As I do, I let my staff sink back into the form of a paintbrush. It hums with a blue-white light I have yet to completely familiarize myself with.

Forcing my eyes back open, I find Reina smiling wistfully, eyes still shut. I realize that while I was caught up in her fantasy, she managed to rest a hand on the Malachite box, but her movements are luxuriously slow now. *She's having a harder time disentangling herself from her own vision than I did.*

Still holding her arm, bathed in that blue-white glow coming off my paintbrush, I gently lift my artifact and let the tip of it trace across the skin of Reina's arm. The hairs there stand on end when I do. I intuitively draw out more of that dream she was having in slow movements, more and more of it until her mouth parts open in happiness. Her eyes flicker behind closed eyelids.

As I work, meditatively, the power of the room rights itself around me—red shifting back to soft green. When the cold dryness dissipates, I recognize the smell of my mother in the air and register a crackle of energy coming from under my palm, which is still clamped around Reina's wrist.

The bracelet I wore every day of my life sparks with a subtle power I never would have picked up on before. It carries information. As I unclasp it from Reina's still arm and let my brush fall from her skin, the bracelet seems to whisper to me. It tells me this collection of jade and metal was how my mother siphoned energy into me as it leaked out of her. I remember, with a pang to my chest, Hathor explaining that gods lose energy the longer they spend on earth. This bracelet was Mom's gift to me, an artifact like my paintbrush. I clench my jaw at knowing Reina's plan. She wants to use my mother to take and take the way so many others have. Anger sharpens my mind to a diamond point. I want her hands off my mother's tomb.

I look back up at Reina's still face and bite the inside of my cheek. She's still completely wrapped up in her fantasy. I slip the bracelet into my pocket and realize that Reina and I are so close our noses are almost touching. I completely detach from her dreams. When I do, Reina's eyes open and clear. For a second they're wide, hopeful, but then they narrow, and she moves as quick as a snake to butt me in the head, sending me stumbling back a few paces.

Reina looks down at her palm. "You can't just take it back!" she whimpers.

Looking down at my own right hand, which is still scarred, I realize it holds the marking Reina took from me. *When did I get it back?*

With a guttural scream, Reina raises up her red palms, her vibrant crimson glow rushing out in a blast. On instinct, I raise my own hands to defend against her energy, which is still amplified by the key in her hand, flinching in preparation for the pain. But then I realize at the same moment she does, that *I now have my marking back.* As I thrust my hands out to block her, instead I absorb the wave she sends my way into my marking. Reina's power flows *into* me, through the circuit she created between us when she used me as an anchor in her spell to unite the keys.

The energy strikes my skin like lightning, and the moment it does, Reina falls to her knees. I taste copper at the back of my throat as the power floods into my marking, the same way the key must have when I thought I dropped it in Jotunheim. My palm is so hot it might burst into flames as Reina's eyes widen in outrage. She tries to pull back her rush of energy, but the damage is done.

I turn the force back on her and she is blasted back hard enough to crack the earthen wall behind her. As she flies back, the key in her hand arcs through the sky and lands at the ground beside my feet.

*Did I kill her?*

"What did you do?" Reina slurs as she pushes herself up against the wall across from me.

I stand completely still for a few breaths before automatically picking up the Malachite box under one arm, then bend down to pick up the key beside me, which is as long as a kitchen knife and lacks the intricacy it had as three separate items. *What did I do? I beat her.* My eyes latch on to the stone tomb as I stand back up. With my newfound strength, and the power coursing through my palm, I press my hands into the loamy moss and push aside the stone lid.

*There she is.* Mom. Her eyes are closed, and her lips are slightly parted. She's wearing the same outfit I last saw her in, before she pushed me into the well that led to Malachite, to my destiny. My eyes well but I still pull my bracelet out of my pocket and slip it over my wrist. When I do, I know that she is in the room with me, all around me, even if I can't see her. *She doesn't want to come back. So, she never will.* I shut the lid.

**I AM THE FIRST ONE** to step foot on the smooth cement of the parking lot; everyone else filters out after me. Once we are all back on the pavement, I can hear the disturbance in the earth quicker than I can see it. We all whip our heads around and watch as the cement, earth, pieces of root, and paint all fold themselves back over each other, covering the stairs to my mother's tomb. A cold shiver runs up my spine as the parking lot returns to normal.

"What are we going to do with her?" Tiana asks as we look at Reina, who now kneels on the ground where the hole used to be.

Basil steps forward instantly, pulling out a set of silver handcuffs crackling with amber light. I take a step back and watch as he takes Reina's red glowing hands. He clamps the metal over her wrists, and when he does, her power dims to nothing.

When it's over, Reina spits at me, "You're going to need me for the labors you signed up for, Thea. The mother goddesses who trapped the Unspoken will not be kind to her only daughter," she says.

"*If* that time comes, I won't need you for anything, Reina. I never did."

She scrambles forward on her knees. "It takes multiple goddesses with a similar energy to trap an Unspoken—you've already met those who were involved and signed your fate to one of them." She grins without cheer. "You might need me more than you think."

My stomach clenches. Hathor, Xiwangmu, La Sirène. I shake my head.

"She's messing with your head. Don't listen to her," Hunar assures me.

"You did it, Thea. We have the keys and the box. We can go home now," Teal follows up.

Tiana wraps her arms around me in a fierce hug, turning me away from Reina and forcing a smile to my lips as I close my eyes and let my joy match hers.

*We did it. It's finally over.*

As Teal wraps their arms around both of us, I laugh with relief and open my eyes, sending my gaze directly into Zero's where he stands with the other Arcana. He looks at me like a bird from a very tall tree, imperious, but a little lonely. I notice Stone holds Reina by the shoulders and I break out of our hug.

"Hey," I shout, as I release Teal and Tiana. "We're taking her with us."

"She has to be tried for what she did," Stone says slowly.

"She comes with us," Hunar backs me up and Zero's eyes flash.

Behind Zero, Ophelia's hands twitch with power; the Malachites beside me square their shoulders. My eyes widen. I can't be a part of another fight tonight. Still, power crackles at my fingertips.

"Fine." Zero says this to me instead of Hunar.

I let out a small breath as Zero motions for Basil to give Reina to Marta, who takes her by the cuffs roughly a moment later, aided by Ness. Afterward we all pause, wondering if this is it, when Tiana breaks the tense moment of silence with a confused clearing of her throat.

"Do you hear that?" she asks the group.

I frown and look over my shoulder at her. *Is this a roundabout way of dissing the Arcana?* Then I register her expression: bright eyes and head tilted on its side in a feline motion. I settle my own breathing enough to focus on what it is she hears. Puzzled, I turn to Teal, who frowns back at me. A low whistle comes from the distance, the kind of whistle you might expect to find accompanied by a steam engine train, *but we're in the middle of a parking lot.*

"Thea," Zero says my name almost accidentally, and I turn to face him as the whistle whines higher, cutting through the air until it's all I can hear.

Then comes a long flash of light like a walkway, cutting over the cement between the Arcana and the Malachites, directly beside me. The shine is horizontal and as wide as I am tall, like the beam a lighthouse might make, but at ground level and without any shore in sight. It comes from far away, though I can't find its origin. When the edge of the light touches my shoulder, the world turns to liquid. Though I am partially still aware of what's going on, my friends who aren't touched by the beam move as if they are in slow motion, while I move more quickly, even if I feel caught in quicksand. *Weird.*

Tiana's claws start to come out and Teal moves back to look at the beam of light. But not one of them manages to turn in time to really *see* the figure walking toward us down the catwalk of this beam at an ordinary pace.

The man is crisply dressed in a long black coat hanging over trousers and a loose white shirt. On his head is a hat underlined with cardinal red. I can feel when everyone finally sees him; none of their bodies react to him fast enough to do anything. The man looks around at all of us, and despite the light, I can't make out any of his features; they are all a blur. I try to move away from him, to stand between him and my friends, but even I can't move quickly enough.

The man walks toward me with the authority of an old friend. Reaching out from the beam of light, he pulls away the box under my arm and takes the key from my pocket. I attempt to tighten my grip, and my power surges up inside of me in response, but I'm too slow.

When the man's bare fingers touch the metal of the key, the world brightens.

From under the shadow of his hat, I catch the side of a sly smile. He takes both items with him into the beam of light separating our group. My body spikes with chill as I'm separated from the pieces of my mother.

I try to summon my power faster. I *will* it—and sort of succeed. Gritting my teeth, I push *everything* through my newly extending staff, which I hold loosely in my free hand. Triumphantly, I manage to reach past the beam of light and into his shin before the mystery man can turn his sights on my bracelet. Energy explodes out of me in a burst that I'm sure could blow a crater into the side of the moon. The man staggers back a couple of paces and seems annoyed, but then quickly shakes off my onslaught like it's a sprinkle of rain. He glances over his shoulder immediately, remembering his true prize.

Full of absolute terror and disbelief, I watch helplessly as this new mysterious man stands idly within a beam of supernatural light. Everything slows down when he picks up the key and the Malachite box and slides one into the other, opening it before the sun can rise behind him.

For a second, the Malachite box remains hovering in midair as his hands fall away from the key. I can feel the connection I had with the two objects continue: a circuit of energy that stretches taut like a string. Watching this scene, unable to move quickly enough to use my staff again, my heart simply stops beating. Even my panic is in slow motion, rising like a kiddie pool filled by a tap. Thankfully, the instinctive magic comes.

When it does, I push with everything I can to reach him, to *CLOSE THAT BOX.* I succeed only at putting myself slightly farther into the beam of light. But, with my shoulder finally touching the current of power and light more fully, I find I can move more easily. I still can't see the man's face, but the rest of him becomes clear: the crispness and detail of his clothes, the softness of his worn leather shoes, the stubble on his jaw, and the feeling of shadow leaking off him.

*This is the face behind the monster who killed my family,* I realize. *This is Kek.*

We exchange no words when I face him, I just reach for the box and slam the lid shut over his hand with my new strength, as fast and as hard as I can. I press so hard, I think I catch the tips of his fingers inside of it, but I *do* manage to close it. For a second, the man—the god—is too shocked to move against me, until he isn't. The second he recognizes what's going on, he is a burst of movement. He pushes me with the force of a planet until suddenly I'm out of the beam of light and skimming across the dark parking lot like a stone over water.

I fall flat on my back but sit up fast enough to watch with disbelief as the light beam disappears just as fast as it came. Time returns to its normal rhythm—and Kek is gone. *But I did it,* I remind myself. Everyone else bursts into action as soon as Kek and the light are gone, looking around wildly to figure out what just happened.

"Thea!" Tiana shouts my name. Everyone turns to find me where I sit, with my mouth open, widening into a baffled smile as I see a slice of golden light rise over the tree line. Sunrise.

*The winter solstice is over. I closed the box before Kek could get what was inside.*

But still, he has the box, and the key. My smile fades while Tiana, Teal, Hunar, and Zero rush to my side, kneeling beside me where I blink dazedly around.

"He didn't get it," I repeat, smiling though my stomach is hard as a rock.

"Come on, let me help you stand," Hunar says, gently taking my elbow.

"What happened?" Teal asks as I rise.

Before I can answer, I lock eyes with Reina across the parking lot. When I do, she smiles. Her blood-red lips part, releasing laughter like ripping fabric.

**33**

THERE WAS A single flower on the entryway table when we got back home. It was cobalt blue and streaked with one line of red that matched the lipstick smeared across Reina's face. Its stem was brown. We put her in the basement, inside a windowless room that appeared when we returned. This house really does provide what we need, though I can't be sure how much longer that will last without the Malachite box to keep it powered.

Marta decided we should keep her there until we figure out what to do with her. No one disagreed, and I was glad we kept the enchanted handcuffs the Arcana provided, surely stolen but ultimately useful.

Now, half a day later, Teal and Tiana are in the kitchen teaching Marta how to make a banana loaf. Through my open door, I have been listening to Tiana calling them Chef Snail all morning.

My bedroom is almost the same as the last time I was here, neutral and earth toned, except now, my curtains are all the way open, displaying the churning ocean broadly, and my bed now has a few soft chartreuse pillows that weren't here before that match the energy in my mother's crypt.

For the first time since my arrival, I sit on my bed and feel a hint of relaxation. I am wearing fresh amber-colored cotton, head to toe, and I am beyond happy to finally be out of that formal gown. On my lap rests an open notebook and pen. I want to chronicle everything that has happened to me. I fill the first line of my new journal with a single word: Amina. I smile as I gaze at the letters.

With my legs crossed under my body, I lean my head against my headboard and remind myself that we really did make it past the winter solstice—and we're alive. Still, the sentence that instantly replaces that self-satisfaction is *But I lost the box and the keys*, after everything.

My shoulders hunch and I drop the pen into the book. Inhaling slowly and closing my eyes, I can still feel the circuit Reina made, connecting me to the box and the key. *If I could focus enough, I could track them both down—I'm sure of it.* The thought fills me with both buttery determination and astringent anxiety.

*Knock, knock, knock.*

My eyes fly open, and I find Hunar standing in my doorway. He raises one hand in a small wave before I nod that he can enter. I close the notebook and move it off my lap.

"So," he says.

"So."

Hunar walks across the wooden length of my bedroom and sits on the end of my bed, looking as cozy as ever in an earth-toned shirt and clay-brown pants. His hair is a little wet, fresh from the shower, and he smells like licorice soap. Still, his eyes appear as shaken as I'm sure mine do.

"Do you remember when you first got here, you asked me all those questions while I was trying to power-nap on the stairs?" he begins.

"I thought you were reading."

"I'm always trying to sleep—that's a great nap spot by the way. Remember when we were in the field, and I told you that at first, I thought you were my mother behind me?" he asks.

"Yeah," I say with a slight frown.

"I wanted to explain that it's because I *felt* you—and even before your awakenings, there was a lot to feel—but also because I was dreaming of her. I dream of her a lot," he confesses without meeting my eyes. "In that dream though, she was saying something to me that I couldn't make out. But when we were in the cave and Reina knocked us against the wall, I heard it again, clearer."

"I'm on the edge of my seat here, man."

Hunar laughs a little. "She said, *it's beginning*," he whispers. "She said it when I was on the stairs, just before you came, and then again in the tomb. It can't be a coincidence." Hunar motions to the blue book he gave me moments after this dream conversation with his mother, which sits on the table beside me. I pull it onto my lap, and he goes on. "When Reina spoke about the other gods imprisoning your mom's spirit to power Malachite, I got to thinking about the book again." Hunar holds out his hand for me to give it to him. After I do, he flips toward the end.

"Here," he says, carefully pointing to the soft-faded paper.

I furrow my brow as I take the book. On the page is a chart of four symbols. The first is just a black scribble, as if someone wrote something down and crossed it out, the next is similar to a triangle, the third an infinity sign, and the fourth a collection of three circles within one another—all four have faint question marks beside them.

I read what it says at the bottom of the page out loud: "It seems that while the Unspoken gods are ancient, there is still a power they are all beholden to—the lines of fate. I hypothesize that when one of them returns to earth, so too will the others. A new cycle, similar to the one that brought forth both their ending and the separation of alternate worlds, will begin again."

I stop when the page does. "Okay, that's not exactly light reading," I try to joke, but my throat constricts.

"I didn't want to worry you, but I thought you should know since—yeah—you probably didn't get a chance to read it," Hunar says.

Looking up into his eyes, I feel, in his gaze, all the emotions that make up Hunar. I let his concern comfort me enough to close the book and set it down.

"It's fine. I'm glad you did."

There's a second when I catch Hunar still looking at me, when I feel a wave of deep affection roll out from him toward me. It warms my cheeks and stirs a similar feeling in my breastbone. *I'm going to have to figure out a way to regulate this hypersensitivity.* Through his eyes I seem so much more capable than I feel.

"That's actually not why I came up here, though," he says, sensing my change in mood and suddenly looking away. "Marta wanted me to get you. We're having a meeting in the library to decide what to do about Kek and the Malachite box, and what it means to all of us."

"What else?" I ask when I notice Hunar's breath pause.

"It's, well, it's already started. The front door isn't moving anymore, we're stationary. Reina's stone doesn't work either," he explains somberly, then attempts to lift the mood. "They also made banana bread, if you're hungry."

I wrap my arms around my legs. Hunar frowns apologetically and mimics my movement, raising his legs up against his chest. *He looks like an acorn.*

I like that he doesn't rush after he's revealed all this. Of course, we have to go—there's so much to do—but I just need a second. We breathe together for a full minute before I can't sit still any longer.

"Library, then," I say, hopping off the bed.

"It's back?" He raises his eyebrows. I look down at the marking on my hand and nod. The reappearance of my stolen mark is old news at this point—we have a god to hunt down.

**THE LIBRARY IS** full of every Malachite who did and didn't come to the cave to defeat Reina. Marta, Teal, Ness, and Tiana sit near the front of the room. Reina's single large white chair is gone, so the four of them sit atop a wide wooden table. The eleven- to fourteen-year-olds sit on the carpet ahead of them, looking up with wide eyes, newly recovered from what Reina did to them. Emilio and Aiko are shoulder to shoulder, little Ani is closest to Marta's legs, and Omari leans against the wall. Seeing all of them better makes my heart swell. Hunar and I join the older group of Godspring at the front of the room.

"Things turned really weird, and we know all of you are scared. Even though a god named Kek has the box, it *is* still closed," Marta says as soon as we join her. "And we're going to get it back." She lets that hang in the air for a few beats, before Tiana chimes in.

"I know we're all used to Reina thinking for us, but that's what got us in this mess. It's up to all of us, together, to figure out how we're going to solve this, and get our house back to normal again," Tiana says simply to the younger kids, who bob their heads in agreement. All of them are excited to be a part of what's going on.

"How did you get out of the tomb under the earth?" Emilio asks.

"That was all Thea," Teal says.

My face heats under the collective awe from all the kids, paired with the respect of my friends.

"Thanks," I say. I've never felt so completely seen before now. Everyone is looking at me the way I always dreamed—like I belong. I beam. "We did it together," I add.

Next, Marta picks up the explanation of how we're going to proceed: with research and more training; and I notice the energy in the room now surging toward her. Of course, we all agree that we'll need to band together to fix Malachite's door and retrieve the box and keys, but Reina left a big hole in the heart of all the younger kids, and they all still need someone to look to for guidance. I remember Xiwangmu's prophecy for Marta: "One destined to lead."

I'm not sure if the sensation in my chest is relief or disappointment at seeing Marta so effortlessly take charge, but soon enough it's replaced with a tickling cough. Turning my head to the side, I catch a spray of blood in the fresh handkerchief I tucked in my pocket. I glance up at the room to see if anyone noticed. Instead, I catch sight of a dark figure just beyond the door to the library. I find myself moving away from the room while the conversation continues with more questions and plans.

The sound of the Malachites fades slightly in the hall outside, where Zero leans against the wall. When I see him, I cross my arms over my chest.

*How do I act around him now? He stole my grandmother's map, and he saved my life.* On one hand, he knew Reina was going to betray us and said nothing, but he also brought us together. Then there's the kiss that I can't deny. It just felt *right*.

*If we're not enemies, what are we?*

Zero is wearing a crisp Arcana outfit, and he no longer looks like he got the shit kicked out of him. His uniform helps me draw a line between us. Still, I lead him away from the noise of the library. He follows beside me until we reach a small alcove seat just past the temple room. Sand grits through the thin fabric of my socks, but I don't mind. I sit down and Zero sinks beside me, pressing the side of his warm leg against mine. The weight of his gaze on the side of my face is hot. I didn't have any time to run over what I wanted to say to him, but when I look at him, I mentally stammer. The feeling is still there—that energy that makes me want to lean over so that more than just our legs are touching.

"I'm sorry for what I've done," Zero says.

"Why did you come here?" I ask at the same time.

My eyes widen and I let out a startled sort of noise when I register his earnest apology. Zero begins to dig into the pockets of his blazer. A second later he pulls out a small vial filled with violet liquid.

"This is for you," he says, holding it out.

"What is it?" I ask, reaching out and taking the bottle carefully.

"It's for your Auroria poisoning. A drop a day should help to heal you."

I look up at him suspiciously. "What do you want for it?"

"Nothing." His eyes are wide and a little moist.

"I—thank you."

Zero doesn't reply, just watches me toss the bottle from one hand to the other. *Is he going to bring it up? Should I?*

"Is there anything else?" I ask tentatively.

"I'm supposed to inform you and the other Malachites that you have the assistance of Arcana to track down Kek. He's exactly the type of deity who shouldn't have the Malachite box," he says.

I exhale. That isn't what I thought he would bring up, but I'm honestly relieved he did. Somehow, in the past two weeks, a conversation about a god stealing my mother's essence is easier to focus on than the tension between him and me.

"Yeah, of course," I say, then furrow my brow when I see his expression. "What?"

"It's just, I thought you'd need more convincing than that," he says with a wry smile.

"Why would I? We need all the help we can get, and I won't let *my* pride get in the way of fixing this mess."

Zero pauses for a second and I squirm under his fixed stare.

"Thea," Zero's tone lowers, "you know this isn't your fault, right? This didn't happen just because of you."

I nod even though I don't really believe him. "Thanks, I guess," I breathe.

Another long pause stretches as we just look at each other. Zero's eyes widen, and I inhale. *There it is*, the electricity, that pull. Again, I can't tell if it's coming from me or him, or if this feeling is something that we create only when brought together. Zero's eyes trail down my face to my mouth and I wet my lips, my eyes already fluttering shut—*ouch!*

I flinch as I recognize a familiar pinch on my right hand. I move the violet vial to my left hand and look down at the surface of my palm. Immediately, my mouth rounds into a small *O* when I recognize the vertical slit.

Grimacing, a shiver runs up my spine as I watch the broken-open skin on my palm crack wider. It oozes, not blood, but peachy-golden goo. The same color and shimmer as the drink Xiwangmu poured us in Kunlun.

I look up at Zero with my mouth still hanging open.

"What—is that?" he asks.

"I made a deal with a goddess in Kunlun and I didn't read the fine print," I confess, half-joking, hoping to alleviate my panic. It doesn't work.

"So, the goo is . . . ?" He trails off, much less disgusted than I'd expect him to be.

"I think it's a reminder," I say. Looking at the thin ribbon of amber, I spot a pair of jade-green eyes staring back at me, as if in a reflection. Gasping, I watch as before my eyes a moment later, the cut mends itself back together just the same as Xiwangmu's did in Kunlun. Leaving behind nothing but my marked palm and the overwhelming sensation of being observed.

"This is going to be weird," I mutter.

# ABOUT THE AUTHOR

**D**RAWING INSPIRATION FROM her love of mythology and her diverse Jamaican, Chinese, and European-Canadian heritage, Giselle Vriesen seamlessly merges mystical themes with the real-world experiences of characters living in the margins. You can find the author dreaming up new stories, crafting forest fairies, and exploring nature at home in Canada's Southern Gulf Islands. *Why We Play with Fire* is Vriesen's debut offering.